Winston Churchill and The Treasure of Mapungubwe Hill

Other Books by Chris Angus

London Underground
The Last Titanic Story
Flypaper

Winston Churchill and The Treasure of Mapungubwe Hill

A Novel

Chris Angus

YUCCA
Publishing

Yucca Publishing books may be purchased in bulk at special discounts for sales promotion, corporate gifts, fund-raising, or educational purposes. Special editions can also be created to specifications. For details, contact the Special Sales Department, Yucca Publishing, 307 West 36th Street, 11th Floor, New York, NY 10018 or yucca@skyhorsepublishing.com.

Yucca Publishing® is an imprint of Skyhorse Publishing, Inc.®, a Delaware corporation.

Visit our website at www.yuccapub.com.

10 9 8 7 6 5 4 3 2 1

Library of Congress Cataloging-in-Publication Data is available on file.

Cover design by Owen Corrigan
Cover photo credit: Thinkstock

Print ISBN: 978-1-63158-003-1
Ebook ISBN: 978-1-63158-039-0
Printed in the United States of America

1.

Blaaw Kranz River, Natal, South Africa

November 15, 1899

THE STEAM ENGINE BELCHED BLACK coal smoke into a blazing Natal sky. The huge machine, nicknamed *Hairy Mary* by the troops, looked like a cross between a rag mop and Medusa's head, every inch hung with heavy braided rope armor. A constant rhythmic panting emanated from the locomotive as though it were a large beast chomping at the bit. But for the moment, the train remained stationary, the eyes of its two engineers fixed on the small figure sitting on the ground on the shaded side of the train. He was dressed in jodhpurs and a dark jacket with a rakish, if crumpled, cowboy hat over his fair hair. His hand fairly flew as he wrote his daily dispatch for the *Morning Post* of London.

One of the engineers leaned out and looked down the length of the track. The town of Ladysmith was barely visible in the distance, shimmering in the late-afternoon heat. In the other direction, a hazy cloud rose against the distant horizon of rolling veldt, whether a dust storm or moving troops was unclear. He grunted and turned to the other man who stood leaning on the catwalk that encircled the engine, staring at the oblivious writer on the ground.

"If that's Boers, we're as good as dead if we don't get out of here now," he said.

"Save it," the second man said. "That's Churchill. I saw him once in India when he was a second lieutenant in the 4th Hussars. Walked through a bloody riot to deliver his dispatch to the telegraph office. We're not going anywhere until Winston completes his writing."

"Stupid," said the first man and spat over the side. "God damn suicide. I'd like to know whose bright idea it was to send an entire train, over a hundred men, straight into the teeth of General Botha's forces. All so that maniac can get close to the action."

"Better be careful. He doesn't take well to that kind of comment. His father was Lord Randolph Churchill, you know. Whole family thinks pretty highly of itself."

The first engineer snorted, but he stared at the man below with more care.

Of course it wasn't an entire train. There were only six cars, three in front of the armored engine and three behind. The lead car was a flatcar with a mounted muzzle-loading seven-pounder naval gun manned by four seamen and commanded by a petty officer from HMS *Tartar*. The next two cars were armor-plated, with slits through which one hundred and seventeen men from the Durban Light Infantry and the Dublin Fusiliers could fire their rifles. Then came the locomotive and tender. Bringing up the rear were two more armored cars, followed by one for the breakdown gang and the guard.

Despite the engineer's remarks, their presence here was not all about Winston. The train made regular forays along this track, designed to reconnoiter the countryside as far as Colenso. The ostensible purpose of the exercise was to mask the weakness of the British garrison at Estcourt through a show of force and activity. Show the colors. It was a laughable military maneuver. The rail route was fixed, the size, smoke and noise of the locomotive precluded any possibility of surprise, and the Boer forces were poised to attack any plums that might fall into their laps.

It was true, however, that this particular excursion, under the command of Captain Alymer Haldane, had the sole purpose of getting journalist Winston Churchill into Ladysmith, which was virtually surrounded and cut off, so he could give his readers the latest news from the front. Most Britons still believed the war would be a short one. How could 90,000 Afrikaners, more or less, fight off the crack British troops that had begun to flow into South Africa? But the guerilla tactics of the Boers were proving effective. It would be three long years before the British broke their resistance and then only by using a scorched earth policy, burning 30,000 farms in the South African Republic and Orange Free State and interning 25,000 Afrikaner women and children. In the lead-up to World War II, the Nazis would remind members of Parliament repeatedly that it was Great Britain that had invented the concentration camp.

The pale twenty-five year-old Winston, head drooped forward in concentration, looked more like a seventeen- or eighteen-year-old. But he was already being lionized in England for his dispatches and for his new book, *The River War,* about the Sudan campaign, during which he had participated in the last great cavalry charge in history. The book had become a best-seller.

Though he'd failed in his recent attempt to get elected to Parliament, everyone knew he was a man destined for great things, most of all Winston himself. And indeed, he was currently the highest paid journalist in South Africa, no mean feat in a war that had attracted such eminent correspondents as Arthur Conan Doyle, H. G. Wells and Rudyard Kipling.

At last Winston stood up, dusted off his pants and folded his notes into his pocket. He rested one hand on the Mauser strapped to his hip, removed the cowboy hat and wiped his forehead, then saw the cloud on the horizon. He stared at it intently before turning to the engineers. "What do you make of that?" he said.

"Boers," the engineers said simultaneously.

"You think so?" said Churchill. He turned and looked again. "How far away do you figure?"

"Five miles maybe," the first engineer replied.

Captain Haldane appeared. "We'd best be getting on, Winston," he said and nodded to the engineers, who wholeheartedly jumped into action.

Winston and Haldane climbed to the catwalk at the front of the locomotive as the train began to move forward. Haldane was twenty years Winston's senior, an experienced officer with a Distinguished Service Order to his credit. But he was deferential to Churchill, whose family connections and burgeoning reputation would have made him a figure of importance even if he weren't also brilliant, impetuous and ambitious in the extreme.

"Look!" Haldane said, pointing to their right.

Winston turned and saw perhaps a hundred Boer horsemen cantering in a southerly direction a mile distant from them. Beyond they could see a low hill occupied by artillery.

"Magnificent!" Churchill said, staring at the riders, his hands gripping the rail tightly. "Aren't they grand? What say you, Aylmer, shall we give them a lesson in marksmanship?"

Haldane nodded at the hill. "They hold the high ground Winston. I don't like the idea of that artillery bearing down on us."

But Winston was eager for action. What a story it would make for his paper! Though he'd been in battle before, he had no experience of artillery bombardment or concentrated rifle fire. Excitedly, he said, "If we move quickly, we can get between the horsemen and their line. We can cut them off."

Haldane hesitated, but young Winston's enthusiasm was infectious. He leaned back and yelled at the engineers to increase their speed.

General Botha's men held their fire until the train reached the section of track closest to them. Then a series of large flashes followed by delayed booms emanated from the hilltop. The Boers opened up at six hundred yards with two large field guns, a Maxim that fired small shells in a stream and a barrage from riflemen lying on the ridge.

Winston and Haldane quickly sought shelter in one of the armored train cars as bullets whined and ricocheted against the steel. The engineers, desperate to escape the onslaught, poured on the speed, rounded the curve of the hill and headed down a steep grade straight into a large boulder that had been placed on the tracks.

There was a tremendous crash as the train came to an abrupt halt. The first car jackknifed into the air landing upside down. The armored cars holding the troops were thrown on their sides, scattering the occupants onto the ground like kernels of rice spilled from a sack. Haldane was also thrown to the ground. Winston, who'd seen the boulder at the last instant, managed to leap from the train just before impact, hitting the hard, baked earth and tumbling head over heels. Somehow, he emerged unscathed. With the captain dazed if not badly hurt, Churchill assumed control, though he held no military rank or authority.

Dodging bullets in complete disregard for his own safety, he ran the length of the train, assessing the damage. Blind good fortune had kept the locomotive from leaving the tracks. "You," he shouted to a group of forty or so soldiers crouched behind one of the overturned cars. "Direct your fire on the hill. I need a dozen men to come with me."

The soldiers obeyed him instantly. At this juncture they could care less who was in charge, so long as it was someone who seemed to know what he was doing. The way things were going, their lives wouldn't be worth six pence unless something happened to alter their circumstances quickly. The big guns on the hill were landing shells all around the train. At any moment one might penetrate the boiler, ending their chances for escape completely.

The damaged cars had to be disconnected from the locomotive and one of them pushed off the track. The men struggled at the task under fire the entire time. Four were killed, but finally the locomotive managed to push past the last obstructing car by running at it full tilt and ramming it off the track. With a screeching and tearing of metal, the locomotive blasted free and the track was clear. Winston now hoped to tow the rear cars and men to safety but discovered that the couplings had all been damaged by shells, leaving the cars stranded some way behind.

Haldane appeared at his side, recovered sufficiently to help organize the men to carry the wounded forward and place them on board the locomotive and its tender to evacuate. The rest of the soldiers used the locomotive as a shield from the blistering Boer fire, as they moved toward the trestle bridge over the Blaaw Kranz River half a mile away. The armored locomotive and the tender were pocked with bullet marks. As the engineer forced the engine to greater speed, the soldiers began to be left behind and the Boers increased their fire even more. At last the train crossed the bridge and was out of range.

Winston jumped off as soon as they slowed down. "Wait here, damn you," he shouted to the engineer above the din. "We can't leave those poor buggers to their fate." He sprinted across the bridge to look for the straggling soldiers and help them back to safety. It was the last time the engineer would see the young journalist. After waiting a short time, he determined no one was returning and headed for Estcourt.

Meanwhile, Winston proceeded along a slight rise between the ambush site and the Blaaw Kranz River, searching for his comrades. He kept low, listening to the whine of bullets hitting the ridge line just over his head. He came to a pile of boulders that offered enough cover for him to climb up and peer over the hill. A hundred yards away, he saw the soldiers standing in the open, their hands held high, guns on the ground in front of them. They had already surrendered, a line of Boers encircling them. He swore and ducked back behind the rocks.

Suddenly the boulder next to him exploded as a heavy bullet struck inches from his head. He was under direct fire from two horse soldiers who had appeared from behind a rock outcrop less than thirty yards away. He dove into the brush and scrambled down into a small depression overlooking the river far below. But there was almost no useful cover. The two horsemen closed on him quickly.

He looked about frantically for some avenue of escape. He calculated he might make it into the river gorge if he fired several shots to delay his pursuers, but as he reached for his pistol, he discovered that the Mauser was gone. He'd taken it off and placed it in the cab while working to free the locomotive. Cursing his stupidity, he slipped farther down the side of the gorge, until his feet ran out of purchase, only barely stopping himself from a headlong fall over a fifty-foot precipice. He could now go neither forward nor backward and was little better than a clay pigeon in a shooting gallery.

Though he'd only recently filed a dispatch in which he railed against soldiers who surrendered too quickly, he now found himself in just such a situation. Alone, unarmed, in open country with riflemen on horseback bearing down on him, surrender was the only option.

Winston was a prisoner of the Boers.

2.

CHURCHILL STARED SULLENLY at the ground beneath his tired feet. This was only the second rest break since their forced march to the Boer railhead at Elandslaagte had begun. There they would entrain for Pretoria, the capital city of the Transvaal where all British prisoners of war were being held. They had already walked thirty miles from the point of their capture in a pouring rain, with an equal distance yet to be covered. A lifelong horseman, Winston was unused to walking such distances. His feet, encased in uncomfortable army-issue boots, were covered with blisters.

The previous day, after ten hours forced march, they'd forded the chest-deep Klip River and made camp. Winston was billeted with the other officers in the black shadow of Bulwana Mountain surrounded by rugged, boulder-strewn hills. His captors were uncertain of his status but assumed he was someone of importance thanks to the deference and even salutes that many of the captured soldiers now gave him following his bravery during the attack. He'd spent much of the evening befriending two Boer guards named Spaarwater and Swanepoel, trying to bribe them into looking the other way so he might escape, but to no avail.

Some might have looked askance at such a ploy and his willingness to leave the other men behind. But it was a typical, impetuous Churchill effort. His head was filled with one thought only, the need to escape and report to his paper what was happening. He was certainly of no use to anyone as a prisoner of war. From his earliest boyhood, he'd always felt in charge of whatever situation he found himself in, his fierce intellect directing his somewhat less than imposing physique. Now, for the first time, he was completely helpless, his fate in the hands of others.

Haldane sat beside him humming softly, anything to distract his thoughts from their potential fate.

"What is that?" an irritated Winston said.

The captain stopped but continued to stare out across the soaking veldt. "I'm not sure," he said. "Something my wife used to sing, but I don't remember what it's called."

"Well try something more military," said Winston. "We ought to be thinking of ways to escape."

Churchill had seen himself furthering his reputation with this conflict by covering great battles and the movements of large forces, writing dispatches, keeping his name in the papers. Instead, here he was, sitting on a dirt path in the Transvaal, soaking wet, surrounded by armed guards. If he was interred for the duration, it would be the greatest lost opportunity of his young career. That he might actually be shot for a spy, since he'd been engaging the enemy while not wearing a regulation uniform, hardly concerned him. He trusted in destiny and firmly believed his own included great things still to come.

Haldane sighed. "A soldier's duty, to be sure, Winston. But you might want to recruit someone else. This . . ." he indicated his leg that had received a glancing shard of shrapnel. It was tightly wrapped with a filthy bandage and although he'd managed to keep up on the forced march, it was obviously an injury that was likely to become infected. Then he would be nothing but a liability in any escape attempt.

Winston put a hand on his shoulder. "You've done well to keep the pace, Aylmer. It must be quite painful." He stared down the line of exhausted men. "Perhaps it would be better to wait until we reach Pretoria and have managed to rest and recuperate . . . but I wonder if conditions will ever be better than now, while we're still in the open. In Pretoria we'll certainly be placed in some kind of stockade."

In fact, the accommodations the Boers offered for captured officers in Pretoria were far better than a stockade. The States Model School, a large, single-storied brick building with a steep, corrugated tin roof and a wide verandah, had housed two hundred students when it had opened as a college in 1897. Now it had been requisitioned to provide quarters for officer prisoners of war.

The building stood at the intersection of two broad, dusty thoroughfares crowded with carriages, carts and pedestrians. The so-called prison with its seventy-yard-square grounds was enclosed by a simple, chest-high ornamental iron fence. The only evidence that prisoners resided within was ten sentries who patrolled the fence. Inside, twelve classrooms on either side of a long corridor had been converted into dormitories with additional rooms for dining and recreation. Churchill found himself sharing a dormitory with Haldane and four other officers. This would be his home for the next twenty-five days.

Escape was ever on the young journalist's mind. He considered and abandoned one scheme after another, all the while attempting to convince his captors that as a non-combatant he ought to be released forthwith. But the Boer commanders had finally determined who they had, Lord Randolph Churchill's son, clearly the most important prisoner of the two thousand or so British soldiers they held. This was a coup they would never give up. They did feel, however, that it was in their interest to permit him to continue making his dispatches to the newspapers and to write letters, though both were subject to censorship. He was even allowed to pen a thousand-word letter to Edward, Prince of Wales.

Ever creative, Winston urged Haldane, whose wound had healed cleanly, to join him, not simply in escape, but in an audacious scheme to seize Pretoria itself through the promotion of an uprising. They were watched by only a handful of guards at a time and Winston felt it would be a simple matter to cut the electricity to the compound, plunging it into darkness, and attack the guards. They would then overwhelm the garrison at the nearby camp where two thousand British soldiers were being held and attack the town guard, which consisted of fewer than five hundred burghers, all deemed unfit for the front. President Kruger would become a prisoner in his own capital.

It was a typical Churchill gambit, audacious, bold and creative … with virtually no chance of success. Haldane and the other officers vetoed the plan.

Meanwhile, Winston developed a friendship with the Transvaal Secretary of State for War, Louis de Souza, whom he described to Haldane as a "kind-hearted little Portuguese." The man brought Winston baskets of fruit and occasionally a forbidden bottle of whisky.

One evening, after most of the men had gone to sleep, de Souza asked Winston to join him for a stroll around the compound.

"What you suggest," said Winston, "might well get us shot. You know we're not allowed outside after dark."

But de Souza merely touched the side of his nose and winked. "It has been arranged, my friend." And he would say nothing more, relying on Churchill's natural curiosity and journalistic fervor to convince him to go along.

The compound was quiet. Most of the soldiers not on duty went to bed by ten o'clock since there was little to do. Sleeping was one way of making the time pass. Winston followed de Souza down the long corridor and out into the poorly lit courtyard. Two guards sitting idly in the dust snapped to attention when they saw the Secretary of War.

They continued to the entrance of the compound, where Winston realized with a start that a carriage awaited them. At his questioning look, his guide merely put a finger to his lips, ushered him into the buggy and climbed in after him. The driver pulled away.

Churchill's nerves were now at fever pitch. This was not what he had expected. It was entirely conceivable, after all, that his captors had decided he was too much of a risk to hold onto. They might not be above shooting him outright, claiming he'd tried to escape— believable enough for anyone who knew the brash young Englishman. Or he might be destined to simply disappear altogether, his body deposited on the veldt for the lions to eat.

The horse trotted amiably enough along the dirt roadway. Only a few people were abroad at this hour. Winston tried again to engage de Souza in conversation, but his friend had become decidedly quiet and withdrawn. Since this had never happened before, it only added to his confusion and sense of impending danger.

After some twenty minutes, they entered a more upscale neighborhood. Stately homes sat back from the roadway. Each had its own wrought iron balcony and fenced yard. It hardly seemed the place for an execution, and he relaxed a bit. Then they passed through a large stone gateway into what appeared to be a private, and very elegant, compound. A guard at the gate house examined them carefully before allowing them to continue down a long, tree-lined drive.

"Here we are," de Souza said at last, seeming to come out of his funk suddenly, as the carriage stopped in front of a large plantation-like residence.

"This really is too much, Louis," Winston said, his anger beginning to rise. "Here we are—where?"

"You are to meet the Commander-in-Chief of the Boer army, Winston, at his request. It's truly an honor. For security reasons, I wasn't allowed to tell you where we were going, but there's nothing at all to worry about."

Winston stared at him. "I'm going to meet Louis Botha?" At his friend's nod, he felt a sudden surge of excitement. Botha was an almost mythical figure. Still in his thirties, he'd only recently been appointed to his new post. He was known as a fierce fighter but also a compassionate leader. He was destined to go on to a long and illustrious career that would include roles as Prime Minister of the Transvaal and first President of South Africa. After the Boer War, Botha would counsel reconciliation with the British and support them in World War I. He would even attend the Paris Peace Conference in 1919, where he would argue against harsh treatment of the Central Powers.

But all this was in the future. For the moment Winston was aware only that the man he was about to meet held his fate in his hands.

They entered a large hall lined with historic African implements of war, spears, war clubs, even early flintlock guns of Civil War vintage. A native woman dressed in white guided them to a second-floor library.

As soon as he entered, Winston's attention was seized by a figure in military dress who rose from a large desk and came forward to greet him. He was of medium build and had a black handlebar mustache, with the rest of his jaw covered in a three-day stubble. He was a good-looking man, but it was the eyes that riveted Winston immediately. He'd seen such eyes only rarely even in the halls of his own Parliament back in London. They were the eyes of a man intensely alive, one who burned with passion, ambition and the pure intensity of purpose. It was impossible not to be drawn in by them.

"Mr. Churchill, a real pleasure!" Botha said, taking his hand and shaking it vigorously. "I hope they have been treating you properly?"

Winston nodded. "Our quarters and treatment have been exemplary, Commander."

"Good. Good! Come sit down." He turned to de Souza. "Louis, sit with us. Bring that chair over."

Botha sat in his own chair, glanced at some papers in front of him with a slight frown and sighed. He waved a hand. "You see all this, my English friend. So many decisions to be made. We appear to have a real war on our hands."

"One you can not win, Commander."

Botha laughed out loud. "Bravely said. But I believe the British Empire may yet find one small spot upon which the sun will set."

"Many others have thought so," said Winston. "We have warred against the Ashanti, Kaffirs, Afghans, Mohmands, Zulus, Egyptians, Sudanese, Burmese, Matabeles and Waziris in the last twenty-five years. British values now guide them all. Good values. Worthy ones."

Botha nodded thoughtfully. "Values such as the invasion of one's neighbors in order to steal their resources." He raised a hand. "You are a student of history. Good. So am I. But nothing is written, despite what our Muslim friends like to say. No matter. I've read reports of your actions during the battle at the railhead. Exposing yourself to heavy fire, returning for your men even though it might result in capture. Very noteworthy. And this is why I invited you here. I believe you are a man made for adventure."

Winston looked at him quizzically. He glanced at de Souza, who stared at a painting with great concentration. Churchill fingered a rip in his still dirt-covered jacket and said, "To be honest with you, Commander, I think I've had enough adventure for a while."

Botha laughed again, stood up, went around the desk and placed one hand on Winston's shoulder. "I like you," he said. "Bravery and modesty are a good combination in a soldier—or a statesman. I wish I had more men with that kind of experience around me." He turned toward the guard at the door and nodded. "There's someone I want to bring into this meeting."

The door opened and a young woman entered. She was very tall, black-haired and dressed in a tunic that was as close to military garb as Winston guessed would be possible for a woman with her curves. She had striking features, with ebony skin and the high cheekbones of her native land.

"This is Zeila, Mr. Churchill. One of my closest aides. She's a member of the Zulu tribe. You will come to know her well before we are done."

Zeila held an object wrapped in an exquisite piece of leopard skin. Handling it with great care, she placed it gently on the desk, then gazed down on Winston from her considerable height advantage with what he thought was an amused look and put her hand out. In perfect English, she said, "I look forward to working with you, Mr. Churchill."

He hesitated, then took her hand and bowed slightly. "A pleasure, though everyone seems to have an idea what I'm doing here but me. If I could ask . . ." He stopped in mid-phrase as his eyes wandered past her to another figure who had come into the room. His mouth fell open.

"Lord Sterne?" He said in astonishment.

Botha smiled. "You see, we have one surprise after another for you today."

Lord Sterne was a powerfully built man of about thirty. He was of average height with broad shoulders and penetrating green eyes. Winston recalled hearing about his days as a top college rugby player. He was dressed in a faddish, khaki outfit that might have come from the display halls of Abercrombie & Fitch. He smiled and took Winston's hand. "It's been two years, hasn't it? I believe we last met during your appearance before the Prince of Wales. He sends his regards, by the way. Appreciated the letter you sent him some weeks ago."

Winston was now entirely bewildered and his face was such a giveaway of his emotions that all of them laughed. It was de Souza who spoke first.

"You are confused, and rightly so, but soon you will understand. We have something quite extraordinary to show you," he said with a smile.

Botha glanced again at the stack of papers on his desk. "Well, let's get on with it. Zeila, if you will."

The men all sat in chairs surrounding the desk while Zeila carefully unfolded the leopard skin and removed the most wonderful object Winston had ever seen. It was the statue of a bird in what appeared to be soapstone. But the stone was the least part of the work's appeal. It was mounted on a kind of pounded gold base that sparkled with precious stones. Most riveting of all were two enormous ruby eyes. There was an aura of age to the piece. The gold shone with such deep amber brilliance that Winston suspected it had to be of great purity.

Gingerly, he took the object from Zeila and examined it from all angles. "Magnificent," he said at last. "It must be very old. Of native derivation?" He looked at Botha but it was Lord Sterne who answered.

"To be sure, Winston." He paused, seeming to calculate how to go on. "Have you heard of the hill of Mapungubwe?"

Winston shook his head.

"One of the most beautiful parts of the northern Transvaal. It lies near the Limpopo River, at a ford that's passable ten months of the year, including just now actually. It's a small 'table mountain' of rough sandstone, very steep on every side, sloping northward toward the ancient ruins of Great Zimbabwe some two hundred miles distant. It is the wildest and most unsettled region of this land. Elephants, lions and remnants of the great Zulu and Ndebele tribes rule. Only a handful of Boers have even hunted there." He leaned forward. "I must tell you, Winston, that this is all highly secret information. If you undertake the mission we have in mind, you'll be working for Mr. Botha here, but also directly for the Prince of Wales and the royal family."

"For the Prince *and* for the Boers?" Winston said in astonishment. "I was under the impression there was a war going on. What sort of mission are you talking about?"

"We'll come to that. Let me continue. Three years ago, a hunter by the name of Max Grundy and his son climbed the hill with great difficulty. In addition to being steep, the sides were dense with thorn and scrub. It was perfect cover for lions. The men were attracted to the hill by a narrow chimney of rock that seemed to offer a way to the top. After they chopped their way to the chimney, they discovered that handholds, very old and very worn, had been cut into the rock, almost like a ladder. They went up the ladder to the summit.

"There, at the edge, they found large mounds of boulders, apparently stockpiled to drop on intruders who might decide to make the climb. Grundy and his son wandered over the hill, finding stone foundations and broken pottery littered everywhere. In the dry soil, their boots scuffed up bits of beads, iron and copper. Then they came to a hillside that had only recently been washed out by a cloudburst. The entire hill sparkled in the sunlight. It was a golden hill."

Winston stared at him. "A golden hill?"

"Very nearly that precisely. They found thousands of gold beads, bangles and bits of thin gold plating. Using only the knives they'd brought with them, they also uncovered many large pieces of heavy gold plate as well as solid gold carvings of rhinoceroses and elephants. In a depression, they found the bones of an ancient burial along with this object you see before you. All told, Grundy and his son packed out over one hundred fifty pounds of gold, all they could carry. But on the way down, they were suddenly attacked by a huge lion who carried Grundy's son off in his mouth as though the poor fellow weighed no more than a doll.

"The hunter was so overcome by the loss of his son that he left the gold behind, everything but this object here, which remained in his small pack. After many days, he stumbled blindly out of the bush and made his way back home."

Sterne picked up the soapstone. "This magnificent object came to me by way of Commander Botha's young assistant here, Zeila. You see where a chip has been taken from the side of the gold band? I had it removed and tested. The gold is of the greatest purity ever seen by the examiners."

Winston looked at Zeila. "How did you come by the piece?" he said.

"My family lives near the edge of this remote area," she replied. "My father had worked with Grundy as a guide. When he came stumbling in half dead, my father took care of him. But the man's ordeal, combined with the loss of his son left him weak and confused. He died about three months ago. Before he did, he gave the soapstone to my father."

"Quite a gift," Winston said. "Ought to set your family up nicely for generations."

She looked at him witheringly. "This is part of our heritage. Here in my native land that you whites, Boer and British, now fight for control of, my black forebears once ruled and developed a kingdom to rival your own Great Britain." She paused. "I have been to Mapungubwe."

"You've been to the site?" Winston felt himself rising to the challenge of this incredible tale. He had a passion for antiquities. Much of the wealth of the ancient world lay in the British Museum, and he'd spent many hours engrossed in those collections.

Zeila nodded. "During my brief visit, we uncovered several more burials, including one skeleton whose legs were wreathed in more than one hundred bangles of coiled wire gold and many thousands of gold beads. This, I firmly believe, is a royal burial ground. I mean to see the contents saved."

"How? By stealing them yourself?"

Botha said, "We live in difficult times, Winston. This war, I fear, may go on for years. I admire the British. You may find that hard to believe, but I do. However, you are in my country and you must go. I understand how Zeila feels. This was her land before it belonged to the Boers. She wants it back for her people as much as I want it back for mine. War makes for strange bedfellows. Zeila and I work together to rid our land of the British. Then, perhaps, she will make war on me." He smiled at her. Zeila's eyes remained fixed on him, but she showed no emotion.

"I'm too busy with the war to direct this mission. But we've agreed that the treasure at Mapungubwe is at risk of looting and should be protected, which means dug up and hidden away. In the event we lose the war, at least the English will not be able to use our own nation's wealth against us. And perhaps it can some day be used to at last rid the Transvaal of our enemies."

Winston looked from Zeila to Botha and then his eyes wandered to Lord Sterne. "If what you say is the real reason for all of this, to keep the treasure from the English, I find it difficult to understand how the Royal Family plays a part."

"A reasonable question," said Sterne. He paused for a moment, as though preparing a response already scripted. Winston realized again how powerfully built the man was. It was something to keep in mind . . . along with his obvious connections.

"I've been serving as a sort of behind-the-scenes liaison between Mr. Botha here and the Prince of Wales who, as you know, with Queen Victoria's age, is likely to soon be king. As you can imagine, it would not be good for our plan to find its way into the press during a war between our two nations. It was one reason we hesitated to confide in you, Winston, since you're a member of the press. We're taking quite a risk, but we feel strongly that you are the man to lead such an expedition. And since you so conveniently fell into our lap several weeks ago, the Commander and I have been discussing the possibility intensely."

"I see," Winston said slowly, "And if I refuse, I'll remain a prisoner for the indefinite future, one who will find his letter writing privileges, I suspect, if not his life, forfeit." He waved a hand as Botha started to protest. "You still haven't told me what the Prince of Wales's interest is," he said.

"The Prince's fascination with antiquities is well known," Sterne replied. "He is, after all, the royal patron of the British Museum. This will be a magnificent, joint effort of two nations, selflessly seeking to save and protect a great heritage from the vicissitudes of war. While he would like nothing better than to have this treasure for the people of Great Britain, the Prince would rather have it protected than become lost in the battles to come." Sterne's eyes took on a faraway look. "Think of it, Winston. Once the war is over, we'll put on the greatest exhibit since the Elgin Marbles in 1816. The Prince will use it as the capstone to his coronation."

Churchill looked at Botha. "You agreed to this?"

"Yes. As Lord Sterne says, once hostilities have passed, we'll hold a joint exhibit in the British Museum before the relics are returned to their rightful home. This promise I have from the Prince of Wales."

Sterne spread his hands on the table. "It's an honor for me to participate in this great work. My place in history will be assured. The Prince has directed me to pursue and protect this unsurpassed cultural treasure at all costs, Winston, and even suggested that you would be a good ally in the venture."

"I'm a prisoner of war," Winston reminded him.

"Indeed. However, I believe you are about to escape."

3.

WINSTON SHOOK his friend hard, watching him rise up out of a deep sleep. "It's time, Aylmer," he whispered.

Captain Haldane raised himself on one arm, looked out at the black predawn sky and groaned. "I ought to have my head examined, Winston. For all you know, this whole thing is a charade, designed to have us escape so we can be shot down like dogs."

They'd had the same argument for days and Winston wasn't interested in continuing it. "Get dressed," he said. "The guards at the back wall have been ordered away from their posts. They'll do precisely what the Secretary of War tells them. Don't worry, I trust de Souza."

"Can't trust any bloody Boer," Aylmer replied, "Not since the Battle of Majuba Hill twenty years ago." But he rose quickly and dressed.

The entire compound was in darkness, itself unusual, since lanterns were generally hung at night to enable the guards to see. They stumbled and tripped their way to the wall and were over it in a moment. Crouching on the street beyond, Winston saw a light flash across the way in an alley. A horse whinnied softly.

Zeila and two men in civilian clothes were there, holding two additional horses. "You're late," Zeila said, handing each of them a set of reins.

"Aylmer, this is Zeila," Winston said. "She's our guide I told you about."

Haldane stared at the tall, striking female intently. "You're Botha's woman," he said.

She gave him a look that could have boiled an egg. "I am no one's woman. Try not to act as stupid as you look," she said. "Keep your mouth shut and don't fall behind." She leaped onto her horse, swung the animal around expertly and headed straight across a field that led toward the distant veldt, just visible in the first light of dawn.

Winston laughed softly at Aylmer's surprised face. "I warned you she was no slouch. Looks like you've made your usual first impression." Before Aylmer could reply, Churchill mounted his own animal and trotted after the others.

An hour later, they were deep in the bushveld as the sun made its first appearance above the shimmering hills. Already, the landscape had taken on a more rugged look with steep-sided rock ledges, deep gullies and stunted trees. Winston could detect no path or trail, but Zeila wound her horse through the undergrowth without hesitation.

With a few words, their guide sent one of the guards ahead to scout the way. The other she ordered to fall back to see if anyone was following them. After a while, he returned and shook his head.

Winston felt himself relaxing for the first time in almost a month. They were free. While their prison had been a comfortable one, it was a prison nonetheless. He was unused to being cooped up for days on end. Now he had a good horse beneath him and the way open ahead. His mount carried a bedroll, canteen, saddle bags containing jerked antelope meat, and a pistol. A rifle rested in a holder at the side of his saddle; he took it out and examined it briefly. His adventurous nature took hold and he found himself enjoying their rugged surroundings. He trotted up beside Zeila.

"How far is it to Mapungubwe?" he said.

She replied without looking at him. "Four days hard riding. We meet Lord Sterne late on the third day near the Limpopo River. He'll have more men and wagons to carry whatever we find."

"And whatever will we find?"

She turned and met his eyes. He was struck again by her handsome features. She made a striking figure atop her horse. She wore tight pants and a white short-sleeved shirt, her strong dark arms contrasting starkly against the material. A rakish brimmed hat sat at an angle on her head. Her black hair shimmered beneath it, pulled back in a tight braid. He noted uncomfortably that even on horseback, she looked down on him.

"You don't entirely believe what Lord Sterne and Commander Botha told you, do you, Mr. Churchill?"

He shrugged. "If we're going to be together for a while, I'd prefer you call me Winston." He chewed on what she'd said for a moment longer. "A lot has happened to us in a very short time. I don't really know anything at all about you or Commander Botha. I've met Lord Sterne before and imagine he is a man of his word, but when large amounts of money are at stake, I've generally found that men sometimes forget their word."

She laughed and seemed to relax. "Commander Botha told me he thought you were a very smart and brave man, *Winston*. I think he may be right. I've known Louis Botha for many years. I can tell you he is entirely trustworthy. As much as any man can be who leads a nation in time of war. As for Lord Sterne . . . I think your evaluation of how money affects people is a good one to keep in mind."

Aylmer moved up beside them. "Am I missing a good joke?" he said.

"Zeila seems to think Lord Sterne is a money-grubbing imperialist," Winston said with a straight face.

The captain stared at him and then his face edged into a smile. "There's many a lord in Britain, Zeila, whose estates have dwindled over the centuries who would do almost anything to improve their status. Perhaps he has only the interests of the Crown at heart. But I'd listen to your instincts in dealing with him. He almost certainly hasn't told us or Commander Botha or even the Prince of Wales his entire agenda."

She gave Aylmer a new look of respect. "Perhaps . . . you are *not* as stupid as you look," she said with a wry smile.

"Don't be too hasty in your evaluation," Winston said.

Aylmer gave him a scowl, but he seemed glad at Zeila's words.

They began to move up a long, rising plateau. This was an arid, subtropical climate. Daytime temperatures could easily reach more than one hundred degrees, although the dryness of the heat made it easier to endure. Acacia trees and termite mounds dotted the red earth. Droughts were common and rainfall erratic in the region.

Zeila grew more talkative. "You are both unfamiliar with this place, and there are some things to remember. You need to take in water at regular intervals to avoid dehydration. At night, check your bedroll before climbing into it. There are many poisonous snakes and spiders. Check your shoes in the morning too. If you need to relieve yourselves, don't go far. The big cats hide in the brush and will take you if they think they can."

Winston nodded. "In India, there was a tiger . . . a man-killer. He stalked the soldiers and killed three men before he was found and shot. The local Indians said that particular cat had been responsible for killing forty people."

She nodded. "A big cat becomes more dangerous as he gets older and less able to catch antelope or other fast prey. Men are easy targets . . . slow and stupid."

Aylmer said, "You don't think too much of men in general do you?"

"Not too much," she replied evenly.

"Tell us about Mapungubwe," said Winston to change the subject.

"My people and members of many other tribes have mined the gold of South Africa for centuries," she said. "They used it to trade with the Arabs and Portuguese along the east coast. Gold and diamonds have brought wealth to the white man in Africa, but only hard labor and death to my people. You've heard of the Rand?"

Winston nodded, but Aylmer shook his head.

"A dozen years ago," Zeila said, "huge gold deposits were found on the Witwatersrand near Johannesburg. Last year, the mines produced eight million pounds Sterling or about one fifth of world production."

Aylmer whistled softly. "Someone once said that all wars happen for economic reasons. That amount of gold might be reason enough to explain why we are here."

She looked at him with a trace of approval. "That and the huge new diamond deposits discovered recently. Your country seems to feel she has a claim to any wealth anywhere in the world. Africa is a rich continent, captain. Fully one third of all the gold mined in human history has come out of South Africa. But we'll always remain poor until we rid ourselves of the British and others who would steal from us."

Winston was a man of his times, and he believed in the positive aspects of British colonialism, but even he could understand the way Zeila felt. He tactfully expanded the discussion. "It might seem to a disinterested observer that the real reason Commander Botha is supporting this mission is to gain more gold to help pay for the war."

"I admit," she said slowly, "that I considered it myself, but I don't believe Louis has ever lied to me. The reason he chooses to work in partnership with Lord Sterne, even though we are at war, is because I think he really wishes to protect the finds at Mapungubwe. Lord Sterne has convinced him that together they can preserve the treasure."

"And you are here, representing Botha, to see that Lord Sterne does the right thing?" said Aylmer.

Before she could answer, a small pebble came flying out of the sky and landed precisely in front of her horse. She looked up at the guard who was riding ahead of them. He'd dismounted and pulled his horse down to the ground, one hand over the animal's muzzle. He motioned for them to come forward silently.

They dismounted and tied their horses to a tree, then made their way up to the top of a ridge. The man said something to Zeila in Afrikaans. She put a finger to her lips, cautiously crawled up a few feet more and raised her head slightly. She stared at something for a long time, then lowered her head and silently backed down to them. In a whisper, she said, "Three men. They look like Boer soldiers, but my guess is they're deserters. They have several prisoners . . . natives. I think they're slave traders. We'll have to go around, give them a wide berth."

Winston said, "If they're slavers, they're breaking the law. We should stop them."

"I don't like it either, Winston, but that's not our mission. If one of them were to get away and report on our whereabouts or if one of us is killed, all our plans would be jeopardized. The risk is too great."

Winston stared at her for a moment, then crawled up and peered at the scene below. The prisoners were two men and a woman. They appeared to be very young, at most fifteen or sixteen years of age. They were completely naked, had their hands tied and were being watched casually by one of the men who held a rifle. The other two men had begun to make camp, hobbling the horses and stringing a piece of cloth between several trees for protection from the sun. As Winston watched, one of the men went over and cut the bonds of one of their captives and ordered the man to begin gathering firewood. He pulled out a leather switch and occasionally lashed the man when he didn't move quickly enough.

Careful not to dislodge any loose stones, Winston backed down to the others. "It shouldn't be too difficult," he said. "We'll wait until they settle down and are relaxed . . . less watchful. Zeila and Aylmer can cover the camp from here with their rifles. We'll send our two guards around to the opposite side behind that gully. When everyone's ready, I'll slip down to that clump of thorn bushes near the camp, then move forward until they see me. When I raise my arm, that will be the signal for the rest of you to move forward and fire if they show any resistance."

"This is not a good idea, Winston," Zeila said. "They're dangerous men, these slavers, capable of anything."

"I'm not going to leave those poor buggers to be dragged off into slavery." He fastened her eyes with his own. "Are you going to help or am I going to have to do it myself?"

She sighed. "Commander Botha said you English might be difficult. All right, but I should be the one to go down there, unless you happen to speak Afrikaans."

They tied their horses a hundred yards away and waited until the men in the camp were sitting by the fire cooking something. The captives sat huddled together away from the fire. It was clear they would sleep on the cold ground with no protection. At that distance from the flames, they might not even make it through the night if a lion happened to pick up their scent.

Zeila directed their two guards to the opposite side of the camp. Then Winston and Aylmer crouched behind the hill with rifles ready. Zeila took a circuitous route around the camp to the clump of thorn trees, from which vantage point she was less than twenty feet from the men. With a glance back at Churchill, she stood up and began to move forward.

Winston had to admire the woman. She showed not an ounce of fear and moved catlike, rifle in hand, toward the men. Just as she came into view and was about to say something, one of the captives spotted her and cried out.

Alerted, the men at the fire leaped to their feet and snatched their rifles. Clearly, they were ready for trouble. Winston suddenly realized that Zeila was totally exposed, less than a dozen feet from three men with guns who would think nothing of killing her instantly. He jumped up, Aylmer a step behind him and began to fire. Almost simultaneously, the guards on the other side of the camp also began to shoot.

The slavers reacted with complete panic, spinning around at this confrontation from three sides at once. Bullets began to fly everywhere. One of the men pumped shots furiously and almost randomly. He hit one of the captives in the chest, killing him instantly. The other male captive jumped up and ran away into the bush, hands still tied. The woman froze and remained where she was.

Zeila had fallen to the ground as soon as the firing started. From her prone position, she calmly shot and killed one of the slavers. A second man quickly fell to the fire of the guards on the opposite hill. Aylmer shot the last man with his pistol and suddenly all was quiet.

Winston ran to Zeila, who was still lying on the ground, but she was unhurt and rose to her feet and went over to the remaining captive. She cut the woman's bonds and then knelt, trying to comfort her in a dialect that sounded like pure babble to Winston. The poor thing was only a girl, very young and clearly terrified. She had no idea she'd been freed, only expecting herself to be shot momentarily.

Winston left Zeila to her task and checked to make sure that no one else had been hurt by the blizzard of ineffective shots the slavers had loosed. Then he set the guards to burying the men as quickly as possible. Bodies could not be left out any time at all on the veldt or they'd attract all manner of scavengers.

Aylmer joined Zeila beside the girl, who was beginning to comprehend that she wasn't going to be killed. Her body was filthy, her feet nearly raw from walking on the rocks and hard earth. She was thin, though not emaciated, with small breasts and a decorative series of black dots tattooed from her shoulders to her elbows. Her hair was tightly bound in corn rows. The hair and tattoos suggested she'd once belonged to a secure family and tribe. She spoke haltingly to Zeila, who stroked her head and murmured reassuringly to her in the strange dialect.

"My God," Aylmer said flatly. "How can people do this to another human being?"

"It wasn't that long ago that millions of Africans were sent to be slaves in America," said Zeila. "There's nothing unusual about it at all. She says she was taken from her village two weeks ago. She didn't know the other two captives who were picked up later. She's sixteen years old."

Aylmer said, "Did they . . ."

"No. One of the men wanted to take her but the others wouldn't let him because she's a virgin and worth a lot of money."

Winston came over. "I've left the guards to burial duty. I think we should make our own camp on the other side of the hill, far enough away that any animals attracted by the blood on the ground won't be inclined to bother us. I saw a small spring there." He looked down at the girl lying naked on the ground. "I've got an extra shirt in my bags I can give her, but maybe you should clean her up first."

Zeila nodded. "She won't know what to do with your shirt. Her people wear virtually nothing as a matter of course. I'll clean her up, though." She stood and faced him. "You acted quickly and may have saved my life, Winston. Thank you. But I still don't think this was a good thing. Four men have been killed, including one of the captives. The other has run off with his hands tied. We'll never find him, and he'll likely be eaten by something before the night is over. Do you still think it was worth the cost?"

"Those men were slavers," Winston said. "I have no problem killing the bloody bastards. I'm sorry for the two slaves, but they're probably better off dead. And we saved the girl. I'd do it again. Such things should not be allowed to go on."

She just shook her head, took the girl by the arm and headed for their campsite.

The night came on quickly. By the time camp was made, Zeila had taken the girl to the spring and bathed her. Then she used a piece of cloth to make her a sort of sarong to wear, more for the Victorian sense of modesty held by Winston and Aylmer than for the girl, who was nevertheless very pleased with the pretty cloth.

"Her name is Wa-Nyika," said Zeila. "I don't know the exact variants of her dialect, but we've been able to communicate all right. The bad part is, it looks like we're stuck with her. Her village is at least two weeks ride to the west. We can't afford the time to take her there."

As darkness enveloped them, the night came alive with the sounds of animals. A lion coughed nearby and hyenas cackled over their stolen prey. The guards had gathered a huge pile of firewood to last the night. Aylmer and Winston lay on their bedrolls smoking their last two cigarettes. Zeila took the first watch. They could just see her tall, dark form at the edge of the circle of firelight.

"She was a good soldier today," Aylmer said with admiration. "It's something to know. We may have more difficulties before we're through."

Winston nodded. "I'd trust her before I would Commander Botha or Lord Sterne," he said. "She's motivated, I think, only by her desire to improve the lot of her countrymen. It would be wise not to forget, though, that white men are not her favorite people."

They watched her move a few feet farther away from them. Then she put her rifle down, dropped her pants and peed. They could see the stream of urine coming from her bottom as it reflected the firelight. She wiped herself with a handful of leaves and stood up, her long, slim legs clearly delineated before she pulled her pants up.

Aylmer whistled softly. "Now that's something you don't see every day in Piccadilly."

Winston said nothing, but he had the clear impression that what Zeila had just done was precisely for their benefit.

For two days they continued northward, the landscape altering little from its rocky barrenness. They skirted herds of wildebeest, impala and waterbuck. Once, a rhinoceros emerged from the brush, running at them full tilt, but the creature veered off before they had to bring their rifles to bear. Wa-Nyika rode behind Zeila, her small extra weight no hindrance to their mount.

At noon on the third day, they halted for a rest under the shade of a large baobab tree isolated amidst the stubbled thorn bushes, its trunk nearly twenty feet in circumference. It was stiflingly hot, close to one hundred degrees. The horizon shimmered in waves from the heat rising off the sun-baked hills. Winston sat beside Zeila, chewing on some jerked antelope, and watched Wa-Nyika, who was eating and humming to herself in a sort of sing-song patter.

"She seems little the worse for her experience," he said.

Zeila nodded. "It's something that frustrates me terribly. The people out here take the existence of things like slavers for granted. One more hard fact of life like all the other every-day things they have to fight constantly . . . hunger, thirst, disease, wild beasts, poisonous snakes. But as long as they accept things with such resignation, they'll never change them." She hesitated. "I'm ashamed that I also sometimes accept the normalcy of such terrible things. I was wrong to want to just leave Wa-Nyika to her fate."

"How did you happen to get so close to Botha?" Winston said, sensing her willingness to open up.

"It's why I feel so strongly about Wa-Nyika, I suppose. My background wasn't all that different from hers. But my father's relationship with Max Grundy became my way out of that life. Grundy helped pay for my education in Johannesburg. It wasn't easy, you know, to educate a black woman at that time—it's still not. It probably wouldn't have made all that much difference except that Grundy sent me to England to live with his sister when I was fourteen. She was a very independent woman, quite wealthy from an inheritance, and she believed firmly that women should be educated to the highest degree. By the time she was finished, I spoke the King's English and had two advanced degrees, including one of the first ever issued by Cambridge to a black woman.

"I had also learned the history of how Africans had been exploited for so long in their own land. That knowledge changed me forever. I returned to Pretoria and was employed at once by Louis Botha, who had need of someone with my talents and knowledge of both worlds, yours and mine."

Suddenly their noonday camp exploded with the sounds of hooves and the clatter of wagons as Lord Sterne rode briskly in out of the heat. He was accompanied by two heavy wagons pulled by workhorses and half a dozen soldiers. The wagons were loaded with supplies including climbing ropes, winch and tackle, and empty crates in the event they actually found anything worth hauling out of this remote backcountry. Sterne cut a dashing figure in his pressed khakis and military-style shirt. He jumped down from his horse and came over to them, excitement on his face.

"Winston! Zeila! Thought we'd never find you. What a mad route we've taken, trying to get these behemoth wagons through this torturous country. Covered ten miles back and forth for every one forward. But . . . here we are!" He smiled broadly, looking around. "This is about where we'd planned to rendezvous, isn't it Zeila?"

"Yes," she said. "Though I hadn't really expected you until this evening and a few miles farther on."

"Good a place as any for our camp tonight, I'd say. Could use a rest before we tackle the last bit to Mapungubwe Hill." He looked around, his eyes coming to rest on Wa-Nyika. "What's this?"

Winston said, "A native girl. We rescued her from slavers two days back. No alternative but to bring her with us."

Sterne considered the girl for a moment. "Not sure I approve. What if she has tribal relatives looking for her? We don't want anyone finding out what we're up to."

"It's unlikely," said Zeila. "Her village is at least two weeks distant by horseback, and they don't have horses. Wa-Nyika said she was taken at night. No one would have known what happened to her. It's entirely likely they wrote her off as being taken away by spirits."

"Well," he gave the girl a last lingering look, "I suppose there's no harm done. Let me situate my men, then I have a bottle of whisky we can share. Lord knows this Lord could use a few stiff ones." He grinned and strode away.

Zeila and Winston exchanged glances. He said, "I never asked. Exactly where will we be hiding this so-called treasure if we actually locate it?" He nodded at the heavy wagons. "It would appear Lord Sterne has some ideas along those lines."

She shrugged. "The idea was to remove any antiquities to a more secure location. If there's anything more specific than that, I haven't been privy to the plans. Lord Sterne spent some time in private talks with Commander Botha, however."

Winston stared about at the bleak and barren foothills that surrounded them. "Hard to imagine any place more secure than this," he said. "It would take a madman to come out here to look for anything, much less treasure."

"Or a madwoman," Zeila said with a wan smile.

4.

THEY REACHED MAPUNGUBWE HILL early in the afternoon of the following day. The landscape had become more heavily covered with brush and it was hard going for the wagons. Sometimes all of the guards had to dismount and cut through a particularly nasty bit of thorn before they could advance. After chopping their way through yet another stand, they emerged at last to see the hill standing majestically before them, the lazy waters of the Limpopo River flowing nearby.

Mapungubwe rose one hundred and fifty feet above the surrounding hills. Perhaps half of that height was nearly vertical, rising above the thick scrub that covered its lower slopes. A sandstone outcrop of great geological age, its vertical sides glowed ocher-red in the afternoon sun. Steep rocks filled with gullies and pocked caves offered a glimmer of hope that there might be a way to tackle the mountain with ropes and sure hands. But it was immediately obvious the manner in which they would broach the flat top of the outcrop.

Zeila said, "You see the chimney? That's how we'll climb. There are ancient footholds cut into the sides. It's steep, but it can be done using our ropes."

The chimney of rock stuck out almost like an industrial smokestack. It stood nearly free of the main body of the hill with only a slim bit of rock attaching it to the rest of the plateau. The base was not visible, for it was buried in thick scrub and thorn. From their vantage point, it looked completely unclimbable.

Lord Sterne stared at the mountain before them. "Incredible. I always wondered what it would actually look like. It must have been a formidable fortress in its day."

"Yes," said Zeila. "The piles of boulders lined along the top to repel attackers attest to that. From the quantities, this place must have been lived in for many hundreds, perhaps thousands of years. Imagine the work required to lift all those rocks into place."

Winston looked around. "I suggest we make camp over there." He pointed to a break in the thorn. "We'll set the guards to unload the wagons while the four of us see if we can climb the chimney for a look around before dark."

Carrying only ropes and a single canteen of water, Winston, Aylmer, Zeila and Sterne approached the base of the chimney. They followed a faint trail in the scrub originally cut by Grundy and then hacked again by Zeila's men the previous year. Still, the thorns grew quickly and they had to use their machetes continuously. While Winston and Sterne hacked away, Zeila and Aylmer stood ready with their rifles in case the activity attracted lions. Finally they stood together and stared silently up at the massive tower.

"Whew!" Aylmer whistled softly. "That's going to be a climb."

Zeila took the rope off her shoulder. "We'll tie together," she said. "If anyone slips, the others should be able to hold him."

"Or her," said Winston.

"I won't slip," she said matter-of-factly. "While I was at school in England, I joined an alpine club. We spent all our weekends going up and down the steep peaks of North Wales, Tryfan, Snowdon and others. It was highly technical mountaineering."

Lord Sterne looked at her with interest. "I, too, have done some climbing . . . in the Alps." He looked up again at the chimney. "This should not be a problem."

Suddenly, the quiet of the late afternoon was interrupted by a strange, high-pitched wail. It went on for over a minute, turning to a distant, reverberating moan before finally trailing off.

"What in the name of heaven was that?" said Aylmer.

They all stared up at the plateau. Finally, Zeila said, "It must be the wind moving through the rocks and caves. It can make strange sounds."

"Interesting theory," Sterne said, "except you may notice there isn't any wind."

"Up there is different," Zeila said confidently. "There will be wind."

Sterne was clearly the strongest of them, so he went first, followed by Zeila, Winston and Aylmer. The footholds appeared some fifteen feet from the bottom and did indeed make the climb much easier. They were cut several inches deep into the hard rock, but their age was obvious, for they were worn completely smooth and rounded. About halfway up, Aylmer's hand slipped off one of the rounded indentations and he fell several feet before the others took in the slack. He clutched desperately for a foothold and then hung on, catching his breath.

As they neared the top, Winston said, "I read once about similar footholds that the Indians of the American Southwest used to reach their hideaways. The thing was, only they knew how to begin their climbs. If you started with the wrong foot, by the time you got to the top, you would be stuck, unable to go forward or back."

"Now you tell us," Aylmer grunted from beneath him.

They finally pulled themselves over the lip of the chimney and stood to take in their surroundings.

The top of the plateau spread before them, rocky, barren and sparsely covered with low scrub. It seemed to slope gently up toward the highest point, where they could make out what appeared to be a series of terraced rock walls and foundation depressions. They detached themselves from the rope and Sterne tied one end firmly around an outcrop, then threw the other end over the ledge. The climb back down would be considerably easier.

Winston stared out across the bushveld, dumbstruck at the stark beauty spread before them. Ridge after ridge of diminishing hills disappeared into the distance. The meandering Limpopo river glinted in the sun and he could see a herd of elephants washing themselves in its shallows. Perhaps a thousand wildebeest filled one large opening in the scrub and he could even see a pride of lions beginning to encircle them, searching for the weak, young or sick. The huge yellow ball of the sun was nearing the horizon. It would be dark in little more than an hour. They had time for only a quick reconnoiter.

"No wonder they chose this place to live," he said. "They could see their entire food supply spread out before them, like Sunday brunch at the Regent Palace. They must have planned their hunts while standing right where we are now."

Zeila said, "I feel a strong pull here, Winston. You English have lords and dukes and princes with a documented history going back a thousand years. But we know so little about our heritage in Southern Africa. This may be one of the earliest sites of my ancestors and here we are, at the dawn of the twentieth century and besides Max Grundy and my own brief foray last year, probably no one has climbed this hill in five hundred years or more." She stared in awe at the foundations lining the hilltop. "It takes my breath away," she said softly.

The sun had begun to dip below the horizon. If they didn't want to spend the night up here they would have to hurry. It would be impossible to go down the cliffs in the dark. Quickly, the four explorers hiked to the central, raised part of the plateau. Here, they found that the ruins were far more extensive than they could have imagined. The rocks hadn't just been piled as dry stone work but showed evidence of having been cemented using a sort of mud paste, probably from the nearby river. They were finely cut and shaped to fit tightly together. By climbing an outcrop that rose above the site, they could see the outline of a low outer wall that meandered for hundreds of yards and had once enclosed the central buildings.

As Zeila and Winston tried to gauge the extent of the site from their elevated spot, Aylmer and Sterne moved to investigate a steep hillside at the center of the compound. The rise appeared to have been washed out by the heavy rains that pounded the region during the wet season. Suddenly, Sterne cried out and beckoned to the others.

"It's true," Sterne cried excitedly as Zeila and Winston came up. "Look!" He waved a hand toward the middle of the compound. "The golden hill!" he exclaimed.

Winston stared, dumbstruck. The entire rise glinted yellow in the evening sun. Mixed with the rocks and red soil were seemingly endless bits of gold. Perfectly round gold beads ranged from tiny pellets to some the size of marbles, pieces of coiled rope gold, tiny bits of gold plate. The wealth extended over an area of nearly twenty square yards. A fortune lay at their feet.

"It appears we have our work cut out for us, literally," Sterne said gleefully. "Cut out of the hillside by the simple rain."

They retreated quickly as dark began to fall, descending the chimney without incident. But as soon as the last of them was down, with the dim light fading, a lion coughed very close by. Keeping their rifles ready, they moved through the heavy scrub. Winston felt himself straining to hear every sound, his eyes aching with the effort to see into the dense brush.

Even Zeila, the most experienced at this sort of thing, was uneasy. "Keep close together," she said softly over and over whenever their line began to stretch out. "The cats can leap in, grab you and be gone in an instant. It's the worst time of day—the time when they hunt. We can't see three feet into the scrub. That's how close they may be."

Finally, with great relief, they were through the dense scrub at the bottom of the hill, and the danger, while not over, lessened considerably. As soon as they entered camp, Wa-Nyika, babbling in her incomprehensible dialect, came running over to hug Zeila.

The guards had gathered firewood and built two separate fires some twenty feet apart. While this took more wood, it offered greater protection and a larger circle of light to keep the lions away. They would sleep between the two fires, taking turns feeding the flames.

After dinner, the guards gathered near one fire, resting and talking quietly among themselves. Winston, Aylmer, Sterne, Zeila and Wa-Nyika did the same near the second fire. Lord Sterne was in a jubilant and expansive mood. He brought forth a bottle of whisky and after filling everyone's glass, offered a toast.

"To the ancients of Mapungubwe Hill," he said. "And to our own successful rescue of their heritage."

Winston raised his glass with the others, but after drinking, he said, "I wonder if the ancients would really appreciate our rooting through their homeland and burial sites . . . whatever good reasons we might invent."

Sterne lowered his glass slowly. "I disagree, Winston. They were primitive people and no doubt would not understand the importance of what we're trying to accomplish here. Were we to leave the site as it is, one of two things would surely happen. Either bandits, slavers or the war itself would lead to looting of the site. And if through some miracle that didn't happen, why then the treasures of Mapungubwe would simply wash out of the hill year after year until everything was dissipated. Who would benefit from that?"

"I think perhaps what Winston was suggesting," said Aylmer, "is that while the long-ago residents here wouldn't understand, as you put it, what we're trying to accomplish, their own preference would certainly be for the place to remain undisturbed. This is a burial site, after all . . . perhaps a royal one. How would we feel if our descendants dug up Westminster Abbey, throwing the bones of kings and great men aside in order to loot their valuables? I don't think the ancients of Mapungubwe would give a hoot for who might 'benefit' from their golden hill."

"Utter nonsense!" Sterne exploded, tossing the dregs of his glass to the ground and refilling it sullenly. "A complete waste to leave things as they are. The dead are dead. The living must go on."

Winston looked at Zeila. "You've been quiet," he said. "But these were your ancestors. What do you think?"

She stared into the fire. She'd washed and changed into clean khaki shorts that exposed her strong, slim legs. Her shirt fell loosely to her waist, but stretched tightly against her breasts. When she moved, they swayed, revealing she had nothing else on underneath. She was an intriguing figure, caught between the two worlds she lived in, traditional African and the imperialist culture of the white man.

"I haven't been completely content at what we're doing," she said. "And I don't believe for a moment the people who lived here would approve of the disturbance of their burials." She straightened her shoulders. "But I agree with Lord Sterne on one point. It benefits no one for the history . . . and, yes, the treasure . . . of Mapungubwe Hill to be stolen or for it to float off, bit by bit, down the Limpopo River." She looked at Wa-Nyika, the blissfully ignorant girl who sat contentedly beside them. "Our preservation of these materials *will* benefit her some day. Perhaps the wealth will help her people out of their poverty or perhaps the simple knowledge of the greatness that was once theirs will encourage them to try for it again. I don't know. But it's for these reasons that I'm here."

Sterne nodded, content once more. "Absolutely correct. Zeila understands better than any of us. One society builds upon the ashes of another." He stood up. The whisky had begun to take effect. "It's been a long day. I'm going to sleep." He moved a dozen feet away and lay down abruptly, pulling his blanket over him.

The others continued to sit by the fire, listening to it crackle loudly from the dry wood fed into it. Lions could be heard in the night, but there was no danger so long as the flames licked high. After a while, Wa-Nyika fell asleep and Aylmer stretched out with his hat over his face, seemingly drifting off as well.

In a low voice, Zeila said, "Your family has royal connections, Winston. How do you think they would feel about all of this?"

He shifted uncomfortably on the hard ground. "My father, Lord Randolph, was the son of the seventh Duke of Marlborough. But he served in the House of Commons and fought for social and political reforms. He believed in looking forward, Zeila. I think he might have sympathized with your idea of helping today's people even if it means uprooting some of the traditions of the past."

A lion roared loudly from just beyond the circle of flames. Wa-Nyika stirred, mumbling in her sleep, and Aylmer raised up on one elbow, then lay back down.

"My father has been dead for almost five years," he went on. "A day doesn't go by that I don't think of him . . . both the good things and the bad. I think the most important thing is that we don't forget the dead. We build on what they started, as Lord Sterne said. It's just that I'm never quite certain that what Sterne says is what he's really thinking." He stood up and stretched. "I'll say good night, too, Zeila. We're going to be very busy the next few days." He went over and lay down a few feet from Sterne.

The night was black and very clear. Winston drifted in and out of sleep. When he was awake, he stared up at the incredible bowl of stars that stretched from horizon to horizon. He thought of Miss Pamela Plowden, his first serious love, waiting for him back home. As much as he cared for her, he wondered if she could ever understand the sort of life experiences he'd had these last few weeks.

Once, he woke to find the fires burning low. He got up quietly to throw more wood on them. He thought he heard something at the edge of the firelight. Suspecting an animal, he took out his pistol and moved forward. Then he realized the sounds were voices. With a few more steps he recognized Zeila's tall figure. She was talking animatedly with Lord Sterne, who didn't appear to be sleepy or drunk any more. As he paused, uncertain, Winston saw Sterne place his hand on Zeila's breast. She slapped it away angrily, turned and walked away. Sterne laughed softly in the dark.

Quietly, Winston retreated to his own bedroll and lay down, wondering what this new turn of events might mean to the success or failure of their venture.

Over the next several days, they set up an efficient operation to remove the treasure of Mapungubwe's golden hill. A makeshift platform was constructed at the top of the chimney using lumber and tools brought by Sterne. The winch and tackle were attached to it so that a large leather bucket could be lowered, filled with the baubles of the ancient people. The guards became workmen, not something they'd bargained for, and they grumbled a good deal at the labor.

Shovel by shovel, the golden hill was sifted through screens that revealed a steady stream of golden bits, rope and beads. At the bottom, Sterne catalogued the contents of each bucketload as best he could, for much of the gold came in pieces from remnants of bracelets or coil. The first day, they uncovered fourteen small gold rhinoceroses. These were the only artifacts found more or less in complete condition. The uniformity of the finds was puzzling.

"I don't understand why there are no gems," Zeila said during a break on the afternoon of the third day. One of the wagons at the base of the chimney now stood filled with crates laden with the treasure. "It's hard to believe the jeweled soapstone bird Grundy brought out could be the only such piece on all of Mapungubwe."

Winston said, "Perhaps we should explore some other areas. The presence of all this gold may have diverted us from other, equally rich deposits yet to be uncovered."

And so, leaving Sterne and the guards to continue sifting the seemingly endless riches of the golden hill, Winston, Aylmer and Zeila began to poke around the remainder of the foundations. Near the heart of the village, they discovered a partially buried temple with decayed columns set back against a steep rise. Winston thought the temple might be the entrance to a burial chamber or at least another room. Together, the three of them, along with Wa-Nyika, who seemed to enjoy the digging, almost like playing in a sandbox, worked to dig out the earth and rocks that filled the space between the columns.

After working all one afternoon, they'd opened up the temple entrance, which seemed to lead to a hallway. As they scraped away the debris of a thousand years, they took turns exclaiming, as vividly colored paintings and rock carvings revealed themselves. Images of elephants and rhinoceroses, giraffes and lions, magnificent paintings of green gardens hanging with flowers lined the entrance.

"This must be how this place actually looked long ago," Zeila said with growing excitement. "It was a very different climate. We're actually seeing the layout of the community in these pictures."

Then Aylmer shouted from inside the temple where he was digging around a depression. "Come see this," he said, a note of awe in his voice.

They all squeezed into the small space. Aylmer said, "You see how this depression in the earth suggests another level?" he said. "I thought it would be worth digging down . . . and look what I found."

There was an exquisite mosaic on the floor of the depression. Aylmer had brought in a bucket of water to wash away the dirt and debris of centuries, as he exposed the floor. The colors, protected for perhaps a thousand years inside the temple, under cover of the hillside, were vivid splashes of green and blue and yellow. Each piece of mosaic was meticulously hand-painted. The scene depicted a jungle setting beside a waterfall. Surrounding the water were animals and birds and . . . three figures, a man and two women.

Zeila squatted on the floor, enthralled by the figures. "Look at them!" she said excitedly. "These could be some of the earliest depictions ever of my ancestors. I might actually be related to one of these people."

Aylmer had crept farther into the depression and was banging with his pick at the edge of the mosaic. Suddenly, a section of the floor gave way and with a cry he disappeared into a black hole. Zeila and Winston exchanged frightened looks as their friend vanished into the earth.

5.

"ARE YOU ALL RIGHT, Aylmer?" Winston stared into the gaping hole that had taken his friend. He spread his weight evenly along the tiled mosaic. The others had drawn back out of fear that the entire floor might give way.

A pained grunt came from the darkness. "Just a minute." Then, "I think so. Banged the hell out of my arm, though. I'm going to need help climbing out, but as long as I'm down here, why don't you lower me a torch so I can look around."

Winston hiked back to the chimney and yelled down to the guards to send up one of the torches they'd made to allow movement outside of the camps after dark. These were simple affairs consisting of a heavy stick with thatch wrapped around one end that was then soaked in coal oil. They burned for up to an hour. By the time he returned to the temple entrance, Zeila had secured a rope and thrown one end down to Aylmer.

Winston handed her the torch along with his cigarette lighter. "Here—light this while I climb down, then drop it to us."

She nodded and watched him descend. As soon as he was down, however, she tucked the torch under her arm, stuck the lighter in her pocket and quickly lowered herself as well. "If you think I'm going to wait while you explore the ancient home of my own people, you are one crazy *mzungu*," she said, using the native word for white man.

She lit the torch and held it up. They were in a sort of hallway carved from solid rock that stretched away for a distance of perhaps twenty feet to where a set of steps descended out of sight. The hall seemed to be a burial chamber, its walls pockmarked with indentations in the stone. As Zeila brought the torch near the entrance of one of these, they saw bones and a skull. Each opening held a similar sight. The bodies had been buried in a hunched-over, seated fashion, and there was evidence in the form of dried bits of hemp-like fibers that they'd been tied into the unnatural positions.

Winston grimaced. "I sure hope the poor buggers were already dead before they were tied. Imagine being roped into such a position and placed in here alive."

"It wouldn't be the first time," Zeila said, "that servants were buried alive to wait on royalty in the next world."

Each body was surrounded by skillfully crafted pottery, still whole and undisturbed, probably food containers for the journey to the next life. There was no evidence of gold or other valuables of the sort associated with royal burials.

Enthralled by each successive discovery, they moved as if in a daze toward the steps at the end of the corridor. Here they found a broad set of stone treads that descended about ten feet before they disappeared, covered with fallen debris from the walls and ceiling. Aylmer stared uneasily at the walls. "This entire place looks like it could collapse any minute," he said.

"Mapungubwe hill is made up of soft sandstone," said Zeila. "It's been washed over by seasonal rains for thousands of years, carving caves and channels. Probably what made all of this possible in the first place. The inhabitants simply had to follow and perhaps enlarge the chambers they found. And carving the individual burial slots would have been easy enough to do in the soft stone."

"Well the place gives me the creeps," said Aylmer. "Let's get out of here."

They backtracked and climbed up the rope into the temple. Zeila extinguished her torch. "We need to dig out that staircase," she said firmly. "There's no telling what might be beyond."

"We'll discuss it with Sterne at dinner tonight," said Winston. "It's the only time of day you can pry him away from his golden hill."

Zeila started to say something, then seemed to think better of it. She turned and went out. Aylmer looked at Winston with raised eyebrows. "What was that about?" he said.

"I'm not certain. But there's some sort of relationship between Sterne and Zeila that I don't understand." He explained what he'd seen the previous evening in camp when Zeila had brusquely rebuffed Lord Sterne.

"I'll be damned," said Aylmer. "You think she's been sleeping with him?"

"I don't know. It didn't strike me that way. Their body language didn't suggest it, and when Sterne touched her breast, she was genuinely angry, as though it was something that had never happened before."

"Maybe you should just come right out and ask her. Something like that could affect all of us and the mission as well."

Winston gave him a dry look. "Feel free to bring it up, old boy, if you want. I don't think she will take kindly to the question, however."

By the end of the day, the treasure of the golden hill had begun to peter out. The two wagons down below were nearly full, however, with golden bits of bracelet, animals, beads, plate and rope coil.

"Must be over a ton of the stuff," Sterne reported gleefully that evening around their campfire. "Still, it's too bad the site seems to have run dry."

"That leads into what we wanted to discuss," said Winston. He glanced at Zeila, who looked away. "We located another chamber. No gold, but it could be significant. We want to spend tomorrow exploring it."

Sterne shook his head. "We've got what we were after. Even if there's something more to be found, we haven't the means to take it out. Our horses will be strained to pull the wagons as it is over this terrain." He paused, gauging their tense faces. "Still . . . I suppose it might be worth a single day's exploration."

Aylmer said, "Where will you take the gold?"

Sterne hesitated. "I'm not allowed to divulge that information. But rest assured that Commander Botha has arranged a safe repository where it will sit out the war."

"And you can also be assured," said Zeila, "that I will be with you every step of the way . . . wherever you are going. This treasure will not be diverted to the war effort or to your own personal plans. I won't allow it."

Sterne looked at her with cold eyes. "I resent that implication. We're all on the same side here. But do as you wish. We'll allow another day to explore your temple. And now I suggest we get some rest."

In the morning, Zeila and Aylmer set up a series of torch holders to illuminate the hallway. An additional stack of torches was piled just below the entrance. The light flickered eerily upon the many burial holes lining the walls, while the smoke of the torches caught in their throats. Sterne somewhat reluctantly contributed three of his guards to help clear the debris on the steps and the work proceeded quickly.

As the steps were revealed, so too were stone walls once again decorated with elaborate paintings of people and the lives they'd led here in the southern heart of ancient Africa. By mid-day, they'd descended twenty feet and the stairs gave way to yet another hallway. They had removed so much debris that they had to install a bucket lift to haul it from the first hallway, for there was no place to deposit all the rock and dirt. The walls of the sandstone structure were soft and porous. Large chunks periodically broke free and collapsed, so that they had to be on guard constantly for cave-ins.

During a rest break, Zeila and Winston sat together on the dirt floor, staring tiredly at the seemingly endless piles of debris yet to be removed.

"It may be hopeless," Winston said. "There's no telling how much farther we have to go. It's just not possible to dig it all out in a single day."

Frustration showed in Zeila's face. "This is much more important than all that gold Sterne has squirreled away. There must be a royal burial chamber, Winston. It just makes sense. The chambers of servants are there for a reason and so is this incredible, decorated hallway. What other reason could there be for it all—to lead nowhere?"

A guard from Sterne's wagon detail came forward from the entrance. "One of the wagons has become stuck near the base of the chimney," he said. "We need to borrow the men who are helping you to get it out."

Zeila waved a hand. "Take them," she said. "But have them back within the hour. We have a lot farther to go here."

The guards departed, leaving Winston, Aylmer and Zeila alone in the flickering hallway. They were too tired to talk and simply lay, sprawled out, staring blankly at the mosaics that surrounded them. When the explosion came, it was muffled and almost seemed insignificant, as though a small section of the structure had again collapsed. But they were quickly enveloped in a cloud of dust and dirt that floated down toward them.

"What the hell . . .?" said Aylmer.

Winston was the first to his feet. He grabbed one of the torches and swore loudly. "Damn! I should have suspected . . . stupid not to."

Zeila and Aylmer stared at him. "What are you talking about?" Aylmer said.

But Zeila quickly understood what Winston was suggesting. "My God, would he really do that?"

"Do what?" said Aylmer.

Winston was already headed back down the hallway to the point where Aylmer had first fallen through from the floor above. The entrance hole was gone, completely blocked by tons of collapsed stone and earth.

They stood and stared at the devastation. Aylmer looked back down the hall. "I hope the air lasts long enough for them to dig us out."

Zeila slumped to the floor. "No one is going to dig us out," she said.

"I think you're right," said Winston, who also sat down and leaned his torch against the wall.

"You're saying Sterne *intended* to bury us alive?" Aylmer said, incredulously.

Winston looked at Zeila. "You have any thoughts on that?" he said.

"I don't know, Winston. I always suspected Lord Sterne had his own plans for the gold if we found any. He tried to feel me out the other night." She laughed bitterly. "Feel me up, might be more like it. I'm sorry. I didn't see this coming."

They were quiet for several minutes, each thinking his own thoughts. The silence of their tomb was almost overwhelming, the loudest sound the beating of their own hearts. Finally, Winston said, "Well, I'll be buggered if I'm going to sit here until I look like these other poor sods buried in the walls. We may already be dead men, but I say we continue to explore. There's always a chance there could be another way out." He stared at the huge mound of earth and rock in front of them. "One thing's certain. We can't dig through that."

The stack of extra torches was buried, but they still had the six that had been mounted along the hallways. They removed each of them as they made their way back down the corridor. Including the one Winston held, they would have light for approximately seven hours . . . provided the oxygen held out.

At the bottom of the steps that had been cleared, they proceeded down the newly opened hallway and stood side by side staring at the wall of debris before them. There was no alternative. They would have to continue to dig.

Winston took off his jacket. The air in the confined space was already growing warmer since the outside entrance had been closed. He picked up a shovel, then handed a pickaxe to Aylmer. Zeila also picked up a shovel. Slowly, with heavy hands and hearts, they began to work their way farther into the debris wall that faced them.

It was backbreaking labor, making them appreciate all the more the work that had been done by Sterne's men. Zeila stripped down to her T-shirt, which quickly became slick with sweat, revealing her breasts almost more than if they'd been bare. Her strong black arms glistened as she worked.

Aylmer pounded his pick into the wall, pulling loose huge chunks, while Zeila and Winston used their shovels to pull more dirt out or to push it behind them. They were no longer concerned about where the debris went, so long as it was pushed back out of the way. After half an hour, Winston paused.

"I think we should put out the torch," he said. "We can work almost as well in the dark. It will save air and torches both." He picked up the light, took one last, self-conscious glance at Zeila's magnificent breasts and thrust the torch into the dirt.

Now they worked in total darkness, keeping at least five feet between them so they didn't get hit by Aylmer's pick. It was a bizarre form of labor to be engaging in in total blackness. The only sounds were those of shovels, picks and their own grunts and heavy breathing. It was as if they labored in the halls of Hades itself . . . and almost as hot, though the flames of that final dungeon would have offered considerably more light to see by.

After nearly an hour, Aylmer said, "I . . . I think I've broken through to something. My pick went through into empty space." He poked some more. "I've definitely opened into another space," he said excitedly, and in fact, they could all feel the temperature cool significantly as new air came into their tunnel.

Winston relit the torch and they gathered around to stare into the opening. Thrusting the brand into the hole, they saw what appeared to be a very large space.

"It's some sort of cavern," Aylmer said. "Must be huge. I can't even see the far side."

Together, they pushed at the sides of the hole until it was big enough to allow them to pass through. Zeila went first, holding the torch high above her head. What was revealed was an enormous, almost circular cavern at least a hundred feet across. The ceiling was beyond the reach of their light, though they could hear water dripping from a considerable height. What captivated Zeila, however, and turned her almost speechless were the carvings.

All around the cavern at ten-foot intervals were sandstone pedestals. Each was five feet tall and held on its flat top a carved soapstone bird with large ruby eyes that glinted as they reflected the torch light.

"Mother of God, what a sight!" said Aylmer.

In front of each pedestal was a platform carved out of sandstone and on each platform was a carefully wrapped corpse. Winston counted twenty in all.

"Who do you think they were?" he said in a hushed voice.

"Not royalty," said Zeila in equally awestruck tones. "Maybe . . . priests or religious figures of some sort." She went up to the nearest body and brought the torch in close. Around the neck of the tightly wrapped torso hung the remnants of a hemplike fiber. Lying on the stone platform beside the head was an assortment of glass and porcelain beads that must once have been part of a necklace of great beauty. "I've heard that such beads were one of the items the ancients coveted most for their trade with the Portuguese and others along the coast," she said.

"Well, it's quite a find," Aylmer said. "But not one we're likely to ever tell anyone about." He gazed at the bizarre congregation. "I think all we may have achieved is the discovery of enough oxygen to allow us to die of starvation instead of asphyxiation."

"I disagree," said Winston. "Look at this place. It's huge. And all that water dripping down has to go somewhere. It has to get out eventually. We just have to search until we find where."

Aylmer looked at him obliquely, "I'm certainly glad that's all there is to it, Winston. Can't imagine why I was worried at all."

Winston ignored him. "Let's split up and search every inch." He lit two more torches from his own and gave one to each of them. Then they separated and slowly began to circuit the cavern.

Zeila made the first discovery, a pool of water near the low point of the room. It was only a few feet in diameter but she drank from it and declared it potable. Winston and Aylmer came over and also drank deeply before splitting up again. Twenty minutes later they recongregated back at the pool.

"No way out," said Aylmer.

"The water must drain through the bottom of the pool somehow," said Winston. He sat down heavily. It was looking as though Aylmer's prediction that they'd only prolonged their deaths might be true after all.

Zeila stood beside him. Despite their predicament, she remained enthralled by the incredible objects surrounding them. The bodies and their platforms appeared to be oriented in an open-ended circle that narrowed toward the opening where the ground began to rise. It was almost as though the entire tableau was designed to point the way forward. But there was nothing there but a solid rock wall with a pile of rubble at the base.

She stared at the pile of rubble. "I wonder where all that debris came from," she said. "Give me your torch, Winston."

He handed her his torch and watched as she approached the base of the cavern wall with both firebrands. She looked up but could not see more than fifteen feet before the light from the torches dissipated. She took Winston's torch, swung it back and forth a couple of times and then threw it straight up into the air.

Winston and Aylmer stared at her as though she'd taken leave of her senses. But when the torch clattered back to the ground, Zeila exclaimed, "Did you see it?"

"What?"

"Come over here and look." Once they joined her, she took the torch and again threw it high into the air. This time, at the top of the arc, Winston saw it. A cave! But not a natural structure. This had obviously been carved out of the sandstone by human hands. The opening was ten feet wide and nearly twenty tall. It was bracketed by columns meticulously crafted into the stone. The columns were fluted and at the top had intricate capitals.

Zeila said, "You see that bit of platform in front of the opening?" It must have been part of a ramp leading up from here at the end of the circle of bodies. It collapsed at some point in the past."

What she said was now clear. The priests must have been an honor guard for the entrance into the room above. But Winston couldn't believe what he was seeing. "Give me the torch," he said. He threw it up into the air again. "Those are Roman-style columns," he said softly. "That's impossible. The Romans never came this far south in Africa. What are we seeing here?"

Aylmer, being practical, said, "Well, what I'm seeing is a way out of this cavern. It may go nowhere . . . hell, it almost certainly does . . .

but it's all we've got. Question is, how do we get up there? It's got to be more than twenty feet to the ramp overhang."

They examined the base of the cavern wall. The pile of rubble reached almost half way to the overhang. "I think between us we can lift Zeila high enough for her to get a hold on the edge of the ramp," said Winston. "It's worth a try, anyway."

They clambered to the top of the rock pile and leaned their torches against the cliff wall. Then Zeila allowed herself to be hoisted to their shoulders. She was still several feet short of the ramp. Shakily, Winston and Aylmer each grabbed one of her feet and, straining with the effort, raised her the full length of their arms.

"I . . . I've nearly got it," Zeila cried. "Just a few more inches." She stretched her long arms out and managed to get the tips of her fingers over the edge. Slowly, muscles rippling, she pulled herself up.

Aylmer and Winston collapsed from the effort and stared up at Zeila's legs hanging over the edge. "Lord knows how we'll get up if she finds anything," said Aylmer. He stood, picked up one of the torches and threw it up. Zeila caught it deftly and turned toward the cave. At that moment, a horde of bats came flying out. Thousands and thousands of the creatures streamed into the cavern.

Zeila waved her arms as the bats swirled around her, catching in her hair and clothes. She fell to the ground and put her hands over her head until the last of them had departed. Shakily, she stood up and stared at an object lying by the entrance to the cave. She could hardly believe what she was seeing. Coiled neatly beside her was a very old-looking hemp rope nearly two inches in diameter.

"Are you all right?" Winston shouted.

"*Ndiyo*—(yes)," she said. "I'm going to throw something down." She tied one end of the rope around a large boulder near the cave entrance and then threw the other end over the edge.

Winston looked at the rope dubiously. "You're kidding, right?" he said. "That thing must be five hundred years old. It'll probably fall apart as soon as we touch it."

But Aylmer took the rope and gave it a tug. "I don't know. Seems strong enough." He grabbed it with both hands and put his full weight on it. It held, and in a moment he stood beside Zeila.

Winston threw their remaining torches up and then prepared to follow. As he glanced one last time behind him, he froze. In the dim flickers from the torch that Zeila held above him, he was certain he'd had a fleeting glimpse of something incredible. For just an instant, he imagined he'd seen an African warrior, a fierce image of finely chiseled muscle, a bone necklace about his neck and carrying a bow in one hand. He rubbed his eyes in disbelief, for the image was gone at once.

"Did you see that?" he said.

"What?" Aylmer cried from above.

Could he have imagined it? Had it been another painting? The darkness had to be playing tricks, calling up an image from the depths of his mind. Yet it had seemed so real.

"I guess it's nothing," he said, finally. "I'm coming up."

Zeila said, "I *hate* bats."

"Maybe so," said Winston. "But they have to mean there's a way out of here somewhere." He stared again at the columns, placing one hand on the elegant fluting. "This makes no sense at all," he said. "I've examined Roman columns in the British Museum. These are exactly the same construction, same style, everything."

"Perhaps there was more contact with the Romans than is generally known," Zeila said.

He shook his head. "If there was, this would be the first evidence ever found. No walls, amphitheaters, weapons, eating vessel fragments . . . nothing . . . has ever been found in the interior of southern Africa before."

"Maybe it's just coincidence that the styles are so similar," said Aylmer.

Winston couldn't accept it, but he put it out of his mind as they moved into the cave. Just before he entered the opening, he took one final glance below, still wondering about the trick his eyes had played on him.

6.

LORD STERNE sat on his horse and stared across the broad expanse of veldt before them. Stretching away to the north was Rhodesia, once known as the ancient Kingdom of Greater Zimbabwe. They had a long, hard journey ahead of them. He'd always known this part of the undertaking would be the most difficult. Beyond the emptiness of the next two hundred miles would come hostile tribes, great rivers to cross, jungles and more. Roads were almost nonexistent. Yet . . . there were a few, and he stared now at the map he'd brought with him. It was the latest available from London mapmakers, yet still held vast empty areas, completely unmarked.

The leader of the guards pulled his horse alongside him. "A miracle if we get these heavy wagons through all of that," he said.

Sterne grunted. "You and your men will be well rewarded. Enough to set you up for the rest of your lives." He put the map away. "Head the wagons toward that river in the distance," he said, "We should reach it in time to make camp for the night."

The man saluted casually and turned his horse away. The guards were Botha's men, but they had no idea where they were supposed to be taking the treasure. They knew only that Commander Botha had placed them directly under Sterne's command. Their fear of disobeying Botha was what Sterne counted on to prevent them from entertaining any notions of seizing the treasure for themselves. As the guard moved off, Sterne watched the two heavily laden wagons lumber slowly down the hill. They left deep tracks, even in the sun-baked earth of the veldt.

He was content with their progress so far. The Prince of Wales would be happy indeed at the outcome of their little venture. Even a ton of gold might not seem of great importance to the future king of England, but in fact, Edward had many debts from his gambling and womanizing. He was also a man terribly interested in history and especially his own place in it. After all, he'd been waiting a very long time for his mother, Queen Victoria, to pass on the mantle to him. Even more than the money, the Prince relished the idea of the adulation that would come to him for enriching the British Museum's considerable treasures. It would be a fitting accompaniment to his accession, which he now expected at any time. The duplicity he and Sterne had brought to their negotiations with Botha was of no account. Were they not at war?

As for Lord Sterne, he'd been promised his own reward for undertaking the dangerous mission. His estates had diminished in recent years, and the future king had promised to remedy that discomfort. If things worked out, he saw no reason why he couldn't also siphon off some of the treasure for himself. No one knew precisely how much there was, after all, except for the guards. Once they reached the safety of the port at Beira in Portuguese East Africa, where shipping transport had been arranged, the treasure would be repackaged as innocuous freight and the guards would become expendable.

As the last of his men passed on horseback, following the wagon downhill, he stared back down the trail behind them. He remained concerned that Boer forces might be sent after him once he failed to return. The Commander wouldn't wait forever for him to appear. Distracted by the war, Louis Botha had been easy enough to deceive. Whether his interest reflected a desire to protect their cultural history, as Zeila believed, or was intended for the enrichment of the war effort, Sterne didn't know and didn't care. What he did know, however, was that the Commander's trust went only so far. His anger might have a considerably longer reach. They needed to put as many miles as possible between them and the Boers.

He was concerned, too, about one other small matter. Wa-Nyika. The girl had disappeared. No one had seen her following the explosion. He cursed his stupidity for not keeping her under guard. Of course, she was only a child, an ignorant native with no idea what was happening. Still, she may have followed them for a time or at least marked the direction they took. If questioned by the Boers, she could put them onto their trail.

For this reason, he continued to look over his shoulder repeatedly, as he made his way down the hill.

7.

WINSTON LED the way into the cave. At once, he felt they'd entered another world, as distant from the one they'd left behind as London was from Pretoria. The impressive entrance gave way to a virtual warren of rooms, all carved out of the soft sandstone. The Roman motif continued with carvings and mosaics displaying the heart and soul of upper-class Roman daily life. There were paintings of baths surrounded by columnar halls, a representation of the Circus in Rome, aqueducts, reliefs of gladiators, servants and senators. Families were depicted going to market, sharing a meal in the open courtyards of their homes and participating in hunting parties. One entire room was filled with eating vessels, exquisitely crafted carafes with fluted pouring spouts and bowls decorated with glazed reliefs.

Curiously intertwined with these images were others showing obviously native figures and symbols. There were pictures of great black warriors holding bows and arrows, of tribal gatherings and native villages. There were images of monkeys and giraffes, huge piles of ivory tusks, panther and leopard skins, ostrich feathers and even pygmies.

Zeila, close behind him, kept running up on Winston's heels as she exclaimed at one unbelievable sight after another. They entered a room whose walls were faced in white limestone. It was filled with intricately carved tables with inlays of mother of pearl and ivory. The tables themselves overflowed with all manner of treasures, jeweled daggers, solid gold figurines, necklaces of precious stones. Large, decorated amphora surrounded the room. When Aylmer bumped into one, tipping it over, hundreds of gold coins spilled forth. Winston picked one up and identified the head of Constantine the Great, Roman Emperor from 306 to 337 A.D. Just when they thought there could not possibly be any greater surprises, they entered a smaller room that was filled to the very ceiling with solid gold ingots.

Winston stared at the riches incredulously. "Each of those gold bricks must weigh seventy pounds," he said. "The contents of these rooms would enrich the Queen of England herself many times over."

"It would seem," said Aylmer, "that our good friend Lord Sterne departed a little too quickly. I'd give a lot to see the look on his face if he ever finds out what he left behind."

"The only way that will happen," said Zeila, "is if we manage to find a way out of here. If we do, I would very much enjoy being the one to tell him—personally."

"You may have to get in line," Winston said. "But this is truly a mystery. How could so much Roman treasure have ended up here, in a part of Africa the Romans never even visited, much less conquered? And how do you explain the mix of Roman and native culture here?"

"I know something of Roman and Egyptian history," said Aylmer. "The Romans took over Egyptian culture in the first century A.D. and you're right, Winston, they never made it south of the Sahara, with the exception of occasional landfalls of their ships along the coast. Some three hundred years later, Constantine moved the capital of the empire from Rome to Byzantium, renaming it Constantinople. Perhaps . . . the capital wasn't all he moved, though it stretches the imagination to see how he could have relocated so much treasure, or why. And it's beyond belief it would end up here. I wonder . . . do you suppose this treasure could have been stolen from the Romans in Egypt and somehow transported here?"

"That doesn't explain the Roman carvings, murals and reliefs," said Zeila. "Can you honestly believe that thieves would construct such a display in order to honor those they had robbed? And where would they get the artisans to do it even if they wanted to?"

"Precisely," said Winston, "These works could only have been crafted by the Romans themselves. Somehow, there was a Roman influence here in southern Africa that no one has ever documented. And from the looks of it, it was a damn sizeable one."

They continued down another corridor. The passageways seemed endless. Deep inside Mapungubwe Hill, they finally entered what appeared to be the primary burial chamber. The room itself was exquisitely decorated with paintings, only this time most of the depictions seemed to reflect an African theme. There was a ten-foot-long reproduction of a river barque, beautifully crafted from ebony, ivory and gold, complete with small ivory oars and sails made of gold leaf. Finely designed spears and war clubs were located about the space, alongside large woven baskets that contained golden fertility figures and arrowheads carved from enormous rubies. One recurring motif was a reclining ram crafted from solid gold. They found dozens of the figures. Each had huge, golden horns and eyes painted brilliant red.

Aylmer pointed to the ram-headed image of a man painted on one wall. Several servants were making an offering to the figure, pouring something from fluted carafes. "That must represent the God Amun," he said. "Amun was worshiped by the Egyptians and Nubians. And the offering is probably water, the most valuable of all things in this dry climate."

All manner of animals swarmed across the vividly painted walls of the room, being ritualistically hunted by life-size images of black warriors. Zeila cried out in alarm as she backed into what seemed to be the body of a complete, stuffed pygmy. In fact, there were half a dozen pygmies around the room.

"Pygmies were important in Egyptian religious rituals," said Aylmer. "More proof of some long-ago connection between northern Africa and this place."

At the center of it all, laid out on a solid gold platform, were the mummified bodies of a man and a woman. The woman's body was replete with jewelry: multiple necklaces, a gold medallion on the forehead, silver earrings dangling from the tops of her ears and from her earlobes, silver anklets around her legs and many silver rings on her fingers. The man was less decorated, but a solid gold ram's head, horns and all, had been placed over his head. The woman, who was naked except for her jewelry, was extensively tattooed on the shrunken skin of her neck, arms and legs. The male figure appeared to be wrapped in linen.

It was clear, even after so many centuries, that the woman was black-skinned. Here, then, were the figures of two obvious representatives of tribal royalty. Zeila was all but speechless at the magnificence of these forebears of her people.

All at once, Aylmer's torch began to sputter and then quickly faded. They were down to their last two firebrands. Soon, they'd be thrust into blackness, destined to die surrounded by the world's greatest treasure, unable to see so much as a single gold coin as they slowly succumbed to starvation.

Standing at the convergence of several corridors, Winston noticed a slight movement in the flames of his own torch. He held the brand in front of each opening. The third caused a pronounced movement of the flame.

"We don't have much time," he said. "There's air coming from somewhere down this passage. We have to follow it. Once the last of the torches goes out, we'll never be able to decipher which way to go in this maze."

Zeila smothered her torch to save it and they proceeded into the corridor guided by Winston's lonely, dim light.

They passed more treasures, gleaming in the fiery glow, but the baubles had lost all meaning now. Soon, if they did not find a way out, their bones would join the dust on the floor, to lie undiscovered for perhaps another millennium.

For half an hour the corridor they followed continued with a slight downward slope. The floor grew rougher. This part of the massive chamber seemed unfinished, as though there hadn't been enough time in the distant past for whomever worked here to complete their task. Winston's torch began to flicker and he relit Zeila's before it went out completely. Aylmer took a turn holding the light and moved ahead.

The corridor took a sharp turn and began to slope downward even more steeply. Several passageways turned off, more like caves now than manmade tunnels. At last, Aylmer's torch began to flicker. They halted involuntarily to gaze upon the last light they might ever see.

"It's been a good adventure," Winston said, reflecting the hopelessness that had descended upon them. "Not the sort of place I ever imagined I'd meet my end. But I couldn't have chosen two finer people to meet it with."

They stood together, looking into each other's eyes. Even if they survived side by side in the dark for another month before perishing, they'd never see each other again. Zeila suddenly smiled at both men. "Here's something for you *mzungus* to take into the darkness," she said. And by the last flickers of the torch, she raised her shirt and allowed both men to see her breasts.

Then the light was gone. Thrust into darkness, Winston and Aylmer each retained a final image of Zeila's glistening breasts, their large, dark nipples the last thing either of them would ever see.

They slumped to the ground. Suddenly, they could feel the weight of a million tons of stone and earth pressing down on them. Winston shuddered at the thought. He forced his mind to better places and times. He imagined hunting on horseback at Blenheim, the place of his birth, thought of the ocean voyages he'd made to India and of the incredible stars that stretched across the heavens above the Sudan. Most of all, he thought of the future that would never be his. He had always believed that destiny held something more for him than an anonymous death in a black hole in the earth. This was worse than death. This was the loss of his place in history.

The others were also lost in their thoughts, searching, like prisoners in a dungeon, for nuggets of memory that might give them something to hold onto. After twenty minutes of silence, Aylmer suddenly scrambled to his feet. "It's madness to sit here," he said, despair in his voice. "I'll go crazy waiting here to die." Before either of them could say a word, Winston and Zeila heard their friend run blindly off down the steep passageway.

"Aylmer," Winston shouted. "For God's sake, stop!"

They listened to his diminishing footsteps and the sound of his body banging off the walls. Then there was a moment of silence followed by a brief cry of surprise as their friend's voice fell away as though disappearing into some great void.

Dumbstruck, they sat listening to the silence. Then Zeila called out, "Aylmer?"

There was nothing but silence. "What do you think happened?" she said.

Winston stood up. "I don't know. But Aylmer was right. It makes no sense to just sit here. Come on." He reached out and found her hand. Together, they moved hesitantly deeper into the darkness.

Winston proceeded slowly, placing each foot ahead to make sure of the footing before putting his weight on it. After several minutes, he came to a place where he felt nothing with his foot. He almost lost his balance and Zeila pulled him back.

"What is it?"

"There's nothing there," he said. "It must be a drop off . . . where Aylmer fell." He knelt down and felt the edge of the hole. He leaned forward and called out Aylmer's name several times. But there was no answer.

He sat back heavily. "No telling how deep it is."

Zeila picked up a stone and tossed it over the edge. It fell for a long time before they heard a small collision at the very edge of their hearing. "A hundred feet, maybe more," she said. "Aylmer could not survive that." She sat down beside him. "What do we do now?"

"Buggered if I know. We can't go ahead with that hole in front of us. I suppose we might find our way back to the main cavern. But what would be the point? We still wouldn't be able to see our hands in front of our faces, so there's nothing to be gained."

Zeila moved in beside him. Hesitantly, he placed his arm around her. The warmth of her body was comforting. They might have been the last two people on earth. The darkness hung over them like a living thing, as though some ogre they could neither see nor hear was drifting above them, just out of reach. Their eyes strained of their own volition to see something, even when closed.

"Are you married, Winston?"

He shook his head, then remembered she couldn't see him. "Girl sort of waiting for me," he said. "Looks like it'll be a long wait."

"I've heard Englishmen have sexual hang-ups."

He would have liked to see her face when she said that. "I've heard African women don't."

He felt her hand on his face and then her mouth found his. She took his hand and put it on her breast and for a while they forgot where they were.

* * *

They must have slept a long time, though time in this dank bit of hell was hardly a relevant part of their lives. Winston woke first. Zeila's long legs were curled into him and he sat up gently, careful not to disturb her. Sleep was worth its weight in gold—even in Roman treasure—for the peace it brought. His hand rested on her bare shoulder. He smiled as he considered what members of his family might say if they could see him now. The careful barriers of class in Victorian England could be punishing and exact. Here in the dark, he mused, a person's color meant nothing at all.

He would have given a great deal to hear the scratch of a rodent or even the buzz of a mosquito around his head. But this deep in the earth, the silence was absolute and stony. Still, there was something . . . he could swear he felt the slightest breeze.

He stood up and, using the wall to guide him, followed the tiny zephyr of air. He located the edge of the gaping hole, expecting it to be the source of the breeze. But it seemed not to emanate from there but from farther along the wall, away from the hole. With his hands on the stone, he crept on until he felt the wall curve away. Another hole? He tested with his foot, edging forward slowly.

The breeze was stronger. He must have found another corridor! That had to be it. It appeared to branch off from the main passage before it ended at the chasm. With a cry of excitement, he yelled to Zeila.

She came awake groggily. Opening one's eyes in this optical void provided no clue as to whether one was awake, asleep or even dead. "What . . . what is it?" she said.

"Wait. Don't move." He was afraid she might forget how close she was to the opening in the earth. Keeping one hand on the wall, he slid back beside her.

"Maybe . . . I've found a way out," he said.

She was instantly awake and listened as he explained what he'd found. She pulled her clothes on quickly. Then, together, holding hands, they crept to the new opening. Zeila felt the breeze and squeezed Winston's hand.

Once again, they moved cautiously along the passageway, measuring each step, Zeila ready to grab Winston should he stagger at the edge of another abyss. The breeze grew ever so slightly stronger and after ten minutes, Zeila said, "I think I see something . . . the dark isn't so dark."

In fact, their image-starved eyes had begun to pick up the smallest change in the intensity of the blackness. Another five minutes and they could actually identify the walls as slightly less grim surfaces against the coal-black of the corridor. Then Winston said, "I smell something. It smells . . . green."

The light grew brighter with every step, their eyes gradually adjusting until at last they emerged at the mouth of a cave and stared out across the African veldt. The colors were so vibrant and rich after their long sojourn in the bowels of the earth that it almost hurt their eyes. They stared in wonder and joy. Below, the sluggish waters of the Limpopo churned their muddy way to a distant sea. Winston looked into Zeila's eyes, something he'd never expected to do again. With a grin, he said, "Thank you. That was the most fun I've ever had in the dark."

"Which part?"

"Very funny. Anyway, if someone asks, you can honestly say we've never seen each other naked. Honor is satisfied."

She looked exasperated. "God save me from Englishmen! It's probably true you all do it without ever taking your clothes off."

He looked surprised.

"I don't give a damn about honor, Winston. We thought we were going to die. To be honest, it wouldn't have happened otherwise. But I'm not ashamed of it. It was fun, and now it's done . . . if that's the way you want it." Before he could answer, she added, "Anyway, I think we have something else to worry about at the moment."

The cave entrance was cut into the side of Mapungubwe Hill. They remained some fifty feet from the floor of the veldt. Fortunately, the hillside here was rough and uneven. Though the descent was difficult, they made it to the bottom in less than half an hour. Exhausted, they fell to the ground. It was late afternoon. Of what day, they had no idea, for their sleep and time in the darkness had been indeterminable.

"Well, this is your land," said Winston. "What now? We've no food, transportation or potable water. It'll be dark in an hour. I expect the lions have already gotten our scent."

She looked back at the cave. "Maybe we should have stayed up there for the night. It offered protection from the animals, at least."

But neither of them had any desire to go back to that awful cave. "We should return to the camp," she said. "Maybe they left something behind we can use. Even a bit of firewood would be a help."

They walked quickly. The sun was low, and they could hear the beginning murmurs of the creatures who ruled the night on the veldt. As they neared the camp, their pace slowed. It was conceivable Sterne could still be there. What hurry would he be in, knowing they were buried beneath a million tons of African rock?

Almost at once, they smelled wood smoke. Someone had a fire up ahead. They exchanged glances. It would be fortune indeed to find their enemy still here. Given their latest run of luck, however, any fortune they might have was more likely to be bad than good. They were virtually helpless against an armed force the size of Lord Sterne's. They'd be forced to retreat onto the veldt.

They crept along the edge of a low ridge until they reached a spot above the campsite. Winston edged forward until his head poked above the scrub and looked down. Zeila saw his shoulders relax and a smile flow across his face. He stood and motioned to her. She scrambled up beside him, then broke into her own large grin. Below them, a small figure sat feeding a fire. Wa-Nyika hummed to herself in her usual sing-song patter.

The girl turned at their approach, started, then leaped up, crying out loudly in her strange language. She ran over, hugged Zeila and even gave Winston a hesitant smile. She waved to the fire and they went over. She had gathered wood for the night and had begun to roast some small, rodent-like creature. Winston didn't want to ask what it was, for it actually smelled pretty good, and his stomach began rumbling with interest.

Wa-Nyika went back to caring for their dinner, babbling away to each question that Zeila put to her.

"She says there was a big explosion that scared her and she ran away into the bush to hide," said Zeila. "After a while, the big white man with broad shoulders came back into camp and began giving orders. Everyone ran around packing up and they broke camp and left. She says she was scared because I wasn't there." Zeila gave the girl a pat on the shoulder. Wa-Nyika continued to talk away. As she did, she broke a leg off the small animal, still covered with singed black hairs, and gave it to Winston, who nibbled ravenously while trying not to look at the thing.

"They apparently spent some time hunting for her," said Zeila. "Search parties went into the bush and called for her, but she didn't trust them and stayed out of sight until they gave up and left. Then she waited here to see if we'd come out of the mountain."

"Brave girl," Winston said. "She outsmarted those buggers and has helped us to boot. Does she have any idea which way they went?"

Zeila asked and a finger pointed across the Limpopo River. Even Winston could understand that.

"They headed into Rhodesia? With those heavy wagons? Maybe we could catch up to them. They can't be moving very fast."

Zeila exchanged several long passages with Wa-Nyika, then shook her head. "They have at least two days head start. And wagons or no, they have horses. We could never catch them."

He nodded. "Our best bet, then, is to turn back and report to Commander Botha. Sterne must be double-crossing him as well as us if he's headed north."

Zeila's face was taught with frustration. "It's my fault," she said. "My job was to keep something like this from happening. Louis entrusted this mission to me and I failed miserably."

Winston put down his braised . . . rodent . . . and stared at her. She was something, this tall warrior, raised in two worlds . . . soldier, native African, Cambridge graduate, expert markswoman and passionate lover. He regretted nothing that had passed between them.

"We'll go on from here, Zeila," he said. "Lord Sterne must be returning to England. We'll track him down. You have my word on it."

8.

"I CAN'T BELIEVE IT!" Louis Botha stared from Winston to Zeila and back again.

"Believe it, Commander. Lord Sterne has disappeared, last seen heading north with two wagons loaded with your gold. He tried to kill us and his actions did kill Aylmer. He'll pay for that some day," Winston said bitterly.

By agreement, he and Zeila had decided not to tell the Commander about the additional treasure and incredible tombs they'd found. That agreement had come slowly. Zeila felt a loyalty to Botha, whom she continued to believe was only interested in uncovering the history of their African homeland. During the time it had taken for them to follow Wa-Nyika to her home, deposit her with her noisily excited family and then locate horses to continue their own journey, Winston had worked tirelessly to convince her that this was the path they should follow.

Botha stood up and rounded his desk to stand before Zeila. "You were supposed to prevent this," he said.

Normally not one to flinch from defending herself, she could only drop her head, for she felt the failure deeply.

"It's not Zeila's fault," said Winston. "Perhaps if you'd had enough trust in us to let us know what plans you'd made with

Sterne, this might have been prevented. By keeping us in the dark, you made it easier for him to surprise us. We were not adequately prepared. If we had been, we might have seen this coming. If you ask me, I think you planned all along to use the gold in your war effort. You don't give a damn about the historical and cultural importance of Mapungubwe Hill."

The Commander stared at him for a moment, then returned slowly to his chair. He sat heavily. "Maybe you're right, Winston. I can't say the idea didn't exist somewhere in my head. War is expensive, and we're fighting an adversary with almost unlimited resources, as you well know. The only thing that has sustained us thus far is the great distance between Britain and the Transvaal. I swear to you, though, I never discussed such a thing with Lord Sterne. My private meetings with him were more to sound him out, to see if he had some other agenda. I never thought he had any alternative but to return here. If he headed straight into Rhodesia, the man may be braver . . . or a bigger fool . . . than I thought." He turned in his chair and stared out the window. "Damn this bloody war! It's made fools of us all."

His tone softened. "I'm sorry about Captain Aylmer. He was a good man. I know what it's like to lose a friend with whom one has been in battle."

"Will you send a force after Sterne?" said Winston.

"I wish I could. But I don't have the men to spare. Lord Sterne probably counted on that. No, we'll have to rely on Africa to deal with him, I'm afraid." He looked at Zeila. "I'm sorry for what I said. I doubt there was anything you could have done. That you made it back to report was no small achievement on its own, and I thank you for it."

Zeila only nodded.

"So what happens, now?" Winston asked. "Do I go back to being a prisoner of war?"

"Reports of your escape have already made it around the world," said Botha. "You may find yourself something of a hero when you get home. I don't know what purpose it would serve to slap you back into prison. I think it best you escape for real this time. I can offer a little help in that regard. And when you get back to England, perhaps you can look up Lord Sterne if he ever reappears and give him a message from me." He leaned forward. "Tell him he's a marked man. I may not have the resources to get him for a while, but it won't hurt for him to know he's made an enemy who won't soon forget his betrayal."

"He has powerful friends, Commander. If what he told us about working for Edward, Prince of Wales, is true, then he may soon be under the protection of the king himself."

"Kings often have better things to occupy them than the protection of self-aggrandizing thugs like Sterne. I doubt the king will lose any sleep over the man." He looked at Zeila. "And what of you?" he said. "Will you come back to work with me? I've missed you. You have skills that are very much in demand here."

Zeila looked at him, then at Winston, who smiled at her, knowing what her answer would be.

"I will miss you, Winston," she said.

9.

London

October 5, 1900

WINSTON STEPPED outside one of the reception rooms at the Houses of Parliament and adjusted his new formal attire. It fit tightly in the paunch that had begun to grow as if it had a life of its own since his return . . . too many of these damn receptions!

He walked quickly down the hallway to his office. It was small by any standards, even for a new member of Parliament, but that he was an up-and-comer was no longer in doubt to anyone. Just five days earlier, he'd won election as a Conservative running for the predominantly Liberal constituency of Oldham.

It had been a close election, so close in fact that, in rushing into print, *The Times* of October 2 had announced his defeat. Winston had pleaded with his American mother, Lady Randolph, to help him with the campaign, but she had instead remained in Scotland on an extended honeymoon with her new husband, George Cornwallis–West, sometimes called the "handsomest man in the army."

Oldham had been one of the first constituencies to vote in an election that was spread over a six-week period. As a result of his early victory, Churchill was in great demand as a speaker for other Conservative candidates still campaigning, including Arthur Balfour, leader of the House of Commons and soon to become

Prime Minister. He found himself speaking on the stump to crowds of five and six thousand at a time.

Winston Churchill had arrived. Just twenty-five years old and only three months back from South Africa, he had established a reputation in the army and made friends in high places. Many of the officers he'd served with would rise to high command in the First World War, when Churchill would be a member of the war cabinet. His widely reported exploits in the Boer War had firmly established him on the world stage.

He had also established his ability to make a living with his pen. His first collection of dispatches, *From London to Ladysmith*, had been published in May and had already sold thirteen thousand copies. A second collection, *Ian Hamilton's March*, had been prepared for publication while he was still at sea. *The River War*, about the Sudan campaign, was about to be reprinted. He had the princely sum of four thousand pounds in the bank.

The only shadow was that he hadn't received a decoration for bravery, something he dearly wanted. But in truth, it was not necessary so far as his reputation was concerned. His actions had proved his courage beyond a doubt.

When the whirlwind of events slowed even for a moment, he reflected on his adventures at Mapungubwe Hill and on Zeila, whose memory and soft allures still tugged at him. He'd told no one about their great adventure. It was not easy to hold back such an exciting tale, especially for one of Winston's nature. But telling it would have also revealed the fact that his *escape* had not gone precisely as the papers had detailed it. That Louis Botha had actually conspired in his escape would not sit well with either his constituency or his fellow members of Parliament. He could well imagine the questions that would fly from those eager to jump on the news that he'd been befriended by an enemy of Britain during a time of war.

He nodded to several staff members who were still setting up his office and then retreated into his tiny private den. Waiting for him was Augustus Dewsnap, a private investigator he'd hired to begin quietly looking into the whereabouts and activities of Lord Sterne. It irked Winston to know that Sterne had to be somewhere in England, yet to be unable, thus far, to locate the man. Given Winston's high profile, his name constantly in the paper, he knew Sterne had to be aware of his activities. This imbalance in knowledge worried and angered Winston, for he had vowed to deal with Sterne one way or another to avenge Aylmer's death.

He settled into a comfortable leather wing chair, bit the end off a cigar and stared at Dewsnap. "Well, what have you found out?" he asked.

Dewsnap crossed his legs, revealing two overlooked and gaping, perhaps permanently forgotten, buttons in the crotch of his pants. In his mid-forties, he wore a ten-year-old tweed jacket and a hat that Winston marveled at every time he saw it. The thing had no shape and seemed to be a permanent part of the man's head, like an enormous boil that desperately needed lancing. Despite his "gone to seed" appearance, he'd been recommended by Lady Randolph, who had employed him to investigate various of her lovers.

"Well, Your Honor," Dewsnap began. "None of my sources here in London report hearing anything about the man. I've also been to his home district, where his estates, I may say, are in some disrepair."

"I know for a fact he's come into considerable money of late," said Winston, irritably.

"Be that as it may, sir, he is apparently not divesting himself of it to better care for his employees and land workers."

"Well where the bloody hell is the man?"

Dewsnap smiled slyly. "Well sir, I can't say. But I can tell you where he was a week ago this Thursday."

Winston sat up, cigar smoke exploding from his mouth. "Well where, man? Out with it!"

"I know a bloke who dispatches carriages off Horse Guards Row—only the finest clients. He told me he took a request for a covered carriage and two last week from none other than Lord Sterne."

"How can he be sure it was our man?"

"Got a good look at him, he did, and he'd seen his Lord-ship order carriages in the past. He was taken to the residence of Edward, Prince of Wales." Dewsnap sat back with evident pride at his accomplishment.

Winston's expression soured. He puffed furiously at his cigar. Sterne in London! Or at least he was, a week ago. And he'd met with Edward. To deliver the gold? Winston wondered, but even if that were the case, he doubted seriously that Sterne had delivered all of it. It wasn't in the man's nature not to keep something back for himself.

His mind worked feverishly. Would Edward at once give the treasure—whatever part Sterne had revealed to him—to the British Museum? It would certainly be a coup—especially during a war—to report that Britain had seized part of the national treasure of her enemies. And yet, he knew the Prince well enough to suspect he had something else in mind.

Queen Victoria had been ill lately. She was very old and many wondered if she might step down in favor of her son. However it happened, Edward would soon be king. Winston could well imagine the pleasure it would give him to announce the presentation of the treasure to the British Museum at the moment of his accession. It was in the Prince's style to want to make a big splash.

He reached into his pocket, pulled out his wallet and handed Dewsnap ten pounds. "Keep after him, Augustus. I want to know where he's staying. I want to know where the bugger is every damn minute!"

Dewsnap stood, pocketed the money somewhere in the folds of his strange attire and gave a little salute. He thoroughly enjoyed being in the employ of a Member of Parliament. "Never you worry, Your Honor. If he's anywhere in England, Augustus Dewsnap will find him." He trundled off.

Churchill sat back and pondered his next move. If Sterne was meeting clandestinely with the prince, then perhaps he should do the same. It would be dangerous, to be sure. He couldn't reveal what he and Zeila had found, but perhaps he could plant the seed of doubt in Edward's mind as to Lord Sterne's trustworthiness, perhaps even suggest that Sterne might be playing the Prince for a fool. If Winston could hint, ever so obliquely, that more had been found than Sterne had revealed . . . well, it was just conceivable that the Prince of Wales might punish Sterne for him. It was certainly an interesting possibility.

The bold move was vintage Churchill. No beating around the bush. Go straight to the heart of the problem.

"Eva!" he yelled.

The door opened and his secretary appeared.

"See what you can do about getting me an audience with the Prince of Wales."

10.

ALBERT EDWARD, Prince of Wales, known as *Bertie* to his family, was sixty years old. He'd spent his entire life waiting to be king. It hadn't been an easy apprenticeship. After a strict upbringing, during which he was forced to endure many grueling hours of study every day, he grew into a troubled young man, joined the army and while on duty in Ireland became involved in a scandal with an Irish actress. Shortly thereafter, his father, the king, came down with typhoid fever and died. However illogical, Queen Victoria blamed Bertie for her husband's death, declaring that she could never look upon the boy without a shudder. For the rest of her life, she steadfastly refused to keep her son informed of official affairs.

In rebellion for this treatment, Bertie filled his life with scandal. Gambling, women, horse racing and the nightlife of Paris and London occupied his time and took most of his money. He had numerous affairs, often with the knowledge and acceptance of his wife, Alexandra. The most famous of these was with the actress Lillie Langtry, the first English woman of elevated social rank to go on the stage. This further soured Bertie's mother toward him.

The Churchill family had also had its ups and downs with the Prince. Winston's father, Lord Randolph, had once become embroiled in a scandal between a friend of his and one of Bertie's many flirtations, Lady Aylesford. In attempting to protect his friend, Randolph threatened Bertie with blackmail.

The Prince was so infuriated over this that he actually challenged Randolph Churchill to a duel. But Randolph refused the challenge and instead sent Bertie an insulting letter. By early 1876, the scandal was all over London. Bertie declared publicly that neither he nor Alexandra would ever set foot in the house of anyone who offered hospitality to Lord Randolph or his wife. For eight years, the banishment continued, causing the Churchills to flee to America for a time on a sort of forced vacation.

But eventually, Bertie and Randolph, who had once been good friends, reconciled. Randolph became leader of the House of Commons in 1885 and later Chancellor of the Exchequer. For the first time, Bertie was kept abreast of official affairs through Randolph, at least until the latter's resignation from the Conservative Party over the matter of some reforms he had insisted upon. For several years, Randolph's health declined and he died in 1895 at the age of forty-five.

By the end of 1900, Queen Victoria's health had begun to decline precipitously. She was now almost totally blind and very weak. Bertie's accession, it was clear, was imminent.

It was with this considerable history that Winston arrived for an audience with the Prince at his home at Sandringham in Norfolk. He found Bertie out walking his hounds on a sunny, brisk, autumn afternoon. The Prince was portly and short, with a thick beard, just beginning its march to gray and then white. Like Churchill, he was fond of whisky and cigars. He welcomed Winston jovially.

"Good to see you, Winston," he said, shaking his hand firmly. "God, but I miss your father. We had some famous times, Randolph and I."

"Thank you, sir," Winston replied. "He spoke to me fondly of you very often."

"Yes, yes," Bertie sighed. "Time goes by so quickly. Now my mother, the Queen, is near her own end, as I suspect you've heard . . . of course you have. It's all they talk about over there at the damn House."

"She'll be badly missed," said Winston. "There are only a few of her subjects left who can remember a time when she wasn't there, providing stability to the nation. I know that will continue with your accession, sir."

"Ah, I hope so, Winston. I hope so. There is so much to be learned, you know. If not for your father the last few years, I would not have been as abreast of affairs as I am. The Queen was quite stingy in sharing information, you know."

Winston knew better than to get into this kettle of fish, for it was common enough knowledge throughout England. He did wonder, though, how engaged the Prince really was at learning the ropes of governing out here at his country home walking with his hounds.

"Well . . . what can I do for you today, Winston?"

"Not a matter of great significance, sir," he began carefully. "And I appreciate your taking the time to see me."

Bertie waved a hand at his own magnanimity, bent down and picked up a stick that he threw for the dogs. They raced lustily and noisily after it midst a flurry of yelps and howls.

Winston continued. "I did want to thank you for suggesting me to Louis Botha as someone you had faith in concerning Lord Sterne's mission to Mapungubwe Hill."

Bertie looked mildly surprised. "Yes, well, as I said, I know your family and your own reputation for bravery, Winston. Perhaps I should even say . . . brashness?"

Winston dipped his head. "A fault, sir, I admit it. But it seems a part of my nature that I am helpless to control. Ah . . . as you know, the details of that mission have never come out."

"Wouldn't do you much good, if they did, eh?" said Bertie. "That whole escape thing was a bit overblown, if you ask me. But . . . no harm done. It helped get you elected to Parliament. I could use another Churchill to assist me in dealing with things up there."

"Thank you, sir." Winston hesitated, then plunged in. "I'm sure the treasure of Mapungubwe Hill will be a real contribution to the British Museum. I've not had the opportunity to congratulate you . . . or Lord Sterne . . . on the success of the mission. I'm sure he filled you in on our suspicions about the hill."

"Suspicions?"

"Well, just that we uncovered some things that suggested it might be worth further exploration once the war is over. Lord Sterne probably told you about the wall paintings and burial evidence that suggest we may have found only the tip of the iceberg."

Bertie stopped walking and stood looking off across one of the many manicured lawns. "Tip of the iceberg, you say? How interesting."

"Of course, it's only speculation, but even the possibility of such a find would be worth pursuing . . . if we can. It might lead to one of the great treasures of our time being secured for the British Museum."

"This is most interesting, Winston. Tell me . . . what sort of treasure do you envision?" Bertie swung another stick, teasing the dogs.

"I'm no expert in the area, sir, but we did find evidence of a Roman influence."

The Prince stopped his stick in mid-throw. "The devil you say! Romans in southern Africa? That's an incredible suggestion. What evidence?"

"There were murals and reliefs of what were clearly Roman sites, baths, the Coliseum, figures in traditional Roman dress."

The prince stared at him in open fascination. His position as patron of the British Museum had long ago spurred what was perhaps his only interest outside of gambling, hunting and women, and that was history. He'd taught himself a great deal and, as a patron of the museum, often went there to look at exhibits and to question the experts.

Winston decided to prod a little further. "Perhaps I speak out of turn, sir. If Lord Sterne didn't tell you about this, it may simply have been an oversight on his part."

They both knew there was no oversight on the part of Lord Sterne. Bertie's face clouded over, but he continued the little masquerade. "Quite likely, you are right, Winston. Have you had lunch? No? What say we go in and see if we can rustle up a bit of fois gras. The bloody French can teach us about cuisine, if nothing else. I should like very much to hear more about your Romans in southern Africa."

11.

AUGUSTUS DEWSNAS stood at the edge of the woods and stared forlornly at the great hulking architectural masterpiece that was Sandringham. Twenty minutes had passed since he'd watched Lord Sterne exit his carriage and enter through the building's main concourse.

The house, surrounded by sixty acres of gardens, a small fraction of its twenty-thousand acre-estate, was a private investigator's nightmare. In a normal pursuit, he might slip up to a house and stare in a window, perhaps even climb to a second floor and peer into a boudoir to determine if a liaison was occurring. But how could he slip up to the window of a building with scores of rooms and hundreds of windows? Bertie and Lord Sterne could be anywhere inside. It was hopeless.

Yet, on more than one occasion, he'd caught his prey through sheer luck, and this was going to be one of those times. Even as he watched, Bertie and Sterne emerged from a side entrance and began to make their way toward a gazebo at the edge of one of the formal gardens. What incredible luck! He quickly reentered the woods and in five minutes had crept behind a dense hedge that ran right up to the gazebo. The King-to-be and his guest had just sat down to a small table and were being served tea by a butler and two maids. As soon as the tea was poured, Bertie dismissed the servants, who went back inside.

Dewsnap removed his ridiculous boil of a hat and raised his head far enough to be able to see the two men. He was less than a dozen feet away and could hear their voices clearly on the quiet heath surrounding the elaborate lawn house.

Lord Sterne spoke defensively. "I confess I don't know what he was talking about, sir. There were no Roman murals or reliefs. I give you my word."

Bertie snorted. "Your word, as we both know, is worth less than the Turkish lira."

Sterne sat deathly still. He was in deep trouble and knew it. Damn Churchill! Somehow, he'd planted this mystery in the prince's head and it was going to be the devil to get it out.

"I'd sooner cut my own throat than lie to you," he said.

"Don't make idle promises," said Bertie. "I just might take you up on one of them. I want the facts. You originally told me that Winston and this girl, what's her name?"

"Zeila."

"Yes. That they were buried alive in a cave-in. That you spent two days trying to dig them out and were finally forced to give up as more and more of the tunnels collapsed. As you can imagine, I was a bit surprised when Winston showed up with his self-serving story of escape from the Boers. Perhaps you recall what I said to you then."

Sterne nodded tightly. "You said if I ever lied to you again, it would be the last time. But sir, I didn't lie. They *were* trapped in the cave-in. That is exactly what happened. I can't explain how they got out. It's a complete mystery to me. I felt we'd wasted enough time and that it was urgent we begin the long trip home to bring you the gold."

"Be that as it may, what I'm interested in now is the possibility there is another great treasure at Mapungubwe. Winston all but insisted there was, and that the Romans were somehow behind it."

Sterne suddenly began to see what the Prince was leading up to, and it didn't make him happy at all. He'd had a long and difficult journey that had nearly cost him his life on several occasions. Now he was finally back in London, considerably richer, both from Bertie's rewards for his triumph and from the two hundred pounds of gold he'd managed to siphon off from the wagons. He was just starting to enjoy himself, making the rounds of the night spots, treating the ladies to his money and his company. Now he saw it all going away.

"Ah, there you are, Cavendish," Bertie said, standing up.

Sterne turned to see a youngish man in a dark suit arrive. He came into the gazebo and bowed to the Prince. "I'm honored at your invitation, sir."

"Sit, sit," Bertie said. "This is Lord Sterne. And this, Sterne, is Charles Cavendish, the leading authority we have at the British Museum on ancient Rome. I've invited him to join us and tell us whether this little hypothesis of Mr. Churchill's is hogwash or not."

Cavendish sat nervously. It wasn't every day of the week that a minor scholar was invited to the residence of the soon-to-be king. Between the two of them, however, it appeared that Sterne was the more uncomfortable.

"There now, let's have it. What do you think of this claim of Romans in southern Africa?" said Bertie.

"Well sir," Cavendish began, "It would be extraordinary if true. No such evidence has ever been found south of the Upper Nile, which the emperor Nero sent legionaries to explore."

"Could the Romans have made port farther south in Africa via boat?" the Prince said.

"There were certainly Roman crafts that traveled the western and eastern coasts of Africa. These explorations were primarily related to naval commerce. Roman ships were not really suitable for the open Atlantic. They were not explorers and were interested primarily in trade toward the Indian Ocean. No doubt, some items could have been traded and made their way inland. But that would not explain the presence of major works of art—mosaics and relief paintings—showing up in the interior." He paused.

"Yes, well?" Bertie said impatiently.

"There really is only one possibility."

"What?" said Sterne, becoming interested in spite of his fear of what was to come.

"Nubia," said Cavendish.

"Aha!" Bertie looked as if he understood something, but Sterne was as baffled as ever.

"The Nubian culture dates from at least three thousand B.C.," Cavendish continued. "It may even pre-date the Egyptian pharaohs. We really know very little about Nubia, for the culture's written language has never been deciphered. Everything we do know comes from descriptions by other cultures of the period. The kingdom stretched from Elephantine in the north almost to Khartoum. It *could* have served as a funnel for trade goods between the Egyptians, that is to say, the Romans, and the interior of Africa. Legend holds they had great wealth from gold mines, ebony, ivory, incense and the fragrant oils—the greatest in all Africa. I've seen objects reputed to have come from Nubia, though it's always been difficult to verify. Many of the kings of Nubia were buried in huge, steep-sided mounds and pyramidal tombs. In fact, it's estimated that beyond the fourth cataract of the Nile, in the Nubian desert of Sudan, there are three times as many pyramids as there are in Egypt itself." He paused, seeming to consider something. "I wonder . . ."

"Spit it out, man!" said Bertie.

"Well, sir, it's the idlest speculation, but I wonder if Mapungubwe Hill could have been used as a natural burial mound by either, or both, the Romans and Nubians?" Cavendish leaned back, staring from one man to the other.

Sterne sat with his mouth open. If what the man said was actually a possibility and if what Winston had suggested was true . . . he felt weak in the knees. He may have left behind one of the greatest treasures in the history of mankind.

There was a sudden sharp *crack*, like the sound of a nearby branch breaking. They all looked in the direction of the sound, from the hedge that grew alongside the gazebo.

Augustus froze, his eyes staring down in disbelief on the offending stick.

"What was that?" said Bertie.

"An animal, perhaps?" said Cavendish.

Sterne stood up. "Someone's over there," he hissed.

Dewsnap heard him and it was all the incentive he needed. He moved quickly down the hedgerow, which ran for a hundred yards before it became part of a formal garden border that surrounded a pond.

The men in the gazebo couldn't see him, but they heard poor Augustus's shambling gate. Sterne started to go after him, but Bertie put a hand on his arm.

"Wait," he said. "He won't get far." He led the way quickly to the house, where he collared one of his servants. "Let the dogs loose," he said. "All of them."

In a moment, a pack of at least thirty dogs, including enormous stag and wolf hounds, went tearing off across the lawns. It was apparent the animals had enjoyed this game before.

Augustus heard the cacophony of barking and howls and picked up his pace, fear suddenly giving him a new fleetness of foot. He tore off his tweed jacket and threw it aside. Perhaps it would distract the creatures for a few moments. His hat soon followed.

As he reached the pond, he leaped in and swam directly across the short span of fifteen or twenty feet. He had no illusions, however, that this would cause the animals to lose his scent. Dripping, he emerged and ran down a steep, grassy swale toward the first woods, still fifty yards away.

The dogs had quickly torn apart Dewsnap's coat, then paused briefly at the pond before one of them circled to where Augustus had come out, and once again the chase was on.

Back at the house, Bertie dismissed Cavendish, assuring the man there was nothing to worry about and that the authorities would be called to handle the intruder. Then he crossed to a cabinet and withdrew two shotguns, handing one to Sterne. "Whoever that was," he said. "He heard too much. Do you understand?"

Sterne nodded. This sort of thing he understood all too well. Both men moved out across the lawns, following the baying of the hounds.

* * *

Augustus was exhausted. He was overweight and cursed his bad habits of smoking and drinking too much port. The most running he'd

83

ever done in his life had occurred several years ago when he'd had to flee a naked husband he'd disturbed in the act of committing adultery. The cheeky fellow had chased him down Tottenham Court Road in full daylight until Dewsnap lost him by nipping into a pub and hiding in the loo.

The incident had been almost laughable, and he remembered actually chuckling at the sight of the man running after him past the startled gazes of ladies on the street. But this was different. He disliked dogs to begin with, and the baying hounds on his trail were getting closer by the minute. He might have been willing to give himself up, but he knew the dogs would be upon him long before their masters could catch them up.

He splashed across a small stream, then paused for a moment to catch his breath. He had an idea. He moved back into the stream and stumbled blindly up the middle of the waterway. The bottom was rocky and he tripped repeatedly on the stones but was careful not to touch either bank. He continued for a hundred yards, following the stream into the woods. It was late October and the water was very cold. But it seemed as though the dogs had fallen behind. Maybe it was working.

He stopped, panting like a dog himself, his chest heaving, taking in huge gulps of air. He wanted a smoke right now, which was the strangest sensation. Adrenalin pumped through him. By God, he was going to send Churchill his biggest bill yet! The thought gave him momentary comfort. Spying on the future king of England ought to be worth a hundred guineas at least. He was tired of giving away his hard-earned talents for a handful of shillings and pounds. What he could do with a hundred guineas!

The dogs had been milling in one spot, but now they suddenly revived their howls, and Augustus knew they'd located his trail. With a curse, he left the stream and headed into the trees. There was a road ahead; maybe there would be people who would help him.

He emerged onto the dirt road and looked right and left. Not a soul around. It was probably a service road for the estate anyway, unlikely to have citizens passing by. He ran along it for a short distance, then crossed and continued into the woods again. The dogs were gaining, the glee in their howls increasing as they ran their prey to ground.

He was nearing the end of his rope. His breathing came in ragged gasps. The underbrush was thick. Thorns tore at his skin. A branch swatted him in the forehead. He entered a clump of brush that hid a drop-off and felt himself tumbling head over heels, down a steep incline. He lay at the bottom, numb and frightened, unable to move another inch.

He heard the dogs arrive at the spot of his fall. Their bays were loud, then died away as the animals snuffled through the brush. They approached from all sides at once. He tried to move, but felt an excruciating stab of pain. His leg was twisted, probably broken. He gasped as the enormous head of a wolf hound stuck out of the brush and growled just inches from his face. Augustus closed his eyes as the creatures, filled with blood lust, leapt upon him and tore into his flesh.

There wasn't much left to see of Augustus Dewsnap, professional investigator, when Bertie and Lord Sterne finally appeared at the edge of the brushy drop-off. They stared at the blood-covered gully. The dogs lay about their prey, panting happily at their triumph and looking up for praise.

Bertie gave it to them, then called them out. "My men will dispose of the body," he said, looking at the depression. "Though this might be as good a place as any to leave it."

"Who do you think he was?" said Sterne.

Bertie shrugged. "Could have been after almost anything. A jealous husband, perhaps. Wouldn't be the first time. Probably has nothing to do with your next job, anyway."

"My next job?"

"You're going back to Mapungubwe Hill and find out what you left behind," said Bertie, as he leaned down to give one dog's ears a playful tug.

12.

WINSTON FIDGETED with his pocket watch as he waited for the Southampton to Isle of Wight ferry to dock. It was a brittle, cold, dreary and utterly typical November day on the British Channel. The boat rocked in the choppy seas, pitching back and forth, as though her captain couldn't quite make up his mind if he really wanted to land or not. Finally, with a deafening blast on the horn, the seamen fore and aft threw their ropes ashore and the deed was done.

He made his way down the gangplank, where he was met by an exotic figure wearing a turban, a great gold belt and buckle and white leggings that emerged from beneath a long white coat.

"Mr. Churchill?" the man inquired in flawless English. "Welcome to Her Majesty's home away from home, Osborne House. We will have a short carriage ride up."

Winston nodded, scrutinizing the incongruous figure. This, he knew, was the Munshi, Hafiz Abdul Karim, Queen Victoria's Indian secretary. Although he'd never met him before, he was well aware of how important a figure he'd become, for this was the man who determined, depending upon the Queen's physical condition on any given day, who might enter the royal presence. The Munshi had been known to refuse audiences to the Prime Minister and members of the Queen's own family, though it was suspected Her Majesty sometimes used him as a convenient excuse to avoid being bored by people she didn't wish to see. It was rumored that Bertie himself had on occasion been Munshi-ed.

They climbed into the covered carriage, a footman closed the door behind them and they lurched away.

"I hope Her Majesty is feeling well," said Winston. Indeed, he suspected Victoria probably felt considerably better than he had since receiving the royal command to appear at Osborne House. He had no clue what the Queen wanted with him, and even half suspected, given her condition, that she might somehow have confused him with his father.

The black beard rimming the Munshi's face, along with cold, stern eyes gave him a fierce countenance. He reminded Winston of a warlord he'd once met during his time in India.

"Her Majesty has rallied considerably in the last few days," said the Munshi. "You will meet her in the drawing room, though that is subject to change if she feels tired. Her strength is limited. I can't tell you how long your meeting will last. It's an honor she's asked to see you. The Queen has called no one to visit beyond her personal staff for weeks." He paused. "You're aware she's nearly blind?"

"So I've heard," said Winston.

"It is not as much of a handicap as you might expect. I and others stay nearby to describe anything she wishes to know about. We are her eyes to the world. Yesterday, she had a number of great works of art brought in and then sat in front of them while I described them to her in great detail. She was an accomplished artist herself, you know."

Winston stared at him in amazement, but before he could say anything, the carriage pulled to a stop after its short journey and the two men got out.

Osborne House, purchased by the Queen and Prince Albert in 1845, had been designed by Albert in the Italianate style with great square towers, an elaborate curved staircase entrance and extensive fountains and gardens. The grounds covered a thousand acres, and the estate had served as a retreat for the royal couple from the pressures of court life at Buckingham Palace and Windsor Castle. Since Albert's death in 1861, the Queen had spent most of her time at either Balmoral Castle in Scotland or Osborne House.

Winston followed the Munshi up the curved exterior staircase, through an ornate entrance and then down a seemingly endless series of hallways, up another long staircase, past dozens of servants padding silently about on their obscure missions and, finally, to a large doorway flanked by uniformed guards.

The Munshi said something to one of the guards, who opened the door and stepped inside. A moment later, a young lady-in-waiting emerged. She looked Winston up and down, as though gauging whether this rather frumpily dressed figure was worthy of an audience with her mistress. Finally, she said, "The Queen has asked to see you privately. This is most unusual. You will enter and proceed to a spot directly in front of Her Majesty. She is sitting in her chair by the fire. Once you have bowed and greeted her, you may sit in the chair opposite, if she offers it. When the Queen is finished with you, she will ring her bell, and I will escort you out."

Curiouser and curiouser, Winston thought. What on earth could this be about? Anxiously pulling at his waistcoat, he tried to straighten his clothes before realizing that, of course, since Victoria was almost blind, she wouldn't see him at all. What she'd be gauging would be his words. He'd give his right arm to know what she wanted of him.

He entered the room behind the lady-in-waiting. It was large and very dark with heavy lace curtains hanging from the bay windows opposite the entry. He was aware of elaborately framed paintings on the walls and a kind of fussy Victorian collection of china in several glass-fronted cabinets. Overstuffed furniture of the most elegant sort filled an area in front of the enormous, marble-topped fireplace that roared with a huge, crackling fire. Shadows caused by the flames danced about, creating a sort of haunted house atmosphere. The room was stiflingly hot, for the Queen was nearly always cold these days.

"Mr. Churchill to see you, Ma'am," said the woman in a loud voice. She waited until Victoria waved a hand and then retreated out the door, leaving them alone. Winston moved forward until he was close enough to see her in the flickering light.

Queen Victoria was dressed all in black, as she had been for the forty years since her husband Albert's death. Theirs had been a good and happy marriage, blessed with nine children, and she had mourned the loss of Albert ever since. Winston stared in fascination at the familiar face he'd seen in person only once before, though pictures of the Queen were common enough. There was the dark hair pulled tightly back, the receding chin and strong nose. She wore a white lace bunting on her head, a pearl necklace, a large emerald brooch and matching ring. Her eyes were sunken and no longer sparkled with the fierce intelligence and wit that he remembered from the one audience he'd attended with his father.

He realized with a start that she must be waiting for him to say something. He cleared his throat. "Your Majesty, I'm honored at your invitation."

"Young Mr. Churchill," she said. "Come sit here." She waved to the chair in front of her. "We congratulate you on your election to Parliament." Her voice was surprisingly strong.

"Thank you, Ma'am. I serve at your Majesty's pleasure."

"As did your father, who had his faults. We wonder if you have the same ones?"

It was disconcerting to look at the Queen's eyes, which focused nowhere and seemed to wander aimlessly about the room. He sat rigidly in the chair and pulled again at his waistcoat. He was sweating profusely in the overheated room.

"Faults I have, Ma'am. But I rather think they are more developed than were my father's."

The Queen laughed out loud, a sort of high chirping sound that trailed off. "You have his wit, sir, we give you that."

"Indeed, I miss him for it," Winston said, adding, "I miss many things about him."

She nodded. "It is good for a young man to revere his father. One of Bertie's many faults was his failure to appreciate the things Albert did for him. Our late husband tried everything to make

89

a man of him. No doubt he pushed too hard sometimes . . ." Her voice ran down, and she said nothing for almost a minute.

Winston couldn't imagine where the conversation was going.

Finally, she spoke again. "We have followed the story of your *escape* from the Boers."

He decided to take a gamble. If he should tell the unvarnished truth to anyone, it ought to be his Queen.

"The escape was a fraud, your Majesty. In truth, Louis Botha freed me in exchange for a service to him. At the time, I was under the impression it was also a service to my own country and to the royal family as well." He shifted uncomfortably. "I should like to explain what we found in the remote back country of the Transvaal."

"Your Roman treasure?" said the Queen.

His mouth fell open. In the silence of the next few moments, he observed the flicker of a smile pass across Victoria's withered face. Though she couldn't see him, she said, "Close your mouth, Winston, or you may entrap one of the royal flies."

"How . . . how did you know?" Winston blurted stupidly before realizing his gaffe. "Pardon me, Ma'am. It is not my place to ask that."

"The cause was sufficient." She paused for breath. "Britain is at war, but we have communicated with Commander Botha. It is always good to keep one's lines of communication open, don't you agree?"

"Botha told you what we found?"

"That and more. It appears Lord Sterne made no friends in South Africa by stealing its heritage. Bertie is a fool. He befriends men . . . and women we might add . . . of the lowest sort."

For the Queen to know about the Roman connection could only mean that Zeila had confided in Botha. He wasn't sure how he felt about that, though he imagined she'd felt the need to trust someone.

"Have you any information for us regarding Lord Sterne?" said the Queen.

"Your Majesty, very little I'm afraid. I hired an investigator to try to find the man, but now my investigator has disappeared. I fear the worst foul play."

Victoria coughed suddenly and the spasm went on for several long moments. She held a handkerchief to her mouth until the fit passed. She seemed weaker.

"We will not be here much longer, Mr. Churchill," she said. "When we pass, Bertie will become King. He is our first-born son and it is his right." She sighed deeply. "We never expected to rule, but one must learn to accept what comes and do one's best. Bertie will need help if he is to succeed. We hope you will give it to him as every loyal subject should."

"Yes, Ma'am," he said, wondering if this pledge of fealty to her son was the reason he'd been brought here, though it was hard to imagine so minor a figure as himself worthy of such a move by the Queen.

But then she said, "Now to the purpose for this meeting. Lord Sterne has been sent back to the Transvaal by Bertie to secure the treasure you found."

Winston's eyes widened. "Ma'am?"

"We have known Lord Sterne for many years . . . since he was a child, actually. His family was always ruthless in its pursuits. It is hardly surprising that he is also quite without scruples. As a result, we have watched him closely for a long time." She leaned forward in her chair, her hand resting on a solid ivory cane, which she tapped on the floor for emphasis. "We will not allow this . . . 'creature' to have such a hold on our son. Lord Sterne will find a reception committee waiting for him when he returns to South Africa. This we have arranged with Commander Botha in exchange for certain other favors. You see, even in wartime, nations must bargain with one another. Your Roman treasure is secure for the time being, Winston. We do not feel so strong a need to add it to the collections of the British Museum as does our son, the . . . *great patron.*"

Winston felt a growing chill. The Queen seemed to know everything, and she certainly seemed firmly in control of events, even from this dark room at remote Osborne House. He realized how fortunate he was to have told her the truth.

"Our final words to you, Winston, are to keep your own lines of information to Louis Botha open. We believe one day he will become the leader of a united South Africa once this war is over, regardless of who prevails. And WE will prevail." She took a long, tired breath. "We wish you to take an interest in this great treasure, for we believe it rightly belongs to those poor souls in Africa. It is their heritage every bit as much as these jewels . . ." she fingered the heavy brooch on her chest, ". . . are mine. We charge you, Mr. Churchill, in this one matter, NOT to support your King."

She leaned back in her chair, seemingly exhausted by the lengthy speech. "You have our leave to go, Winston."

He stood and looked at her for a moment longer. He knew he would never see her again. She was the only Queen he had ever known, indeed, the only one his father had ever known.

"Could . . . Your Majesty, could I kiss your hand?"

The old woman smiled and raised her arm. Winston moved forward and gently pressed his lips to the back of her hand. "You have meant so much to England, Ma'am. I think now, I truly understand how much. I will not forget your words."

"Few words are more quickly forgotten than those of a dead monarch," said the Queen. "But we sense a strength in you. We think you will serve our nation well. Follow your instincts, Winston. It is all any of us can do."

13.

Buckingham Palace, London

January 1920

MARTIN RAND stared down the vast entrance hall of Buckingham Palace. He never tired of the magnificence of this place, with its red carpets and golden chandeliers, its ridiculously clad footmen and horse guards. Yet for all its ostentatious symbolism, it represented values he'd fought long and hard for, and it always caused a lump to rise in his throat.

He'd been here several times before, though the visits had always been clandestine, in keeping with the invariably secret missions with which he was charged. For he was without a doubt one of Britain's best-kept secrets. Just twenty-six years of age, he already had more experience than most men twice his age. His father had been posted as an official in the British colonial government in Cairo. There, Martin was educated in a school for the children of British officials. At fifteen, he'd been kidnapped by a group of Sudanese tribesmen. The Sudan was also under British rule, but the resistance of its fierce tribesmen remained almost continuous. The Sudanese attempted to ransom him in exchange for the release of prisoners held by the British in Cairo.

When the British colonial government refused to be black-mailed, Martin's father resigned his post, hired a guide and several mercenaries, and went looking for his son. By the time he found him, seven months later, Martin had already won the hearts of his captors with his bold spirit and had become one of them, a sort of honorary Sudanese warrior. His father died from malaria just one week after locating his son. Feeling little desire to return to the boring life of an English schoolboy, Martin had instead gone on to fight in brush wars across the Sudan and northern Africa.

He picked up native dialects with ease. He was an expert shot with a rifle and pistol, had killed his first man at fifteen and knew how to survive in the desert living on nothing but snakes, insects and the morning dew. He learned to ride with the best horsemen on the African continent. Because of his fluency in languages, he was frequently called upon to serve as an interpreter between a wide array of tribal factions and the British.

When World War I broke out, he felt the tug of his native land and offered his services to Great Britain. For the duration of the war, he served across north and central Africa as an agent at large, an "Our man in Khartoum" figure. The British government of David Lloyd George used him repeatedly to help foment trouble for the Germans in Africa. When the war ended, the Treaty of Versailles gave Britain most of Germany's empire on the Dark Continent, and Martin was awarded the rank of major in His Majesty's service.

He paused at the top of the great staircase while his credentials were checked for the third time. Though he generally received his orders from the War Department, he'd twice been decorated by the King, who had taken a liking to him. At last he was ushered into the presence of King George V, who had acceded to the throne following the death of his father, King Albert Edward, known as Bertie, in 1910.

He approached the King, who stood behind his desk staring out at the crowds that now daily filled the streets of war-released Britain.

"Look at them," the King said. "Over a year since the war ended and they still celebrate. I wish I could join them, but there's so much to do now to recover. My days are filled with meetings and decisions. One wonders, sometimes, what the point of our Parliamentary system really is. The members of the House seem unable to agree on anything." He sighed. "Well . . . it's good to see you again, Martin. I hope you are well?"

Rand enjoyed the King's company. His Majesty could be an informal man in private, avoiding use of the royal "we" in conversation and honestly appearing to be interested in the lives of his subjects.

"Very well, thank you, sir."

King George smiled. "By rights, given what your country has asked of you over the last four years, you ought to be retired and living off a damn good pension in Devonshire."

Martin sat in the chair offered by the King. "Retirement would bore me, sir. I'm afraid I got a taste for a more active lifestyle during my boisterous teenage years."

"And that boisterousness has survived even the late war? You may be one of the few men on Earth, Martin, who is not tired after this last conflict. My God, I can still hardly believe the carnage in Europe."

"They did have the worst of it, sir. I've read about it and would not have wanted to be there, lying in a filthy, soaking ditch waiting for a German tank to drive over me."

The King looked amused. "You managed to find enough excitement of your own in Africa." He nodded at the medals lining his guest's uniform. "My feeling is that the map of that continent is going to be in flux for a long time. We're going to need someone with your knowledge and expertise, Martin, to help the Prime Minister and me make the right decisions there. If I thought it would be the right thing, I'd bring you to London and put you in the foreign office, like your father."

"My father was good at what he did," said Martin. "I miss him . . ."

"But you're different." The King finished his sentence for him. "I know. Which is why I'm sending you to South Africa."

"Sir?"

"I need someone to keep me informed of the political situation. It's an important place now and will grow more so in the years to come. Since Louis Botha's death last year, the situation is in flux down there. The country is rich beyond anyone's dreams . . . diamonds, gold . . . Lord knows what all is buried in that place.

I want you to get your hand on the pulse of what makes the Union of South Africa tick. As you know, the Union was formed in 1910. What a messy alliance it's been! By combining the British Cape Colony and Natal, the Boer Transvaal and Orange Free State, along with the native states of Zulu Land, Basutoland and Swazi Land, there's just so much to learn. I know you pick up dialects like other men pick up a glass of whisky. Send me regular reports."

Martin felt his pulse quicken. It was precisely the sort of assignment he'd hoped for. He'd been to South Africa only a few times, but he knew the central part of the continent like the back of his hand. This would broaden his expertise and he, too, had long felt the region would be the key to the entire continent.

"I'll do my best, sir."

"Good fellow!" The King shook his hand. "Now, I'd like you to meet someone who's expressed an interest in meeting you."

King George pulled a cord that evidently rang a bell somewhere. At once the door opened and Winston Churchill entered the room, striding in his slightly stooped gait to the King and bowing formally.

"Winston, this is the young man I told you about, Martin Rand. Martin, this is the Secretary of State for War . . ."

"No need, sir, to introduce Winston Churchill. It is a great honor. I've read your books and followed your escape from the Boers in the newspapers when I was no more than six or seven years old. My father read the accounts to me himself."

Winston shook the young man's hand. "Well, don't believe everything you read, Mr. Rand. Especially when a man is writing about himself. But I can assure you, the honor is mutual. The King has mentioned your exploits in Africa to me on a number of occasions. Quite impressive. It appears you were practically a one-man army and caused the Germans no end of misery. I hope to be able to read your own memoirs some day . . . though I imagine I'll have to wait a while for that privilege."

King George looked pleased at the exchange. "I've arranged for us to have lunch on my closed terrace overlooking the gardens. I'm sure you two will have plenty to talk about."

They followed King George down a long hallway to a set of open doors that revealed a glass-enclosed terrace. There they sat at a small table, elegantly set, that looked through leaded glass windows down on the small lake and snow-covered lawns of the King's private garden.

After settling themselves, the King said, "Tell me Winston, how goes our tank production?"

"Well sir, it's been a struggle. As you know, when David Lloyd George appointed me Minister of Munitions in 1917, the development of our new tanks became my number one priority. Now that the war's over, I'm charged with supervising the demobilization of the army. I firmly believe we must never again let our guard down, as it had been a few years before the war. So . . . I find myself attempting to demobilize with one hand and build up with the other. Some days, I feel like I'm treading a very slim wire."

Martin used the exchange over affairs of state to sit back and observe Winston Churchill. He'd heard all of his life about this pale, rather odd-looking man who, in his mid-forties, was already a giant in the fields of war, politics and literature. Of course, Churchill had been born with the correct pedigree. That never hurt a career in public life. Still, he was a man who didn't shy from saying what he thought, which had gotten him dismissed from high office in the past. Rand admired any man with that sort of "Damn the torpedoes, full speed ahead" mentality, for it mirrored his own.

He realized with a start that the King had said something to him.

"Uh . . . I'm sorry, sir. I wasn't listening."

King George roared with laughter. "What do you think of this chappie, Winston? Having lunch with two such high fellows as ourselves and day-dreaming. Well . . . probably thinking about more important things than all this bureaucratic mumbo-jumbo."

"I'm afraid not, sir," Martin said. "Actually, one of the things I was thinking about was the last king I shared a meal with. He was buck naked and had a bone run through his nose."

"By God," said the King, "you two ought to get together and talk about Africa. Between you, I've managed to learn quite a bit about the Dark Continent over the last few years."

Winston eyed Rand thoughtfully. "I understand you spent quite a spot of time in the Sudan, is that right?"

Martin nodded.

"Know anything about the Nubians?" said Winston.

"A great race once upon a time. Historically very powerful and wealthy. For a period, they ruled all of Egypt, you know. Nubian pharaohs controlled all of the territory from Khartoum to Palestine. Eventually, they were thrown out of Egypt but continued to flourish in the Sudan for another thousand years. The last Nubian kingdom collapsed some twenty years ago and most of her people converted to Islam. They are only a fraction of what they were . . . for the most part. But still a noble, prideful people. The women are beautiful and the men powerfully built."

King George nodded approvingly. "I told you, Winston, that he knows as much about Africa as anyone."

Winston said, "You mentioned that the Nubians are only a fraction of what they were 'for the most part.' What did you mean?"

Martin considered for a moment. "There's a group of Nubians that refuse to be Arabized . . . a sort of secret society that has attained an almost mythical stature in central Africa. They are said by those who fear them to be giants . . . or ghosts. They use traditional weapons, primarily bow and arrow, with which they are extremely proficient. The men live, work and train together, patterning themselves after the great Shaka Zulu's men. There have been a number of political assassinations attributed to them, though no one knows for sure."

"Have you met any of them?"

"I have fought both with them and against them. Given a choice, I'd rather they were on my side. They are fierce warriors, but they hold honor above everything. That makes them easy to deal with on one level, for you can trust their word, a rarity in this world."

Winston said, "Ever hear of a place called Mapungubwe Hill?"

"Yes . . . some sort of sacred place to the Nubians. A burial location, I would guess, though I've never seen it. It's far south of the Sudan, which is unusual."

"I would be interested," said Winston, looking away, "in anything you might learn of the place."

Martin stared at him curiously. "Are you interested as a matter of politics or culture?"

"As a matter of . . . history, I would say," said Winston, obliquely. "Ancient history." He shrugged his shoulders, as though throwing off a great weight.

The remainder of the meal passed with mostly political conversation and a bit of spirited talk about an upcoming soccer match between France and Britain. At the end of the meal, the King rose and offered his hand to Martin. "You must excuse us now. Mr. Churchill and I have some more serious matters of state to discuss."

Winston stood and also shook hands. He looked into Martin's eyes and said, "Africa needs strong young men, Mr. Rand. So does Britain. Do you think it possible to serve both at the same time?"

"I love both, sir. I hope I shall never have to make a choice between the two."

"A wise woman once told me," said Winston, "that if I always did what felt right in my heart, things would work out in the end."

"A fine sentiment, sir. Could I ask who she was?"

Winston nodded. "Queen Victoria."

Rand left, and the two remaining men sipped their tea silently for a couple of minutes. At last, the King said, "Still can't give up thinking about it, can you, Winston?"

"There are more important matters," Churchill replied in a tired voice. "But it's a rare day that passes without my seeing a vision of that incredible place from twenty years ago. I've always wondered if the treasure remained where it was. Victoria wanted it that way, though your father did not. She felt it belonged to the people of Africa. But I've often wondered what good it does them if it remains in the ground, unbeknownst to any of them."

King George said, "Bertie admired you, Winston, as do I, and he relied upon your daily reports of events in the House of Commons. I'm aware also that he was a help in your career, appointing you to your post in the Privy Council. But as you know, shortly before he died, he told me about this Roman treasure of yours. He had tried throughout his reign to bring it to England, without success. He always believed you had something to do with that failure."

"Forgive me for saying this, Your Majesty . . ." Winston hesitated. "Your father did promote my career, and I've never quite known why, though perhaps it was because of his friendship with my father. But . . . I always detected a certain ruthlessness in him. I think he was capable of almost anything. It amazed me how popular he was with the citizenry. He had two completely separate personas, one public and one private."

"He was a much more complicated man than many had grown to think from his earlier years," replied the King. "He was a very skillful politician, as you well know, setting up the Triple Entente, the alliance between Great Britain, France and Russia, and supporting your efforts to build up our war capabilities in anticipation of the worst." He sighed. "There are those who still believe he was responsible for creating the nightmare world of crossed alliances and mobilizations that led to the war. Ruthless? You may be right, but having been in his shoes, now, for a decade, I can tell you that a King can not be successful without a certain amount of ruthlessness."

"No doubt you are right, sir. But your father's alliance with Lord Sterne did not make this loyal subject confident of either King Edward's choice of associates or his principles at times. I still have a personal debt to settle with Sterne if he remains alive, though your grandmother, Queen Victoria, once assured me that Lord Sterne would be well taken care of if he ever returned to Africa."

"Indeed. Then perhaps she took care of the matter. As you know, Sterne disappeared many years ago without a trace. Victoria was never fond of the Sterne branch of the royal house. She told me once they were a bunch of money-grubbing, adulterous, mentally deficient throwbacks, probably spawned by the invading Vikings a thousand years ago." He shook his head. "Lord, but Grandmum had a way with words."

14.

Nubian Desert, Upper Sudan

January 1920

MARTIN GUIDED his horse up a steep rise overlooking the Nile River and paused to stare out across the vast Nubian Desert that stretched away to the east as far as the eye could see. His lungs filled in a deep sigh of contentment. This was home. He'd spent the first eight years of his life in England before his father was posted abroad, but didn't care for the dark, wet climate. He *felt* British, for it was his birthright, and the country's history was the history he'd been taught in school. But it was here, surrounded by desert and savannah, that he knew he belonged. This was where he had come of age, and the stark beauty of Sudan penetrated every fiber of his being. His father had been the only family he had. Africa was now his family.

He and his companion could more easily have journeyed to South Africa by ship, but he preferred to travel overland, through territory that was rife with bandits, poisonous vipers, wild animals, thick jungles and warring tribes of every description. There were few roads where they were going, but they would shorten the journey, when possible, by using those intermittent sections of the Cape Town-to-Cairo railroad that had been completed over the past forty years. They traveled cross-country, living off the land, alternately enjoying the hospitality of old friends and the enmity of traditional enemies.

Two days earlier, they'd skirted the valley of Wadi Allaqi. Extending sixty miles into the mountains east of Quabban, it was the site of the great Nubian gold mines of ancient times. The region was one of narrow gorges and rocky outcroppings, known in Arabic as the Batn el-Hajjar, the "Belly of Stones." It was the enigmatic words of Winston Churchill about ancient Nubia that led Martin to detour here from a more direct route.

Nabeel al Hussein rode up beside him. Nabeel had fought many battles at Martin's side. He was Moroccan, a huge, powerful man who always looked like too much load for whatever poor mount had drawn him. His hair was jet black to match his handlebar mustache and blazing eyes. He carried a brace of pistols, a rifle and a sword that had belonged to his father. Nabeel was the sole companion Martin had chosen to accompany him on his long journey.

"We near the valley of the Nubian kings," Nabeel said, matter-of-factly, although Martin knew their presence here made him nervous.

"I haven't seen anything unusual," he said. "We'll cross above the fourth cataract. There should be a good place to camp near there."

Nabeel grunted. "What is unusual, *Marteen*, is our presence here. I don't relish a Nubian arrow in my back."

"The Nubians are a proud people," said Martin. "They do not shoot their enemies in the back. Anyway, we're not their enemies and they will leave us alone."

"Huh!" was the only answer his friend gave, and he moved away, his eyes continuing to scan the horizon.

They crossed the river without incident. The valley ahead was formed by a rift in the earth with stone cliffs, many of which had been carved into great temples, homes and burial places during the age of Nubian greatness, more than two thousand years ago. This was the site of Jebel Barkal, the sacred mountain of the Nubian rulers. Desert sands had long since reclaimed most of the ruins.

Nubians buried their rulers here in giant earthen pyramids so large that in modern times they were often mistaken for hills. Martin had once been taken through a tomb by Kwesi Ayoub, a Nubian who'd fought at his side in a skirmish with bandits. Encircled and trapped, Kwesi had led them through the tomb's maze of underground tunnels to escape. Though they'd since become friends, he'd always been aware there was something different about Kwesi. He suspected he was a member of the "Clan of the Bow," the secret society of Nubian warriors.

The tomb had consisted of brick-lined chambers filled with the bodies of hundreds of sacrificed retainers destined to serve the departed king. There were also scores of horse, camel and donkey remains. It was an entire nether world of winding corridors and strange, cadaverous forms that seemed to leap out at them in the flickering light of Kwesi's torch. Martin had never been more glad than when they finally emerged into the daylight, a safe distance from their enemies.

Today, they traveled through a landscape of acacia and tamarisk trees, with dense thickets of thorny shrubs that sometimes necessitated wide detours. Game was surprisingly abundant in the arid climate. They surprised Barbary sheep, Dorcas gazelle and wild asses at regular intervals. In mid-summer, temperatures reached 120 degrees Fahrenheit, but now, in January, nighttime temperatures could fall below freezing. It was a hard, unforgiving place, but like the animals that eked out a living here, Martin felt relaxed and in his element.

It would take months for them to reach South Africa via this tortured route, but the King had given no instructions on when he should begin sending his reports. This way, he could take measure of the heart of the continent, from which all things flowed. Central Africa served as a feeder belt as trade goods of all sorts made their way to the coasts, everything from gold, ebony, silver and copper to furs, ivory, ostrich feathers and live animals destined for zoos. Even slaves were still dealt in unsupervised marketplaces. Everything he would observe, be told by native tribesmen or simply intuit along the way would help to inform his opinions on what was happening on the great land mass. This ability to take the pulse of Africa was precisely what King George expected of him. What he reported to the great colonial power of Britain would ultimately direct policy, determine which areas might be opened to exploitation and affect the lives of tens of millions of people. It was an enormous responsibility and one he did not take lightly.

They began to move down a narrow, rocky gorge filled with patches of thorn. The horses picked their way carefully, ears pricked up. Even they understood the potential for ambush in such a place by panthers. Martin knew, however, it was unlikely one of the cats would attack humans. He was more concerned with bandits.

Nabeel guided his steed down the opposite side of the rift. Both men kept their eyes peeled, even relying on their sense of smell to detect any human presence. Once, Martin pulled his horse up and sniffed the air. There was a faint whiff of smoke . . . perhaps a nearby boma. He turned to ask Nabeel if he'd detected it when a sudden, rhythmic chanting split the stifling late-afternoon heat. The sound seemed to emanate from the very rocks that surrounded them.

Nabeel sat rigidly, pistol in hand, every fiber of his fierce countenance at fever pitch. Slowly, he walked his horse over to Martin's side.

"What do you think?" Martin said softly.

"I think . . . we may be dead men," Nabeel said.

The chanting stopped abruptly. Without any sound or apparent movement, they were suddenly surrounded by at least fifty nearly naked warriors. The fierce figures held spears and bows, and Martin also saw rifles. The men were tall and very dark-skinned with corn-rowed hair and painted slashes on their bodies. He recognized them immediately: Nubian warriors, the last of a breed whose lineage stretched back more than four thousand years. The ancestors of these men had once ruled the pharaohs; indeed, Nubian kings had served as pharaohs themselves for hundreds of years.

Today, they were a sad remnant of that glorious past. Martin knew there were not many of this sort left, living in the wild, eschewing all contact with modern men. They could manage it only by living in such incredible remoteness. Yet the presence of the guns suggested that trade reached even here.

One of the painted figures padded silently through the rocks to a position a few feet in front of the intruders. He spoke in a dialect Martin recognized as a partly Arabized vernacular of the Upper Sudan.

"Why are you here?" The man said.

"We seek only to pass through to the south," Martin replied. "We'll take nothing from your land but what we need to eat."

"Perhaps we will eat you," said the tall figure.

Martin smiled. There was no cannibalism in this part of Africa. It was an idle threat. "Then you should feed us well," he said. "So we will taste better."

The man laughed out loud and shouted something to the others, patting his own stomach. A smattering of cries and hoots answered him.

"We will feed you well," said the man. "At our boma. Put your weapons on the ground."

Martin shook his head. "We are friends to the Nubians. I am a friend of Kwesi Ayoub. Friends do not need to surrender their weapons."

The man peered at him with new interest. There were not many Nubians living in this region. It was likely he'd at least heard the name of Kwesi Ayoub. He moved back and consulted with a small group of his warriors. Then he came forward again.

"Maybe you are a friend of Kwesi Ayoub. Maybe you only heard his name. We will see. You will come to our boma and you may keep your weapons."

Martin nodded. The warriors fanned out, some of them moving behind, others alongside. The man who'd done the talking led the way up the steep slope and into the granite mountains that surrounded them.

They didn't have far to go. The smoke Martin had smelled had indeed come from the men's boma. In short order they approached the wall of the compound, constructed out of a hodge-podge of tree trunks and thorn bushes. The dense mix made an impenetrable barrier in which not only the villagers but also their animals sought refuge from lions at night. As they neared the enclosure, a lookout shouted. The leader of the warriors called back and a moment later an opening appeared in the wall of thorns. They entered to a collection of huts surrounding a central hard-baked earthen square. This was home to several hundred people. Women and children gathered around them, noisily chattering away with excitement. Most of the women were bare-chested and wore colorful, patterned skirts that also signified trade somewhere along the line with western elements.

A young warrior, no more than eighteen, but a magnificent, muscled fellow with an intricate design of tattoos on his shoulders, ran up to Martin and slashed him on the leg with a knife. The cut was not deep thanks to his thick hide pants, but the challenge could not go unanswered. He stared at the wound and then slowly raised his head to look at the man who stood defiantly in front of him.

Slowly, he wrapped his reins around the pommel of his saddle and spoke loudly in the dialect of the lead warrior who had brought them here. "Your children play funny games," he said. "They should be careful with knives until they grow up. I will take the knife from this boy so he will not hurt himself." He swung one leg over the saddle and jumped lightly to the ground.

The young warrior's face contorted at the insult given him in front of the entire village. He yelled something and rushed at the *mzungu*, slashing the knife viciously. Martin sidestepped the thrust, grabbed his attacker's wrist and twisted it around until he had the hand bent behind his back. Then he put his other arm around the boy's neck and choked off his wind. Calmly, he removed the knife from the twisted hand and shoved the boy forward, where he stood, choking, as he regained his wind. Then Martin turned his back on the boy and tossed the knife to the warrior he'd exchanged words with.

"Your children need better instruction as warriors. If I had more time I would help you teach them." He turned to his horse and glanced at Nabeel, who made a slight motion with his head, indicating that the young warrior had regained his composure and was coming at him again.

This time, Martin barely glanced over his shoulder before slamming his elbow back into the boy's forehead. He fell like a stone, out cold on the ground. Martin remounted and sat passively staring at the warriors encircling them.

For a moment there was silence, then everyone in the village began to laugh uproariously. Apparently, the rash young giant was not particularly popular. A few children threw sticks and stones at the figure lying on the ground and then everyone ignored the prostrate adolescent as they looked at Martin and Nabeel with new respect.

"Do you not offer *chakula* to your guests in this part of Nubia?" Martin said.

The lead warrior, who was still laughing, nodded. He yelled a few words to a group of women, who hurried to set up a feast. Meanwhile, as Martin surveyed the crowd, a figure of perhaps thirty-five years of age moved forward. He was not outfitted as a warrior, but instead wore heavy, leather leggings similar to Martin's.

"It has taken too many years for you to return, *Marteen*," said the man.

"Kwesi!" He leaped from his horse and clasped the man by the forearms. "It's good to see you. Your men wanted to eat us. What kind of welcome is that for old friends?"

Kwesi laughed. "You're lucky. We don't eat our enemies like those to the south." He looked at the youth lying on the ground. "I'm sorry for your welcome. The boy has just received his tattoos and become Takatifu Wapigani, a sacred warrior in the Clan of the Bow. He was showing off. Come, you shall have your *chakula*."

He led the way to one end of the square. Here, the women had already roasted a Dorcas gazelle and were busily preparing other foods. Kwesi motioned for them to sit on a pile of heavy fronds that had been placed on the ground. He produced an ancient, worn pipe and spent considerable time lighting it. "What brings you here, *Marteen?*" he said between puffs.

"I've been ordered by my King to travel far to the south and tell him how things go there."

"Why?"

"It's difficult to explain, Kwesi. It has to do with politics. The King wishes to know who will control the region and what goods they might trade, among other things."

"We trade with white men," Kwesi said. "With hunters who come through looking for monkeys, giraffes and ostriches, sometimes gold. They give us cloth and guns—but not enough of either. I don't like these men. They are untrustworthy."

"It is often so," Martin said, making a long face. "One of my King's subjects is interested in the burial place at Mapungubwe Hill. Do you know of it?"

Kwesi sat still, the smoke from his pipe rising straight up into the air. He said, "It's a place we do not speak of. It is forbidden. You must not go there."

Martin shrugged. He'd heard this sort of thing many times. Most of the tribes were superstitious and had numerous and often elaborate taboos. As he decided what to say next, the women began to lay out food and drink.

"Do you know who is buried at Mapungubwe Hill?" he persisted.

Kwesi threw his pipe on the ground and spat. "Enough! We will not speak of it." He made a sharp motion with his hand and the women brought gourds filled with a drink that Martin recognized. As soon as the vessels were delivered, the women and children disappeared to allow the men to partake of the religious drink in seclusion. He took a small sip. It was a pungent, fermented drink that he knew also contained hallucinatory herbs. If he took too much, he might not wake up for days. He pretended to take another mouthful and then handed the gourd to Nabeel, who, as a Muslim, did not drink alcohol. But he knew enough to play along, also pretending to take a sip.

Suddenly there was a loud wail from within the hut immediately in front of them. Instantly, the boma grew silent. There was a low moan followed by a series of howls and laments the like of which Martin had never heard. Then an incredible figure leaped through the door of the hut and began to chant and gyrate around the compound in front of them. He wore the head of a wart hog over his own and even had foot coverings made from the animal's hooves. His body was entirely naked except for a tiny loincloth and painted designs that covered him from head to toe.

This was the tribe's magic holder, or, more accurately, its witch doctor. Kwesi and the others watched the man in a kind of trance, as he leaped high in the air, spun around like a dervish, made pig-like snorts and occasionally swatted someone in the crowd with a bundle of magumbo sticks that must have hurt like the devil. As the entertainment wore on, more and more of the assemblage became impervious to the beatings, as they drank deeply from the gourds.

Martin and Nabeel continued to pass their own gourd back and forth. Every third or fourth time, Martin would surreptitiously spill some onto the ground when no one was looking too closely. They also ate, since there was no telling when they might get another meal as tempting as Dorcas gazelle. Meanwhile, other natives appeared with drums and various noisemakers and began to rhythmically accompany the gyrations of the witch doctor. It appeared that the strange scene might go on for a long time, perhaps all night.

But eventually, the witch doctor began to wear down. He'd put away an astounding amount of the powerful drink. He shouted something into the open doorway of the hut from which he'd leaped. Martin glanced at the hut as he bit into a piece of meat and then stopped in mid-chew.

A woman emerged, unlike any female he'd ever seen. At first, he thought she was wearing tightly-fitted clothing covered with designs and patterns, but then he realized she was completely naked, her body painted white with black figures of animals and evil spirits sketched on top of the base color. She was tall and slim with magnificent, large breasts. Every inch of her skin was painted.

She moved forward until she was only a half dozen feet from them. It was apparent the woman was not in control of herself. Whether she was drugged or simply in some kind of spiritual trance, her head dipped unsteadily and her body swayed drunkenly. Yet her eyes caught Martin's and he thought there was something bewitching about them.

"Who is that?" he said softly to Kwesi.

"Spirit Woman," Kwesi replied, as though that explained everything.

The woman began to move about the opening between the hut and the men, swaying and moving her hands languidly in elaborate patterns. She appeared to be mumbling something, but he couldn't hear what it was. Wherever she went, her eyes held onto Martin's almost as if they were a lifeline of some kind.

"Look," said Nabeel, motioning to the witch doctor, who had removed the warthog's head from his own.

Martin stared into the man's face and saw mad eyes. The witch doctor began to chant something. He picked up the bundle of stout magumbo sticks and waved them over his head in a ritualistic fashion. Though Martin had witnessed many tribal ceremonies, this was unlike anything he'd seen before.

"What's happening?" he said to Kwesi.

His friend was terribly inebriated himself by this point. He waved a listless hand at the tableau in front of them. "Spirit Woman to be beaten until she moves no more," he said. "To appease the spirits that haunt her."

"What?" He stood up, but even as he did, the witch doctor raised the bundle of sticks and struck the woman on the back as hard as he could. She staggered at the blow but didn't fall down. Once more, the man raised his arm. Before he could hit her again, however, Martin moved in and deftly relieved him of the sticks. He heard Nabeel rise, swearing, and saw his companion's pistols appear suddenly in his hands.

The drumming stopped and the entire congregation froze. The witch doctor looked puzzled at what had happened. He couldn't believe anyone would dare interfere with his elaborate and time-honored rituals. He said something to Kwesi, who looked more panic-stricken than puzzled.

"What are you doing, *Marteen?*" Kwesi said.

"I can not allow this woman to be beaten in my presence," he replied. He knew what he was doing was terribly risky and required some explanation that the warriors might somehow relate to. Otherwise, he and Nabeel and the girl might all be dead in very short order. "It is against my own gods," he said, quickly. "Any warrior in my clan who allows a woman to be killed in his presence will die a terrible death. It is written." He glanced at Nabeel who rolled his eyes at his friend's stupidity.

The witch doctor was having none of it. He spewed a tirade of invective and grabbed one of the Spirit Woman's arms, attempting to pull her away from the intruders. Other warriors were now also standing. They were all so drunk or doped, however, that they hardly seemed to understand what was happening.

Nabeel edged closer to Martin and said, "You are going to get us killed. The woman knows what is expected of her. You can't interfere."

"I won't let this happen, Nabeel. I'm going to take her out of here." He looked at Kwesi. "It is a matter of honor. I'm sorry, my friend. I will take the woman with me, but we can no longer accept your hospitality. Nabeel, bring our horses and one extra for the girl." He took a spare revolver out of his waist and handed it to Kwesi. "This will pay for the horse."

He broke the witch doctor's hold on the woman and began to move toward the entrance. Nabeel, cursing the entire situation, moved to the edge of the boma, where the horses were corralled. Leading the three animals, he pushed aside the thorn entrance and the three of them left the boma.

The witch doctor continued to yell and try to arouse his soldiers. A number of them staggered forward, but Martin knocked them aside with little effort. Indeed, they were hardly more than automatons, practically out on their feet from the strong brew they'd been taking in for hours. Once outside, Martin threw the girl onto one of the mounts and jumped up behind her. Nabeel led the extra horse and together they moved off into the night, leaving behind the strange fire-lit tableau of staggering warriors and screaming witch doctor.

Nabeel yelled at Martin, "You crazy *mzungu*. Last damn party I ever go to with a white man!"

15.

THEY PUSHED hard through the night, a torturous task on horseback over the rocky terrain. At dawn they stopped for a ten-minute rest, then continued on through the day. Not until evening did they feel comfortable that they were finally beyond the reach of the Nubians.

They halted in a remote spot above the fifth cataract of the Nile. The Spirit Woman had still not said a word. Martin sent Nabeel to reconnoiter the surrounding area and try to find something to eat. Then he led the woman down to the river. She still moved as if in a trance, the drugs not yet worn off. He tried to get her to wash herself, but her arms were limp, and finally he had to do it himself. Using handfuls of river water and a piece of rough cloth, he scrubbed her entire body until all of the paint was gone and her skin was red from the harsh treatment. She stared off into the distance throughout the procedure, even during his attempts to clean her most private parts.

When he was through, he put a shirt on her and found her a pair of extra pants. He had to cut several inches off the legs to make them fit. Then he guided her back to camp and sat her down by the fire. She immediately curled up on the ground and went to sleep.

Nabeel returned with a brace of wildfowl, which they cooked and ate ravenously, sitting before the fire. They didn't wake the woman, but saved her some choice pieces for later.

"Well, *Marteen*," said Nabeel, "That was quite an adventure. Exactly what do you plan to do with her?"

"Take her along," he said. "No other choice. We can't leave her in her present condition. She's completely helpless. We'll be in Khartoum in two or three days and should be able to find some place there to leave her."

"Showing up that witch doctor in front of his entire clan may be the stupidest thing I've ever seen you do," Nabeel said, "Though it might be a close call. We were fortunate they were all out of their minds with drink. But I still think we may be in danger. Allah alone knows how far they might be willing to go to find us." He finished eating, licked his fingers and stood up. He grabbed his bedroll and pointed to an overhang some thirty yards away. "I'll be on watch up there."

Martin nodded. "I'll spell you in four hours." He watched his friend climb up to the ridge, then gathered some more firewood and fed several sticks into the flames. He stared at the woman's face in the flickering light.

She was quite beautiful, with light chocolate skin, broadly set eyes and a firm tilt to her chin. She was definitely not a traditional Nubian. He wondered if she might have been captured for purposes of the ceremony they'd interrupted. As he contemplated her, those big eyes suddenly opened. They remained focused on him for a long time. Then she sat up, and the mind behind them seemed to come back from a long journey. When she spoke, his jaw dropped, for the words were in English.

"This is perhaps a stupid question," she said. "But who are you?"

He gave a little bow of his head. "Martin Rand at your service." He pointed up to the ridge line. "That charming fellow up there is Nabeel al Hussein."

Her eyes moved from the ridge back down to Martin and then seemed to notice her strange clothes for the first time. She fingered the heavy pants. "Where did these come from?"

"You had no clothes of your own. I washed you in the river to remove the body paint and put those on you."

Her eyes held his for a long moment. "I hope the cleaning was no trouble," she said, with just the hint of a smile.

"None at all. You were most cooperative. The Nubian fermentation process is quite an effective one. I've seen it take four days to wear off. Sometimes it never does and the person remains permanently deranged." He looked at her curiously. "What's your name?"

"Kesi."

"Well, Kesi, we've had quite a time. You were about to be beaten to death by a Nubian witch doctor. We brought you with us instead. I'm curious how you came to be in the position you were in."

Instead of answering, she stood up slowly and unsteadily. She moved as if her entire body ached, which was not an unusual side effect of the drugs. She took a few steps, stretching her arms over her head.

"I feel as though I'm made of glass," she said tiredly.

He leaned into the fire, picked up a piece of fowl and put it on a tin plate. "Here, eat this. It will help. You haven't eaten anything for quite a while."

She took the plate and sat back down. A tentative nibble soon awakened a ravenous hunger and she ate the meat along with several more pieces before asking for some water. Then she leaned back and stretched her long legs out in front of her.

"I must thank you for rescuing me," she said. "I was in the Nubian camp as a sort of volunteer. To study them. Their culture has always interested me. They're one of Africa's oldest races."

"It would seem," he said, "That you got a pretty close take on their intoxication rituals."

"That was not my intention. The witch doctor decided he wanted me for himself. I rejected him, though I tried to do so . . . diplomatically. They offered me drink I didn't realize would have the effect that it did."

"You came here alone?" he said incredulously.

She shook her head. "I had two male companions . . . a fellow student, Edgar, from Cape Town, and Akil, our guide. Edgar died of some intestinal disease shortly after we arrived. Akil was killed by snake bite, or so I was told. Without my guide, I couldn't leave."

She was either very brave or incredibly naive, he decided. "You come from Cape Town?"

"That's where I was born and grew up. I've been in London for my education. I'm doing research for my anthropological studies at the University of London." She contemplated the figure in front of her. He was tall and lean, almost hard, but there was a warmth behind the eyes. She decided she liked him. "Where will you take me?"

"The first place of any size is Khartoum. We should reach it in two days. From there, I'm sure you can arrange transport to wherever you want to go."

"And what do you do out here, Mr. Rand? Search the wilderness for young maidens to rescue?"

He laughed. "All part of the service. We rescue 'em, wash 'em up and point them in the right direction." He stopped, embarrassed at having brought up the fact that only a short time ago he'd been running his hands over every inch of her naked body. At the time, it had seemed very businesslike. Now, looking into her dark eyes in the firelight, he remembered the curves of that body in detail.

She met his eyes, knowing exactly what he was thinking. "I believe I can take care of the washing up part myself from now on," she said.

He was grateful for the dim light, that she couldn't see his face turn red.

"And where do you go after Khartoum?" she said, letting him off the hook.

"Nabeel and I are traveling to South Africa. I suppose you could say I'm doing some research of my own."

"For whom?"

He hesitated. "The King of England."

She stared at him with wide eyes. "King George? What does the King want with you?"

"I've had some experience of Africa. He's interested in the future of the Dark Continent. I rather think he doesn't expect it to stay dark forever. I'm just trying to fill in some of the blanks for him . . . politics, history, resources and so forth."

"I've been at school in London for three years. I've never even *seen* the King. What's he like?"

"He's informal and takes a real interest in people. I like him very much. He wants the best for England, but he also has concern for and interest in other nations. I hope to help him develop that concern with regard to Africa. I grew up in both countries. It would be nice to see them work together for a change."

She looked away from the fire. "That would be a very good thing."

"And what about your research? You say you've studied the Nubians. Do you know about the Clan of the Bow?"

Her face clouded. "It's difficult to know about. No one speaks of it. It's a rite of passage for young warriors. But only a few are selected. Part of the test is a series of tattoos on their shoulders, which I understand are very painful."

He nodded. "Tattoos are involved in many such rituals." He looked at her for a moment, then pulled up his shirt. On his lower back was a tattoo about three inches long of a brutal-looking dagger. "This I got when I was fifteen as part of my initiation as a Sudanese warrior."

She stared at him with wide eyes, then touched the marking. "Did it hurt?" she said.

He laughed. "I don't know. I was too drunk." Then he asked, "There have been rumors that members of the Clan of the Bow have been assassins, even killed tribal leaders. Did you ever hear anything about that?"

She shook her head. "I never heard what they did after they were initiated." After a moment, she said, "You and Nabeel are going to South Africa. I also wish to go to South Africa. Will you take me with you?"

He looked startled. "It really would be simpler if you arranged transport via ship. Khartoum is only three days travel from the sea. Nabeel and I will be many weeks, even months, traveling through the heart of the continent. It will be a very difficult trip."

"More difficult than what I've been through already?"

Grudgingly he said, "Probably not much."

"I won't be any trouble. I promise. Besides, I have no money, no papers." She looked down. "I don't even have my own clothes. I couldn't pay for my own transport."

"I can give you money," he said.

"The way you speak of Africa ... it's how I feel too. The trip you plan has been a lifelong dream. Imagine ... to pass the length of the continent. There would be so much to see and learn. When we reach South Africa, my family will pay you for your trouble."

He stared at her beautiful, anxious face. The feel and smell of her body was still embedded in his mind. He couldn't just let her disappear into the streets of Khartoum, never to be seen by him again. It would be a huge responsibility to take her with them, but he realized he wanted to do so more than anything he'd wanted in a very long time.

The only question was how he was going to convince Nabeel.

* * *

They crossed the winding Nile twice more, swimming the horses across where the water was shallow in the heat of mid-day and the crocodiles were sluggish. At last, they stood on the heights above Khartoum in Anglo-Egyptian Sudan. The city sprawled below them, a brown mass of mostly one-story mud brick buildings. Smoke from thousands of hearth fires gathered in a thick haze beneath the relentlessly blue and cloudless sky.

"The place where Gordon was killed by the Mahdi," said Kesi reverently. "I always wanted to see it." She stared at the spot where the Blue Nile entering from the east and the White Nile from the west joined to form the main body of the great river. Looking back to the distant horizon, they could see the main part of the river begin its long northeastern curl. It resembled an upturned elephant's trunk, which was in fact what the word Khartoum meant.

"Will we go into the city?" she asked.

Martin nodded. "It's under British colonial rule. I think we could all do with a bit of civilization for a day or two."

Civilization may have been too generous a word for the Khartoum of 1920. There was a languorous, still quality to the place. Isolated, poor and colorless, its streets were filled with refugees from whichever war happened to be going on currently. Children in the streets did not play in the manner of children around the world. Malnourished, they sat on reed mats in the dirt, too bereft of hope to even beg from the occasional *mzungu* who passed by.

They guided their horses slowly through town to the center, where a large brick building advertised itself with a faded sign as the Palace Hotel. Kesi looked at the building and then back at Martin.

"They won't want my business," she said, matter-of-factly. "Certainly not dressed like this."

He knew she was right. She was colored and soldiers of the British Raj would not be happy if she were to enter the big hotel.

"There's an Indian store down the street," he said. "You can get more appropriate clothes there."

"I'll try," she said. "I don't think it will make a difference, Martin."

He took her to the store and paid for a colorful Indian-style silk dress that covered her completely. She still looked exotic. Perhaps the locals would make an exception in deference to her beauty. Life was dull in the city of Khartoum.

Inside the Palace Hotel, a taste of colonial opulence was still to be had in the form of a large foyer with cathedral ceiling, slow-moving fans operated by servants, and a polished mahogany bar imported all the way from India. A handful of British soldiers lounged at the bar and stared at them with the single-minded fascination of the extremely bored.

Martin went to the main desk and secured rooms for them, one to share between him and Nabeel and another for Kesi. The proprietor started to say something when he saw Kesi, but changed his mind when Martin gave him a cold look. Then they split up, agreeing to meet in the bar after cleaning up.

Nabeel and Martin arrived first and ordered drinks, a beer for Martin and soft drink for the Muslim, Nabeel. They struck up a conversation with a British lieutenant.

"We're headed south," Martin said. "Any obvious hot spots we ought to avoid?"

The man laughed. "Stay away from Abyssinia, especially if you're traveling with a woman. Slavers have been active. They'll take one look at your companion, slit your throats and sell her at the slave market in Addis Ababa."

"If they can," Martin said.

The lieutenant stared at him. "Well, I grant you look like a man who can take care of himself and as for this one," he nodded at Nabeel. "I wouldn't want to come on him in a dark place. But you still want to be careful. No need to go looking for trouble in East Africa. It'll find you on its own."

"Thanks for the information," Martin said. "We'll follow the Rift Valley south to Lake Victoria."

The man nodded. "It's the main route going north to south for anyone traveling in East Africa. In any case . . ."

The lieutenant's voice trailed off as he and every other man in the room looked up at Kesi's arrival. Fresh from the somewhat dubious shower facilities available at the end of her hallway, she displayed clean hair tied back in a simple knot. Her eyes sparkled with the excitement of being in Khartoum, an excitement hardly shared by any citizen of the drab city.

Martin watched her approach across the room with an emotion he realized was something akin to pride. He knew her body in the most intimate way, yet now that she was covered in the colorful Indian sarong, he felt as though he was seeing her for the first time. One of the soldiers whistled softly and Kesi gave him a dazzling smile that almost made the poor fellow fall over. None of the soldiers showed the slightest inclination to question the presence of this incredible beauty in their midst.

Nabeel gave her a bow when she joined them. Among his own people he was known as a ladies' man. Like many Arabs, he treated foreign women with something like awe and his own like virtual slaves. It was a cultural oddity that Martin had never been comfortable with. But Kesi had lived her whole life steeped in the misogynist attitude of most African men. She could handle Nabeel with ease.

Martin ordered a drink for her, as a horn sounded somewhere in the distance and the soldiers all trooped out, called to some tiresome military duty. The three of them settled at a table with their drinks.

Nabeel said, "I don't think we should stay here, *Marteen*. The desert and jungles are far safer than a city, especially this city."

"But why?" Kesi said. "I wish to see the place where Gordon was killed. All my life I have wanted to see Khartoum."

Martin said, "Nabeel has a point, Kesi. You have no papers of any kind. Even under colonial rule, if someone should decide to question you, we'd be hard pressed to explain who you are and why you're here. You could be detained. And detentions in a place like this have a way of lasting indefinitely. I may have been wrong to bring you here."

She placed a hand over his. "*Sawa*— (Okay). You haven't made a wrong move yet, Martin. If I'm to go with you all the way to South Africa, I'll do what you say. Though I would rather stay."

Half a dozen extremely unsavory-looking men dressed in loose-fitting desert clothes entered the room noisily. Nabeel looked up at them and stiffened. Martin glanced at him, then turned and looked sharply at the newcomers. Kesi caught the change in her companions' demeanor.

"What is it?" she said. "Who are they?"

"*Mamluki*," said Nabeel, softly. "Mercenaries. I've seen one of them before. A slaver from Uganda. They're out of their usual territory. What do you think, *Marteen*?"

But he already knew what to think from the way the men stared at Kesi. To them, she was nothing but a walking cash register. She stood out in this part of the world like a peacock at a pig farm. He slipped one hand into his lap and loosened his pistol. One of the men, the slaver Nabeel had recognized, came slowly toward them. He was a fierce-looking character, deeply sunburned from the desert, with a purple scar on one cheek, broad shoulders and a demeanor that clearly said he was used to getting his own way. The bartender took one look at the impending situation and disappeared out the door.

Kesi said nervously, "What's going on?" But even she had a sense what this was about. She was no longer an educated, aspiring anthropologist from two of the world's great cities, Cape Town and London. In an instant, she'd become a piece of meat to be bargained over. She felt a stab of real fear as her eyes met the slaver's cold appraisal.

The man pulled out a chair at their table and sat down. With something approximating a smile, he said to Martin, "Interested in selling the woman? I will pay well for her."

Martin glanced at Kesi and seemed to consider. "You probably wouldn't like her," he said. "She talks too much."

Kesi kicked him under the table. The slaver laughed at this. "Good spirit is worth money—to a point," he said. "But nothing is more easily controlled. We will cut her tongue out and she will not talk too much any more, eh?"

"She's not for sale," Martin said, his face expressionless.

The slaver's smile died away. He raised one hand and the other men approached the table. "Maybe we'll take her anyway," he said.

Nabeel's hands didn't seem to move at all, but suddenly there were two pistols pointed at the other men, who stopped uncertainly. Martin took his own gun out and placed it on the table.

"Of course, we don't want to be unreasonable," he said. "If we don't sell her to you, you might think it will be okay to bother us later on. I wouldn't like that . . . so what do you say we make this between you and me? My friend here will keep your men honest. There's my pistol on the table. Put yours beside it and we'll determine which of us will keep the girl."

The man's face lit up at the prospect of winning the girl simply by overcoming this rather slim-looking opponent. He pulled his gun out, put it on the table, stared at Martin for a moment, then pushed his chair back noisily and stood up, fists clenched.

Kesi gasped and put her hand on Martin's arm. "No, Martin, don't do this. He's too strong." She looked to Nabeel for support.

"It will be all right, Kesi," Nabeel said, quietly.

Martin stood up slowly and moved away from the table. What happened next was almost comical. The slaver lunged at his opponent, missing him as his target slipped sideways and then delivered a solid kick in the slaver's backside that sent him sprawling. The other men stared at their leader on the floor and one of them gave a little laugh that halted abruptly as the slaver glared at him.

With a roar, the man got to his feet and lunged again, fists swinging lethally. None of the blows landed. It was unclear how this happened, but his target simply rocked back and forth. After the third swing, Martin grabbed one of the man's arms and, using the fellow's own momentum, tossed him halfway across the room, where he crashed into a table. He got up more slowly this time, reached into a boot and brought out a deadly-looking blade.

Martin stood waiting calmly. He even reached over and picked up his drink and took a sip. This made the man livid. He lunged with the knife. Again, Martin barely seemed to move. There was a flurry of twisting arms, a yell of pain and suddenly it was Martin who held the knife.

This time the man looked scared. He realized he'd miscalculated badly. Thus far, he'd been unable to even touch his adversary. He backed away from what moments before had seemed a remarkably vulnerable opponent. Martin took the knife, flipped it so the blade rested between his fingers and threw it all in one motion. It sliced through the man's left ear, leaving a notch that spouted blood. He screamed and grabbed the side of his head.

"All slavers should be marked with a slit in their ears," Martin said. He sat down and casually put his pistol back in its holster. With a snarl, the injured man motioned to his companions, and they left the room.

Kesi looked stunned. She'd seen fights before, but never such a one-sided affair as this. "I think maybe you really do work for the King of England," she said in a small voice.

He shrugged. To Nabeel, he said, "Now, unfortunately, I think you may be right. It wouldn't be wise for us to stay here any longer. Those men may try to cause further trouble."

"They looked scared to death of you," said Kesi. "I don't think we'll see them again."

"They may be scared to deal with us directly. But they are men who make their own rules. They'd just as soon shoot us from behind a tree and take you that way if they got the chance."

She shuddered as the realization of how close she'd come to being sold into slavery sunk in. Growing up in Africa, she'd heard the stories about women who simply disappeared from their families. Everyone knew they'd been taken for the slave and prostitution markets that still flourished. Now, Martin was telling her the danger was far from over.

"If I had a gun," she said bitterly, "I swear I could kill those men with no more regret than I'd shoot a rat. They're nothing but parasites feeding on the weak." Then her mood changed and her eyes sparkled. "My God, Nabeel, did you see the way Martin kicked that big fellow in the seat of his pants? I'd give anything to have done that."

Martin finished his drink in a single gulp. "Come on," he said. "Time to head for the hills."

16.

The Hills of Africa

MARTIN WAS CONCERNED that their overland trip would take too long and delay his reports to the King. To shorten their travel time, he decided that where possible they would book passage on the Cape to Cairo Railroad.

Pieces of the transcontinental railroad, the vision of the great Cecil Rhodes, founder of the DeBeers Diamond Company, had been under construction since the 1880s. It had been a very haphazard undertaking, the routes selected driven by the vagaries of war, terrain and the discovery of mineral deposits. Still, it would save them considerable time and they'd be able to bring their horses with them at very little additional cost. This would become part of their regular travel routine. On several occasions, as they stared out the railcar windows and saw spectacular scenery, they got off at the next stop and proceeded on horseback.

After following the White Nile a long way, sometimes using local guides, many of whom Martin and Nabeel had dealt with in the past, they began the long climb to the Equatorial Plateau. The great savanna plains of Africa enveloped them, filled with large cats, wildebeest, water buffalo, zebra and giraffe. After two unforgettable weeks, they stood, finally, on a steep hillside and gazed down at the spot where the Victoria Nile River drained the second largest body of fresh water in the world, Lake Victoria.

Kesi stood beside Martin and watched as a strange sort of transformation came over him. His thoughts seemed a thousand miles away.

"It *is* beautiful," she said. "I've always wanted to see it." He nodded. "I was thinking of the Queen for whom it is named. Here, even in the very heart of the Dark Continent, is a sign of the strange partnership between two worlds, Great Britain and Africa. I want more than anything to see those worlds coexist rather than collide in a conflict of cultures." He rubbed a hand across his forehead. "I don't know if it's possible. People naturally resist outsiders. No one wants to be told what to do by foreigners. The British have had more experience at it than most, but things are changing. I believe the future for Britain lies not in controlling other nations but in influencing them through the example of her institutions."

"And I think you are the perfect person to make that happen," said Kesi. "You know both worlds, Martin, and you have influence with King George."

"Perhaps," he sighed. "It's been in my mind to try at any rate, ever since the King gave me this commission."

They heard a chanting sound and turned to see a long line of native bearers carrying enormous loads head down a nearby trail toward the lake and the town of Jinja below.

"We'll follow them," Martin said. "I hope you like fish. There's a big fishery at Lake Victoria, primarily a species called ngege. Some of the best you'll eat anywhere, and the local people know how to cook it."

Kesi was staring at the bearers. "Martin, do you see?"

"What?"

"The last two men . . . they have the marks."

"What marks?" Nabeel said.

"I see them," Martin replied. Large, muscular fellows, they bore their loads bare-chested. They looked very young but carried themselves with obvious dignity. Along the top of each shoulder were the same tattoos that the Nubian boy in Kwesi's camp had exhibited.

"What does it mean?" Kesi said. "Surely members of the Clan of the Bow don't go this far south."

"I've never heard of Nubians this far south either," said Martin.

"They may not be from Nubia," said Nabeel, "but members of the same cult, or religion, if you prefer. They may even be Maasai. Many of the tribes of East Africa are related and sometimes share beliefs."

Martin nodded. "The spine of Africa has a great many tribes. There's a sort of central network that runs down the Rift Valley. Many tribes communicate via this traditional pathway. Their ideas, beliefs and customs are often shared."

"Yes, I know this," Kesi said. "I hadn't thought of it before, but I've seen young men with such tattoos even in my own South Africa. I didn't know what it meant."

"Well, let's hope it doesn't mean that another of them will try to stick me with a knife," Martin said.

At the lakeshore, Martin and Kesi shared a marvelous fish chowder prepared and sold right off a fragile dock held up by poles sunk into the lake bed. Nabeel scorned the idea of eating fish over the traditional Arab meat diet. Instead, while they ate, he negotiated passage for them and their horses on a small steam launch. They would make good time by using the lake as a highway through this part of the continent, for Lake Victoria was the size of Ireland.

Their boat was a fifty-foot steamer of indeterminate age. Kesi thought it must have been built in the days of Dr. Livingston. As the craft belched and rattled its way down the lake, following the Rift Valley, they sat in comfortable chairs on the upper deck, from where they had a magnificent view of the wildlife and the surrounding hills. Before long, Nabeel was lulled to sleep by the motion and clatter of the engine.

Martin stared at the whitecaps licking the lake's surface and rocking the picturesque dugout canoes with their lateen sails. "Incredible they go so far out in those flimsy boats," he said. "I've seen storms sweep across this lake powerful enough to sink any craft that floats. But what a magnificent highway it is for the heart of a continent," he enthused. "Victoria touches on three nations, German

East Africa, Uganda and British East Africa, which has only just been renamed the East African Protectorate. Names change quickly in this part of the world. This region could become the breadbasket of Africa. Look." He pointed at the rolling hills. "They're already well cultivated with coffee, tobacco, maize, sugar cane and cassava, but so much more could be done. The people of all three countries could benefit enormously. If it weren't for the tsetse fly and malaria, it might even become a tourist destination. Who knows, perhaps one day it will, if they ever learn some way to control the insects and disease."

Kesi looked dubious. She was a bred African and disease was a part of life that seemed incontrovertible. "Control the tsetse?" she said. "I wouldn't count on that as a route to development. But I couldn't agree with you more about the beauty of this place."

They passed an enormous flock of flamingos, tens of thousands of them, standing in the shallows off the port bow. As their belching craft got closer, the birds took to the air in a mass that seemed to fill the sky with their graceful forms and raucous calls. As if in answer, a dozen hippos roared at the sky and dove beneath the surface. Crocodiles sunned themselves on sandy banks not a hundred yards from where young children swam, unconcerned, in the same water, their mothers washing clothes in the shallows nearby. It was a tableau of peaceful coalition between man and wildlife, surviving side by side.

"Just look at it," said Martin. "What you're seeing hasn't changed in a thousand years, hell, maybe ten thousand."

"Except a thousand years ago, I don't think we'd be traveling in this noisy contraption."

He looked at her. "What will you do once we reach South Africa? Have you learned your lesson, or will you turn around and go back to Nubia to continue your studies?"

"I don't know, Martin. I haven't been home in almost two years. It will be nice to spend time with my family. But then I must go back to London. I still have a year of school left. When I'm finished, I shall return to Africa. Maybe to teach. I'm not sure. They need teachers so very much here."

"Where's your family?"

"They live on a farm north of Cape Town. My mother, father, sisters and their husbands. It's a beautiful place. I'd love to show it to you some day."

"I'd like that." He rubbed his face with one hand. He was suddenly very hot in the mid-day sun. "I think I'll get something to drink," he said, starting to get up. Then he staggered, grabbed the ship's railing and almost fell down.

Kesi looked at him in alarm. "Are you all right, Martin?"

His eyes were glassy and unfocused. In a moment, he slumped to the deck.

She cried out, "Nabeel!"

The Arab stirred and opened his eyes.

"Something's wrong with Martin!" she said.

Nabeel got up quickly and came over to his friend. He put a hand on Martin's forehead and grunted.

"*Joto*. Fever. He's having a malaria attack. He gets them periodically. They come out of nowhere. Help me carry him below to our cabin."

With difficulty they carried Martin down to the small cabin and deposited him on the bed. He was unconscious, burning with fever and drenched in sweat.

Nabeel said, "Don't worry. I've seen him come through many of these. I'll tell the captain what's happening. Maybe he has some quinine which can help shorten the attacks. There's fresh water on the dresser. Keep cool compresses on his face."

After he left, Kesi sat beside Martin and held his hand. She took a wash cloth, wet it, and wiped his face. He mumbled something, moving about restlessly, his eyes closed tightly. She could see the pupils moving rapidly beneath the lids. She hoped his dreams were better than her own had been after her experience with the Nubians.

His shirt was soaking with sweat. She unbuttoned it and struggled to lift his torso enough to remove it. Then she washed his chest and underarms with the cool water, which seemed to comfort him. He stopped thrashing around. She marveled at the muscles that rippled tightly across his torso. His body was perfectly proportioned, the chest deep and shoulders broad, narrowing to his hips.

She dipped the wash cloth in the water and wrung it out, then took the bowl, tossed the contents out the cabin window and refilled it with fresh water. She felt a real connection with this man of two worlds, for she was equally connected to the same two lands. He had big plans for Africa. What a huge loss it would be if he were to succumb to a simple case of malaria

She patted him dry with a towel and covered him with a sheet and several blankets. He slept more peacefully now. Nabeel came back in and handed her a small bottle.

"Only a little quinine left. The captain said to give him this. Then, we'll see how he's doing. I'll be up on deck if you need me."

She managed to get some of the pills into Martin. Then she retreated to a chair and sat staring at him, wondering about her feelings for this unusual man.

17.

ARTIN RECOVERED QUICKLY from the malaria attack. By afternoon of the second day aboard the steamer, he was sitting up and drinking tea. He made no comment to Kesi about who had cared for him. He knew it hadn't been Nabeel.

They landed the next morning at Mwanza, with Martin apparently none the worse for wear. To save time, they again booked passage for themselves and their horses on a newly constructed section of the Cape to Cairo railroad. It was wonderful to sit in comfort for a day and gaze out as the African landscape passed before them.

When the rail line petered out once more, they disembarked and hired a guide, for they were entering a part of Africa that none of them were familiar with. For the next three weeks they proceeded in a southerly direction. There were a few roads, but much of the time was spent traveling cross-country. Their guide avoided several well-known trouble spots where civil war had flared up. Occasionally they passed streams of refugees on the dusty roads, heading nowhere in particular, their only purpose to leave death and destruction behind them.

After they had passed still another such group, consisting mostly of women, children and old men, carrying virtually nothing in the way of food or supplies, Martin said, "This is the part of Africa I want to put an end to. If the British people could just see something like this, I think they'd do whatever it took to help."

He insisted on making camp on the spot, while he and Nabeel went hunting. They brought down two impala, which they proceeded to cook over open fires and feed to the starving refugees. It was little enough to do, and they knew their efforts could only stanch the suffering for a short time.

They continued on, fording rivers with their horses, avoiding hippos and crocodiles, traveling down the spine of Africa, the great East African Rift. There were many semi-active volcanoes along the rift and they encountered a series of boiling hot springs rising up out of the hot earth.

They each reveled in the experience of traversing the heart of the continent. Kesi especially was enthralled by the Rift's spectacular scenery. Its long valleys running north to south made travel much easier. They frequently ran into other groups, more refugees, traders and occasionally even rugged individuals using the continent's great natural highway.

"The Rift must have been used by tribes to travel the length of Africa for thousands of years," Kesi mused one evening, as she and Martin sat around the campfire. Nabeel had taken his bedroll off to the far edge of the circle of light and gone to sleep.

"Yes," he replied. "It's been a major trade route and undoubtedly helped the various tribes exchange ideas, customs, religious practices, probably even wives. It's a natural melting pot of cultures."

They sat companionably, staring at the flames and listening to the sounds of the night. Martin never tired of the wildlife and the ever-changing landscapes of Africa. He could easily live this way all the time. He was grateful King George understood his true nature and didn't call him back to work in some office in London.

"We should reach the Limpopo River tomorrow," he said. "Have you heard of a place called Mapungubwe Hill?"

"Heard of it—yes," she said. "There was some speculation it had been a burial ground long ago. We talked about it a little in one of my classes in London. My teacher passed by there once during an expedition, almost by accident. When he learned I was a native of Cape Town, he considered me the resident expert on the place, which was ridiculous since I've never even been there. Almost no one has, actually. It's never been the site of any serious excavation."

"Before I left London, at a meeting with the King, I was introduced to a member of Parliament, Mr. Winston Churchill, who inquired about Mapungubwe."

"Really?" She looked interested. "I certainly know of your Mr. Churchill. His exploits during the Boer War were talked and written about a great deal in the south. I can't imagine what his interest would be or even how he would have heard of the place."

"Nor can I. But I'd like to detour slightly and take a look. It would be nice to have something to tell him the next time I'm in London. I've always found it's a good idea to follow up on suggestions that come from people in positions of power, no matter how abstruse they may seem at the time. They usually arise for some reason, even if it isn't always a readily decipherable one."

Kesi shivered and moved closer to the fire. She glanced at Martin out of the corner of her eye. They'd been traveling through some of the world's most remote and unexplored regions for many weeks now. No matter what the danger or risk, he had always known what to do, and he always thought first about her safety or Nabeel's or even the refugees' on the road before his own. She'd never known anyone like him. She realized, too, that since caring for him during his malaria attack, she thought a great deal about his broad chest and narrow waist. She was thinking about it now.

She stood up and stretched, letting the blanket that had been over her shoulders fall to the ground. He watched her movements. He found that he enjoyed watching her. Aside from her obvious beauty and that soft, mocha-colored skin, she moved with a comfort in her own body that was a joy to watch. And he felt a strange sense of connection to her in their joint love of the wild land they were passing through.

He stood up and stretched in almost the same manner. Their eyes met, almost laughingly. She said, "Martin . . ."

He moved forward and put his arms around her. Their bodies molded perfectly together as he kissed her long and passionately. When he finally released her, she took his hand and led him over to her bedroll. She gathered up his blankets and arranged them so the two were side by side, all the time looking into his eyes.

"It's funny, isn't it," she said, as she pulled him down beside her.

"What?"

"You must have examined my body in great detail when you cleaned me and washed the paint off."

In mock outrage, he said, "I didn't examine you. I was *rescuing* you."

"Ah—that's what you call it." She kissed him on the mouth. "Well, I *examined* you, Martin Rand," she said softly. "And now I want a closer look."

* * *

They reached Mapungubwe Hill late the following morning. The sky was overcast and the wind had picked up. As they stood in the shadow of the hill, they could hear a distant, ululating wail that seemed to emanate from somewhere near the top of the massive outcrop. The branches of the trees undulated back and forth in the gusting wind and dark clouds blew across the rim of the mountain.

"What *is* that?" Nabeel said uneasily, staring up at the unusual sound.

"Just the wind," said Martin. "See the caves and pockmarked indentations all over the cliffs? They must funnel the wind somehow, causing it to make those sounds. It's almost musical, isn't it?"

""More like voices than music," Kesi said. "Like someone moaning or chanting. It's pretty eerie. But you're right. It has to be the wind."

"Maybe it's the ancient spirits protesting our arrival." Martin winked at her.

Nabeel didn't take such talk lightly. "We are not wanted here," he said. "We should go away."

"Well, I want a closer look," said Martin. "Why don't you two make camp, while I explore a little. There seems to be a rough path up through the brush toward the cliff. I want to see where it goes."

Nabeel grunted and turned away, but Kesi said. "I'll go with you. This is my chance to say I've actually been to Mapungubwe Hill." She looked up. "I've heard there's a way to the top via that chimney of rock. Come on. Can you keep up with me?"

Martin grinned at the challenge. Her excitement at being able to explore this place she'd heard about in her studies was infectious. To Nabeel, he said, "It's getting late. If we find a way to the top we may have to stay there overnight rather than attempt the climb back down in the dark, so don't worry about us. We'll be safer from lions than you will be down here, even with a fire."

Nabeel looked dubious. "Why not wait until morning?"

"We've wasted too much time already making this detour. We'll be all right."

They carried two lengths of rope, a canteen and Martin's rifle, for the thick undercover leading to the cliff was obvious lion territory. Ten minutes of bushwhacking brought them to the base of the rock chimney. The wailing sound had diminished, though strangely, the wind had not.

He tied the shorter rope around their waists, connecting them with about twenty feet of slack. Then he slung his rifle and the long rope over his shoulder, and they were ready. "Hold on tight once we get up higher," he said. "A strong gust could knock you right off the hill."

He climbed the first fifteen feet effortlessly, selecting tiny cracks in which to place his fingers. Kesi marveled at his strength, as he pulled himself up with just his fingertips. When he reached the first of the ancient handholds, he continued another five feet, then paused. "Okay, come ahead," he called.

With Martin pulling her, she scrambled easily up to the first handholds. She marveled at the rounded indentations, imagining how difficult it must have been to carve them out of the rock while hanging by one hand. If this was the only way up, Mapungubwe must indeed have served as a very effective refuge in ancient times.

A single sentry could easily prevent anyone from climbing up by simply dropping stones on them.

It took half an hour to reach the summit. They untied themselves and Martin secured the longer rope to a boulder, leaving it coiled on the ground. He left his rifle beside it, for there was no way lions could possibly be on top of the hill. They stared out at the incredible view of the African veldt below. Heavy, low clouds and the strong wind gave life to the scene, putting everything in motion, along with a large herd of wildebeest far in the distance.

"This would certainly qualify as one of those top tourist destinations you were talking about, Martin . . . assuming they ever conquer the malaria problem, that is."

"It is magnificent, isn't it?"

They began to hike toward the elevated part of the plateau where they could see foundations and walls of rock. They'd scarcely taken their first steps before the strange wailing began again. This time it seemed to coincide with a decrease in the wind. They continued without comment, but Martin found himself growing uneasy. The wailing was very human-like, a series of high-pitched, wavering cries that would deteriorate into something resembling whimpering before it died away, only to begin again. As they neared the first foundations, the sound stopped all together.

Kesi cocked her head at the silence. "A good thing Nabeel didn't come," she said. "This place is downright spooky. He'd be a nervous wreck. I don't give any credence to spirits and ghosts, but I have to admit Mapungubwe could make me a believer."

"It's just the setting, the weather and the wind. Most of the Arabs I've known like Nabeel are fiercely brave in battle, but they blanch at anything even slightly suggestive of the supernatural."

They explored the foundations at length. Kesi was dumbstruck at the extent of the site. "There must have been hundreds of people living here," she said.

The sun had already set by the time they stumbled upon the remnants of Lord Sterne's golden hill. It was obviously a place where someone had dug indiscriminately some time in the past. Now the golden hill held only an occasional glimmer of the yellow metal. Kesi picked up a bit of braided gold rope and exclaimed at its intricate beauty.

"We need to find a place for the night," Martin said. After looking about, they settled on a depression where the crumbling remains of two stone walls came together. It would offer protection from the wind. They hadn't brought their bedrolls and were resigned to lying side by side on the hard earth, though the night was warm and they would not suffer in that regard. Martin pulled from his shirt a small pouch that contained jerked antelope meat. That and water from the canteen was their dinner.

After eating, Kesi snuggled in beside him as he leaned against the wall. A full moon came up and they watched its light reflect off the Limpopo far below. "I could almost believe we're the only two people on earth." She kissed him. "And that's all right with me."

He squeezed her contentedly, started to say something, then stopped. He lifted his head slightly and sniffed the air.

"What is it?"

"I don't know. I thought I smelled something."

They lay silently for a few minutes, then Martin took his arm away from her and got to his feet. He walked a few paces, climbed up onto the rock wall and stood, smelling the night air. A lifetime on the savanna and deserts of Africa had given him a highly advanced ability to smell. He could identify a herd of elephants half a mile away from their odor and could detect the ugly scent of a native Kraal from farther still. But this was different.

Even in the moonlight, Kesi saw his body suddenly stiffen, his fists clenching.

"What is it?" she said again.

He jumped down and came over to her quietly. "*Mbaya,*" he said. "Something very bad. I've only smelled it once before, so maybe I'm wrong . . . but I don't think so."

"You're scaring me, Martin. What?"

Instead of answering, he put his finger to his mouth to caution silence. Then she heard the wailing sound of the wind rise again. Only this time, it sounded much less like wind and much more like something alive . . . or perhaps like something that wished it weren't alive. She shivered as a chilled finger of sweat trickled down the base of her spine.

"Come on," he said. "We'll take a look, but be quiet and Kesi . . .?"

She looked into his eyes. They were dark and hooded.

"The smell? I think it's something burning . . . I think it's *someone* burning."

* * *

They moved across the plateau cautiously, making as little sound as possible. Fortunately the full moon enabled them to avoid the obvious pitfalls of holes and depressions in the ground. The wailing continued, guiding them ever closer to the edge of the cliffs. There was a strange, flickering light emanating from beyond the drop-off.

"I don't understand where that's coming from," said Kesi. They were almost at the edge of the precipice. The sound and the flickering light both seemed to be floating in on the wind, directly out of the void of space over the edge.

A depression in front of them fell away between two slightly higher rock formations that marked the drop-off. As they neared it, they realized it was a path that wound down to a hidden, hanging ledge below the main body of the plateau. In fact, it was considerably more than just a ledge. It was almost like a hanging valley, a mini-plateau attached to the larger one, a hundred feet long and perhaps fifty wide.

Once they climbed halfway down the path, the rock walls pulled back enough for them to see down over the entire area. The source of the light they'd seen was immediately evident, for there were several fires, more or less arranged in a circle. In the center of the circle of fires was a large, flat stone and on the stone was a naked man. He lay on his back, spread eagled, his hands and feet tied down with ropes that ran across the rock to stakes buried in the earth. The wailing came from this figure, whose cries continued, though in a more subdued fashion.

Even as Kesi gasped at the sight, a tall, naked warrior, one of half a dozen who worked away at the fires, walked up to the spread-eagled man and, almost as an afterthought, drew a knife blade across his throat, effectively ending the wailing. Blood spurted and the body lay still. The man proceeded to cut the tongue from below and pull it out through the throat. What happened next Kesi would never forget.

The warrior was a fearsome-looking figure with a glistening, oiled torso. His wrists and ankles were wrapped with coils that appeared to be made from pieces of bone. He put down his knife, picked up a small war ax and chopped the man's chest open. Then he pulled back the bones of the rib cage so he could remove the blood-red dripping heart. He also sliced out the liver. Then he picked up his knife again and sliced off the man's genitals. In a very businesslike manner, he gathered up the body parts and handed them over to one of the other men, who proceeded to grill them over the open flames.

"Mother of God!" Kesi said, so appalled she forgot to whisper. "They're eating him."

Martin grimaced. "Not just him," he said. "I count four other bodies on the ground by the fires. They've all been split open."

"Those tall warriors . . . do they look like Nubians to you?"

"Yes. At least the markings look similar. Maybe now I understand why my friend Kwesi wouldn't talk about Mapungubwe Hill. He said it was forbidden to talk about the place."

"Can you blame him if this is what goes on here? They're cannibals."

"I've never known Nubians to engage in anything like this," he said in mystification. "It has to be some sort of aberration. Kwesi would never be a party to something like this."

"Eating the bodies of your enemies is considered a way of augmenting your own power," Kesi said. "There's a pretty long history of such atrocities in central Africa. A number of tribes have used it purely as a way to terrorize those they want to subdue. I've heard about it, but it's something else to actually see it."

138

She turned away, suddenly overcome by a wave of revulsion. Her foot struck a loose stone and she slipped, causing a mini-avalanche of rocks that bounced noisily down to the valley floor. They both froze.

But the damage was done. The warrior closest to them stared up at the noise and saw them clearly outlined by the light of the flickering fires. He immediately screamed to his fellows.

"The game's up," Martin said. "Come on." He grabbed her hand and they scrambled up the slope. There was no need to look back. The yells were enough. The warriors were coming after them, perhaps to secure an additional after-dinner snack.

They ran as fast as they could across the torturous landscape of the plateau. It was an almost impossible task and they fell repeatedly, sprawling in the dirt, banging their bodies on sharp pieces of rock. Their pursuers had the advantage in the dark, since presumably they were more familiar with the landscape and whatever obstacles and holes there were.

Kesi glanced back only once as they topped the high, central portion of the plateau. Half a dozen large black figures swarmed across the terrain behind them. They held knives that glinted in the moonlight and two or three also carried bows.

"Head for the rope," Martin yelled, as they flew over the rocks. When they reached the edge, he threw the coiled rope out over the rim, far into the night. He put Kesi's hands on the rope, kissed her roughly on the lips and literally threw her over the edge. Then he knelt and picked up his rifle.

She yelled up to the top of the cliff. "Martin, come on!"

"I'll be right behind you. Now go down fast." He turned and shot the lead warrior, who was no more than a dozen yards away, through the head.

He knew there was no way they could both make it down. Either the warriors would cut the rope as they descended or throw rocks down on top of them. He had to make a stand here to allow Kesi to reach the bottom safely.

He shot another man. The others slowed and sought cover behind the boulders. The two men with bows began to fire arrows that ricocheted perilously close to where he crouched. They were deadly accurate with the weapons, he grudgingly admired. He fired another shot, then leaned over to see how Kesi was doing. It was too dark to see her.

"Are you down?" he yelled. He heard a faint cry from far below. She must have made it.

The pause in his firing emboldened the warriors, who again swarmed forward in a mass. He brought his rifle up to shoot and the weapon jammed. He had only an instant to find the rope and get over the edge, but before he could, they were upon him. He fought with a ferocity that surprised his attackers. He kicked one man between the legs, pummeled several others with his fists, head-butted another. His hands and legs were both weapons. He sent one man screaming out over the rim. But finally a warrior got behind him and smashed him over the head with a rock.

The fight was over. Martin Rand was carried back to the sight of that awful feast, where his body was tied to the still blood-spattered boulder. His captors settled down to await his return to consciousness, so his dispatch might be all the more enjoyable.

18.

THE SUN APPEARED as a hazy orange ball just above the horizon as Martin returned to consciousness. His scrambled brains felt as though that fiery orb was located somewhere between his temples. He could turn his head from side to side but found he was unable to move either his arms or legs. Gradually, he determined that he was tied down, and in another moment, as reality finally flooded into his aching brain, he became totally aware of his situation. He was tied to the very rock where they'd witnessed the horrible death of that other poor soul. He had no doubt whatsoever that he would soon share the same fate.

As if to confirm his worst imaginings, the fierce visage of a warrior suddenly appeared, seeming to float in the sky above his face. The man stared at him intently, searching for signs of alertness. He wanted this victim, who had fought so viciously, totally aware when he was dispatched. It would make the transference of his abilities to those who ate his vital parts all the more effective.

The warrior grunted and his head disappeared. Martin heard him shout to the others and then movement as they began to build up the cook fires in anticipation that there would soon be more choice cuts for grilling.

When he turned his head to one side, he could see the mutilated bodies of the others who had so recently undergone the treatment he was about to receive. He'd always known he would die in the bosom of his adopted land, though perhaps not in its stomach. Still, the end result would be the same. He'd never feared death, even one of the most horrible sort. The life he'd led virtually guaranteed that something like this might happen one day, and he'd long since reconciled himself to it. His only regret was that he'd had so little time with Kesi.

The warrior reappeared, floating again above his head. This time he held a particularly wicked looking blade in one hand. His shoulders were covered with the now familiar pattern of tattoo markings. Curious to the end, Martin decided to see if he could talk to the fellow. He spoke in the Nubian dialect.

"I've not eaten in a long time," he said. "My liver will taste better if I'm given a good meal first."

The warrior's eyes grew wide. The last thing he'd expected was for a *mzungu* to speak to him in his own tongue. "How do you know the language of the lost people?" he said.

"I have many friends among the Nubians. Why do you call them lost?"

"If you have many friends, then you should know. You've broken the most sacred of taboos in coming here. For that you will die at the hands of Mbari Wauta."

A thin veil of mystery lifted from Martin's thoughts, for he recognized the strange words. "You are Clan of the Bow? I didn't know that Nubians, the bravest of all warriors, feared across Africa, ate their victims like hyenas."

Comparison to hyenas, the scavengers of the veldt, was the greatest insult he could make to these proud, fighting men.

The man's face turned to fury. "We are not Nubian," he said. "We are Takatifu Wapigani."

"Sacred warriors?" Martin said, puzzled. "Yet you speak the language of the Nubians."

"For thousands of years," the man said, "Takatifu Wapigani have guarded the sacred burial grounds of Mapungubwe. It is a great, sacred honor to be chosen. Only the fiercest among us bear the mark of Mbari Wauta." He turned so Martin could see the tattoos on his shoulders.

In spite of his predicament, Martin was fascinated by what the man was saying. "You say you are not Nubians, but I've seen similar marks on Nubian men in the Sudan and even farther to the south."

"They are the lost people," the warrior said, spitting out the words. "Only a few Nubians still follow the ancient ways. But Mbari Wauta may be found the length of Africa. Many tribes provide sacred warriors for the task. It is a rite of passage. All the young men wish to be Takatifu Wapigani. Only a handful are chosen," he said with obvious pride.

"Chosen to do what?" said Martin. "Guard this empty hillside?"

"Each generation must absorb the strength of any who trespass here, so we may grow even stronger." He waved a hand at the mutilated bodies that lay scattered about the plateau. "Those men were nothing. Grave robbers. Hunters of trinkets to sell to *mzungus*. They deserved their fate. *They* are the *fisi* (hyenas)."

Martin might have agreed with him, but he now understood what Kwesi had been so afraid to discuss. No doubt his friend didn't approve of the disgusting practices maintained by the Clan of the Bow, most of whom were now apparently not of direct Nubian descent. But Kwesi was too scared to do anything but bow to the ancient traditions. To do otherwise would certainly have meant a terrible death. For how many generations, he wondered, had this gone on? How many men had been carved up and cooked over open fires here on this blood-drenched plateau? He closed his eyes, disgusted at this terrible aberration that had somehow mutated out of the once noble Nubian culture.

"Kill me now," he said, his eyes still shut, "for I don't want to look again upon the face of one so evil, upon a betrayer of his own people, a creature lower even than the *fisi*."

The warrior spat on Martin in disgust. "You speak this way to Takatifu Wapigani? The chosen of all Africa? You say you have friends among the Nubians? I think you lie. Let this be your last thought, *mzungu*. Your death will make me even stronger."

Martin felt the hand with the knife at his throat. The blade bit into his skin and then stopped, as a rifle shot reverberated across the plateau. He opened his eyes to see the warrior fall straight back away out of his line of sight, the blade clattering across the rocks.

Suddenly there was a flurry of shots. More warriors fell. He could hear men crying out and running in all directions, but the open terrace of the sub-plateau offered no shelter from the withering fire. In a matter of moments, the remaining warriors of the Clan of the Bow lay dead beside the bodies of their own victims.

"Martin!" Kesi ran to him and a moment later it was her head that appeared in the sky above him in place of the fierce warrior. She put her arms around him, her head resting on his chest. "I thought we were too late," she cried.

Nabeel appeared beside her. He picked up the dead warrior's fallen knife and cut the bonds that held his friend. "She is something, *Marteen*. This new woman of yours. When we came to the path and saw that fellow's knife at your throat, she reacted even before I could, raising her rifle and shooting him through the head in one instant."

He sat up and swung his legs over the edge of the rock. Kesi said, "I waited at the bottom until I heard you fighting with them. When the fighting stopped and you didn't come down, I knew you had to be dead."

"But she came to get me anyway," Nabeel said. "Walking through the thicket with lions all around her until she saw my fire. We came for you . . . or your body. Nabeel came to avenge you if nothing else," he said. "I am glad you are still alive, *Marteen*."

Martin put out his arm and grasped Nabeel's. "Thank you, my friend. I owe my life to both of you."

Kesi said, "There's an old African proverb, you know. When a woman saves a man's life, she owns him from then on."

He smiled. "I can live with that."

19.

Casablanca, North Africa

January 14, 1943

WINSTON CHURCHILL settled into the chair in his hotel room with a groan of relief. He was tired beyond words. The secrecy and security revolving around his conference with Roosevelt had been exhaustive. Now, he wanted nothing more than a belt of whisky and a good cigar. His secretary, who knew him well, obliged on both counts without being asked.

"When does Franklin arrive?" Winston said.

"No one seems to know, sir," said the secretary. "It will be the first time a sitting president has ever been to Africa, you know, and the first time one has ever left the United States in time of war. The Americans are treating it like some sort of second coming."

He grunted. He liked the American president. Their relationship, as much as any single factor, had likely saved the free world ... thus far, at any rate. He was aware that Roosevelt's health was deteriorating, and that the long trip was likely to increase his frailty. The Casablanca Conference had been billed as a get-together of the Big Three, including Joseph Stalin. But Stalin had declined at the last moment, citing the extreme strain Russia was under with the siege of Stalingrad. So now it would be the Big Two. Which was fine as far as Winston was concerned. He didn't trust Stalin anyway.

In the coming week, Winston and Franklin would engage in intense conversations about the war, interrupted only by occasional jeep forays into the town's medieval market. The tide of the conflict was changing. A month earlier, British forces under Montgomery had pushed the Germans out of El Agheila in North Africa. In another week, the Battle of Stalingrad would come to an end in the bitter cold and snow of Mother Russia.

Even Hitler, in his madness, had begun to see the beginning of the end. In February, illustrating his growing desperation, he would order the mobilization of the entire German population between the ages of sixteen and sixty-five. In March, there would be two failed assassination attempts against the German leader by officers of his own army.

The cascading events, already beginning to build in January, emboldened Churchill and Roosevelt. The primary achievement of Casablanca would be their agreement to seek unconditional surrender. They were determined to permanently eliminate the threat of Germany to the world. The conference would also help unite the Allied Powers and mark the beginning of the decline of Hitler and the Nazis. The Soviets, assured that the United States and Great Britain were in the fight to the end, would be encouraged to keep fighting on the Eastern Front while a cross-channel invasion was planned.

Despite his exhaustion, Winston managed to enjoy himself. In addition to his marketplace forays with Franklin, who was holding up remarkably well, he found time to visit with the troops. The familiar, rotund figure, cigar thrusting out from beneath his desert hat, was greeted wherever he went by cheering soldiers. His presence was a sign to the men that the end of the war was now in sight and no longer in doubt.

*   *   *

Yet Winston's optimism would have been tempered if he'd been aware of the actions of another British citizen who had appeared on the scene in North Africa at this time. For Lord Sterne had risen again like the fabled Phoenix.

Now in his early seventies, Sterne's own path had taken him in a decidedly different direction from Churchill's since they'd last met more than forty years earlier. The vigorous young rugby player now walked with a stoop, his face lined and pockmarked from the typhus and other maladies he'd suffered during his thirty years in a Boer, and later, South African prison. True to her word, Queen Victoria had succeeded where Winston had failed. She'd orchestrated Lord Sterne's punishment herself.

Barely off the steamer that had taken him once again to the Transvaal at Bertie's command to continue the search for the treasure of Mapungubwe Hill, Sterne's worst fears had been realized. He was arrested by Louis Botha. His trial was little more than a perfunctory ritual. Still, he'd remained confident that the new King, Albert Edward, would not allow him to rot in prison. Even after he was sentenced to thirty years at hard labor, he fully expected to be freed, either by an exchange of prisoners or through a commando action. Only as the years passed and no such actions occurred had he finally begun to realize the degree to which he had been abandoned.

Louis Botha had died in 1919 and for a time, Sterne had hoped the South African leader's death might pave the way for his release. Instead, the vagaries of new governments and turmoil on the international scene left him withering away for another decade. At last, at the age of sixty, his health poor, forgotten by the world and no longer considered a threat to anyone, he was quietly released. He spent the Depression years moving about Africa, earning what meager wages he could and gradually repairing his health. One thing he never stopped thinking about in all those years, however, was the treasure of Mapungubwe that Winston had once suggested might have been left behind. In Sterne's mind, it now rightfully belonged to him. He'd paid for it with the bulk of his life, and he'd begun to scheme to retrieve it. Nothing would get in his way, not even a second world war.

Indeed, in his search for allies to help him, Sterne approached the one group that, in 1943, was just as desperate to find gold as he was. The Nazis. His first attempt to contact the Germans went through Erwin Rommel, the Desert Fox. The Field Marshall listened to his incredible story with little interest. There was no proof, after all, of anything, unless one counted the gold Sterne had brought to England and that now rested in the British Museum beneath a plaque crediting King Albert Edward with the find.

But the war situation was desperate, in Rommel's mind virtually hopeless. If nothing else, he felt a responsibility to the Fatherland to seek out any avenue that might help alleviate the suffering of his people. And so, in late January of 1943, Lord Sterne found himself being transported to Germany aboard a U-boat. Rommel accompanied him, ostensibly to report to the Fuhrer on matters in North Africa, but in reality to be on hand to earn any credit that might come his way if Hitler seemed interested in Sterne's plan.

The two men met with the Fuhrer at Berchtesgaden, high in the Austrian Alps. As the war went badly, Hitler spent more and more of his time here, far from Berlin and the pall that hung over that once great city. They met the German leader on his magnificent terrace with its panoramic views of the surrounding mountains. Sitting with him was the mercurial Eva Braun, who melted into the background at once whenever matters of war were discussed.

Hitler seemed to be verging on madness, as the terrible state of the German war machine grew more obvious every day. Failure and defeat beckoned on every side and it was this, as much as anything, that caused the Fuhrer to latch on to Sterne's scheme with the same single-minded intensity with which he had once gone into Russia.

Sterne recognized obsession as well as any man. He'd lived with it in that prison for three long decades. Now, he realized that he could enlist the German leader's assistance through the simple use of one word . . . gold. Germany was starved for hard currency to pay for the war. The Deutschemark was growing more worthless by the hour. Even the wealth looted from Europe's museums and chateaus and from the Jews, right down to the gold removed from the teeth of those pitiable creatures, was insufficient. Suddenly, Hitler saw a man standing before him who promised to bring a fortune in gold home to Berlin.

"How much gold?" said the Fuhrer, staring at Sterne with those lifeless eyes.

"In just two days digging," Sterne replied confidently, "we brought out nearly two tons. But it's been suggested by Winston Churchill himself, who accompanied me in my first trip to Mapungubwe, that we missed the mother lode. I believe, sir, that the remaining treasure would surpass the entire gold reserves held by Great Britain and the Americans combined."

Hitler stared out at the crags and valleys below, but he wasn't seeing them. "With such treasure, we would win the war!" He pounded his fist into one palm. "And to think that the man who set us on the path to finding it is Churchill himself. What I'd give to be able to see his face when he finds out. That would make the cigar fall out of his fat mouth!"

To Sterne's amazement, the Fuhrer suddenly broke into a little jig, pulling out the sides of his pants and dancing gleefully. To Rommel, he said, "What do you think about that, Field Marshall?"

Rommel now regarded the Fuhrer with little more than disgust. He believed Hitler had squandered their chance to win the war through his mad plans, most especially the invasion of Russia. He chose his words carefully, however, as everyone did now when meeting with the German leader. It was never good to oppose something the man had already sunk his teeth into.

"My Fuhrer, I think it may be a chance worth taking. There's no real proof that the treasure is there or that we'll be able to find it if it is, but our need is great. With that amount of gold, we might indeed change the course of the war. I recommend we send troops to secure the treasure if it is to be had."

"I concur, Field Marshall," said Hitler. "And find it we shall, even if my soldiers have to dig out the entire mountain." His small eyes gazed off at the horizon. "I'll authorize a ship. Nothing too conspicuous . . . perhaps a small coastal freighter. Our best remaining SS troops will lead the effort, and Lord Sterne here will serve as their guide. I'll have to consider who to put in charge of the mission." He looked slyly at Rommel. "You are no doubt too busy with your other duties, Field Marshall?"

For a moment, Rommel felt ill at the thought of being placed on a freighter for an indefinable amount of time on a wild goose chase as potentially pointless as this one. "I fear that's the case, My Fuhrer. But I'll put all my resources in North Africa at the mission's disposal. Anything they need . . . men, materiel, diversionary tactics . . . they shall have."

"Good! Good!" Hitler took Sterne's hand and squeezed it tightly. "A British Lord and the Prime Minister himself responsible for turning the tide of the war. It would be exquisite justice, don't you agree? Now off with you both. I must continue my war planning. You've given me new hope."

Rommel and Sterne departed down a set of stone steps and past Eva Braun sunning herself in the garden in a one-piece white bathing suit. Eyeing the Fuhrer's mistress with barely disguised distaste, the Field Marshall said, "For both our sakes, Sterne, I hope there's something to this treasure." He stared forward glumly, as he contemplated returning to the deteriorating situation in North Africa.

Sterne said nothing. In his mind he was already back on Mapungubwe Hill. He knew precisely where he would begin the search: Beneath the rubble where he'd once believed Winston and Zeila had breathed their last.

20.

KAPITAN HEINRICH BOEHME leaned out the small, open window on the port side of the bridge and yelled to his first mate, "Let go fore and aft lines. Prepare to make way." Slowly, the seven-thousand-ton trawler, only recently rechristened with the colorless sobriquet *Coast Princess,* slipped away from the dock, her engines churning in reverse. Once free of obstructions, she moved forward, threading her way past several islands and out into the Gulf of Guinea off West Africa.

Lord Sterne stood on the foredeck watching their progress. He hadn't been impressed with the choice of craft, though he had to admit that the trawler offered ample space for both the SS troops on board and any gold they might find. What he found most distressing was that the craft was slow and would take at least two weeks to wind its way down the coast, around Cape Town and then north to a spot off the shores of Portuguese East Africa that had been selected as a staging area for their push inland to Mapungubwe. The British had an increasing influence in the region through various British companies, but he didn't believe that would be a problem politically. Their plan called for a night landing of soldiers and equipment followed by a blitzkrieg inland push to the plateau. With any luck they'd find the gold and retreat to a rendezvous with the ship before any serious local government resistance could be organized. It was a Hitler plan through and through.

The slowly passing African shoreline was frustrating in the extreme, but he understood the reasons behind the selection of the freighter. The *Coast Princess* was about as innocuous a looking craft as one could imagine. In addition, by purchasing her in situ, as it were, in French West Africa, they were already out of the mainstream war theaters. It was highly unlikely anyone would question their ostensible reason for being at sea, the coastal transport of freight bound for Portuguese East Africa.

Sterne had taken to daydreaming about the riches that would soon be his, and about the look on Winston Churchill's face once he learned what the source of Germany's newfound wealth and resurgence really was. His only regret was that he wouldn't be around to witness it. That what he was doing made him a traitor to his country never entered into his calculations. As far as he was concerned he was the one who'd been dealt with traitorously, by King Edward who'd left him to rot in a Boer prison.

He had few illusions regarding either the Nazis or the SS. He considered them creatures of the lowest order, which was pretty low indeed to scrape beneath Sterne himself. His only concern was the money. He felt confident there would be enough to enrich both him and the Nazis. He was experienced, after all, in the siphoning off of treasure. The portion he'd secured for himself years ago before handing the remainder off to Bertie had long since disappeared. How and by whom, he had no idea, but thirty years in prison had been long enough for someone to discover it and siphon it away from Sterne himself. It was even possible, he thought dismally, that King Edward had located the gold and used it to pay off his gambling debts.

SS Sturmbannfuhrer Erich Rathke lowered himself down the iron ladder to the main deck and came up alongside Sterne. He was a spit-and-polish SS Major, the sort Sterne couldn't stomach at all. But he made the effort to get along, since for all intents and purposes he was under the Major's command. Hitler had endorsed Rathke to head the expedition.

"An important mission, Lord Sterne," Rathke said, putting one polished boot up on the railing and taking out a pack of cigarettes. He offered one to Sterne, who took it and leaned in to accept a light. The Major had blond hair, broad shoulders, a square chin and penetrating blue eyes. Hitler could not have come up with a better specimen of the master race out of central casting.

Sterne took a long drag and exhaled slowly. "It is important . . . and because of that, maddening to be on this clattering, slow-moving tugboat."

The Major looked at him with interest. "We were lucky enough to get her. Spare craft of any sort are hard to come by these days. I can't quite figure your angle in all of this. You're a British Lord, yet here you are, aiding and abetting the enemy, as the saying goes."

Sterne looked out to sea. They'd cleared the harbor and the engines had settled into a rhythmic chugging. "You could say my country gave up on me before I gave up on it. England saw fit to let me sit in a South African prison for thirty years. I figure she owes me something. I can't get those years back, so I'll take it out in gold."

"So a portion of whatever we find will go to you?"

"It's not in writing, Major, if that's what you mean. Call it a partnership. You'll never find the treasure without my help. In any event, if we find what I think we'll find, there will be more than enough for Germany and me . . . perhaps even a little extra for an enterprising SS Major."

Rathke lowered his foot from the railing and turned to face Lord Sterne. "What I do I do for the Fuhrer and the Fatherland . . . not for money."

"Don't be so superior, Major. We all have our price and from what I've seen of the SS, you fellows can be had as cheaply as any. Even with the gold, Germany's survival will be a long shot. And if you lose the war, SS officers aren't going to be the most popular commodity around. A hundred kilos or so of African gold could pave your way to a life of leisure in Argentina. A hell of a lot more attractive option than a prison cell or hangman's noose."

The Major leaned back against the railing. Sterne couldn't read his face but felt he'd struck a nerve. All over the Fatherland and indeed around the world, German officers and even some regular soldiers had begun to wonder what life would be like in a defeated Germany after the war.

Rathke threw his cigarette over the side and said, "Come. I want to show you something." He led the way down into the ship. They passed rows of bunks hastily installed for the seventy-five SS troops. The men were relaxed, many with their shirts off in the stifling confines of the ship. During daylight hours, they weren't allowed on deck for fear a passing airplane might see them, a proscription, Sterne realized, that apparently did not apply to the Sturmbannfuhrer.

The Major didn't acknowledge his men. He merely passed them by, exited through a passageway, and continued down two sets of metal steps to the main cargo area. Sterne hadn't been in this part of the ship and couldn't imagine what the Major wanted to show him.

Finally, Rathke stopped and gestured at the two massive objects in front of them. Sterne stared incredulously at two hulking Tiger tanks. "My sweethearts," Rathke said. "What do you think of them?"

Sterne walked all the way around one of the huge vehicles. "By God," he said in a low voice. "I wish I'd had one of these forty years ago instead of two bloody draft horses."

"They're a new design," Rathke said. "Only been making them for six months. The Fuhrer authorized them himself. Heavy plate armor with 88-millimeter guns. Not overly fast, and we'll have to carry our own fuel. But they should take care of any resistance we might come up against. And they can pull a lot of weight. We have heavy wheeled carts to carry the gold . . . as much as we find, I would imagine."

Sterne rested his hand lightly on one of the impressive tanks. For the first time, he found himself believing they might actually pull it off.

21.

London

January 28, 1943

CLEMENTINE CHURCHILL fussed over Winston's coat. "Really, Winnie," she said with exasperation, "You look more like some frumpy thing let out the back door of a pub than the Prime Minister of England. You simply must learn to put your best foot foreword."

"The British people aren't the slightest bit interested in my feet." He playfully batted her hands away. "Anyway, that's what I've got you for, old girl. To make sure I'm presentable and that I don't go off to address Parliament with my fly open."

"Oh, I see," she replied. "The British people aren't interested in your feet but they *are* interested in your fly?"

He gave her a baleful look. He loved his wife dearly. She was the rock that allowed him to function at the highest level. Sometimes, he was so scattered trying to keep track of all the balls he had in the air that if he hadn't had her to rely on, the entire house of cards might have come tumbling down and England and the free world along with it.

They exited their home at No. 10 Downing Street and climbed into the car waiting to take them on the short drive to Parliament. Winston was scheduled to give an address on what he had accomplished at the Casablanca Conference. He truly believed they'd turned the corner in the war at last, and that even the Hun was beginning to take alarm at the effect of so many concurrent disasters, from North Africa to Sicily to Stalingrad. It was a day he'd long feared might never come.

As they entered Parliament, Clemmie kissed him, wished him luck and left for her seat in the gallery with some friends. As Winston sat going over his notes one final time, a stern-looking figure in civilian clothes but with an obvious military bearing strode up and sat down beside him. He was Sir David Petrie, head of MI5, one of Britain's intelligence services.

"I need a few words, Mr. Prime Minister."

Winston looked at him in exasperation. "I'm trying to get my thoughts in order, Petrie. Can't it wait until after my speech?"

"I'm afraid not, sir. It's most urgent."

"Oh, it's *always* most urgent. Very well, what is it?" He threw his notes down on the bench next to him.

Petrie looked up and down the hall, which was filled with members milling about. "Could we just step into a private room, sir?"

Winston raised an eyebrow. "Very well, but this had better be good."

They moved across the vast hall and entered a small reception room that was empty. Petrie closed the door behind them.

"Our MI6 branch in North Africa has intercepted a message sent from the German Chancellery to what appears to be a small freighter somewhere off the west coast of Africa." MI6 was the secret service with responsibility for counter-espionage outside Britain.

"Well, what's so special about that?" said Winston. "For God's sake man . . . West Africa? We don't even have any troops in the region."

"That could be part of the problem, sir. Thanks to Enigma and our ability to decipher the German code, we've learned that this freighter's mission is one of Hitler's highest priorities."

"Highest priority? Talk sense. What's so bloody important on the West coast of Africa?

"Gold."

"I beg your pardon?"

"The freighter is apparently planning to transport a large amount, possibly a *very* large amount of gold into German hands. Frankly sir, if they're successful, it could rejuvenate their war machine, maybe even affect the outcome of the entire conflict."

"Well where the bloody hell is the gold coming from?"

"We don't know. That information wasn't revealed in the communiqué. However, there would seem to be a British national involved."

"A British citizen? Bugger the man! Who is it?"

"His name is Lord Sterne. We've done some research on him ..." Petrie stopped and looked at the Prime Minister curiously. "Sir?"

Churchill's normally pallid face had grown suddenly red and for a moment, Petrie thought he might be having an attack of some kind.

"Say that name again," he said in a quiet voice.

"Uh ... Lord Sterne, sir. Have you heard of him?"

The Prime Minister let loose a stream of invective that might have made a lesser man blanch, though not the head of MI5. Very little in this world surprised Sir David. Nonetheless, he'd never heard Churchill react in such a manner. As he tried to think of some reply to the extraordinary outburst, Winston waved a hand at him.

"I'm sorry, Petrie. It was just a shock to hear that name again after more than forty years. Can there be any doubt as to the decoding? Might it be a mistake?"

"No sir, I really don't think that's possible," Petrie said, adding, "Do you know something about this, Mr. Prime Minister?"

"You might say so. I think I know where the gold is coming from."

"Sir?"

"It's a place called Mapungubwe Hill in the northern Transvaal. I've actually seen this gold and believe me, the estimates being discussed are not exaggerated. It's a trove of unbelievable wealth." Winston's mind raced as he realized the significance of the information. The changing tide of war could well turn again if Lord Sterne managed to direct the Nazis to the ancient treasure, a small part of which he'd stolen so many years before. It was a nightmare scenario.

Sterne rising up again, virtually from the dead, to make such a blow against his own country. That the man was capable of being a traitor, Winston doubted not for an instant.

"This is news as foul as death, Petrie. We must take action. What military vessels are within striking distance of the freighter?"

Sir David looked uncomfortable. "I'm afraid, precisely none, sir. As you pointed out, we have few resources in the area."

"Bugger all!" Winston thought feverishly. "Is the boat still off the west coast?"

"To the best of our knowledge. It's been less than twenty-four hours since the message was intercepted. The freighter was at that time south of the Gulf of Guinea. We estimate her top speed at no more than twelve to fifteen knots."

"Good! They must be planning to round the cape. It would be too far of an overland push to go in from the west. From the east coast, it can't be more than a couple of hundred miles to Mapungubwe. That has to be their plan. So we have some time to intercept them. And I know exactly who I want for the job . . . Martin Rand."

Petrie nodded. "We thought of him also. He's been useful to us throughout the war. The man knows everyone in Africa, from heads of state to native chieftains. There is one unfortunate matter, however."

"What's that?"

"I'm afraid he's not in Africa at the moment, and it will take some time to get him in position."

"Why? Where is he?"

"He's returned from South Africa to report directly to King George. At this moment . . ." Petrie looked at his watch. "At this moment he's at the Royal Theater with his wife. *Hamlet,* I believe."

Churchill stared at his intelligence chief. "He's in London? Why the hell didn't you say so? Arrange a meeting with him tomorrow morning at eight at 10 Downing. Now get the hell out of here. I have to give a damned speech and I haven't an idea in my head."

22.

TWO DAYS LATER, Kesi and Martin were shown into the Prime Minister's private office at No. 10 Downing Street, and the door was closed behind them. Surprised to find them left alone, Kesi wandered about looking at pictures of Churchill with various heads of state as well as family members. His desk was piled high with the papers of war.

"I can't believe they just leave people alone in the Prime Minister's personal office," she said, incredulously. "We could be spies or assassins or . . . or anything."

Martin smiled. It was her first visit to No.10, a place he'd grown familiar with over the years. He knew not just anyone would be left alone in such a situation, but he was well known inside the government of Winston Churchill. Indeed, this was his second visit since he'd received the summons to see Churchill alone two days earlier.

Another door opened and Winston entered. He crossed to Martin and shook his hand warmly. "Martin, thanks for coming so promptly. England can not begin to repay you for the work you've done in Africa during this latest German mess. Now, here we are calling on you again."

"I'm glad to help in any way I can, sir."

Winston nodded and turned to Kesi. "It's a pleasure to finally meet the woman who tamed Martin Rand, my dear."

"Thank you, sir, though I'm not sure *tamed* is the right word. It's been twenty years, and I'm still working on the problem."

Winston smiled. "By God, a good choice, Martin."

"Like my husband," Kesi said, "I'm anxious to help, and I was thrilled that my services were also requested. But I can tell you, Mr. Prime Minister, that it took a while to convince Martin I should be involved."

"Frankly," said Winston, "I had my own doubts. This mission will be dangerous in the extreme. The stakes for the Nazis could not be higher. Their backs are to the wall. But Martin convinced me much as I suspect you convinced him that your skills would be essential for our success. Your knowledge of Africa, and of the history and anthropological aspects of Mapungubwe Hill, along with the same command of dialects that your husband has, makes you downright indispensable. Especially given the urgent nature of events. We simply don't have time to find anyone else. You're a very brave young woman to agree to go along." He turned and waved them to two chairs that faced his desk. "Please, sit down."

They sat in the chairs offered and watched as Winston set out three glasses and poured a healthy jot of scotch into each. He handed them around. "I'm afraid scotch is all I have here, but I believe the beginning of an important mission deserves a toast."

He held his glass aloft. "To your success and safe return . . . and to an end to this bloody war."

Martin and Kesi each took a sip.

"I know you've been up half the night, Martin, discussing plans with the War Office. You must be very tired. I leave the operational details to them . . . and you. I have other duties, I'm afraid. But I wanted the opportunity to thank you both personally and to wish you Godspeed."

"Thank you very much, sir," said Rand. He remained seated.

Kesi also stayed in her seat. Winston looked from one to the other. "Is there something else?"

Kesi said, "I'm afraid there is one other matter, sir."

"Yes? What is it?"

She looked at Martin, then back to the Prime Minister. "What I'm going to tell you, sir, I tell you not because you are the Prime Minister, but because it's something I think you should know. Something . . . personal."

Winston cocked an eyebrow. "Personal, you say. Well, what is it?"

Kesi looked again at Martin. She reached out and took his hand. He squeezed it tightly. She seemed almost unable to speak. "Martin, would you please tell the Prime Minister my mother's name."

Winston stared at the little tableau in puzzlement.

Martin said, "Her mother's name is Zeila, Mr. Prime Minister."

Winston rocked back in his chair. "Zeila?" he said. For the second time in two days, a name . . . an ancient memory, came flooding back to him.

"Yes," Kesi said. "What I'm about to tell you I found out only a few weeks ago from my mother. I have no way to prove it, other than to say that I believe my mother, because she's the most trustworthy person I've known in my life. The only other person who has ever come close is Martin. I've been so lucky to have both of them in my life. I don't know what I would have done without either of them."

Winston's normal pallor seemed somehow to have grown even whiter. He stared at Kesi with a strange sort of fascination.

"I'm not telling you this because I want anything from you, sir, other than this opportunity to help in the war effort. But because it's a dangerous mission, I felt I had to tell you now."

"Tell me what?" Winston said in a very small voice.

"That you are my father," she said, looking into his eyes.

Winston's mouth fell open. He stared at her in stunned silence. Even after a lifetime of adventures around the globe, this portly, grandfatherly figure, the last great hope of the free world, was speechless.

"Oh, my," he finally managed to say. "Oh, my." He stood up, walked around the desk and stared at Kesi, who had also risen. There were tears in his eyes. "So many memories," he said. "There's hardly been a day in my life that I haven't thought of your mother . . . our

time together was short, but when people expect to die, they feel . . .
very intensely."

Kesi smiled shyly at him. "My mother said much the same thing
to me. She was a student of the Swahili language. It is a Swahili name
she chose for me. It means 'born when the father had difficulties.'"

"Oh, my dear," said Winston. "What difficulties we had!" He
put his arms out and Kesi, hesitantly, went to him. He held her
tightly, feeling her body shake as her own emotions overwhelmed
her. After what seemed a long time, he let her go and held her out
at arm's length.

"Good Lord, but you were lucky, girl. You got your mother's
looks, with the exception of your skin color, which I rather imagine
I had a bit of a hand in." He brushed a tear off his cheek.

"I can't prove anything," Kesi said again.

"Not a doubt in my head, dear girl. Because I knew your
mother and I know Martin, and there would be nothing that could
ever make either of them concoct such a story. I'm so very glad you
told me. I *must* tell Clemmie and my own children. To think that
they have a new sister! And one so brave and beautiful to boot." He
stopped. "Tell me, have you any children of your own?"

She dipped her head. "No, sir. We've been unable. It's a great
sadness for us."

"I'm truly sorry." He hesitated. "You know, I've never really
liked being called 'sir.' Conjures up unpleasant memories of my
school days at Harrow. I don't suppose I could convince you to call
me . . . what? Father? Winnie?"

She laughed, delighted. "I'm not quite sure I can make the
transition so quickly from Mr. Prime Minister to Daddy. Sir may
have to do for now."

"Ah, well, it will come in time. But then, you have a new family
to meet! Oh, it will be a shock, but you'll see. They'll take to you in
a minute. They'll . . ." He looked suddenly stricken. "But there's no
time for that now, is there?"

He leaned against his desk. "No time for anything in this bloody
war. But Martin, you make damn sure you bring my daughter back

to me, you understand? I intend to spend many hours talking with her . . . maybe even meet with Zeila again, somehow."

"I had it in mind to do just that," Martin said.

Winston looked at him. "I suppose I've also gained a son-in-law. Couldn't imagine a better one. What a day! What a day! How the past rears up and surprises us all."

23.

THE AGING VICKERS Victoria troop transport sat on a military runway at a base outside of Cairo, awaiting takeoff instructions. The Victoria had a crew of two and could carry up to twenty-three fully equipped troops. The bi-planes were already obsolete by the outbreak of the war, but the shortage of transports had kept them in service, particularly in the Middle East, where they were sometimes pressed into offensive duties as light bombers flying night attacks.

On board were Martin, Kesi and a single squad of British commandos. These eight men were all that Rand had requested, for they needed to be able to move quickly. In truth, he would have preferred to go in with Nabeel and a handful of his Sudanese comrades. But there was no time to locate and recruit them. On boarding at RAF Northolt airport outside London for the first leg of their journey, he'd been introduced to the squad commander, Major Jeremiah Sandys. Fortunately, he warmed quickly to the Major, who exhibited an easy-going but professional demeanor.

"I must say, sir, you come with very high recommendations," Sandys said upon their first encounter. "To tell you the truth, my men have only been back a week from our last mission. We'd been looking forward to a bit more R & R, but when the Prime Minister calls you in . . . well . . . off you bleeding well go."

Martin realized that Winston must have ordered up the very best in the business to protect the mission . . . and his new daughter.

The Victoria, with a maximum speed of 130 mph and a range of just under a thousand miles, required repeated refueling stops during the noisy, roundabout flight, leap-frogging via Lisbon, Malta, Cairo, Khartoum, Addis Ababa and Nairobi to Sofala in Portuguese Mozambique. Martin and Sandys spent the seemingly endless trip working out the details of their mission. Their destination was a deserted air strip north of the port city of Sofala. The Victoria would drop them off, then fly on to Mombasa, where it would await a call for pickup at the completion of the mission.

There'd been no further information about the freighter. Perhaps the Germans had begun to realize the risk of using open communications. With few, if any, British naval and air operations in the region, the chances of the boat's position being reported were slim to none. It could make land almost anywhere between Cape Town, Sofala and points north. A glance at the map made it likely that a landing would occur where the ocean was closest to Mapungubwe, to speed transport of the gold, but this still left hundreds of miles of open coastline. Their only hope of intercepting the Nazis, then, was to go as quickly as possible to the one spot where they knew they had to show up eventually—Mapungubwe Hill.

"The worst part," said Major Sandys, "is that once we reach Mapungubwe, we aren't going to know if we're arriving there first or if the enemy is already in position, perhaps just waiting for us . . . if they have any fear at all of interception, that is."

"No reason that they should," said Martin. "We only know about their plans because of a message intercept that was translated via our code people. The Germans don't know we've broken their code, so they shouldn't be expecting anything. Actually, they probably feel pretty damn safe and cocky . . . for the same reason we don't know where they are at the moment . . . because there are no Allied forces anywhere in the area."

Sandys grunted. "Perhaps, but I don't much like going to an unknown location with no idea whatsoever if the enemy is on their way in, already there or on their way out. We might as well be parachuting into Deutschland on a black, bloody night."

It had been decided, in the interests of speed, that the British party would make no attempt to remove the gold themselves for safekeeping. That would have meant a huge effort involving heavy transport vehicles and many more troops. There was simply no time. The War Department believed this would be the Nazis' only attempt to secure the treasure. Hitler's leadership was becoming more and more erratic. He no longer maintained interest in any strategic move that failed to produce immediate results—his ill-fated Russian venture had seen to that. Martin's orders were simple enough. Stop them, then leave the gold where it was.

"There is one other variable," he said to the Major.

"What's that?"

"We don't know the size of the force we may have to face. If they plan to transport the gold, they're going to have to have a lot of men to do the work, along with heavy transport and, no doubt, Nazi soldiers to guard the effort. The freighter they're using can hold a lot of gold and soldiers, perhaps hundreds of the latter."

Sandys whistled. "I don't like those odds."

"Nor do I," said Martin. "But they must also be prepared to move quickly and, as much as possible, without raising the suspicions of the locals. So I think they'll try to keep it to a minimum, say, less than a hundred men all told."

"Oh well then, that's not a problem is it?" Sandys said with a big smile. "Everyone knows one British commando is worth any ten Nazis." More seriously, he added, "What about local conditions? Slipping into a foreign country without bothering with such niceties as customs can sometimes annoy folks on the ground."

Kesi had been listening to the discussion quietly. Now she said, "None of these small countries are terribly efficient in their border control operations, Major. Hardly surprising for a nation like Portuguese Mozambique that's been responsible for the export of more than two million slaves to Brazil and Cuba during its bloody history."

The Major whistled. "I had no idea."

"They don't advertise it," she said. "Another thing to keep in mind . . . there are at least eight native languages in Mozambique alone, including Swahili, Yao, Shona, Makonde, Nguni and many other local dialects. Between us, Martin and I can manage in most of them, but it makes communication between the various regions difficult, even for local officials. They're used to not really knowing what's going on—that should work to our advantage."

"And to the German's," Martin added. "Though I recall that Lord Sterne was something of a linguist. I imagine the time he spent in a South African prison only helped to increase his knowledge of dialects."

The landing, just at dawn, went smoothly enough, considering that the air strip was little more than a bit of cleared upcountry grassland. The plane mowed down numerous small scrub bushes before finally coming to a halt and turning around immediately in preparation for departure as soon as everyone disembarked. Martin had arranged for a Moroccan friend, who had once fought with him and Nabeel many years before and who now lived in Mozambique, to have horses waiting for their party of ten. True to his word, the horses were precisely where they were expected, though the friend was not. He apparently had too much at risk to be caught in such a venture. A lone native man was in charge of the mounts, his primary job to ensure that they weren't eaten by lions before Rand's party arrived. As soon as delivery was made, the man melted away into the bush.

Kesi was now their primary guide. She was more familiar with this part of Africa than was her husband. Fortunately, the light forest and open grassland made horses quick and reliable transport. They would stay away from villages and skirt the few dusty roads.

The first couple of hours were almost comical. Most of the soldiers had never ridden horseback before. A couple had taken brief rides as children twenty years earlier. Kesi gave instruction as best she could, starting with how to cinch on the saddle and hold the reins. These weren't race horses, but neither were they nags. Several of the mounts had spirit, and the soldiers looked like desperate, bouncing Pogo stick riders.

"If the horse decides to run away with you, the best advice I can give is to let him go and hang on," Kesi said to the concerned faces. These men had faced death dozens of times in the last four years, but the thought of a horse running away with them gave them pause. "Eventually, he'll tire or get distracted or bored and simply stop. If you try to pull the reins or kick him, you'll probably just make him go faster."

Martin followed at the rear of the column, ostensibly to help pick up anyone who fell off his mount, but really he just wanted to ride behind Kesi and watch her. She was dressed for the bush in loose-fitting pants, a shirt tightly tucked into them and leather boots that came to mid-calf.

Even after more than twenty years together, he enjoyed watching her move. She was as much at home in her own skin as any woman he'd ever known. He still loved her as much as he had after the very first time they'd made love. And she'd hardly changed in all those years . . . gained no more than a pound or two, her face smooth, barely a hint of a crease around the eyes, and her rear end, moving up and down gently as she rode, as tight as a drum.

Of course, being unable to have children was partly responsible for her shape. It was something she would have surrendered in a moment for the joy of giving them a child. But they had come to accept the laws of nature. They could be happy enjoying each other and their work.

They rode in a southwesterly direction, the elevation increasing gradually as they approached the Chimoio Plateau on the border of Southern Rhodesia. The forests grew denser here, and they saw occasional patrols, which were easily avoided. Indeed, the men they saw appeared remarkably uninterested in any sort of serious policing and likely had very little in the way of formal training.

Wildlife was rich in the sparsely populated region. Elephant, giraffe, hippos, lions and water buffalo were prolific. They heard and once or twice saw baboons who screeched in protest at the strange posse that passed them by. Kesi warned the men to beware of cobras and adders, which could kill a man every bit as efficiently as a Nazi.

By mid-afternoon on the second day, Martin estimated they were halfway to Mapungubwe. Most of the men had begun to manage their mounts more or less capably. They were approaching the entrance to a narrow rift in the landscape, and Martin marveled at the change in terrain and the stark beauty of the place. It was this astonishing variety of landscape that had kept him so fascinated by Africa all of his life. The walls of the rift naturally funneled them into the canyon. Too late, he realized his appreciation of their surroundings had distracted him . . . the gorge was a natural spot for an ambush.

The first shot struck one of the soldiers in the chest. He fell off his horse without a sound and lay still on the ground. In a moment, a barrage of gunshots ricocheted off the boulders around them.

"Ambush!" he shouted. "Take cover!" Everyone jumped off their horses, which were frantic at the sudden noise, and sought cover. Kesi yelled at the men to hold onto their mounts, but several of the soldiers let go of their reins and the horses bolted back down the gorge and out of sight. Martin tried to gauge where the shots were coming from. The valley floor was a scant fifty feet wide here and he saw movement among a pile of boulders above them and perhaps sixty feet away. At that distance, they were fortunate to have lost only one man.

Major Sandys lay behind a large boulder a few feet away, Kesi and two other soldiers beside him. The rest of the men were spread out behind smaller rocks. "We're not in a good position," Sandys said. "They've got elevation and position on us. I can't even tell exactly where they are."

Martin nodded. He peered cautiously around the edge of his rock. About fifteen feet to his left was the side of the gorge, which offered shelter from the enemy fire. The cliff wall was steep but had many obvious cracks and fissures. If he could climb it, he could reach a narrow ledge that was out of the line of sight of their attackers. With luck, he could move along it to a position that would allow him to flank them. He didn't see any other options. The only trouble was that he would be completely exposed for at least two or three seconds as he crossed the open ground.

He shouldered his rifle and came up on the balls of his feet. "I'm going to make a dash for the cliff wall over there."

Kesi and Sandys looked where he indicated. What he planned was obvious . . . and obviously dangerous, but it was clear they had few alternatives. Kesi met Martin's eyes. "Be careful," she said simply.

He looked at her for a long moment, absorbing her love as an almost physical source of energy. "I intend to be," he said.

"We'll make a diversion at the other side of the gorge," said Major Sandys. He called to several of the soldiers who were near the far side of the rift and prepared them to fire on his signal. He turned back and nodded. "Good luck."

Rand crouched, preparing for the dash. He took a deep breath and nodded once at the Major who raised his arm and waved it sharply downward. At once, the soldiers farthest away thrust their rifles over the rocks and began firing, almost blindly, in the general direction of their attackers.

Rand leaped forward and crossed the distance to the cliff wall before a single shot could be fired at him. Quickly, he began to climb the cliff. He reached the ledge in less than a minute, then moved along it until he could look down on their attackers. There were at least a dozen men and any doubt he might have had as to their origins was immediately dispelled by the black uniforms of the SS.

He lifted his rifle and sighted carefully. His first volley would be the most important, for although he had the advantage now, the men would quickly move to protect themselves. He fired three quick shots, each finding its mark. The SS soldiers were surprised and scrambled to find protection from this new threat. But Martin still managed to hit two more before they were hidden.

He looked back toward his own group and saw with horror that another German force had crept up from behind them. It was a classic pincers operation, and they'd fallen into it. Even as he opened his mouth to warn the British commandos, the SS opened fire and killed two of the men instantly. The Nazis were very close. The British had to crawl around their protective boulders, away from the oncoming soldiers at their rear. But this made them sitting ducks to their original attackers. Martin fired rapidly and steadily, keeping the heads of this group down and preventing them from firing at his now completely exposed comrades.

Several of the SS had moved alongside the cliff wall until they were just a few feet from the boulder that Major Sandys and Kesi crouched behind. With a quick glance, Rand saw the Major crawl a few feet away from Kesi to get a better line of sight. Then he watched helplessly as two SS soldiers dashed forward and grabbed Kesi, whose attention was in the other direction. One of the men struck her a blow on the head. She went down and they hauled her limp body back with them to their main group.

He turned his fire away from the SS on the ridge and fired at the new attackers below with deadly accuracy. He killed four men in a matter of seconds, then turned back and shot two more above him who had emerged as soon as he'd turned his fire away. The ambushers had had enough of this withering and almost superhumanly accurate gunfire. A loud cry in German echoed through the canyon and all of the enemy soldiers faded away.

He scrambled and slid his way back down to his men. They heard the engine of a truck fire up farther down the gully. "No!" Martin shouted and started to run after it. Major Sandys and the remaining commandos followed, but by the time they emerged from the rift, all they could see was the dust cloud moving off into the distance.

"Kesi!" Martin yelled, his rifle hanging at his side uselessly, as he watched the vehicle disappear. He started to move after it, but Major Sandys held him back.

"Martin, listen to me! You can't catch them on foot or even on horseback. But we know where they're going. To Mapungubwe. That's the direction we have to go. They've no reason to kill her outright."

Martin shook his head grimly. "No. They have no reason to kill her right away. That's what scares me. They'll want information from her as to who we are. And they'll do anything necessary to get it." He felt more helpless and frustrated than he'd ever been in his life. But he knew the Major was right. They couldn't catch up to the truck. They could only go on and hope to meet up with the Germans at Mapungubwe. And if they hurt one hair on her head, they would pay for it dearly.

They spent two frustrating hours tracking down the horses. With the loss of three of the commandos and Kesi, they now numbered only six. Martin refused to allow himself to consider how woefully undermanned they would be in any future encounters.

"Major!" One of the men called out. "Come look at this."

They all gathered around the soldier who pointed at a deep rut in the earth at his feet. "Tanks," the man said.

"Mother of God," said another of the men. "If they've gone to the trouble of bringing tanks and feel confident enough to leave at least twenty men to guard their rear . . . Lord knows how big a force we're dealing with."

But Martin was having none of it. Every minute, Kesi was being taken farther away. "Let's move," he said. "We're going to ride all night. Maybe they won't."

24.

KESI SAT on the floor of the military truck, propped uncomfortably in one corner. Mercifully, her hands were tied in front of her body so she was better able to adjust to the swaying and lurching as the vehicle careened over the rough terrain. Her head still ached from the blow she'd received. She'd come awake slowly and when one of the men saw her eyes open, he'd lifted her into a sitting position.

There were six men in the back of the truck, and she could see two more sitting in the cab through a small window. They were all dressed in black SS uniforms. The uniforms struck her as ridiculous in the hot, dry African climate, evidence that these men were clearly out of their element. It might give her an advantage when and if the opportunity to escape ever came.

But she wasn't optimistic. In her worst nightmares, she'd imagined being a captive of the Nazis. Now, after almost three years of war, it had finally come to pass. That it had occurred here in the very heartland of her people only made the injustice more poignant.

Her first thought upon waking had been Martin. She knew he'd blame himself and do whatever it took to try to save her. She also knew, however, that his anger could cloud his judgment, especially when it came to her safety, and she hoped he wouldn't do something rash or plain stupid. If these men had wanted to kill her, they would already have done so. Obviously, they wanted something from her—information, no doubt. What they might be willing to do to get it caused a shudder to run down her spine. She'd heard plenty of stories about Nazi atrocities.

None of the men in the truck appeared to be officers. They talked quietly among themselves. She knew only a smattering of German, though her general command of languages helped her to decipher occasional words. She decided to play dumb regarding the language, which was not too much of a stretch, in hopes she might learn something. The soldiers mostly appeared to be tired following the battle. Perhaps they'd also been awake through the night. She gathered, slowly, that they must have been stationed in the gorge for several days to watch for any possible pursuers of the main force.

It took nearly ten hours for the truck to negotiate the hundred miles or so of rough country between the gorge and Mapungubwe. When they finally pulled to a stop, at dawn, in the shadow of the hill, she was hot, tired and bruised from being tossed about in the truck. She was pulled roughly from the vehicle and led toward a clutch of tents. Nearby, she saw a tank facing away from the hill, its crew sitting about eating breakfast from tins. A handful of other soldiers appeared to be on guard duty. She assumed the main force must be on top of the hill.

A hand on her shoulder stopped her outside one of the tents and she stood waiting as one of the men announced their presence. In a moment, Sturmbannfuhrer Erich Rathke emerged. In deference to the already growing heat of the day, he had removed his jacket, but was otherwise immaculately dressed and groomed. He stared at her with interest.

"They radioed they'd taken a woman prisoner." He appraised her openly. "Very much a woman, I would say."

Kesi didn't respond, shaking her head slightly to indicate she didn't understand him.

Rathke nodded. In perfect English, he said, "You work for the English, yet you're Negroid. Not completely, obviously. Too bad. The purity of the blood is important." He walked all the way around her. "Still, not unattractive, I give you that. My soldiers report your force was small but clearly made up of British soldiers, apparently good fighters. What is your mission?"

She took a deep breath. She'd been planning how to deal with this moment. To be openly uncooperative and belligerent would only hasten her torture and the probable revelation of everything she knew. She had no illusions about her ability to resist for long. Instead, she had decided to play dumb. The fact she was a woman and of "impure" blood just might make the pose more believable to these cretins.

"I don't know the nature of the mission," she said. "I was hired as a guide because I grew up in this part of Africa and I speak many native dialects. I was only told where we were going, not why. I can tell you that it was clear to me that the British soldiers had no idea they might be attacked. They were very surprised by the appearance of German soldiers in this part of Africa."

Rathke smiled at her. "And what was this destination that you were leading them to without knowing why?"

During the long drive in the truck, she'd racked her brain trying to think of some plausible explanation she could offer that might explain the presence of a group of British commandos. Nothing she thought of made any sense. She finally decided to fall back on the truth. The Germans would no doubt suspect the British goal was Mapungubwe regardless of what she said. The truth, then, would only make her story more believable and make little difference to her friends. "The destination was here," she said. "Mapungubwe Hill. But I don't know why."

"Even if I believed your story," said the Major, "You were nevertheless supporting British troops, and for that I could have you shot."

"I am nothing more than a hired guide," she said. "This isn't a war zone, Major. We consider ourselves neutral here. If you like, I offer my services to you and your men. I have no feelings of loyalty to the British."

"A true mercenary, eh?" He considered her. "Perhaps you could be useful. Outside of Lord Sterne, not a single man of us can understand all the gibbering languages these people speak."

She managed not to react at the mention of Lord Sterne. She'd known she might encounter this enigmatic figure once she undertook the mission. Zeila had told her about Sterne . . . and his treachery so many long years ago. Kesi felt a strange fascination with the man. He'd attempted to kill her mother and, as it turned out, her father too. But if not for his actions burying Zeila and Winston alive, she would never have been born. Her life seemed to be connected to his in inexplicable and mysterious ways.

Sensing she just might have pulled off her deception and avoided the wrath of the Nazis, she decided to try to cement her innocence in the Major's mind by distracting him from the current line of questioning.

"If I'm to be an interpreter for you, Major, I wonder if you'd let me clean up and rest for a while. It's been a very long day and night."

He contemplated her for a few more moments. Finally, he seemed to come to a decision. "Come with me," he said. He dismissed her guard and led Kesi around to the back of his tent where the troops had rigged an open shower by mounting a barrel of water over a large pan punched with holes.

"Here's your shower," he said. He went into the back opening of his tent and emerged a moment later with a shirt and pair of pants. He handed the clothes to her. "These will have to do, I'm afraid, until you have a chance to wash your own clothes. I can't really leave you alone. I'll be in my tent and will check on you every few minutes. Please don't consider trying to run away. It won't do you any good."

She stared at him until he went into the tent. He could probably see her from where he was, but she undressed and stood under the shower, bathing as quickly as possible. After she was dressed, he said, "Now I'll show you something quite wonderful."

She followed him to the base of the hill. The Germans had constructed a small lift using block and tackle and a derrick at the top that stuck out over the edge. It was a hastily built construction but appeared serviceable enough. They stepped onto the small platform.

"Hold onto the ropes," Rathke said. Then he waved a hand and a truck to which the rope was attached began to move forward slowly. They were raised smoothly to the top of the hill in less than a minute.

She followed the major to the central part of the plateau. Though she was apprehensive, she couldn't help but once again admire the incredible view out across the veldt that had captivated her and Martin twenty long years ago.

Set back against a rise at the center of the hilltop she saw something they'd not seen in their earlier visit. It appeared to be part of an ancient temple. Columns flanked an opening that disappeared into the ground. All around were soldiers stripped to their undershirts. Huge mounds of rock and debris lay about the entrance. They appeared to have been at it for days and looked exhausted. Nevertheless, they stared at Kesi appreciatively. She was an unanticipated diversion for the female-deprived men.

"Come," the Major said, taking her hand.

Her skin crawled at his touch, but she forced herself forward. They went down a hallway lined with relief paintings and mosaic scenes of an Africa long since past. It was every bit as beautiful and mesmerizing as Zeila had described.

They reached a second set of steps that took them even lower into the Earth. Here, torches had been set up to light their way. Finally, they reached the end of the hall where a hole had been opened into what looked like nothing more than a dirt wall. Two soldiers stood beside the hole.

"Where is he?" Rathke said.

"He went in some time ago," said one of the men. "He was in a hurry. Grabbed a torch the moment the opening was found and disappeared. Told us not to let anyone in. I think he wanted to see whatever there was to see alone." The man shrugged his shoulders in the time-honored manner of soldiers who didn't understand their superiors.

Rathke stood for a moment, weighing the man's words. Then he took two torches from the wall, handed one to the man and kept the other for himself. "Go ahead," he said. "I'm in charge here."

The soldier hesitated only a moment before stepping into the gloom. The second man followed and Rathke motioned Kesi to go ahead of him. "You might as well see what we're after . . . if it's here," he said. He'd always had his doubts as to the seriousness of this mission.

Kesi gasped as she moved forward. The gloom of the tiny corridor gave way at once to a huge, cavernous space, the dimensions of which she couldn't guess. But the combined light of both torches was enough for her to see the sandstone pedestals before her, each holding its carved soapstone bird with ruby eyes glinting in the torchlight.

"My God, they're beautiful," she said. Then she saw the decayed bodies of the ancient priests who guarded this place from intruders. Evidently, they weren't doing too good a job, she thought morbidly.

Rathke grunted and moved past her. One of the soldiers pointed ahead to a flickering light that seemed to float in the darkness. As they got closer they realized the light was coming from a cave entrance some twenty feet above them. Even as they stared at the cave, a stooped figure emerged holding a torch up high. He looked down at them.

"You won't believe it, Major!" said Lord Sterne. "It's greater than anything we could have imagined. Come see for yourself." He indicated the rope hanging down.

Rathke moved forward. He handed his torch to one of the guards and told them to remain at the foot of the cliff. To Kesi, he said, "Go ahead," and gave her a boost by putting both hands comfortably on her rear end.

She scrambled up quickly and found herself face to face with the man she had to thank for her very existence.

Lord Sterne was obviously distracted by his discovery, but he looked at her curiously. "And who might you be?" he said.

Before she could answer, Rathke pulled himself up beside them. "She's the prisoner our men took at the fight in the gorge," he said. "She claims to only be a guide with no knowledge of what they intended."

"And you believe this?" Sterne said, his voice dripping with sarcasm. "You bring her *here*? You're a bigger fool than I give you credit for, Major." Sterne looked again at Kesi. There was something oddly familiar about her. He couldn't put his finger on it, but clearly she was no immediate threat, and he was too excited to be bothered about her now.

"Never mind," he said. "Come . . . prepare yourself for a shock." He led the way into the cave.

25.

Neasdon, London

WINSTON STARED around the table. He'd called this special meeting of his cabinet to discuss what everyone agreed was a nebulous subject, the state of Adolf Hitler's mental health. The meeting was being held in one of Winston's two underground bunkers, this one codenamed Paddock, the alternative to the Cabinet War Rooms beneath Whitehall. Unlike Whitehall, Paddock was completely bombproof and could withstand a direct hit. Designed as a final refuge to accommodate the entire war cabinet and two hundred staff in the event the Battle of Britain was lost, it was located in Neasdon in northwest London.

"Our latest intelligence suggests, Mr. Prime Minister, that Hitler is becoming increasingly erratic in his decision-making and spends a great deal of time worrying about his personal security," said Foreign Minister Anthony Eden.

"And well he should," said Lord Beaverbrook. "His own staff must see what's going on. They're scared of him, of course. He's a madman and utterly unpredictable. I think we can expect more attempts on his life. Who knows? Maybe we'll get lucky."

Winston chewed on his cigar. "Luck," he growled, "is one bit of war materiel that has been in short supply in recent years. Are we giving adequate assistance to potential assassins? And are we actively recruiting for the position?"

"We do have some operatives concentrating on this," Eden replied. "And there's a secret working group, assisted by the French underground, that's been attempting to find disaffected Germans interested in doing away with Hitler. But it's very difficult to get close to the Fuhrer, either at the Chancellery or Berchtesgaden. Only his most trusted aides are allowed anywhere near him. Of course, this works to our advantage in one sense. He's isolated and not really aware how quickly things are deteriorating. No one wants to tell him bad news."

"I fear," Lord Beaverbrook said, "that we'll have to rely on those within his private circle to do the deed for us."

"He's not too mad," said Winston, "to have realized the potential of seizing the gold at Mapungubwe Hill."

Lord Beaverbrook looked exasperated. "This is the second time I've heard mention of this so-called gold. It's a fantasy, if you ask me, pure and simple . . . a good thing if it diverts his attentions."

Winston stared at Beaverbrook witheringly. "It would brighten my day considerably," he said, "if my cabinet ministers were to read their Prime Minister's memos. I called this meeting, among other purposes, to get your predictions concerning what might happen to the war effort should the Germans suddenly come into virtually inexhaustible wealth."

Lord Beaverbrook attempted to salvage his position, for he'd obviously not read the memo. "I tell you, sir, it's a pipedream. I don't know who's been feeding you this incredible story, but . . ." He stopped as Anthony Eden placed a hand on his arm.

"The Prime Minister has seen the gold in question personally," Eden said, quietly.

Lord Beaverbrook stared incredulously at Winston. "You've seen it?"

Churchill snorted, blew a cloud of smoke and turned his eyes away from Lord Beaverbrook, dismissing him entirely. He turned to his Chancellor of the Exchequer, Sir Kingsley Wood. "And what does my financial expert think?" He said.

In the manner of all economists, the Chancellor hedged uneasily. "Of course, the potential is there to do great mischief. The Germans could purchase more war materiel from their allies and others willing to sell. They could use the funds to bribe other nations and leaders, to hire assassins of their own, to install puppet governments. They might even be able to manipulate the financial markets. The list is endless. But they'd be restricted in some ways also, regardless of the new money. There are only so many German people, for example, upon whom to draw troop strength. I think it unlikely they could hire any significant number of mercenaries, especially given the current state of things. The RAF is ascendant in the air and the Luftwaffe has suffered great losses. It takes time to build new planes, ships and tanks no matter how much money you have. And we can disrupt those building programs with our air superiority. Meanwhile, America can produce far more war materiel and deliver it far faster than the Germans, regardless of how much money they have." He looked around the table. "All in all, I'd say their obtaining the gold could lengthen the war but not alter the final outcome."

"And that's not a cost I'm willing to pay!" Winston pounded the table. "A longer war means more casualties. We've squandered enough of our young men fighting this scourge. We must not allow Hitler to get his filthy hands on this new source of wealth.

"When I first saw the gold of Mapungubwe, it was 1900 and the area was utterly isolated," the Prime Minister continued. "Virtually no one had visited it in hundreds . . . perhaps thousands . . . of years. Some of you may recall the name. The *Illustrated London News* reported in 1933 the discovery of a grave of unknown origin, containing considerable gold. The hill had been forgotten since an Iron Age metropolis was located there on the Limpopo River and ruled by an African king more than a thousand years ago. A local resident revealed the existence of the place to the University of Pretoria in the 1930s."

"Excuse me, sir," said Eden. "Surely, if the hill has been excavated over the past decade, the gold would have been found."

"I think not," Winston said. "My interest in Mapungubwe led me to keep abreast of the university's work at the site. The hilltop and its extensive subterranean depths are vast enough that they couldn't possibly have examined it all. Indeed, a number of scientists and workers disappeared during those excavations, which led to periodic abandonment of the work."

"Disappeared how, Sir?"

Winston's eyes seemed to glaze over, as he remembered the past. Finally, he said, "That is something I don't know. However, it's my belief that the gold of Mapungubwe came from another civilization, a thousand years farther back in the mists of time than even that Iron Age tribe."

Eden and the others listened to the incredible tale, spellbound. "What other civilization?" Eden said.

"One unknown to mankind, a melding of Nubian and Roman culture."

"You can't be serious," Lord Beaverbrook blurted, then caught himself as the Prime Minister cast a wintry eye on him.

Winston settled back in his chair. "Now . . . We've sent a very small group of men—and one woman—to do what may be the most important job left in this war. We had to restrict the size of our force in order to get them quickly where they needed to be. But I want backup for them, God dammit! Eden, I want you to send two of our submarines to the east African coast. They're to search for the enemy freighter and if they find it, they are to sink it."

"It's a tall order, Mr. Prime Minister. The vessel in question is undoubtedly unmarked or flying under a flag of convenience. Small freighters are a dime a dozen. A needle in a haystack would be child's play in comparison. And, I should add, we don't have submarines to spare from the main war theater."

"This is not a negotiable directive, Mr. Foreign Minister," said Winston.

Eden cocked an eyebrow. "Then may I ask, *if* we can locate it, is the boat to be sunk before or after the gold is on board?"

"I don't care. If the gold is already on board, then it's too bad. It will be a loss to mankind, but mankind is what we're trying to save here. If it's not on board, then they'll have at least lost their ability to transport it. We'll have bought some time." He stared about the room. "Hitler is mad, gentlemen, have no doubt of it." He chewed his cigar so fiercely it looked in danger of coming apart. "But we can't *rely* on his madness. I've known other madmen who made proper decisions when it was necessary. Stalin is the prime example. KBO! KBO! We have to Keep Buggering On. We must get inside the madman's head and think like a madman ourselves. Our countrymen and the entire free world are counting on us." He stood up and started to leave. "And read my bloody memos!" he said over his shoulder.

Then he was gone, down a dank hallway and up the tiny elevator to the surface where his driver waited with an umbrella against a relentless and cold mid-winter drizzle. It took only a few minutes to return to Downing Street, where he was scheduled to have lunch with Clementine. He didn't anticipate the sort of relaxed occasion he was used to. He and Clemmie had a near-perfect working marriage. There were many reasons for this, but at the root of everything was the simple fact that they were comfortable with each other. He didn't relish the prospect of upsetting that apple cart. But since his first—and last—meeting with Kesi, he'd begun to realize that however much he'd been overjoyed to discover he had a lovely new daughter, explaining it to Clementine was going to be anything but easy.

The tumultuous cabinet meeting was probably a good preliminary to the main bout, he thought glumly, as he entered No. 10 and greeted his wife. They sat down to lunch, and he waited until they'd been served and were alone.

"How did your meeting go?" Clementine asked. She was a master at politely inquiring after her husband's day, even though she knew he often couldn't tell her about most of what he was doing. Her inquiries served their purpose, however, by allowing him the opportunity to vent his feelings.

"Beaverbrook's an ass. Don't know why I keep him around. But as you know, my dear, the main reason I enjoy being Prime Minister is because everyone has to do what I say."

"Almost everyone, Winnie," she replied.

"Present company excepted," he admitted. He took a deep breath. "There's something I need to talk to you about, Clemmie."

She nodded and gave him her attention.

"This is going to be most buggered difficult," he said. "Do you remember my telling you about a place called Mapungubwe years ago?"

"Why, yes. It was when you escaped from the Boers and then were almost killed by that awful scoundrel, Lord Sterne. It was all years before we came together. But I remember your telling me about it very well. Wasn't there some incredible treasure involved . . . Roman? Or African?"

"A bit of both, apparently. It seems that our Mr. Hitler has designs on it—to pump up his war effort."

"I certainly hope then, dear, that you're doing something to stop him."

He sighed. "I have to stop beating about the bush, Clem. When Lord Sterne caused that cavern to cave in on me, you recall I was trapped with two people, Aylmer and a woman named Zeila."

"Yes."

"Aylmer was killed shortly afterward, in a fall we believe, though his body was never found. Zeila and I were alone in that black cave and knew we were going to die."

"It must have been horrible."

"It was. We had nothing to hang onto but each other and . . . we made love."

Clementine was silent. Then she placed her hand on Winston's. "It was before we were together, Winnie. The cause was sufficient. You needn't have told me."

"She was a native African, Clemmie."

She shook her head. "I don't need to know this."

"I'm afraid that you do, my dear. I would never have told you if there was any way to avoid it. I'd do anything to spare you, you know that."

"Spare me what, Winston?" she said quietly.

"A week ago, I sent a group of commandos to Africa to attempt to dissuade the Nazis from taking the treasure at Mapungubwe. I put Martin Rand in charge. You've met him."

She started to say something but Winston put up a hand to stop her.

"Let me get through the rest of this, my dear, as best I can. I met with Rand and his wife, a very beautiful, very brave . . . very light-skinned . . . African woman. Her name is Kesi. After I thanked them for taking on such a risky venture for us, this young woman told me something quite extraordinary."

His wife watched him with the kind of innocent focus he'd seen so many times before, as he explained some intricate piece of the war effort.

"She told me that her mother's name was Zeila and that I was her father." The last came out in a rush and Winston leaned forward in his chair, his face beet red, as he stared at his wife.

Clementine Churchill's mouth fell open. She stared at her husband and, for perhaps the first time in her life, wondered if she really knew him.

"You . . . you're telling me you have a Negro daughter?" she said softly.

He nodded. "I know it's a shock. It was to me. But it's fate, that's all. Can any of us really have too many children in this world, Clem? I have to be proud of her. If you could only see her . . . meet her. She is strong and beautiful and brave . . . willing to risk her life to help end this bloody war. And she's a little bit sad too, I think, because they are unable to have children. I can't deny her existence, Clem. I won't do that."

"Can you be sure she is who she says she is, Winston? You're the Prime Minister of England, after all. It could certainly be worth the girl's while to be related to you."

"There can be no absolute proof. I did have a relationship with her mother. Kesi is about the right age. She is light-skinned while her mother and, I am told, current stepfather are both very dark. And per-haps most of all, I don't believe either Zeila or Martin would concoct such a tale. As for her wanting something from me, all I've managed to give her is the very real chance to be killed."

Clementine pushed her chair back and stood up. She moved to the window and stared out across the shiny, wet cobblestones of Horse Guards Row.

"It will cause a scandal, Winnie. You know that."

"I know it only too well," he said sadly. "It will sell a lot of papers. But I don't give a damn about that. All I care about is what you think, my dear."

She turned back to him. "Why, Winnie," she said, "I think it will be quite nice to have another daughter."

Relief washed over his face. He stood and went over to her and took her hands in his. "I am the world's luckiest man, Clemmie, to have a wife like you to see me through all the difficulties I've had."

She smiled and kissed him. "You most certainly are, Winnie," she said.

26.

K ESI SAT in front of a roaring fire the SS troops had built to ward off the lions. She was feeling slightly ill. The dinner they'd just finished had consisted of salt pork and beans straight from tins. That this was now standard fare for Germans in the field had to be a sign that the great, invulnerable war machine of the Hun was beginning to grind down. But her stomach grumbled uncomfortably nonetheless. The urgency of their mission evidently left little time for such niceties as hunting local game to eat. The days were spent unburying and, beginning tomorrow, transporting the gold. By nightfall, it was all the soldiers could do to stay awake.

She was keenly aware this exhaustion might provide her with an opportunity to escape, provided her story was accepted and she wasn't watched too closely. For the time being, she sat between the Major and Lord Sterne, the latter of whom continued to stare at her periodically as if trying to place her.

Surrounding the fire was a circle of tents and farther outside this perimeter were the bulk of the German troops, who had several smaller fires of their own. Already, the men were lying down following the evening meal, most too tired to even converse.

Kesi's thoughts were still spinning from the images of gold, jewels and treasures of almost unimaginable magnitude that she'd seen inside the cave. She fingered a gold ring with a huge ruby that the Major had plucked from a basket filled with similar ones and insisted gallantly on putting on her finger. The ring served only to remind her how dangerous the treasure would be if it ever found its way to the Third Reich.

Suddenly she cocked her head. There was something at the edge of her hearing. Something almost . . . familiar. She glanced at Lord Sterne, who had also heard it.

"What's that?" he said, getting up and walking to the edge of the firelight.

Major Rathke shook his head. "I don't hear anything," he said.

But then the sound grew louder, and even the Major heard it over the crackling of the fire. He also stood up and stared into the darkness.

"It sounds almost human," he said. "Like a baby or a child crying. Could it be an animal of some kind?"

In that instant, Kesi realized what she was hearing. It was something she recognized from long ago, during that awful night when Martin had been nearly eviscerated by the Clan of the Bow. Could they still be here, she wondered incredulously . . . after all these years . . . still guarding the treasure of Mapungubwe Hill? It seemed too fanciful. And yet, she remembered what Martin had been told, that the warrior caste that guarded Mapungubwe had done so for thousands of years.

The strange sound also sparked an old memory in Sterne, something barely retained from more than forty years ago. "It's the wind," he said. "I've heard it before. The wind makes strange noises as it blows through the cliffs and caves." He returned and sat back down but continued to stare off into the darkness as the strange, distant wailing rose and fell. From his new position, he could look at Kesi's face, blackened in profile against the firelight. All at once, he started.

"By God!" he said. "I knew there was something about you. You're the spitting image of someone I once knew . . . what was her name?" He thought back over forty years of triumph, tragedy and imprisonment. "Zeila!" he said with satisfaction finally. "She was much darker, though. Ah, what a woman she was. A real African beauty."

188

Kesi turned her face away from him, but she knew the damage had been done.

He continued to stare at her, his eyebrows furrowing as a new thought began to form. "Major . . . Don't you think it unusual that a party of British troops should appear here in the middle of the bush, right on our trail?"

"Yes," Rathke said, "I do. Obviously, they found out somehow about our mission. Perhaps the girl knows nothing as she suggests, perhaps not. But that they're here because of us, I think is indisputable."

"How could they have found out?" said Sterne.

"The secret was kept to only a handful," replied the Major. "The Fuhrer himself would have had anyone who revealed it shot . . . he thinks what we are doing is that important. The only feasible explanation I can see is that some communication about our mission was intercepted."

"That's always a possibility, of course," said Sterne. "But think about it. Even if our destination was found out, what could the English make of it? Almost no one knows about Mapungubwe Hill. I could make a fairly short list of those who ever knew anything about the treasure," he mused. "There's myself and Rommel, Hitler and two or three of his most trusted confidants. Then there was King Edward . . . Bertie . . . that traitor who left me to a Boer prison. He suspected there might be a treasure still unfound. And Churchill, of course, if he actually found something, along with the two I buried him with, Aylmer and Zeila." He paused. "Now that's something. If word reached Churchill about where we're going, he'd understand in a moment what we're up to. Yes! By God. It has to be that bastard, Churchill. He sent the troops, and he knows what we're after!"

Kesi stared into the fire. She was frightened. Sterne was edging much too close to the truth.

"And that leads us to one other rather strange coincidence," he said, looking at Kesi again. "This young woman here claims to be only a guide. But she's a guide who knows the way to Mapungubwe. And she's also a guide who bears an uncanny resemblance to Zeila, one of those on our short list of people who knew about the treasure."

She couldn't hold still any longer. "I don't understand what you're saying. That I look like some African woman you knew forty years ago? How many African women do you know? I thought we all looked alike to you, just as you *mzungus* all look the same to us."

Major Rathke had been listening to Lord Sterne with one ear and the distant wailing with the other. Now he said, "You're suggesting she looks like this Zeila woman you once knew. But you said Zeila was black as soot. The only way this woman could be related to her would be if she mated with a very light-skinned African."

"Or a white man," said Sterne, absently. He yawned, suddenly tired. "It's a puzzle, but I'll sleep on it. The answer will come to me. In the meantime, nothing has changed. We still know the British troops are here because we are." He stood up, stared lingeringly at Kesi one more time, then disappeared into his tent.

Kesi felt a wave of relief but also knew it would only be a matter of time before Sterne put two and two together. The idea that the Prime Minister of England had a Negro daughter was so preposterous that it made the final connection difficult to see.

It was a beautiful, clear night, with the stars so close it felt as though she could reach up and touch them. She knew Martin was out there somewhere, looking up at those same stars and planning her rescue. It was a comforting thought.

Rathke stood up, threw several more sticks on the fire and then motioned for her to get up. He took her hand and led her into his tent. "I don't know if you're who you say you are or not," he said. "But I'll keep you close."

He tied a rope tightly around her wrist and then secured the other end to the center pole of the tent. She'd have to sleep on the tent floor beside the Major's cot. He laid out two blankets for her, watched her lie down and then removed his boots and lay on the cot. In a few minutes, he was asleep, snoring softly and regularly.

She lay uncomfortably on the ground, which was cold even through her blankets. She was living on borrowed time. If Sterne ever made the final connection that Winston Churchill was her father, he might well order her killed simply to spite the British leader.

She lay quietly for an hour, listening to the Major breathe. He slept soundly. Clearly, little troubled the dreams of Nazi slumber. The camp outside was quiet, the men all asleep except for the two guards she'd seen.

Ever so slowly, she turned over on her side. She slid the rope that tied her securely to the tent post down until it touched the earth. Then she tried to lift the post up high enough to allow her to slip the rope underneath it. After several tries, she gave up. The post was too heavy and securely set. Next she tried to untie the binds themselves, but the Major had used an elaborate set of knots and pulled them very tight. She was unable to loosen them with only one hand to work with.

Finally, she began to dig out the dirt around the base of the pole. First she dug all around the pole down to a depth of several inches. Then she loosened the soil directly under the pole, removing it a handful at a time. With the pole now resting in the hole, she had decreased the amount of tension sufficiently to enable her to raise it just high enough to slip her rope beneath it. She was free.

She lay still, listening to the Major's even breaths. Then she crawled on her hands and knees to the tent door and looked out. The fires had died down considerably, which made her suspect that the guards, who were supposed to continually feed them against the lions, had probably dozed off at their posts.

She slipped out of the tent and, keeping low to the ground in case any of the troops chanced to open their eyes, crept through the camp, passing only feet from the sleeping men. Finally, she reached the edge of the firelight. She felt safe enough now to stand and begin to move forward onto the veldt. Her fear of the lions she knew were everywhere was only marginally less than her fear of what would happen if Lord Sterne figured out who she was.

She was thirty feet from the fires when suddenly, looming up in front of her, was a figure out of her worst nightmares. A tall, fierce-looking, black warrior, covered in bones that ringed his neck, wrists and ankles stared at her from only feet away. His hair was piled high on his head and was thick with a shiny, black grease. His body was daubed with white slashes of paint and he held a long bow in one hand.

She screamed at the shock of the sudden encounter and stumbled back from the man. In an instant, the camp was awake with people calling out and running in all directions. The dark warrior melted away as though he'd never been there. Before Kesi could recover from her shock, Major Rathke appeared and grabbed her by the arm.

Lord Sterne came up beside them, holding a pistol in his hand. "What is it?" he said.

"She tried to escape," Rathke said.

"That's not true," Kesi said, desperately. "There was a man . . . a warrior . . . he grabbed me in the tent, covered my mouth and carried me out of the camp. He loosened his grip for a moment once we were clear of the fires and that's when I screamed. He dropped me and ran away."

The two men stared at her. "What did this man look like?" said Sterne, obviously curious at her account.

"He was a warrior of some kind. I didn't recognize the markings. He wore bone decorations all over and was painted with white slashes. They . . . they looked like *human* bones. If I'd been trying to get away why would I have screamed for help?"

"Why indeed?" Lord Sterne repeated. "Human bones you say?" He grabbed a torch from one of the soldiers and walked forward a dozen feet into the bush. After a moment, he stopped and knelt down. "Major, come look at this."

Rathke went over and knelt beside him. Clearly delineated in the soft earth were the bare footprints of what had to have been a quite large man. They disappeared into the gloom.

"Well, I think we have to believe our own eyes," Sterne said. "What do you make of it, Major?"

"Damned if know. But I don't like it one bit. As if we don't have enough to worry about with lions all around, that strange wailing on the wind, British soldiers somewhere out there on our trail, and now we've got African warriors appearing like ghosts out of the dark." He turned to one of his men. "I want the guard doubled and you tell them any man who falls asleep will be put to sleep permanently. You understand?"

"Yes, sir," the man said and rushed to do as ordered.

"I begin to wonder a little, Sterne, if there might be a curse on this place and your treasure," the Major said. He took Kesi by the arm and led her back to his tent.

Sterne stared out into the night, quiet once more after the turmoil. He had to agree with the Major. Too many unexplained things were going on. As he headed back to his own tent, his thoughts turned again to Kesi and her uncanny resemblance to another woman, one whose breast he once briefly held forty years ago. He could still vividly recall the warmth and heaviness of it.

He would sleep on it—long his solution for difficult problems—assuming he was ever allowed to get any sleep in this God-forsaken place.

27.

MARTIN AND MAJOR SANDYS pushed hard through the night, their horses struggling over the difficult terrain. The two men soon left the other, less experienced riders behind. But there was little fear of getting separated. The rut marks of the heavy truck provided an easy trail to follow in the moonlight. They also periodically saw the track marks of the tank. How they were going to overcome a force so much bigger than their own, including tanks, was something Martin refused to dwell upon. Kesi was his only concern. He'd faced long odds before and come out on top. He knew she was counting on him.

Just after dawn, they topped a long, gradual rise and saw the hulking mass of Mapungubwe Hill on the horizon.

"Should be there in a couple of hours," Sandys said. "Not good to arrive in full daylight, though."

Martin knew he was right, but the prospect of waiting around the entire day until dark was simply not something he was willing to do. Anything could happen to Kesi in the next twelve hours. Still, the risk was his to take, not the soldiers.

"You wait for the others to catch up," he said. "I'll scout the Germans' position." He held up a hand as Sandys started to protest. "Don't worry, I'll be careful, but I have to know if Kesi is still alive.

We'll rendezvous at dusk on the far side of the hill. You see where that slightly lower ledge sticks out? It's a hanging plateau attached to the main body of the mountain. It doesn't look like much, but it could be another way to the top."

He left his horse behind. Covering the remaining ground on foot would take a little longer, but he couldn't risk the animal being seen or making some sound. He carried a canteen of water, a few pieces of dried meat, his rifle, his knife and his pistol.

By ten in the morning, he knelt in thick brush twenty feet from the German tents. In circling the encampment, he'd located two sentries. They were well concealed, but this helped him to sneak up on them, and he disposed of them efficiently. The remainder of the camp appeared to be deserted. He could see movement near the base of the stone chimney, and at the top more men were loading something heavy onto a makeshift lift. Gold ingots glinted in the sun. They'd found the treasure, then, and were beginning to remove it, starting with the most valuable portion.

He started to move forward. If Kesi were still alive, she was probably on top. But he stopped as he caught movement out of the corner of his eye. Beyond a stand of baobab trees, partially hidden, was a tank, its crew relaxing on the ground beside the huge machine. He considered what to do. This was a chance to even the odds considerably. He knew if he took out the tank crew, it would advertise his arrival on the scene. But there was really no choice. The tank must be removed from the equation. Besides, once the two sentries were discovered, any hope of surprise would be lost.

He moved cautiously through the brush until he was within a few yards of the tank. Three men sat in the shade, sharing a bottle. He'd have to dispatch them without using his guns to at least avoid immediately alerting everyone on top of the hill.

He placed his firearms on the ground and took out his knife. It seemed a pitiable weapon against a tank crew, but of course, the idea was to keep them from using their advantage. He wished he had a second blade. He could have killed one man by throwing the weapon, then close in immediately, relying on surprise to momentarily stun the Germans, allowing him to dispatch the remaining two in hand-to-hand combat. He had no doubt of his ability to do this. Three men, however, made the odds longer. He could still probably take them, but the fight might last long enough for at least one of them to raise a cry or possibly even get off a shot.

Then he got lucky. One of the men, a big fellow, stood and stretched. He said something to the others and moved away behind a thick stand of scrub, apparently to relieve himself.

The moment he was out of sight, Martin moved with lightning speed. He was on the two remaining men in a moment, killing one instantly with a stab through his windpipe so there was only a gurgling sound. The other barely had time to open his mouth before Rand's hand clamped over it and his blade flashed once, in and out. There'd been virtually no sound at all.

He crept forward until he could see the last man. The German was facing in the opposite direction, urinating. Martin started forward, but something on the ground crunched beneath his boots. The man turned and stared at him. His mouth fell open, the stream of urine stopped abruptly and he took off like a bat out of hell toward the tank where the men had laid their guns. Martin cursed and threw his knife, but the blade was deflected by a tree branch. He charged after the German at full tilt and tackled him just short of his weapon.

The man was powerfully built. He managed a full, looping swing of his fist that Martin only partially blocked. The blow staggered him. The soldier turned toward his comrades and then hesitated, staring at their bodies in disbelief. He started to call out to the soldiers on the hill, but Martin had recovered enough to get an arm around his neck and choke off his cry. They fell over backward together, rolling in the dirt, as Martin's arm closed like a vise around the big man's throat. Slowly, the German stopped struggling until his arms lay limp at his sides.

Martin released him and lay back, taking deep, heaving breaths. No alarm had been given. When he was able, he stood and pulled all three bodies into the deep brush. The lions would have a treat this day. Then he returned to the tank and stood staring at it. It was likely that these three were the only ones who knew how to operate the machine. Still, he couldn't be sure. He had to disable it somehow. There was really only one way to do it with any certainty while also not making a sound. He opened the fuel cap and poured in half a dozen large handfuls of sand.

He retrieved his weapons, cleaning the knife by thrusting it into the earth. Then he spent several minutes peering up at the hill. He counted at least a dozen men working around the lift at the top of the chimney. There must be others at the bottom to unload, though he couldn't see them. There was no way he could get to the top from this side.

Keeping out of the line of sight from the figures on top, he worked his way around to the back side of Mapungubwe. Here the sides were still steep, but he thought he might be able to climb them using the thick brush that grew on the rocky cliffs to pull himself up. It turned into more of an effort than he'd imagined. The crumbling sandstone cliffs were treacherous and several times small bushes he grabbed for support came out by the roots. Once he actually lost his balance because of this and tumbled down nearly ten feet before his hands found something to hold onto. When he finally pulled himself over the edge, he was scratched and torn from head to foot.

But he was on top. He could almost sense that Kesi was close by. The sub-plateau appeared to be deserted as he made his way to the opening between the rocks that led up to the main body of the mountain. He knew what he was doing was foolhardy. He should wait for Sandys and the rest of the men. To move across the hill in broad daylight, where cover was sparse, was asking for trouble, but his need to assure himself as to Kesi's welfare drove him forward.

Using the various depressions and the stone walls that had been built hundreds of years in the past, he crept ever closer to the central plateau. He could see men working, coming out of a hole in the earth, heavily weighted down with a variety of wondrous objects. There didn't appear to be any guards posted, the feeling evidently being that there was no way for anyone to reach the top except via the chimney. He filed the information away—it might prove useful.

He picked a spot slightly higher in elevation than the opening where most of the men were working. He was still thirty yards away but had a clear view of the operations through a hole in a stone wall that gave him perfect cover. He settled back to watch.

The Germans had a virtual assembly line operation. Soldiers came out of the earth carrying baskets of jewels, gold ingots and silver medallions. A number of men had placed necklaces or wristlets of incalculable value around their arms and necks. The abundance of wealth was apparently so great that no one seemed to begrudge the men these trinkets of their own. Each man here would likely come out of the war, win or lose, with substantial personal wealth.

The objects were carried to the lift at the edge of the stone chimney and lowered. The weight of the ingots was so great that no more than a handful could be lowered at one time. It was clear the removal operation would have to go on for days. He counted at least fifty men on top of Mapungubwe, though it was difficult to be certain he wasn't counting the same men more than once. Including those at the bottom of the lift, he estimated a force of at least sixty.

As he watched, a man obviously much older than the others emerged from the hole in the ground. He walked with a stoop, had gray hair and limped slightly. Behind him came a German officer, the only German Martin had seen who still looked relatively clean and fresh. Whoever he was, this fellow was not soiling his own hands. He held what appeared to be a jewel-encrusted spear that he examined with obvious delight.

Suddenly Martin tensed and sat bolt upright as a familiar figure appeared at the entrance to the opening. Kesi. She looked bone-tired and moved away from the entrance and sat on a boulder next to a stone wall. His heart swelled at the sight of her. Not until this moment had he any real reason other than blind hope to think she might be alive.

The German officer, SS by the color of his uniform, crossed over to Kesi and displayed the spear to her. She said nothing, merely looking away. He said something harshly and grabbed a handful of her hair, pulling her head back. It took all of Martin's willpower to keep from bursting down on that scene and breaking the bastard's neck. But he waited. The officer released her, laughed and moved away. As far as Martin was concerned, his fate was sealed.

It was now late afternoon and he realized the work day must soon be over. The soldiers and Kesi would undoubtedly ride the lift down and spend the night in their tents below. Once that happened, they would discover that their tank crew and sentries were missing. All chance of surprise would be lost.

He made his decision. He couldn't wait for Sandys and the rest of the men. The SS officer had retreated to the edge where the gold was being loaded onto the lift. The older man was there too, and the two were engaged in conversation. It was the best chance he would ever have.

Quickly, he moved along the warren of stone walls toward the opening. There were still other soldiers emerging periodically from the ground to deposit their loads on the wheeled carts. But these men appeared beyond tired and hardly glanced up at their sur-roundings. In just minutes, he worked himself up behind the wall where Kesi sat. When he was only a few inches from her, he said in a low voice, "Don't make any sound, my love. We're going to take a little stroll."

She sat bolt upright. "Martin? Oh my God, I knew you'd come. But this is crazy. You're just going to get yourself killed!"

He slipped his hand over the wall and gently squeezed her arm. From their position, they could barely make out the men standing at the lift, whose attention was directed away from them. "You have a better look at the entrance into the ground than I do," he said. "As soon as you see no one about to emerge, I want you to slide back-ward right over the wall. I'll help you. Don't stand all the way up."

He felt her nod. Two soldiers came out of the ground, glanced at Kesi, dropped their loads and turned wearily back again. As soon as they were gone, she slipped over the wall, then followed her husband until they reached the opening leading to the sub-plateau. Here he stopped, put down his rifle and embraced her fiercely.

"Don't squeeze me to death!" she said, but she held onto him out of pure joy.

"Are you all right?" he said. "Did they hurt you?"

"No . . . not really. Martin, what are we going to do? They'll miss me at any moment."

"I know. They aren't going to know what happened to you, but they'll certainly initiate a search at once. We'll wait here to see what happens. If they come this way, we can slip down to the sub-plateau. With any luck, they won't find the entrance to it. If they do, we can still try to escape by climbing down. It's steep, but possible."

"Thank God you came. Did you see that older man? Do you know who he is?"

He shook his head.

"Lord Sterne. The man who buried my father and mother down there in the ground forty years ago. Can you comprehend such a thing? He was so close to figuring out who I am. I knew at any minute it might come to him and then he would have killed me. I know it, if for no other reason than to spite Winston."

"All these years, and he's still after the same thing," Martin said, shaking his head. "Gold. A lifelong fixation. Only this time he's working with the Nazis. An English lord. It's incredible."

Twenty minutes passed and it was beginning to grow dark. They had a clear view of the entire hilltop from where they were. The tired soldiers emerged regularly to deposit their loads. No one noticed that Kesi was no longer on the boulder. Finally, the Major and Lord Sterne began to make their way back. Halfway across the opening, Rathke stopped and stared. He looked in all directions. Kesi was nowhere to be seen. He yelled to Sterne and then ran forward, calling to the men in the cave at the same time.

Rathke climbed up onto the boulder that Kesi had been sitting on and turned all the way around searching for her. He jumped down as the soldiers began to stream out of the hole. He yelled at the men to grab their weapons and begin a search of the plateau. His manner was urgent, but it was clear he didn't believe she could possibly evade them. There was only one way down from the hilltop.

"Time to move to the lower plateau," Martin said.

They crept silently down the narrow opening. He cut some bushes with his knife and piled them up to hide the obvious entrance. Maybe it would be enough. Then they crossed the smaller ledge, skirting the flat rock where Martin had once stared up at a knife blade bent on cutting him open. They crouched at the spot where he'd climbed the plateau. The light was growing dim, and he hoped they wouldn't have to risk a descent unless it was absolutely necessary.

The soldiers called to one another as they continued their search. A few had flashlights and Kesi and Martin could see the beams swinging back and forth.

"They've been digging and hauling all day," she said in a low voice. "They're exhausted. Maybe they won't do a thorough search."

But the beams of light moved ever closer. The men were spread out widely across the plateau. Martin could see one fellow who clearly would come the closest to the entryway. The man seemed poised to enter the narrow depression despite the fact that it looked like it contained nothing but brush.

"Stay here," he said to Kesi, and before she could reply, he was away, running crouched over toward the entrance. The guard was beating at the brush with his rifle and seemed puzzled that pieces were flying off, apparently not attached to the ground at all. Then he brought the flashlight to bear and at once saw the narrow trail. In that instant, Martin stood up and threw his knife, striking the poor, conscientious Nazi full in the chest. The man fell over without a sound.

Martin retrieved his blade, picked up the man's flashlight, and dragged the body out of sight. Then he rearranged the fake bushes and returned to Kesi.

"Do you think they'll miss him?" she said.

"I don't know. It's pretty dark now. They might give up and head down, figuring if they leave a guard at the lift there will be no way for you to escape during the night. There's a chance he won't be missed in the crowd."

But Major Rathke was not in a mood to stop the search until he found Kesi. He was at the forefront now, working his way along the ridge. They watched as the flashlights began to coalesce near the narrow path leading to the sub-plateau.

"It doesn't look good," Martin said. "I think we'd better start down the cliff."

But as they turned to begin the extremely dangerous descent in the dark, there was a sudden rattling of gunfire. They both naturally ducked but then Martin said, "That was too far away. They're not shooting at us."

They heard more fire. It seemed to be coming from the base of the hill. The steady rat-tat-tat of machine guns was now almost continuous. Somehow, a fierce firefight had broken out below.

"It must be Sandys and his commandos," Martin said, excitedly. "We were supposed to rendezvous at dusk. Maybe when he couldn't find me he decided to go after the bastards on his own."

"Look!" Kesi said, pointing up at the searchers. The men were retreating rapidly, their flashlights dipping out of sight one by one.

"They must be going back to the lift to go down and help their comrades. I think we're safe for the time being. But perhaps we can help our boys below. They'll be badly outnumbered."

"What can we do?"

"Come on. We'll tag after them. Maybe we can pick off a few somehow. Never hurts to open up a second front."

They climbed back up to the main plateau from where they could see the Germans with their flashlights coalescing at the lift.

"It only holds three men," Kesi said. "Two minutes down, two more to come back up, another for loading and unloading . . . five minutes per trip. It'll take an hour at least for all of them to descend."

"Your Major will probably leave a few on top to keep an eye out for you."

"He's not *my* Major."

They kept going until they were some forty feet from the lift, then settled down to wait behind one of the stone walls. The device noisily repeated its trip up and down. It actually appeared to be taking longer for each round trip, probably because the truck driver at the bottom who controlled the operation was coming under fire himself.

After nearly an hour, only a handful of men were left. They seemed prepared to stay for the night. The gunfire below tapered off, but every so often another flurry took place. It was impossible to know which side had the upper hand.

"I'm going to put those Nazis to work," Rand said, checking his rifle.

"Not without me," Kesi said. "Give me your pistol."

He hesitated but knew it was hopeless to argue with her. "We'll keep behind this wall all the way down," he said. "See where the stones veer off about ten feet from the lift? We'll make our stand there."

Cautiously, trying to avoid disturbing any loose stones, they took ten minutes to get into position. From so close, they could count the men, who were illuminated by their lantern. There were six. It would be like taking potshots in a shooting gallery.

"All right," he said. "Let 'em have it."

It was an uneven contest. Martin and Kesi were completely invisible to the soldiers whose eyes had adjusted to the light from their lantern, and there was almost no cover at the lift site. In less than a minute all the men but one were dead. The last one hovered behind the slim protection of the lift itself. Martin finally got him with a near perfect shot, and the soldier fell backward against the frame of the lift. The flimsy contraption, weakened by its long day of transporting heavy loads, collapsed. The entire framework tumbled over the cliff and fell to the valley floor with a tremendous crash.

Kesi whistled softly. "Well, that was decisive," she said. "Now what?"

"I guess we're stuck here. Until morning anyway. We should be able to get down from the sub-plateau. It's a hard climb but doable . . . in daylight. Looks like we can't do anything more to help out Sandys, though."

They found supplies of various sorts stored close to the lift. Martin located some food tins, but Kesi took one look at the rank pork and beans and declared that she'd make do with his dried meat. They found an assortment of jackets, shirts and a few blankets left by the men. Kesi piled them all together and made a comfortable place for them to lie down.

They sat watching and listening to the firefight going on far below. It became clear where Sandys and his men were, as all the fire from the Germans was concentrated in one area. The commando weapons also made a different sound from the Nazi machine guns. One by one, the commando positions fell silent.

"Isn't there anything we can do?" Kesi asked.

He was also in anguish, but their friends were hopelessly out of reach. Finally, only one British gun still fired. After a few minutes, it too ceased, and the battle seemed to be over. It was hard to accept that Sandys and all of his men were really gone. They were completely alone now.

"We'll wait till morning and see what the Germans intend to do," Martin said quietly. "They'll have to climb up using ropes now. That means only two or three at a time and they'll be exposed. If we shoot a few, they may give up."

She shook her head. "They'll never give up, Martin. They have orders to get that gold or die trying. The Fuhrer himself handpicked these men. I've watched them, especially the Major and Lord Sterne. They won't stop until they have the gold or they're all dead."

He knew she was right. "There's nothing we can do about it now. Might as well try to get some sleep. We're probably going to need it."

They stretched out together. For a time, they'd both feared they'd never see each other again. Now they touched and held one another close.

"Do you know what I'll regret the most if we don't make it out of here?" Kesi said. "Not getting to know my father better. I still can't quite believe my father is Winston Churchill. If I could have chosen any man in the world to fill that role, I might well have selected him. It's so strange."

"Not at all. He's a great man. Possibly the only man I would have said was worthy enough to be your father . . . but then, I could be biased."

After a while, they made love for perhaps the last time. It was achingly sweet and passionate and familiar. They knew each other so well. Then they slept soundly. Martin woke just before dawn, a lifelong habit he'd formed in the bush. He stood and peered down at the bottom of the cliff. Everything was quiet.

He shook Kesi awake. "Come on," he said. "We'll try to go down the other side before they wake up."

By the time they reached the sub-plateau and had begun to cautiously work their way down, the sun was up. Birds called and floated on warm thermal updrafts, watching the strange intruders disturbing their nesting area.

They were a third of the way down, hanging on to a variety of thorny bushes, when the first shot rang out. The bullet whistled close by Martin's head. The Germans had anticipated them and posted a guard.

"Come on," he cried. "We have to go back up. We're sitting ducks here."

Fortunately, there appeared to be only one soldier shooting at them. Guards must have been placed all the way around the hill. This man was not a very good shot, but they could hear shouts as others ran to join him.

Martin, who was below Kesi, kept pushing her upward so fast she almost felt like she was on a lift of her own. Bullets whistled all around them as they reached the lip of the plateau and pulled themselves out of range. They sprawled, breathing heavily. The birds were now screaming indignities at the noisy interruption of their routine.

"I think," Kesi said, trying to catch her breath, "I'd rather have breakfast first the next time you decide to do something like this."

"Looks like we've got all the time in the world for breakfast now." He crawled to the edge and peered down. Several men had begun to climb up, while others crouched, prepared to offer covering fire. "Damn! They're coming up. Unless I miss my guess, the Major will have more men climbing up using the handholds on the chimney."

"Then we're surrounded." She looked at him. The depths of her feelings for her husband overwhelmed her. She knew he'd fight until he was killed before he would surrender her to the Germans. They were both as good as dead.

Martin sat reloading his rifle. "We'll take some of them with us," he said.

Suddenly, she put her hand on his arm. "No! I have a better idea. Come on." She jumped up and began to run toward the main plateau. He had no choice but to follow. He caught up with her as they emerged onto the main hill.

"What are we doing?" he said.

"We'll go into the caverns. My mother told me all about them, what a maze it is down there. We can at least hide. And there's a way out, the same way she and Winston escaped. We may never find it, but at least it's a chance. More of one than we have out here."

They reached the opening and slipped inside just as the first soldiers scrambled over the edge by the broken lift. Martin pulled out the flashlight he'd taken from the soldier dispatched at the entrance to the sub-plateau.

"I don't think they saw us come in here," Kesi said.

"Good. With luck, they'll spend hours looking for us before someone figures out where we went."

He aimed the small beam of light into the gloom ahead, and they began to move downward, past the glimmering, painted images of African natives and wildlife, into the deep caverns of Mapungubwe Hill.

28.

SIR DAVID PETRIE, MI5 Intelligence Chief, examined the directive in his hands for the tenth time. Not a word had changed from the first nine times he'd read it. He rubbed his forehead in frustration. It was sheer madness. Yet who was willing to tell that to the Prime Minister? It fell to him, and he did not relish the task.

Churchill had requested that two British destroyers, H.M.S. *Blackmore* and H.M.S. *Anthony,* be placed at his disposal. The ships were already en route from India across the Indian Ocean to East Africa, where the British leader planned to rendezvous with them via his personal plane. The Prime Minister intended to direct operations revolving around the mission to Mapungubwe Hill personally. The trip would take the Prime Minister from London to Gibraltar to Cairo to Addis Ababa and finally to Mombasa. Sir David felt ill. Churchill had always been a hands-on leader. His wartime travels were legendary. Already he'd been to the battle fronts of Africa, to Turkey, Malta, Athens, Moscow and many other locations. He'd logged over 100,000 miles since the outbreak of the war. The man considered himself a tactical expert. It was something Sir David couldn't deny, but the folly of risking the leader of the free world on a mission the size of this one was beyond ludicrous. There had to be some other reason for Churchill to insist on the action, but Petrie was damned if he could figure out what.

He arranged a meeting with the Prime Minister, the volatility of which they could both well anticipate. He arrived at No. 10 and was shown into the PM's private office. Before he could utter a word, Churchill said, "This is a bunch of tosh, Petrie. My mind is made up."

Petrie stared at him for a moment, then sat across from his desk.

"I'm sorry, Sir, but I can't accept this decision. It is absolute folly. Put one of your top aides in charge or give it to the military intelligence services. They have plenty of experienced field operators. You put the entire outcome of the war at risk—millions of lives could be affected by this action."

"I'm not that important," Churchill said gruffly. "You speak of military intelligence? No one else knows the situation like I do or has the personal understanding of what we are dealing with. I've been to Mapungubwe. I understand what this gold could mean to the Third Reich and to the war effort. The rest of my staff hardly believe what I've told them. It's clear to me I can't leave something this important to anyone else. You say millions of lives are at stake? So they are, if this bloody war is extended, or God help us, lost."

"I believe you overstate the import of the mission, Sir," Petrie said. "It's just one more commando action out of hundreds. Do I have to say those words again? Commando action. Pardon me, Sir, but you're no spring chicken. You'd be the weak link in any operation and might well put that mission at risk."

"I won't argue this any more, Petrie. My mind is made up. Need I remind you that I am both Prime Minister and Minister for Defense. The decision is mine. I have to be there. Precisely because you and all the others don't really believe there could be such a treasure. I've seen it, and it will alter the outcome of the war. This mission is as vital as D-Day."

Petrie looked away in frustration. There was no arguing with the Prime Minister when he was in this sort of mood. "How long will you be away?" he said, resigned.

"I'll be gone two weeks—in and out—it will be surgical."

"Whose surgery is what worries me," said the MI5 Chief. "May I have a week to arrange your transport and put out the usual misdirections as to your whereabouts?"

"I leave tomorrow," Churchill said. "I've made my own travel arrangements. You may handle the other however you wish."

* * *

True to his word, Winston left for Gibraltar the next day. He flew in his new Avro York, a conversion from the Lancaster Bomber. The journey took three full days of flying. Coordinating the plane's stops across the war-torn Mediterranean theater had not been easy, but late on the second day, he landed at an airport outside Mombasa. He transferred to a launch, which took him directly to one of the destroyers. The former First Lord of the Admiralty knew all the ins and outs of getting around the navy.

Sir David did what he could. He issued a communiqué via sources known to be compromised in which he discussed the Prime Minister's intention to take a vacation in Scotland. Daily notices would also appear in all the papers outlining Churchill's schedule, including long country walks on the moors and private get-togethers with family and friends. With luck, no one would suspect the real location of Britain's wartime leader. It was all the intelligence chief could do, and it was precious little.

* * *

Winston steadied himself and jumped from the heaving launch to the gangway of the Destroyer H.M.S. *Blackmore*. A seaman grabbed onto him but was brushed away, as Churchill pulled himself up to the main deck. He wore a white navy uniform, his head bare and the traditional cigar planted firmly in his mouth. As the ship's loudspeaker blasted *Rule Britannia*, Winston shook the hand of Captain Edwin P. Nevins and gave a salute to the cheering sailors. Then he disappeared, climbing directly to the bridge.

"A fine day for sailing," he said. "Thank you for having me aboard, Captain."

"A pleasure, Sir," the Captain replied, completing the fantasy that it was not Winston himself who had invited Winston aboard. Captain Nevins was a good naval officer, one of the youngest captains in His Majesty's service, and he was an admirer of the former First Lord of the Admiralty. For all that, no captain in his right mind relished the prospect of having a power superior to his own on board. It could only lead to trouble.

The ship's commander had been forewarned about Churchill's arrival and was already carrying out orders to conduct a search for a specific enemy vessel, but beyond that the captain remained in the dark. To his mind, it was rank folly to risk the Prime Minister's life by placing him directly in the theater of war, albeit the somewhat less active one of the western Indian Ocean. "We've established communications with our two submarines in the area, Mr. Prime Minister."

"Good!" Winston said. "Have they located the German freighter?"

"Nothing definite, sir. They're watching three vessels at the moment that might be prospects. There's no way to know, however, without boarding them. For that, we need your direct order, since they are all flying under neutral flags."

"I want to be kept informed of all communiqués, Captain, and all tracking procedures." He stared out the window. "She's out there somewhere, and by God we'll find her. Have you had any radio contacts from Major Sandys and his commandos?"

"Two days ago, we received a message from the Major. They'd been attacked by the Nazi force and suffered some casualties, but were continuing on to Mapungubwe. The contact was sporadic and weak but the impression we got was that they were considerably outnumbered."

Churchill grunted. What had he sent Kesi and Martin into? "All right, Captain. Show me the way to your radio control. I intend to live there."

* * *

Winston stood alone on the open deck and stared out to sea. The ocean was immutable. He'd always felt a visceral attachment to it. Everything in life eventually made its way to the sea. He had once intended his own ashes to go there some day. But he now knew his body would be demanded by his countrymen for the pomp and ceremony of a ritualized burial and interment.

Since his only meeting with Kesi, he'd been astonished by the intense feelings boiling up within him. The memories of Zeila and their moment of passion deep under Mapungubwe Hill still hung vividly in his thoughts. That something so wonderful as another human being had come of it thrilled him. And the more he thought of Kesi, the more he regretted his decision to send her off on such a dangerous mission. What if he never saw her again? It was an inconceivable thought.

Zeila had sent her only daughter to him. She would have known Kesi would feel a need to seek him out once she learned the story of her own incredible beginnings. What could he ever say to Zeila if Kesi were to die horribly at the hands of the Nazis?

"Bugger all!" he cried out loud to the wind, his hands gripping the rail until they turned white. He'd come here because he truly believed what he'd told Sir David about the import of the mission and his own personal knowledge of the situation. War was sacrifice. He preached this to the nation every chance he got. Yet there was no denying in his innermost thoughts that he was here, too, to be prepared in case the time came when he could do something to help Kesi and Martin.

His sense of helplessness drove him to despair. He was one of the most powerful men on earth, but he didn't know where Kesi and Martin were or even if they were alive or dead. He turned away and made his way once again to the radio room.

29.

"INCREDIBLE!" Martin stared at the images of Roman and African cultures, blended together in a rich montage of daily life. Even as they moved quickly down the halls and into the huge cavern of the priests, he felt a part of something extraordinary.

"Hard to believe we were so close to this twenty years ago and didn't suspect any of it," he said. "It's not simply a treasure . . . This is a wealth that needs to be studied by scholars. There's a part of history here we know almost nothing about. Mapungubwe Hill could become one of the great tourist destinations of the world, rivaling the pyramids."

"You haven't even seen the burial rooms yet," said Kesi. "It's absolute madness to think of it all being plundered for gold to pay for still more Nazi murder." She paused to catch her breath. They stood surrounded by the circle of pedestals holding the ruby-eyed soapstone birds.

Martin picked up one of the magnificent carved figurines and ran his fingers over the enormous ruby eyes.

"Listen!" Kesi said, putting a hand on his arm. There were shouts coming from the entrance. "Turn off your light."

He flicked the light off and they were plunged into darkness. He could feel the walls closing in on them. What must it have been like five hundred or a thousand years ago, coming down here to toil for months, maybe years, carving burial rooms out of the soft sandstone, working by the light of smoking torches? How many died here? Did they do it as slaves or were they willing participants, expecting their reward in the next life?

"Come," Kesi said, taking his hand in the dark. "I think I can find the ladder that leads to the burial cave. It lies just ahead. The Nazis attached a fixed iron ladder to the cliff wall to speed up their looting."

They moved forward, stumbling over the rocks and boulders that constituted the ramp that had collapsed eons ago. Glancing back, they could just detect the smallest flicker in the darkness. Men with lights were working their way down from the hallways above.

"Here it is!" she said in a whisper. "I'm going up."

He climbed quickly behind her. At the top, he risked the flashlight for a moment to orient themselves, then they moved forward into the cave, turning several times as corridors branched off until they were certain they were deep enough inside that their light wouldn't show. Then he turned the flashlight on and stifled a cry as the first thing the beam focused upon was the gruesome, tortured face of a stuffed Pygmy just a few feet in front of him.

"Mother of God! That's worse than any nightmare I've ever had."

Kesi, who'd already seen the Pygmies, continued forward. "Take a look around," she said. "It may be the only chance you'll ever have."

He pivoted his light about the room they were in, picking out gold and jewels and baskets laden with wonderful things. He saw the bodies of the two royal figures, dried and wizened, yet still retaining, somehow, part of their majesty. Much of the richness had been disturbed as the Nazis searched for only the most valuable and easily moved items. Baskets of precious stones were tipped, their contents spilled across the floor. Polished and intricate pieces of exquisite furniture had been thrust aside and broken in the Germans' haste to locate the real valuables.

"They'll be here quickly," she said. "They know their way around down here better than either of us. We have to keep moving . . .

go deeper." She shuddered. "Can you imagine what it must have been like for Zeila and Winston down here with no source of light? Surrounded by all of this, certain they were going to die. What a horrible place to be conceived in."

"I don't know. I'd say there was something rather magnificent about it . . . that they actually managed to connect with each other, if only for a few moments, in such a place. No wonder it affected your father so deeply."

There were more cries behind them, closer now, echoing through the cavern.

"They're in the chamber of the priests," Martin said. "Come on."

He led the way through a maze of passages. Always they went lower, the halls growing narrower, the floors damp with subterranean runoff. They left the wall paintings and mosaics far behind. Still, they could hear the sounds of men pursuing them.

Once, they took a side passage that seemed to double back and then deposit them abruptly into a higher chamber where suddenly the voices of men were louder. Martin turned off their light and they backed into a tiny cul-de-sac that turned out to be a small burial chamber. Half a dozen decayed bodies shared the space with them as they huddled, listening to heavy footsteps that pounded back and forth. The Germans were being thorough, exploring every passage.

Two men passed their side chamber, shadows from their lights flickering ominously as they went by. Then one man returned, apparently curious about the small cul-de-sac. As he turned his flash into the opening, Martin grabbed his arm, pulled him in and dispatched him silently with his knife. He picked up the man's light and pistol and gave them to Kesi. After a few moments, the German's companion returned, wondering what had happened to his friend.

The soldier approached the chamber, but before he could look in, there was a loud cry from farther off. Suddenly, the entire mountain seemed to explode with noise. There were cries of alarm, guns firing and heavy boots running. It was impossible to tell where it was all coming from. Sound echoed through the myriad passageways. The German looked alarmed at the outcry. He called out for his friend, then hurriedly moved past their tiny burial room.

Major Rathke stood at the entrance to the subterranean burial chamber, directing the soldiers. Once a dozen of the Germans had made the climb to the top of Mapungubwe, they crafted a rope sling and hauled Lord Sterne, who was too old to make the difficult climb, up the cliffs. The handful of dead soldiers lying beside the ruins of the lift was proof enough that Kesi hadn't simply wandered away or attempted to try to escape on her own. Someone was helping her.

Even as the men spread out across the hill and eventually met up with their counterparts who'd climbed up the back side, Rathke gravitated to the chamber. Almost intuitively, he realized there was only one avenue of escape for Kesi and that was into the underground. As the men returned, the Major sent them into the darkness in teams of two and three with orders not to come out until they found Kesi and whomever was with her. The risks of getting lost were somewhat ameliorated by the sheer numbers of soldiers. With at least fifteen separate search parties, it was unlikely any of them would be out of shouting distance of the others, no matter how intricate the maze below. Indeed, the bigger danger was that they might mistake one another for the enemy and fire blindly.

Lord Sterne, pistol in one hand and flashlight in the other, stood beside Rathke. He was agitated. "This is a waste of time," he said. "The girl doesn't matter. We need to rebuild the lift and get the gold out."

But the Major was fixated on Kesi, furious that she'd deceived him. When he caught her, he'd decided he would show her a thing or two. And besides, he rationalized, they couldn't allow enemies to remain undetected in their midst. "I'm in charge of military matters here," he said. Then he waved a hand. "Take six men if you want and put them to work on the lift. I'll direct the search until the woman is caught."

Sterne stared at the Major for a moment longer. The Nazi would obviously do what he wanted. It was the nature of the beast. He turned abruptly, pointed to several men to accompany him, and left for the ruins of the lift.

Rathke joined the last team of soldiers and headed into the chamber. It was a surreal world. German soldiers were everywhere, their heavy boots and shouts echoing through the vast network of corridors and caverns. Lights flickered, forming shadows that seemed like living things. It was impossible to make sense of any of it. The Major directed any groups he came upon to go lower into the maze, certain that that would be Kesi's only chance of avoiding them.

After an hour, the Major found himself deep inside the mountain. The cries of other men were more distant now. He moved forward with three soldiers, checking each side passage and burial cul-de-sac.

One of his men yelled, "In here, Major!"

He joined the soldier in a tiny burial hole and stared as the man played his light over the body of one of the Germans. Rathke knelt and examined the corpse. The man's throat had been neatly sliced open and he lay in a pool of his own blood.

"All right," he said, standing up. "He hasn't been dead long. Continue searching." He led the way down a steep incline and very nearly walked over a drop-off that disappeared into the darkness below. Aiming their lights into the hole, they couldn't see the bottom. As they stood contemplating the obstacle, they heard a distant scream that seemed to emanate from higher up in the maze of corridors.

Suddenly, there were other shouts and the sound of guns firing. Rathke and his men backtracked and headed toward the sounds. They climbed up through several corridors until they came upon a group of soldiers cowering in a dead-end passage. The men very nearly fired at them before realizing who it was. They were almost catatonic with fear.

"What the hell's going on?" Rathke said, grabbing the nearest man by the collar. The poor fellow stared at him blankly but pointed to the floor a few feet away. Rathke saw two dead soldiers lying on the ground. One had an arrow sticking out of the center of his chest. The other figure seemed foreshortened somehow, until the Major realized the man's head had been neatly cut off and was lying on the ground separate from his body.

In spite of himself, the Major gave a shudder as he looked at the dead men in front of him. There was no way Kesi had done this, alone or otherwise. They weren't the only ones down here.

* * *

"What's happening?" Kesi said.

Martin shook his head. "They're shooting at something. I don't know what. At least it's not us."

They moved back out into the main corridor and began walking forward tentatively. Shots continued to echo above them but there didn't seem to be any sounds coming from below. That was the direction they had to go.

His flashlight was beginning to show signs of getting weaker. Soon it provided barely enough light to reveal the ground at their feet. He took the spare light they'd taken from the man he'd killed and they continued on. Neither of them wanted to contemplate what would happen once this last light gave out. In total darkness, they couldn't hope to find a way out of this hellhole.

A narrow passage came in from the left. It seemed to continue down but in a slightly less steep manner. They decided to take it, but after a few minutes, it began to ascend again.

"We can't go up," Martin said. "We'll have to go back to the other passageway."

But as they turned to start back, they heard the sounds of men approaching. Martin looked around frantically for someplace to hide. Just above their heads was a series of small openings that must have been burial chambers for servants or other lesser figures in the Mapungubwe hierarchy.

"Up there," he said in a whisper. He boosted Kesi up and into one of the holes. Then he pulled himself up and they backed farther inside, kicking something behind them which felt uncomfortably like bones that cracked like match sticks. Kesi almost choked at the sound, but they were finally able to get their heads out of sight. Martin moved his rifle up beside him, ready if he needed it.

The footsteps of the Germans were almost upon them now. Except it didn't sound like the Germans. Instead of the heavy pounding of leather boots, they heard a softer pattering. Instead of anxious cries in German, they heard only the steady breathing of men exerting themselves. As the sound grew close, they raised their heads just enough to see who or what was passing. What they saw set their hearts to thundering.

A half dozen warriors, naked black bodies slathered with white slash marks, bone ringlets hanging from their arms, wrists and necks, and carrying long, lethal blades and bows and arrows trotted barefooted past their chamber. The men looked like some strange sort of demons flashing past. They carried no torch, yet somehow Martin and Kesi could still see them. The warriors said nothing, only moved quickly and with a sense of purpose. Once they'd passed, Kesi and Martin realized they hadn't taken a breath in half a minute.

"My God!" Kesi said. "Is it possible? They're still here . . . the Nubian guards? After all these years?"

"Maybe not Nubians," he replied. "And I doubt the few we killed twenty years ago even fazed them. They've been doing this for thousands of years. I won't soon forget what that warrior said to me as he was about to slit my throat. He said they were sacred warriors. *Takatifu Wapigani.* As near as I can determine, it's some sort of religious cult that has taken on the mission of protecting Mapungubwe. Their members seem to be spread throughout East Africa, with a virtually inexhaustible supply of young warriors willing to take on this gruesome business."

She shuddered. "I doubt your tourist industry at Mapungubwe Hill will ever happen," she said. "I don't think watching the happy natives is going to be a real attraction." She put her head on Martin's shoulder and closed her eyes, but the image of the fierce warriors remained fixed in her head. "I don't understand how we were able to see them," she said. "They had no torches."

"I know. It's pretty strange." He brought one hand up and gently stroked her cheek. "We're going to get out of this, I promise you." He buried his face in her hair. "With Germans and the Clan of the

Bow both running around, I think we're probably safest right here for a while."

So they lay side by side in the stygian darkness, afraid to use their light, aware whenever they moved of the splintering bones of whomever this space belonged to for all of eternity. They hoped it would not soon belong to them for the same time period.

30.

WINSTON PEERED through the binoculars that he somehow managed to hold up to his eyes without interfering with the cigar that puffed away furiously beneath them.

"You're sure she's the one?" he said, staring at the small freighter anchored in a bay, partially hidden by a long spit of rock.

"We can't be sure of anything till we board her," said Captain Nevins. "But she's the only one our submarines have tracked that's at anchor. The other two have moved on up the coast and are no longer considered likely suspects. This one hasn't moved since she was first sighted. And it's a pretty strange place for a freighter to drop anchor. No port, secluded location. Not likely to be patrolled by local militia, even if they have any in these parts, which I doubt. Weather's fine, so she's not trying to avoid high seas. Only other reason to be here would be if she was having some sort of engine trouble."

Winston grunted, considering how best to proceed. If this *was* the German boat, it might make sense to stay out of sight and just watch her. Sooner or later, Sterne and company would have to return. On the other hand, if it wasn't the right boat, then they'd waste valuable time and do Kesi and Martin no good at all. He gripped the rail, frustrated. It was his nature to do *something*.

"Prepare a boarding party," he said at last.

"Are you sure? She's not going anywhere. Maybe we should observe her for a while."

"There's no bloody time," said Winston. "If she's the wrong one, we need to get on with it." He put the binoculars down and buttoned up the flap of his coat. "I'll go along," he said.

Captain Nevins looked aghast. "I don't recommend that, sir. You might be boarding a ship full of Nazis. If you were to be captured . . . well, I wouldn't want to have to admit to my grandchildren that I was the one responsible for handing Winston Churchill over to Hitler's blackboots."

"I give you complete absolution, Captain," Winston said with a straight face.

The destroyer approached from the freighter's stern just in case she was some sort of Q-ship, an enemy craft disguised as a harmless trawler but actually carrying hidden deck guns. Several attempts to contact her via radio and bullhorn proved futile.

"She looks like a bleeding ghost ship," said the captain. "Hard to believe they'd leave no one on board."

"Especially if they intended to use her to evacuate the gold," said Winston. "Unless . . . she's meant to be a decoy."

The captain raised an eyebrow. "You think they would do that?"

"That boat's presence here has already delayed us while we discuss what to do about her. They might well expect us to simply keep her under observation until something happened. That could keep us locked up here indefinitely, while they rendezvous with another ship. Do I think the Nazis are capable of being that devious? You bugger-all bet I do!"

As dusk came on, the *Blackmore's* launch was lowered and sixteen armed sailors, the ship's security chief and the Prime Minister of England motored off.

"Look at him," said the captain incredulously to his first mate, "Like he's on a cruise up the Thames to Greenwich."

"More balls than brains," said the officer flippantly. But then he gulped and shut up as he remembered who it was he was talking about. It was Winston's "damn the torpedoes" mentality, after all, that had given so much spark to England in this war. The entire nation revered the man precisely because they knew he had both brains *and* balls.

The launch pulled alongside the *Coast Princess* and her crew tied off to a gangway that hung down, a few feet above the water, yet another sign that all was not as it seemed on this vessel.

With half the sailors training their arms on the deck, the other half climbed aboard. Winston was right beside them, carrying a cigar as his only weapon. The men kept a tight circle around the Prime Minister. They weren't about to let anything happen to him on their watch.

But it took only a few minutes to determine they were the only ones on board. Winston climbed to the bridge and looked around. There were a few personal items, coffee mugs, foul weather gear, cigarettes, but no men.

The security chief climbed a set of metal steps to the bridge and stuck his head in the door. "You better come see this, sir," he said to Churchill.

Winston followed the man down to one of the lower decks. It had been fitted out with sleeping quarters for at least a hundred men, an extremely unusual setup for a freighter trying to maximize her cargo capacity. This boat was obviously being used to transport people as well as freight, and the size of the possible enemy contingent caused Winston to once again fear he'd sent his daughter off on a desperate mission against fearsome odds. As he walked down the rows of cots, staring glumly at the empty beds, the chief said, "There's more, sir."

Again Winston followed him down, deeper into the bowels of the ship. At the far end of the main hold, the chief stopped. "No freight on board, sir, which makes me suspect they planned to pick up cargo, not deliver it . . ." He stepped a few feet farther along. "This is what I wanted to show you." He pointed to the floor.

Winston leaned over to see what the security chief was indicating. On the floor of the hold, midst the normal debris and refuse, he saw the clear impressions of a tank track. His eyes followed the track marks all the way to the main cargo door, where they halted abruptly.

"Sweet Jesus!" he said in a low voice. They were using tanks to defend, and probably to help transport, the treasure. What had he gotten Kesi into?

"I don't understand," he said to no one in particular. "Why would they simply drop anchor and leave the boat here?"

"It's got to be a decoy, sir," said the security chief.

"Perhaps," Winston said. "Though there's one other possibility."

"Sir?

"The Germans left to make their push inland. But maybe whomever they put in charge of the freighter got nervous waiting around here like a sitting duck and simply took off, abandoning the ship."

"If that's the case," the Chief said, "Then the Nazis might still be planning to rendezvous back here once they secure the gold. We could wait around, maybe even put our own men on board and surprise them when they return."

"It's an idea," said Winston. "But the Germans must be in radio contact with the ship. When they get no reply, they're going to be suspicious."

"Suspicious or not, if they have no other way to get the gold out, they're simply going to have to come back and see what happened to their ship."

"So it would seem, Chief. So it would seem."

When they returned to the ship, Captain Nevins met Churchill as he came over the side. "We're in contact with Major Sandys, Sir. You should come to the radio room immediately."

Inside, Winston reached for the operator's headphones.

"They're at Mapungubwe," said the radio man. "Under attack from a much larger force." He hesitated. "It doesn't look good, Sir."

Winston swore, then raised a hand for silence. "Sandys?" he said. "Are you there?"

The reply seemed far away, the signal weak, but he recognized the Major's voice.

"Yes. Who is this?" said the voice.

"Winston Churchill."

There was a moment of silence, during which Winston could hear sporadic gunfire.

"Say again," said the Major.

"It's the Prime Minister, Major. What's your situation?"

"Sir . . . Sir, we are badly outnumbered. Only three of us left. We're surrounded at the base of Mapungubwe Hill."

"Sandys . . . Are Martin and Kesi with you?"

"No," came the faraway voice. "Kesi was captured. Martin went to rescue her. He was supposed to rendezvous with us here, but we've been unable to find him."

There was a flurry of gunshots, men shouting. The radio contact went in and out, as though whomever was handling the device kept diverting his attention to the conflict.

"What's happening, Major?" Winston shouted.

Sandys's voice came on again, weaker. "My men are all dead, Sir. I've been wounded. They're closing in. I'm sorry I failed you . . . and England, Mr. Prime Minister."

"Sandys? Sandys? Listen to me. Your nation will not forget you and your men, for all the missions you've carried out. I promise you."

The line went dead.

31.

MAJOR RATHKE organized the men he had into a compact group. There were ten of them, including himself. He placed two men with lights in front and two more facing the rear. Each group was supported by three men who would concentrate their fire in each direction as they moved along the passageways.

He'd all but forgotten about Kesi. Let whomever was murdering people down here take care of her too. His only goal now was to get out of this maze alive.

They moved slowly and quietly, listening as hard as they could while staring into the blackness beyond the reach of their lights. Rathke kept them moving upward at every branch. He no longer had a clear picture of where they were and there was no sound from the other groups of soldiers wandering around somewhere down here. Either they, too, were unwilling to advertise their positions, or they were already dead.

"There! What's that?" One of the men said in a hoarse, terrified whisper.

The little formation stopped, as they all strained to see down the hall in front of them.

"I tell you, I saw something move down there," he said.

Then they heard a faint whispering sound as an arrow came flying down the passage and buried itself with a thud in the chest of one of the lead gunners. The soldier fell to the ground and lay still.

Every man in the group turned his gun down the hallway and sprayed a long burst of fire into the dark. The corridor flickered with the ricochets of bullets off the walls, the sound deafening in the enclosed space. The shooting went on for almost twenty seconds before Rathke could finally get them to stop.

"Turn off the lights!" he shouted, and they were thrust into darkness. Several of the soldiers cursed, their fear palpable.

"Shut up!" Rathke said, "Listen. Try to hear something."

They were silent for several long minutes, but there was no sound.

"Maybe we got him," said one of the men hopefully.

"Assuming there was only one," said another.

"Easy, now," Rathke said. "Remember . . . you're SS, Germany's finest. We're not going to let some damn darkie with a bow and arrow scare us."

But it was clear they couldn't just sit there in the blackness. They had to have the lights in order to continue. Finally, Rathke ordered one light in front and one in back. When they came on, the soldiers cringed visibly. They were sitting ducks and they knew it.

"Move ahead," said the Major. They began to walk slowly forward. The soldiers bunched together, almost as if they felt a certain safety with their comrades close around them, offering at least the illusion of cover.

They reached the end of the corridor where there was another branch. Again, Rathke selected the branch that led upward. No one commented that they had obviously not hit anyone with their shots. No bodies. No blood. Whomever or whatever had killed one of them was still out there.

They continued on past numerous small burial alcoves. As the last soldier in line passed one of these, there was a wet, rasping sound. Rathke turned back at once and shined his light on the man. His head had been nearly severed by some kind of blade. The next two men in line shoved their weapons into the tiny alcove and fired bursts of their guns. Then Rathke played his light into the tiny space. There was clearly no place that a man could have hidden. It was as if a ghost had killed their friend.

"We're all going to be killed down here!" one of the soldiers cried. His words only affirmed what every one of them, including the Major, was now beginning to contemplate.

"Quiet!" Rathke ordered. Despite his own fear, he knew if he lost control of the men they'd have no chance at all. "Move out . . . that way!" He indicated the rising passage. "Give the men on the right and left sides of the corridors flashlights. If we pass any more side chambers, shine your lights into them and be prepared to fire."

They continued on, a human train passing through an endless tunnel, with lights at the front, back and sides and men holding onto one another like separate rail cars connected fore and aft.

They turned down several more passageways. The Major had never felt more lost in his life. The only method to their progress was to move upward whenever possible. At one point, they froze as they heard distant shots being fired. A furious firefight was going on somewhere. The shots echoed through the cavern and it was impossible to tell even if the sound was above or below them.

By now, they were all so spooked that their fingers rested on the triggers of their weapons ready to loose a barrage at the slightest provocation. After turning into yet another passage, they heard the familiar whispering sound and the man holding the lead flashlight crumpled, an arrow lodged through his neck. Again they fired blindly down the corridor to no effect. From then on, each time they came to a branch, Rathke ordered the lights turned off and the men fired volleys down the dark corridor ahead.

The mystery of who their attackers were was paralyzing. How could anyone move through this black maze without the use of lights? So far, they'd seen nothing except arrows and the bodies of their own men. But then they got lucky. Upon extinguishing the lights as they approached a new hallway, they fired into the dark and heard a cry. The men cheered their first success against their invisible foe.

Rathke and two men edged round the corner and moved forward toward something lying on the ground. When they reached it, they played the light over the figure and stared in stunned silence.

"What is it?" yelled one of the men left behind.

"Come forward," Rathke said, and the rest of the men joined them.

The Major knelt by the body and rolled it onto its back. There was a collective gasp. It was a huge black man, naked, his body painted with white slash marks. Strings of bones encircled his neck, wrists and ankles. A series of unusual tattoos lined the tops of his shoulders. The man's eyes were wide open in death and here in what felt like the middle of the Earth, he could have been a demon straight from hell.

Rathke said, "There's your ghost. Just a man with nothing more than a bow and arrow against our guns. And obviously he can be killed."

"But why are they doing this?" said one of the soldiers.

"Forget that," said another, "How *many* are doing this?"

There were no answers. But at least they'd seen the enemy. It was a close call, however, which was worse, the mystery of ghosts in the darkness or this frightening-looking warrior lying on the ground in front of them.

"Let's move," Rathke said. "We're getting out of here. I think I recognize this corridor. If I'm right, we're not far from the royal burial chambers and from there it's only a few minutes out the cave, through the cavern of the priests and back to the surface. Keep your heads and we'll get out of this yet."

32.

LORD STERNE had put his time to good use. Quickly realizing the lift was unrepairable, he had the men reinforce the rope sling as their only way to descend. It wouldn't be feasible for transporting the gold, however, and he was determined to get as much gold out as possible. A large quantity of the ingots had been carried to the surface and stockpiled at the lift site. He directed the men to heave the heavy bricks over the side.

It took two men to lift each ingot and cast them into the void, the seventy-pound weights plummeting to the bottom of the chimney with enormous crashes. Many would be lost in the dense undergrowth at the base of the plateau, but that couldn't be helped.

Once all the stockpiled ingots were dropped, Sterne led them back to the temple opening where additional gold bricks had been piled, awaiting transport to the cliff edge. His six soldiers were becoming exhausted, but Sterne didn't care. He intended to get as many ingots over the edge as possible. Periodically, they heard shots coming from the caverns far below, along with the faint cries of men. The soldiers grew increasingly uneasy. Their comrades had gone down into the earth in search of what they assumed was a single woman. Now there appeared to be a full-blown war going on beneath their feet.

Once all the ingots had been removed, Sterne led the men back into the cave. Such was his greed that he wanted to bring out some of the many baskets of precious stones as well. He convinced the men by telling them they could each take as many gems for themselves as they could stuff into their pockets.

When they reached the cavern of the priests, however, the sounds of battle coming out of the cave entrance were almost debilitating. The men milled about nervously, all thought of treasure gone. Something very bad was happening, and they wanted no part of it.

Even Sterne was having second thoughts. Maybe he had enough treasure. They retreated to the temple entrance.

Sterne was more than prepared to leave Rathke and the other Germans behind. But he needed the help of the six men under his command if he was going to get any treasure at all out of Mapungubwe. As frightened as the soldiers were, they wouldn't be happy abandoning their comrades.

"We'll wait here at the entrance until we can figure out what's going on," Sterne said. 'I want explosives set inside that will collapse the tunnel once our men come out. Whoever they're fighting down there will be trapped inside."

Two of the men familiar with explosives placed the charges, laying a fuse to set them off from just outside the temple entrance. Then they waited.

It didn't take long. The sounds of conflict rose quickly through the passages and the cavern. The explosions of firearms echoed up from below and they began to hear cries and screams from men obviously fighting for their lives. The closer the sounds came, the more terrified the men grew.

One of the soldiers said to Sterne, "If our men aren't the first ones out, it may be too late to close off the tunnel. There's no way for us to know who will emerge first."

Another agreed. "We sent fifty men down there. But they seem to be on the losing end based on what we're hearing. If whoever they're fighting gets through first, we'll be dead men. The seven of us won't be able to stop them."

Sterne looked around at the faces next to him. This couldn't have been better. It was exactly what he'd hoped would happen. He didn't even need to bring the matter up first, which he'd fully intended to do if no one helped him out.

"We're all agreed then?" he said. No one said anything.

He reached down and ignited the charge.

33.

KESI AND MARTIN had been lying in the tiny alcove for a long time, listening to the sounds of battle rage around them. More fiercesome giants ran past, the only sound the padding of bare feet and their rhythmic breathing. The sacred warriors moved without light of any kind, though there seemed to be a glow as they passed.

Another group flashed by and Kesi whispered, "How can they do that? Run through these black halls without light?"

Martin shook his head. "It's pretty extraordinary. The only thing I can think of is that they actually practice for this sort of thing. What else have they got to do with themselves year in and year out? They must know these tunnels and corridors like a blind man knows how to get around his own home."

The sounds of fighting now seemed to be far above them and no other warriors had passed for some time.

"I think it's time to move," he said.

"I don't ever want to leave this hole," said Kesi. "It's an awful place, but it feels safe somehow. Once we're in the corridors . . ."

"I know. I feel the same way. But this may be our only chance. If the warriors have chased the Germans up toward the surface, we may be able to move in the opposite direction without running into anyone."

Cautiously, using their single flashlight, they crawled out of their cramped quarters. At every branch of the passageways, they took the descending path. The floors of the halls grew damp, rough and uneven.

"It'll be a miracle," Kesi said, "if we manage to find the same escape that my father and mother used."

"Yes, but there may be more than one way out. This entire bloody mountain's like a Swiss cheese." He stopped suddenly, throwing his arm out to prevent Kesi from going forward. The ground at his feet had disappeared under a stream of water. "I think we've come to a dead end here," he said.

Kesi played her light across the water. It was about twenty feet wide. On the opposite side, she could see where the corridor picked up again.

"This section of corridor must have collapsed at some point," said Martin. "Seems to be a pretty good current." The water passed underneath an overhang and disappeared out of sight. He stared at the stream curiously and then turned off his light.

"What are you doing?"

"Just a minute. I want to let my eyes adjust."

"Adjust to what? Your eyes can't adjust down here. There's no light to adjust to."

"I know . . . but I swear I see something down there . . . Look!" He pointed to a strange phosphorescence in the water that illuminated the surface.

Kesi realized with a start that she could see. It didn't make any sense. They were hundreds of feet beneath the surface. "What do you think is causing it?" she said.

"I've heard of tiny creatures that give off light in the water," said Martin. He dipped his right arm into the stream all the way up to his shoulder. When he removed it, the arm glowed with a faint, greenish cast. "Incredible."

"It must be how the warriors move around down here without light," said Kesi. "They swim in the pool and the glow attaches to their bodies, allowing them to see."

Martin continued to stare at his arm in fascination. "Pretty neat trick." He looked up quickly. "Listen!"

They could hear the soft padding of bare feet again. More warriors were coming. But this time they seemed to be approaching from both directions, behind them as well as from across the pool.

Kesi grabbed Martin's hand as they both backed up to the stream. In a moment, two groups of warriors appeared, one across the pool and one directly in front of them. All of the men glowed with the phosphorescence of the water. They were an unearthly, almost preternatural sight, their huge, muscled bodies draped with human bones, glistening with a greenish hue.

Kesi and Martin were trapped. No more passages to turn down, no alcoves to hide in. The warriors began talking animatedly among themselves at their good fortune. Several took their bows from their shoulders and began to fit arrows while others drew terrifying-looking knives.

"Hold my hand tight," Martin said.

"What do you think I'm doing?"

"Don't let go."

Then he pulled her back violently, thrusting both of them into the pool. They disappeared beneath the surface. Kesi just managed to grab a breath as she realized what Martin intended, but her eyes remained open. In astonishment, she found that she could see under the water. A brisk current pulled them beneath the overhang, leaving the sacred warriors of the Clan of the Bow staring at each other with their bows poised uselessly.

They tumbled end over end in the fast water. It was difficult to tell which direction was up, but the phosphorescent glow continued to light their way. At any moment, their underground river might spill over a cliff or plunge through solid rock, cutting off their air. Then their troubles would be over permanently.

The water was unusually warm. Eventually they oriented themselves and began to float side by side through an underground grotto. The walls of the passage glowed with that strange greenish-blue hue. The ceiling above their heads was only a few feet high, enough for them to breathe, however, and after two or three minutes, Martin said, "I think it's getting brighter."

A few moments later, they bubbled out of the depths of Mapungubwe Hill and into the bright African sunshine. They found themselves floating down the sluggish Limpopo River past a herd of hippos that bellowed their displeasure.

They swam to shore and pulled themselves out. They were several hundred feet from the mountain and as they sat dripping in the sun, still stunned at their incredible good fortune, they heard a thundering crash from within the dense underbrush that cloaked the trail leading to the rock chimney.

"Look!" Kesi shouted, pointing up to the top of the hill.

In the late afternoon light, they could clearly see a small group of men at the top of the chimney. They seemed to be struggling with something that glinted in the sun. Then, a moment later, the shimmering object went tumbling over the cliff and struck the ground with a huge blast.

34.

MAJOR RATHKE LED his men quickly through the treasure rooms and past the wizened bodies of the royal couple whose ancient rule, perhaps two thousand years in the past, was responsible for this ghastly place. Only half a dozen of his original party of ten were still alive, and as they reached the cave opening into the chamber of the priests, another whistling arrow embedded itself in one of the soldiers, cutting their numbers still further.

The men scrambled and all but fell down the iron ladder onto the chamber floor. With barely a backward glance they raced past the carved soapstone birds, which stared at them through their sightless ruby eyes.

Then the warriors appeared at the cave entrance. Rathke looked back long enough to estimate their number at about twenty with more appearing every second. Some stopped to shoulder their bows. Arrows began to fly through the cavern, forcing the Germans to duck behind boulders near the entrance to the lower hallway that led to the temple opening.

The Germans fired back, but the arrows flew about them with such deadly accuracy that they hardly dared raise their heads and were able to get off only wild shots of their own. In a matter of seconds, one of Rathke's men was killed with an arrow through his throat and two others received injuries in their legs.

"Fall back!" he screamed, retreating into the hallway. The men limped and struggled down the corridor as two of the soldiers knelt by the entrance and offered covering fire. Meanwhile, the warriors descended the ladder and swarmed across the chamber of priests toward the retreating Germans.

Mbari Wauta, the Clan of the Bow, was in full fury now, filled with a blood lust thousands of years old. The cavern rang with their cries and the sound chilled the very marrow in the soldiers' bones. SS they were. Germany's finest. And to a man, they were so panicked that some of them had trouble getting their limbs to function. Terror had taken hold of their hearts, for they truly believed they were going to die . . . here, so very far from the Fatherland.

The Major paused at the entrance to the final hall leading to the surface. He had only three men left now. The wounded soldiers had been unable to keep up, and none of their comrades were of a mind to go back for them. The stragglers were quickly and brutally dispatched.

Rathke raised his gun to fire, but the weapon jammed. He cursed and clambered up with his last three men into the first hall. He played their only remaining flashlight across the peaceful scenes of ancient Roman gardens and on to the end of the corridor. All of the soldiers felt their hearts leap as they caught the glimmer of daylight. Somehow, just making it out of this cavern of horror and back into the light of day seemed to offer hope. They would still be outnumbered, but perhaps Lord Sterne and his handful of men could help hold off the screaming horde of Africans.

"There it is!" Rathke shouted. 'We're almost there . . ."

And then an explosion rocked the narrow hallway, throwing them off their feet. Dust and dirt swirled over and around them, billowing all the way out into the chamber of the priests.

With that blast, sunlight disappeared forever for Major Rathke and his remaining soldiers.

"Mother of God!" One of the Germans cried. "They've closed us in. We're dead men."

"Get behind the boulders," Rathke shouted. "Make a stand. We'll take as many of them as we can."

But it was pure bravado. Unable to get his own rifle to fire, the Major was left with just his pistol and five rounds of ammunition. The others were almost out of bullets as well.

The warriors had backed away after the explosion, but as the dust settled, they began to come on again.

Rathke balanced his light on top of a flat stone so it faced down the passageway. He held his pistol in his left hand and a knife in his right. Beside him, his three men also crouched, waiting. None of them could believe this was how they were going to die . . . here in the dark, choking in thick dust, at the hands of the strangest and most brutal-looking adversaries they'd ever encountered.

For long moments, nothing happened. The hall resounded with silence following the deafening blast. Then one of the soldiers cried, "Here they come!"

But the warriors, now well aware that their prey was trapped, changed tactics. They no longer charged in a mass, allowing the Germans to pick them off with rifle fire. Instead, they gathered at the entrance to the final hallway, pushing rocks up to form a wall of protection. As the wall grew several feet high, more and more of the warriors climbed into the hall, spreading out, facing the Germans.

Rathke realized what was coming. Their own positions were untenable. The rocks they crouched behind were barely sufficient to offer cover. Parts of their bodies were invariably exposed to the varying angles that the warriors now held. A foot here, a shoulder there. If they tried to return fire, they had to show even more flesh.

Their opponents were making a game of it! They chattered amongst themselves, exclaiming animatedly as they took turns showing off their marksmanship. An arrow struck the man next to Rathke in his heel and the poor fellow screamed, dropping his rifle and grabbing his leg. The Major ducked as another arrow missed his head by barely an inch.

Two warriors had climbed high up on the rock pile, one on either side of the corridor, and were taking aim carefully. The first loosed an arrow that struck another German in his shoulder. Before the other could shoot, Rathke put a bullet through the bastard's head with his pistol. Another warrior took the man's place even before the body had stopped rolling to the bottom of the rock pile.

He now had only four shots left. He heard someone scream and realized it was his own voice he was hearing, as an arrow struck him in the thigh. The pain was excruciating. He suspected the impact had shattered the bone. He lay back, whimpering in agony, and watched as the rest of his men were patiently picked off, until he was alone.

As the guardians of Mapungubwe began to move forward, Major Rathke hoped through a cloud of pain that he'd meet up with Lord Sterne in the next life, if there was one. He peered around the rocks. They were almost upon him. He shot three more warriors with his pistol, careful to save the last bullet for himself.

35.

THE SECOND of the Germans' two Tiger tanks pushed through thick vegetation at the base of Mapungubwe Hill, creating a track all the way to the chimney. By a stroke of good fortune, the tank and its three-man crew had been on a patrol of the surrounding countryside looking for any native troops that might have been in the area when Martin had arrived on the scene.

Now, Lord Sterne directed his men to attach the heavy wheeled cart to the tank and begin filling it with the gold ingots they'd thrown from the top of the mountain. It was backbreaking labor. The heavy gold bricks were strewn across an area of fifty square yards that was filled with thick, dense undergrowth. The men kept wary eyes out for lions, though the beasts weren't the main concern, having been scared off by the noise of the tank. More worrisome were the many poisonous snakes and spiders that inhabited the rocky terrain.

Some of the bricks would never be found. Landing in clefts in the rocks or burrowing straight down into the soft earth as they struck, they ended up completely hidden. But this was the minority. By the end of a full day of searching and hauling, the heavy cart was filled with almost sixty ingots, more than two tons of gold. The cart groaned under the weight and even the tank had to struggle to pull the load down the steep path to the more easily managed terrain of the veldt.

Everyone was on edge. The soldiers couldn't help but wonder what had happened to the comrades they'd abandoned beneath Mapungubwe Hill. Most felt guilty at what had happened and more than a little confused at the train of events that left a civilian, Lord Sterne, in charge of the operation. They were afraid that whatever force had destroyed Major Rathke and the others might still be out there and might somehow find a way out of the underground maze.

This fear was a good thing so far as Sterne was concerned. It gave the men incentive to get the work done quickly so they could leave this place.

With the cart loaded at last, the soldiers piled into the truck and the little convoy set out.

It was slow going. The tank struggled to maintain just a few miles per hour and had to stop every couple of hours for a few minutes to avoid overheating from the great weight it pulled. The stops angered Sterne, who eventually ordered the tank commander to forgo them. He wasn't concerned about damage to the tank in the long term, just so long as it lasted until they reached the coast.

Periodically, he used the tank's radio to attempt to contact the *Coast Princess*. He wasn't certain what the range of the radio was in this terrain. But as the first day drew to a close and he'd still not raised the ship, his concerns began to grow. Any number of things might have gone wrong. The ship could have been attacked by Allied forces. It might have been boarded by local authorities and ordered back to port to explain what it was doing. The world was at war after all, and an unexplained freighter sitting in a remote bay was sure to arouse suspicions. He supposed it was even possible that the crew had become concerned at the length of time the operation was taking and had abandoned the vessel.

But there was nothing he could do about any of these possibilities. The freighter was their only avenue of escape with the tons of gold they hauled with them. He had to hope it was still there. Otherwise, all was lost.

36.

WINSTON SAT at the tiny table in his quarters on board the H.M.S. *Blackmore,* composing a letter to Clementine. The roll of the big ship had increased substantially over the last twenty-four hours, causing his pen to create numerous extended lines, giving the letter an almost weeping quality. Clemmie's acceptance of Kesi had brought him great relief, and he was trying yet again to express to her the intensity of his feelings for both his new daughter and for the rock in his life, his wife.

On one level, he understood that what he was doing was the sheerest folly. He was exposing himself to unnecessary danger. For all his insistence to Petrie that he wasn't so important, he knew otherwise. He'd long had a sense of his own destiny and believed in his heart that no other leader could defeat the Hun. If he was killed, it might very well affect the outcome of the war.

Kesi was his daughter. His own flesh and blood, created out of a moment that had fused passion with impending death and despair in the black, subterranean depths of Mapungubwe Hill. He had convinced himself that his personal knowledge of the gold and of Mapungubwe required his presence here. But there remained a suppressed, niggling doubt that this wasn't the only, or even the main, reason he was here. Could it possibly be for personal reasons? He couldn't bring himself to consider it.

There was a rap at his door and Captain Nevins stuck his head in. "We've intercepted radio messages to the *Coast Princess* from someone calling himself 'Meridian.' Whomever's sending the communication isn't using code, and the message is in German."

Winston slammed his fist on the table. "I want to hear it!" He followed the captain to the radio room.

"Anything new?" the captain said to his radio operator.

"No sir. The same message every time. It's very short. They repeat it every twenty minutes or so. Our translator has written it down." He handed a sheet of paper to the captain, who read it out loud: "Meridian to *Coast Princess*. Will deliver cargo late afternoon tomorrow. Please acknowledge."

"You've given no response?" said the captain.

"None, Sir . . . wait . . . here it comes again."

"Quick, man, give me your headphones," said Winston.

He closed his eyes and listened to the words as they flowed through the ear pieces. He didn't speak German, but even after more than forty years, he recognized the voice as though he'd heard it only yesterday. He took the headphones off, handed them to the radio man and looked at the captain.

"It's Sterne," he said.

"No doubt?"

"A little weaker. A little older. In a language I never heard him speak. But there's no doubt. I'll never forget that man's voice."

The captain motioned to the Prime Minister to accompany him into the corridor. "Do you think he'll still come if there's no answer?" he said.

"They could have a backup plan," said Winston. "But I'd bet against it. They had to put this whole thing together on short notice. With tons of gold to move through hostile territory, they won't have much in the way of other options." He stared out at the sea, which was growing rougher. A storm was moving in.

"We could send a reply," said the captain. "My man speaks perfect German."

Winston shook his head. "They might have a password or some coded reply. If we didn't use it, they'd know something was wrong. Sterne will be suspicious of course, when they get no answer. I would be. But one possibility he'll be forced to consider is that their men on the freighter simply ran out on them. They'll have to come and see if the ship is still here."

"But if they have no crew, how can they hope to operate the ship?"

"Some of the soldiers may be experienced seamen. I know for a fact that Lord Sterne was once a topnotch sailor. I remember reading about him captaining a number of trans-Atlantic Clipper races when he was only in his twenties. That was back in the 1890s when the Clippers were the fastest ships around."

Captain Nevins looked skeptical. "There's a hell of a difference between a Clipper ship and a modern freighter."

"No doubt, captain. But Sterne knows the sea and I know him. The word 'hubris' was invented for the man. He won't doubt his ability to do it for a moment. Most especially when the motivation is untold millions in gold."

The captain nodded slowly. "So what do we do? Send men ashore and try to intercept them?"

"We won't have any idea precisely where they are until they're on the coast, nearing the ship. They must have a launch hidden somewhere along the shore, but in this swampy bit of heaven, we'd never be able to locate it. Besides, I want to avoid an international incident if it's at all possible. Let's keep any confrontation out to sea. That's where we have the advantage with our destroyers and submarines. We're going to put our own men on board the *Coast Princess* and wait for them to walk into our arms."

What he didn't say and tried to avoid thinking about was what might have happened to Kesi and Martin if Lord Sterne was already on his way to the coast with his stolen treasure.

"All right," the captain said. "I'll prepare a force, say twenty armed men, to wait on board the freighter. We'll also bring the submarines in to guard the bay entrance so there will be no possibility of their escaping."

Winston said, "As soon as your men have embarked, take the *Blackmore* far enough out to sea that there will be no chance she can be seen. I don't want anything to spook them."

Captain Nevins had already turned away to put a call on the ship's intercom. "I'll put Lieutenant Spencer in charge of . . ."

"I'll be the one in charge," Winston said. "But your Lieutenant may come along."

Nevins stared at The Prime Minister. "I can't allow that, Sir. It's too dangerous."

Winston's mouth turned up in a brief smile. "Really, Captain," he said. "I would have thought an officer in Her Majesty's Navy would have a better understanding of the chain of command. Last time I checked, the Prime Minister was a bit higher up the duty roster than an officer of the line."

"Sir, I have to protest!"

"Protest noted. Sandys and his commandos are all dead. They were brave men, but now it's up to us. One leads from the front, captain, not the rear. I won't allow Hitler to have this gold and give new life to his war machine."

37.

KESI AND MARTIN hid in the bush as they watched Lord Sterne's men manhandle the gold bricks out of dense brush and into the heavy cart attached to the tank. Martin estimated there were no more than ten Germans left, though he never had the chance to see them all at once, so it was difficult to be certain. He briefly considered trying to pick them off one by one with his rifle. But the odds were too great and he didn't want to put Kesi in any further danger. Then, too, there was the tank. A single, well-placed round could end it all.

They struggled to find something to eat by scavenging the German camp after dark. They couldn't risk firing their weapons to shoot animals, and even if they had managed to snare a bird or other small creature, they couldn't risk a fire to cook it.

"We could just head for the coast," Kesi said. "They've got to go there eventually."

"I know, and it's tempting. But we can't risk losing them. Our mission is to keep that gold from reaching Hitler. We can't let it out of our sight."

"They've got a truck, you know. How are we going to keep up with them?"

"With the load that tank's pulling, we'll probably be able to walk as fast as they can drive. Anyway, we can take short cuts cross-country, while they'll have to keep to the open veldt." He looked at her with a grin. "Besides, I thought you natives were supposed to be able to run like bush bunnies."

"Bush bunnies?"

"Maybe it was gazelles."

Late on the afternoon of the second day, it became clear the Germans were preparing to leave the following morning. To get a head start, Kesi and Martin hiked to the top of a distant rise in the direction the soldiers would have to go. In doing so, they skirted the German camp, passing the spot where the battle had taken place between the commandos and the Nazis.

There wasn't much to see beyond red stains in the earth and bits of clothing. Their friends' bodies had been left where they fell. Lions, hyenas and vultures had done their work efficiently.

"It's so awful, Martin," Kesi said. "I wouldn't leave a dog lying in the bush for scavengers."

"I'm afraid to admit I did the same with the men I killed, though if I'd had time, I would have buried them. Somehow I don't think Lord Sterne is overly concerned with the niceties of a decent burial. Hell, he probably figures it's a good way to keep the lions from bothering them for a few days."

She stared at a bloody piece of shirt lying in the dirt. "They were good men," she said. "They deserved better."

"A lot of good men have died in this damn war. We need to keep our focus on that gold. If it ever reaches Hitler, a lot more brave men will die."

"Do you really think Sterne cares if the gold reaches Germany or not?"

"Not for a moment. If he can figure some way to keep it all for himself, he'll do it. I'd say he probably likes the way the odds have changed in his favor with most of the Nazis having been killed already."

They woke early the next morning and watched as the Germans headed off. The tank moved excruciatingly slowly. In addition to its normal weight, it was piled high with spare fuel containers, since there were no fuel depots where they were going. The men who rode in the truck drove ahead, then parked and waited in the shade until the tank caught up. The pattern contin- ued throughout the day and well into the evening, Sterne keeping them at it until almost dark.

Kesi and Martin took great care not to be seen. Martin slipped away and made contact with a native village, where he bartered for food for the two of them. At night, they bivouacked without a fire, which was extremely dangerous in lion country. It took four long days for the Germans to reach the coast.

On the last day, Martin stood atop a final rise and took a deep breath. The smell of salt was in the air. Below, the coast of Portuguese Mozambique spread before them beneath a sky black as coal. A strong wind had begun to whip the water's surface into small whitecaps.

"Storm coming," he said "Looks like a big one."

The Germans had also noted the weather and begun to pick up their pace. While the tank chugged along like a faithful tugboat, the truck filled with the rest of the troops bounced and rattled its way down to the sea.

Kesi and Martin moved along the ridge, until they came to a spot where they could see a partially hidden bay. It emerged from a swampy area north of where the Limpopo entered the sea.

"Look!" Kesi said, pointing.

Sitting at anchor in the bay was a small freighter.

"That's got to be their destination," said Martin excitedly. As they watched, the truck suddenly seemed to disappear into the swamp. But then it emerged farther along and it was clear that a hidden road skirted the marsh. The truck pulled to a halt and the men jumped out, tiny figures in the distance.

"What are they doing?" said Kesi.

But it was immediately clear as the soldiers began moving brush and fronds, revealing a carefully camouflaged, thirty-foot launch.

"That's how they intend to get the gold on board," Martin said.

"You plan to tell me how we're going to stop them, right?"

"I don't have the foggiest notion. But it should take them a while to transfer the ingots from the cart to the boat. We've got that much time to figure something out. One thing's for certain . . . we can't do anything from up here. We've got to get closer."

They made their way down to the shore, keeping out of sight by avoiding the road and keeping to a strip of dry ground at the edge of the swampy area. Working their way to within fifty yards of the activity, they crouched in tall weeds. The Germans were working feverishly. Sterne barked orders while standing to one side with the collar of his jacket turned up against the growing wind. The launch was already settling deeply into the sea under the weight of the ingots.

"Martin, it's more than half loaded already!" Kesi said in a harsh whisper.

He nodded. "Sterne wants to get on board before that storm hits. It's damn risky if you ask me. That thing will float like a coal barge. Maybe the storm will do our work for us and turn their boat over."

"We can't rely on that. We have to do something."

He stared at her for a moment, appreciating for the hundredth time how much he admired her spirit. "All right," he said finally. "We can't take them on here. Maybe we can find some way to get on that freighter. If we could just get on board first, we'd be able to shoot at them as they pull alongside. It'd be like picking off ducks in a shooting gallery."

They crawled back out of sight and followed the road that skirted the swamp. It had to be there for some purpose. After hurrying along for half a mile, they discovered what that purpose was. The primitive home of a native fisherman stood at the end of the rutted dirt road. It consisted of a wooden hut with palm fronds for a roof, a ramshackle barn and a flimsy dock no more than four feet wide precariously balanced on poles shoved into the muck along the shore.

"This whole place looks like it would fall down and wash away in the first good storm that comes along," Kesi said.

Martin looked uneasily at the sky. "We may get to find out." He stared for a while at the tiny homestead. "I don't see any sign of life.

Either it's abandoned or its owner is off fishing somewhere. Come on. I want to look in that barn."

He pushed on a leaning barn door that fell off its hinges the moment he touched it. Inside was a low-slung dhow about twenty feet in length. Normally dhows were rigged with a lateen sail, but there were no sails in evidence for this craft.

He worked his way to the rear, where he found that the boat had an engine and, surprisingly, a full tank of petrol. Everything looked more or less functional, though they wouldn't know if the engine would turn over until they launched her. Kesi found a pair of oars which she put on board. They'd be virtually useless appendages, however, in the growing winds.

She gave the rudder a turn. "It looks operational enough," she said optimistically. "For a short voyage anyway."

Martin was a bit less enthusiastic, but they were out of time and options.

"Help me pull it down to the dock," he said, as the first drops of rain pricked the ocean surface.

* * *

Lord Sterne stared worriedly at the threatening sky. During his long years in Africa, both in prison and later, wandering the continent, he'd grown to recognize the large storms that sometimes roared out of the Indian Ocean. They could last for days, and this one had that feel. He fully intended to be on board the *Coast Princess* before it set in. If the ship was abandoned, as he now feared, it might not survive the storm. Their only hope of successfully completing their mission lay in getting on board and piloting the ship to safer waters before the full brunt of the storm struck.

Even this plan, he knew, was fraught with peril. The Nazi soldiers knew little about the sea. He had faith in his own ability, however, and would have to rely on being able to organize the men and instruct them in what they had to do.

The clouds were dark and increasingly roiling as the launch finally accepted the last of the ingots. Stern ordered the men immediately into the boat. It rode dangerously low in the water with its rich cargo. The Nazi foot soldiers looked petrified at the prospect of putting out into that storm-tossed bay. However, the heaviness of the boat's load seemed to steady the craft against the rising wind. After a few nerve-wracking failures to fire, the engine coughed to life, and they pushed off.

The launch floated much like the tank had driven. "Take her round to the leeward side," Sterne yelled. "It'll take time to load the cargo. We can use the ship to protect us from the wind."

The men managed to tie the boat off at the gangway and soldiers swarmed up onto the ship. One of the ship's winches was swung into place and the slow process of lifting the ingots on board began. The sea was a maelstrom, the wind blowing harder by the minute. The men struggled to load the heavy ingots from a tossing launch into an only slightly less heaving freighter. They were all inexperienced with the sea and they stumbled about like drunks, their bodies pummeled by the blasts.

It took several hours to complete the task. But at last Sterne ordered the launch let loose into the storm, for there was no time to lift it on board. The boat quickly disappeared into the rain.

Sterne gathered his men together and began to divide them into groups, explaining to each what their duties would be, some to the anchors, some to lash the holds against the storm, others sent down to the engine room. Two of the soldiers had experience with diesel engines, though they'd never operated ones as large as those that powered the *Coast Princess*.

The storm intensified, if that were possible, as Sterne scattered his men to their stations. Several of the soldiers were already sick from the storm-tossed seas. He showed them no sympathy. Keeping them moving despite the adversity they faced was paramount. These were crucial moments. The future Sterne envisioned for himself as one of the world's wealthiest and most powerful men would soon be determined.

38.

WINSTON had changed into full navy raingear, including a floppy brimmed hat that, from the rear, seemed to be on fire as his cigar smoke curled around the rim before being whipped into the storm-filled sky.

He strode past the line of sailors who stood in their own raingear, nervously holding their rifles. "We'll earn our keep today, men," he said. "England will defeat the Hun in this war, you have my word on it. And some day you can tell your children you played a major role in sending that blighter Hitler down to his allotted place at Satan's table."

The men cheered and seemed suddenly more at ease. After all, weren't they heading into battle with Winston Churchill himself? It was as great an honor as any man in His Majesty's service could hope for. They reveled in Winston's cocky confidence.

Captain Nevins came out onto the deck and watched as the launch was lowered into the water on the lee side of the ship. Once the craft rounded the protected side of the *Blackmore*, the wind would show it no mercy.

Nevins angled over to Churchill's side and in a low voice said, "We've picked up weather warnings from shipping as far as fifty miles out to sea. It's a real typhoon. Impossible to predict its course.

It might only brush us or it might strike head on. I think we should consider postponing the operation until it passes."

Winston shook his head. "The Germans won't postpone, captain. They can't afford to. And neither can we. We're done with waiting. The storm changes everything. We can't let Sterne and his men reach the ship." He waved a hand at the wind-tossed seas. "Your submarines can't guarantee they'll bottle them up in the bay in this weather. They could slip away under cover of the gale. It can't be chanced. We need to scuttle the freighter."

Captain Nevins contemplated Winston with a look that was a cross between admiration and exasperation. This stubborn, pudgy figure was going to get the captain's name placed in the history books as commander of the vessel that lost the Prime Minister of England. His notoriety would equal that of the captain of the *Titanic*. He sighed out loud.

Winston turned from the lowering of the launch and smiled suddenly, placing one hand on the man's arm. "Don't worry, captain. I haven't used up my nine lives yet." He hesitated. "There's a letter to my wife sitting on the desk in my stateroom. Would you see that it gets to her?"

Captain Nevins nodded solemnly.

The launch hit the water and sat banging against the hull. Lieutenant Spencer ordered the men over the side. Winston saluted the captain jauntily. "Time to see how much agility the old boy has left in him, eh?" he said.

He grabbed the rigging and lowered himself, showing consider-able strength, though he swore as his cigar fell into the sea. The boat rose and fell a dozen feet with each swell, so timing his step onto it was tricky, but a dozen hands reached up and helped him make the transition. He took a seat in the middle of the craft, and turned to face the long spit that hid the *Coast Princess* from view. The *Blackmore* couldn't come any closer if she wanted to remain out of sight from anyone approaching the freighter by land.

As expected, as soon as they rounded the protective hulk of the ship, the wind hit them hard. The center of the storm was still far out to sea, but the winds were already near gale force. The launch's propeller sputtered each time it came out of the water as the craft poised at the top of each massive swell. The temperature had fallen thirty degrees in the past half hour.

As the seamen sat hunched over, uncomplaining, backs to the salt spray, Winston surveyed them with pride. These sailors were the backbone of what had made England great throughout her long history. During his tenure as First Lord of the Admiralty, he'd grown to appreciate their skill and grit. Almost overcome by the grandeur of the scene, he reached out and placed a hand on one sailor's shoulders. The man turned and looked at him and then smiled as the Prime Minister squeezed him, nodding reassuringly.

The freighter sat like some enormous, hulking iceberg, seemingly immutable against the wind. She was held fast, for the time being at least, by her two anchors, fore and aft. But the wind was coming at her across her beam, which caused the ship to roll heavily from side to side.

As the launch approached the gangway, the metal stairs banged noisily against the side of the ship. They seemed to be fastened securely, however, in little danger of coming loose. The steps were on the leeward side of the *Coast Princess*, offering protection from the wind, but the roll of the ship made bringing the launch alongside a devilishly tricky maneuver.

Time and again, the small craft attempted to cozy up to the gangway as the sailors tried to grapple onto something. The roll of the ship was so severe that it was impossible. Finally, Lieutenant Spencer shouted they'd have to remain free of encumbering lines and each man would have to time his leap onto the gangway. An experienced seaman might expect to achieve this fairly easily as the boat came level with the gangway platform at the top of each swell. But in addition to the swells, they'd have to time the roll of the freighter as well. A split second would make all the difference between success and being crushed between the sides of the two vessels.

Even Winston felt a chill at the prospect of what they were about to do. But he'd brought them this far. He moved to the side of the launch, intending to be one of the first.

A young sailor made the initial leap. He managed to time it perfectly, but still sprawled on the gangway, nearly losing his rifle before getting a grip on the railing. He pulled himself upright and turned just in time to see the Prime Minister of England virtually leap into his arms. With a look of horror on his face, the sailor grabbed Winston by the collar and for a moment they teetered as the ship rolled heavily. Then Winston grabbed the rail with one hand and the two men stood facing each other, smiling broadly. They were safe. Quickly, they climbed to the main deck, since space on the gangway was limited.

Meanwhile, the launch had lurched away, caught by a blast of wind. Slowly, her pilot fought to maneuver her back alongside. Winston watched as she moved closer. He had to continually wipe his hand across his face to clear away the salt spray. He could see the tense faces of the lieutenant and his men.

Each time the launch sank into a trough and the freighter happened to roll in the opposite direction, the *Blackmore*'s small boat seemed to disappear into a hole thirty feet below where Winston and the sailor stood. It was clear the operation was becoming more dicey by the moment.

Again and again the launch moved toward them, only to be driven back by fierce gusts or by the pilot's pulse-pounding fear of collision with the side of the larger craft. The wind and storm were now furious. The rain blew horizontally, and the skies above were so dark they could scarcely be distinguished from the sea itself.

Again the launch moved in toward the gangway. Suddenly, a terrific blast of air hit them. The freighter shuddered, pulling against its taught anchor lines. The launch pilot looked like a toy figure to Winston as he disappeared into a fifty-foot-deep trough alongside the *Coast Princess*. At that moment, above the wind, Churchill heard something snap.

The sailor standing beside him screamed, "One of the anchor lines has given way!"

Without the stabilizing line of the stern anchor, the freighter rolled over on top of the launch as it neared the bottom of the trough. Winston stared in horror as the hull of the bigger ship crushed down on the smaller craft, forcing it straight down into the sea. The boat and her fifteen-man crew disappeared in an instant, pushed straight to the bottom. Not a man escaped.

The sole remaining sailor who'd come aboard with Winston stood frozen, holding onto the rail, staring down at the place where his comrades had been just moments before. Winston, too, was stunned by the rapidity of the disaster, but he grabbed the young seaman's arm.

"We've got to go aft and see if there's another anchor we can drop," he said. "She won't hold otherwise."

The sailor clutched the rail and didn't move.

Winston put his face right in front of him. "What's your name, son?" he said.

The frightened face seemed to focus on the familiar figure. "C—Campbell, sir. Mitchell Campbell, Able Seaman."

"All right, Seaman Campbell. We can't help those poor buggers. They're standing before their maker. Do you want to join them?"

"No . . . no sir!"

"We've got a job to do. Follow me."

He led off toward the stern of the *Coast Princess,* which seemed to be holding on by a thread, a single chain-link thread that was all that separated the ship from the rocks in the cove. Seaman Campbell followed close behind him. As soon as she was freed of the aft anchor, the ship had changed her disposition. She now drifted directly back from the blasting wind, which lessened the degree of rolling, but Winston feared the new direction of stress on their remaining anchor might pull it free from the bottom. There was no time to waste. He glanced momentarily in the direction of the *Blackmore,* wondering if there was any chance her captain might have witnessed what had happened to the launch, but the destroyer was nowhere to be seen in the gloom of the storm. He hoped she'd be safe in the face of the rampaging winds.

The two men stumbled down the deck, grasping onto whatever they could until they came to the anchor hole. Winston felt his heart leap as he stared at a second anchor still in its harbor.

"There's a manual release," said the sailor. "So you don't have to operate it from the wheelhouse in case of emergency. I know how to work it."

Winston stood aside, as Campbell grabbed a hammer that was secured to the side of the winch and used it to bang the release. It took several tries and then the anchor was free, falling straight down to the sea floor. Now they were a little safer, though if the other anchor should break or come free upwind, the ship would be spun around in the storm and might well capsize. Their troubles were far from over.

"Good man!" Winston said. "Now let's get up to the bridge and see if there's anything we can do. We've got one hell of a storm to ride out."

Like two drowned rats, they entered the darkened bridge and shut the door behind them. For the first time, the noise and fury of the storm seemed to separate itself from them. Winston took off his hat and wiped the salt from his eyes.

"There must be a light somewhere," he said. "Assuming the generator is still working. Look around."

But the room was suddenly flooded with light. Winston blinked in the sudden brilliance and wiped his eyes again. Standing before him with a look of astonishment almost as great as his own was an aging caricature of a man he'd last seen forty years ago.

"Winston Churchill?" Lord Sterne said in disbelief. Then his face slowly broadened into a smile. "There must be a God, after all."

39.

T TOOK every ounce of their combined strength to haul the dhow out of the shack and down a gangway of logs to the water. Kesi held the boat steady from the flimsy dock while Martin jumped aboard and tried to figure out the engine. The rain and wind were relentless now.

"Has it occurred to you," she shouted above the wind, "that what we're doing is suicidal?"

He gave her a thumbs-up sign. "Most of what people do in war is suicidal," he said. "If they all stopped to think about it, they'd probably never go to war in the first place."

He managed to hook up the gas line to the fuel container and squeezed a small pump in the line to feed fuel into the engine. Then he pushed the starter and, incredibly, the thing turned over the first time and caught with a satisfying rumble.

"Whoever has this place keeps his boat in a lot better shape than his house," he said. "Hop aboard."

Kesi jumped down from the dock and sat near the middle of the boat. It was a heavy, plank-bottomed craft with only ten inches of freeboard above the water line. It seemed to float stably enough, though, even in the wind.

"She doesn't present much above water for the wind to catch," Martin said. "Probably how she was designed. It should help us keep her from turning broadside. On the other hand, we're going to get pretty wet."

"I couldn't be any wetter if I was a mermaid," Kesi said.

He laughed. "You're a right pretty mermaid at that," he said. "Though I never heard of a chocolate-colored mermaid before."

Then they were into the bay and the full weight of the wind bore down on them. The *Coast Princess* was barely visible, about five hundred yards off, a rocking, gray form against the black sky. They'd lost all track of how long it had taken them to find the fisherman's shack, haul the dhow down to the sea and figure out the engine. There was no sign of Sterne and the rest of the Germans in their launch anywhere on the horizon, though visibility was poor.

"What if we don't get there first?" Kesi said.

He shrugged his shoulders, as he needed both hands on the rudder to keep them straight into the teeth of the storm. "Either way, we're committed," he said. "If we manage to reach the ship at all, we're going aboard. This wind's gaining strength every minute. I seriously doubt we could turn this thing around without tipping over."

They crept forward slowly. The small engine was only a few horsepower at best. At times, it seemed as though they were standing still. Mostly they kept their heads down. The wind was so strong it hurt their eyes and took their breath away if they stared into it. Martin adopted a policy of looking obliquely at the distant target of the *Coast Princess*.

Kesi found a bucket and bailed continuously, for the waves that broke across their bow deposited great sheets of water. The dhow seemed to hold the extra weight well, partly because it carried no cargo other than the two of them.

The air was cold, even this close to the Equator. The combination of being soaked to the skin and sitting in high wind made for a significant wind chill.

When they were only a hundred yards from the *Coast Princess*, the wind suddenly changed direction. The combined force of the wind and beating waves began to drag the lighter-weight reserve anchor at the stern across the ocean bottom.

"She's turning," Kesi cried. "She's coming right toward us!"

He could see for himself what was happening. The big freighter was being blown sideways by the wind against the fulcrum of the bow anchor and directly toward them.

"Turn us away!" she shouted.

"I can't. The dhow will turn over if I broadside her to the wind."

"Martin! The freighter will crush us."

"I know. It's going to be damn close . . ." He cut their speed as much as he dared without allowing the wind to take control of them.

The huge bulk of the boat bore down on them like a ghost ship looming out of the storm. The wind was so strong that the drama was over in less than a minute. The freighter swung past, missing them by fewer than a dozen feet. They stared up at the side of the vessel and could clearly see the letters of her name, *Coast Princess*, as she slipped by.

"Sweet Mother but that was close," said Martin.

The freighter rolled far over on her side but somehow managed to keep from turning turtle. Martin turned the rudder slightly and nudged the dhow in alongside the gangway.

"Get ready to jump," he said. "You'll have to time it carefully."

"What about you?"

"I'll be right behind you."

"That's what you said when you threw me over the cliff. When the Nubians were after us on top of Mapungubwe. You lied, and I had to come back and save your hide."

"Good to know I can rely on you . . . now jump!"

The boat rose up on a swell and Kesi neatly stepped onto the gangway, timing it perfectly. She turned and watched anxiously as Martin maneuvered the rear of the boat closer to the platform. This was clearly going to be a lot trickier, since he'd have to abandon both the engine and rudder once he prepared to jump.

Several times he came close to going, crouching, with one hand on the rudder, but each time the boat moved too far from the gangway at the last instant. Finally, the craft moved in close and banged against the hull. Rand dropped the rudder and leaped, just catching the railing with one hand. He swung wildly by his arm as the freighter rolled from side to side.

Kesi leaned down and grabbed him by the collar and pulled as hard as she could. Slowly, he clambered up onto the gangway and collapsed. She held onto him tightly.

"There's an old African proverb . . ." she began.

"I know, I know. But I can only belong to you once." He kissed her hard and then they watched as the dhow disappeared into the storm.

40.

LORD STERNE DANGLED his pistol lightly as he stared at his old Mapungubwe comrade from forty years earlier.

"I ought to kill you right now, Winston, and be done with it. I always suspected you must have had something to do with my being imprisoned by Botha."

Seaman Campbell stared at Sterne with a look of horror on his face. "You're a bloody Englishman!" he said. "How can you talk of killing the one man who can save England from German invasion and occupation?"

"Oh, he's English, all right," said Winston bitterly. "A lord, if you can believe it, a member of the royal family. But he's as twisted as they come. There are always a few bad worms in any apple."

"You have that right anyway," said Sterne. "Bertie could have arranged an exchange to free me, you know. I was good enough to do his dirty work, but once I landed in a Boer prison, I was expendable."

"Tut, tut," said Winston. "You've always been unappreciated, haven't you? Of course that might have something to do with the fact that you're a duplicitous, cruel, self-serving bastard of the first order, one of the most eminently *expendable* people I've ever had the misfortune to meet."

Sterne's gun focused directly on Churchill. "At the moment, I'd suggest you are the only one who is expendable around here. I've wasted enough time on you."

Seaman Campbell shouted, "No!" and threw himself in front of Winston just as Sterne fired, taking the full impact of the bullet in his chest. He fell to the floor, dead instantly. Winston groaned aloud and fell to one knee beside the poor sailor.

Suddenly the big ship lurched violently. One of the soldiers who'd been staring out the window yelled, "The bow anchor line broke! We're turning broadside."

Sterne and the other soldiers turned to look out the window, though there was nothing to see. Winston stood back up. "She'll never make it around," he said, quietly. "She'll turn turtle in this wind. Looks like we'll meet our maker at the same time after all."

Sterne looked back at him, his face taught with fear. It lasted for only a moment, and then he yelled with rage and brought his gun back to bear on Winston. He fired just as the *Coast Princess* yawed violently, leaning far over onto her port side. The shot went wide of its mark as everyone on the bridge fell down.

Winston staggered back against the door to the bridge, which blew open. He went right through it and out onto the catwalk. He held on for dear life as the ship slowly, miraculously, came back from the brink of disaster. As soon as it was clear they weren't going to go over, he flew down the steps and hurried along the deck searching for some place to escape from Sterne's gun, which at this point represented a demise only slightly more certain than the one that beckoned from the storm.

He glanced for a moment over the side and thought he saw a small boat. It couldn't be, of course. No one would be out on these waters in a craft that flimsy. He stumbled along. A shot rang out and a bullet ricocheted off the steel next to him. Then he was flung again to the deck as the ship rolled once more far over on to her side. He scrambled back up, cursing his lack of agility. "Too damn much whisky and cigars!" he muttered.

A German soldier, one of those left on deck to deal with the hatches, loomed up out of the dark. He had no knowledge that anyone was on board other than his comrades. He started to say something but Winston, with a ferocity born out of four long years of fighting an enemy he'd never confronted personally, turned on the man and struck him with all the force he could muster. The soldier staggered back, dropped his rifle and fell over the railing into the roiling sea without a sound.

Winston stared at his own fist in surprise. "Well, bugger my old boots!" he said. He picked up the rifle and continued along the deck, chambering a round as he went. He turned around long enough to fire a shot back in the direction of the bridge. Wouldn't hurt to let them know he was now armed.

The ship was stabilizing as she reached the end of her light stern anchor line, which seemed once again to be holding for the moment. The rocking of the deck eased. Now the Germans would come after him more seriously. He knew he had no chance against eight or ten fully armed German soldiers. These were the cream of the crop after all, handpicked by Hitler himself. The best he could expect would be to take a few with him. He needed to find a place to make a stand.

He picked his way across the freighter to the other side, clambering over bulwarks, hatches and all manner of obstructions. He was beginning to tire. He was no spring chicken any more. Petrie had been right about that. Still, he wished Clementine could see him now. Fighting the Hun in hand-to-hand combat, by God! *There* was a story for the bloody tabloids!

He stumbled around yet another bulwark amidships and ran straight into Martin and Kesi, who were running in the other direction. In the gloom, they nearly tried to shoot one another, but Kesi thought she recognized something familiar about that stout profile and bald pate shining in the dim glow coming off the ship's running lights. She grabbed Martin's arm at the last instant and yelled, "Wait! Good lord, it's Churchill!"

A light went on in Winston's heart as he heard the familiar voice. "Kesi? Martin? Thank God! I never thought I'd see you two again." He grabbed Kesi and hugged her tightly. "I'm sorry I sent you here, my dear," he said fiercely.

A shot sounded and a bullet rang off the bulwark next to them.

"We'll do the reunion thing later," said Martin. He fired his own weapon in reply and heard a satisfying cry. Then they ran to an open, swinging galley door and entered the lower deck.

They passed quickly down a long corridor and into what appeared to be a dining room. Winston collapsed gratefully into a chair. Kesi knelt beside him.

"What on Earth are you doing here, father?"

He smiled. "I came to hear you say that," he said.

Martin stood by a crack in the door watching the corridor, his pistol in hand. He glanced over at Churchill. "Damndest thing I ever heard of," he said. "The bleeding Prime Minister on the front lines. Have you lost your mind? We can't afford to lose you."

"Ah, you overvalue me, Martin. I think you always have. I was getting a bit stale back there in London."

Martin just shook his head. He peered out the door suddenly and put a finger to his mouth. Everyone froze.

Two soldiers were coming along the corridor. They looked into each room as they passed. Martin closed his door all the way and stood with the pistol ready. When one of the men opened the door, Rand shot him quickly, then leaned out and shot the other before he could react. He dragged both bodies into the room and closed the door again.

"Any idea how many of these blokes there are?" asked Winston.

"I estimated no more than ten when we watched them loading the gold onto the launch," said Martin. "I've killed three so far. That leaves seven . . . plus Sterne."

"Six," said Winston. "I got one of the buggers."

Martin looked at him and smiled. "Six, then."

"I take it," said Winston, "That the gold is on board?"

"We didn't see them unload it but it was on the launch and they certainly didn't throw it into the sea. I suspect it's in the hold."

"Then we've *got* the buggers!" Winston said, slamming his fist on the table. "We have two British destroyers standing offshore and two submarines guarding the entrance to the bay."

"Glad to hear it, sir. That means all we have to do is stay alive until the storm runs its course. But we're still outnumbered and outgunned."

The *Coast Princess* shuddered and then a loud thrumming sound pulsed through her, growing in decibel level until it was clear what they were hearing.

"They've started the engines," Winston said. "Sterne has to know if I'm here, there must be British vessels around. He's going to use the cover of the storm to get away. I'd bet Clemmie's best silver on it."

"Can they do that?" Martin asked. "I thought you said we had them bottled up."

"In a storm like this, anything's possible. If they can maneuver along the shoreline, dangerous though it may be, they just might slip past the submarines. The destroyers won't be able to come inshore until the storm ends."

"What can we do?" Kesi said soberly.

They could feel the *Coast Princess's* engines firing in reverse. She was attempting to reduce the tension on her sole remaining anchor line, and in a few moments, they heard the grating sound of the winch drawing in the anchor, followed by the sound of the engines grinding into forward thrust.

"We've got to finish the job," said Winston.

"Scuttle her," Martin said.

Kesi gasped but bit her tongue. "It's why we came. To make certain none of the gold gets back to Hitler."

"Come on then," said Winston. "Time to finish that traitor Sterne, once and for all."

"All right," Martin said, "but I propose it serves no useful purpose for us to go down with the ship. I saw a lifeboat near the stern as we were approaching in the dhow. Maybe we can get off on it."

"I imagine there will be some competition for it once they figure out what we've done," said Kesi.

"Hmm . . . maybe not," said Winston. "It'll take a good twenty minutes once we open her cocks before anyone will notice her beginning to list . . . longer if they put it down to the storm. Time enough to get her boat launched."

"I sure hate to see all that gold go to the bottom," said Martin. "Seems like a waste."

"We're in shallow waters," said Winston. "Perhaps some day, the local government can salvage it."

"Which local government?" said Kesi.

"Good question," her father answered. "South Africa? Rhodesia? Mozambique? Hell, I don't know . . . Nubia? Maybe some day, all of Africa will be united and they can do it together. Establish a museum to the betterment of all her people."

"Before we get too far along establishing museums and all, we might want to see if we can find the damn cocks first," Martin said. He peered out the door and then motioned for them to follow.

The sound of the engines was louder in the hallway. The *Coast Princess* had begun to work up a pretty good head of steam. Martin led the way down several stairwells and opened a door that clearly led to the engine room. The chugging diesels resonated. They descended a set of metal steps, Martin again cautioning silence. There were certain to be soldiers down here.

He saw the Germans first. There were two of them, leaning over trying to open a stuck valve. The men had placed their weapons to one side and had stripped to their waists. One of them looked up and cried out.

Martin shot him in the forehead. The other man grabbed his gun and dove out of sight.

"I'll keep him busy," said Winston. "I'm too bloody tired to go roaming around down here, anyway. You two look for the scuttling cock."

The German was trapped between the hull and the engine and was going nowhere. The only way out was up the stairs. Winston took a shot at the fellow's position and nodded to Martin and Kesi. They slipped past him and moved down toward the lowest part of the ship.

Periodically, the German raised his head and attempted to get a shot off, but Winston had the high ground and there was nothing the man could do. The only worry was whether or not the other Nazis would hear the gunfire. Winston was betting that between the engines and the storm, they would not.

"What are we looking for?" Kesi said.

"It'll be a sort of hatch on the floor," Martin said. "It could be locked, in which case we're done for. But most of the time they're simple enough to open. In a freighter like this, I wouldn't expect there to be any special security mechanisms."

They heard Winston firing behind them. After each shot, he exclaimed gleefully, "How do you like that, you bugger?"

"He is something," Kesi said. "My dad."

"Yeah, he's something, all right. You two are a lot alike. Can't tell either of you a thing."

"That's kind of what I like about him," she said. There was pride in her voice.

"There it is!" he cried.

He handed his pistol to Kesi and knelt down by the cock. There was a wheel mechanism and nothing that smacked of a lock. He grabbed hold and tried to turn it. It wouldn't budge. He repositioned himself, braced his feet and tried again. The muscles in his arms bulged with the effort. He stopped again, breathing heavily.

"I think I moved it a little," he said. "Give me a hand."

Kesi got on the other side and together, they loosened the screw. Sea water began to flow in steadily, faster and faster as Martin opened the cock all the way, finally removing it entirely. Water gushed into the room in a geyser.

"All right," he said. "That's done it. I'll take the cock with me and throw it overboard. They won't have any way to stop it."

They backtracked to where Winston was waiting. There hadn't been any more shooting and they found the Prime Minister sitting on the steps with his rifle across his legs.

"Got the bugger," he said with a contented nod. "Only four left now besides Sterne. Wish I had a damn cigar."

"We don't have a lot of time," Martin said. "Let's get the hell out of here."

41.

LORD STERNE STARED out the window of the freighter's bridge. He had control of the boat's column and was directing the craft toward the end of the half-moon beach that marked the entrance to the bay. There was no time to study the charts for hidden shoals. He intended to stay as close to shore as he felt comfortable with and pray there was enough depth to make it into the open sea.

It would have been a lot smarter to wait until the storm died to attempt the risky maneuver. But the discovery of Churchill could mean only one thing: There were British naval vessels at hand, destroyers, possibly even submarines. If he waited, the freighter would be helpless in the face of that sort of firepower. The storm could prove to be a godsend, giving them cover to slip away.

The *Coast Princess* was the largest vessel he'd ever controlled . . . by a long sight. He could feel the vibration of the big diesel engines far below right through his shoes. It might have intimidated a lesser man, but he'd been through more than most in his long life. Even his years in prison had strengthened him in terms of his resolve. He didn't know how many years he had left but had convinced himself that he deserved to live them in comfort. Not just comfort. He would live like the ancient kings once had, with wealth unsurpassed.

He could feel the presence of the gold bars almost like a living being. They were a promise of wonderful things yet to come. No one was going to deprive him of his final reward. Not this frustratingly slow freighter, not the storm, not even Hitler.

Least of all that bastard, Churchill.

It was still almost too incredible to believe that Winston was somewhere on board. His first sight of Churchill had stunned him, literally taken his breath away. Not just because he hadn't seen the man since burying him with Zeila under tons of rock and earth forty years earlier. But also because it was simply impossible to accept that the Prime Minister would be here, unprotected, on a freighter in the Indian Ocean. It was madness of such a high order that it had taken him several moments to believe his own eyes.

That delay had been costly. He should have shot the son of a bitch the very instant he saw him. Now his nemesis was on board somewhere. His men had reported that one of their comrades had disappeared and Churchill had fired at them. Was there no end to the man's luck?

Two soldiers remained on the bridge with Sterne. He'd sent two others to deal with Winston. Now, one of them was back, bursting onto the bridge, dripping wet.

"No sign of him," said the man. "But I found Bayer and Kuhnke dead in one of the cabins and Greger's body was out on deck, shot through the chest."

Sterne stared at him as though he were insane. "He's a bloody fat old man! Are you certain he's alone? He couldn't have killed four SS by himself."

He turned his attention back to the ship. He was furious that Churchill had eluded them for the time being, but not entirely unhappy at the disposal of more of the Germans. He had only a handful of men left now, though still enough to help him operate the vessel. With luck, they should be able to limp into a foreign port. Once there, he was confident he could arrange for the disposal, or at least dispersal, of the last of the soldiers. The SS were used to taking orders without question and had come to accept his leadership even though he wasn't one of them. He might yet manage to divert Hitler's entire treasure to his own purposes.

The second man he'd sent to look for Churchill also appeared on the bridge. The soldier was obviously frightened about something. He stood unspeaking, staring blankly at the others.

"Well, what is it?" said Sterne.

"I . . . found Kreisch and Schreiber, both dead in the engine room."

Sterne cursed like a sailor. Churchill was proving to be a bloody one man army. He couldn't possibly be alone.

"And," the soldier continued, "someone opened the scuttle cock. The entire engine room is flooded. The ship is sinking."

As if to put an exclamation point to the man's horror, the engines sputtered and then died completely, engulfing them in a sudden silence punctuated only by the wind outside.

Sterne backed away from the controls like a man who has suddenly seen a ghost . . . or perhaps his own death. If the scuttle cock had been opened, then the ship was doomed and the gold that was intended to transform his miserable life would soon be on the bottom of the Indian Ocean.

"No!" he swore. "By God, I won't allow it!" He turned and headed off the bridge. "I'm going to see for myself. Come with me. All of you."

Three of the soldiers started to follow, but the man who'd reported the damage stood rooted in place. "Sir! There's nothing you can do. The engines are flooded, and we have no power. We're adrift. We have to get to the lifeboat."

But Sterne was gone. The other SS men stared at their comrade for a moment, but the habit of obeying was too strong in them. They turned and followed after the Englishman.

The remaining Nazi soldier hesitated only a moment, then left the bridge and headed in the opposite direction, toward the aft lifeboat station.

42.

ARTIN LED the way up from the depths of the sinking ship and out onto the deck. As they reached the open, the ship's engines died.

Winston grunted. They weren't going to have their twenty minutes before the listing ship clued the Germans to what was going on. "That'll warn them something's up," he said. "When they can't raise anyone on the intercom, they'll send someone to the engine room. As soon as they see the extent of the flooding, they'll head for the same place we are."

"I thought it would take longer for the engines to go," said Martin. "She must be flooding quickly. We've got to hurry."

One positive effect came of the rapid flooding. The ship was growing heavier and lower in the water, which made her more stable. The *Coast Princess* was now drifting and doomed, but she was no longer in danger of capsizing as she drifted broadside to the wind. Indeed, the wind appeared to be slacking off.

Even as they made their way aft, the ship began to list to the stern so that they were heading down an incline.

"Hurry!" Martin shouted. "She's going fast and by the stern. If the lifeboat gets swamped, we won't be able to launch her."

They stumbled and banged knees and elbows as they struggled over, around and sometimes through the multitude of obstructions that seemed to decorate the freighter's decks. Winston lagged badly. He'd had a lifetime of exercise and adventure in the past twenty-four hours. Kesi hung back, helping him negotiate around the obstacles.

"We're going to make it," she said over and over, encouraging him on. She held onto one of his arms and he leaned on her heavily.

"Of course we will," he said breathlessly. "The bloody Nazis couldn't get us and neither will the sea."

"That's the spirit," she said. "England has things for you to do."

"There's the boat," Martin cried. He clambered around the final obstacles, handed his rifle to Kesi and looked over the railing. The water was only a few feet away. The boat's angle had shifted because of the list, causing the lifeboat to lean against the rail. "You two be ready to fire if anyone shows up. I'll see if I can figure out how this thing works."

A maze of ropes and winches were designed to manipulate the craft over the side and into the water. Winston, more familiar with ships than Martin, offered suggestions.

"She's got to have both sides released . . . that's it . . . those levers there." he said. "She's supposed to slide right over the side now if you push on her."

Martin struggled mightily to push the craft, but her hull was jammed against the railing. "I can't get her over the rail," he shouted. "We've got to use the winch to pull her higher. You'll both have to help."

Kesi and Winston put their weapons down and got on one side while Martin grabbed the rope for the other. But the boat was designed to move only if both sides were raised in tandem. Pulling with every fiber of his being, Martin couldn't equal the weight and pull of Kesi and Winston together.

"Halt!" said a voice in German.

They all looked up to see a soldier in black SS uniform pointing a gun at them. Slowly, they let go of the ropes and stood facing the man. Martin glanced over the side. The water was very close to them now. Once the ocean came over the stern it would flood everything quickly and make launching impossible.

"Kesi," he said slowly, "You know the most German. You've got to convince him to help us . . . or we're all going to die. Make him understand."

She took a step toward the German. He was young for an SS soldier at this point in the war. Many of the older ones had already died. Haltingly, she tried to explain the situation to him.

"We can't get the boat into the water," she said hesitatingly. "Das boot!" She pointed to the ropes, then to the water. "Schnell, schnell!"

The soldier stared at her without moving.

"What's the matter with the blighter?" said Winston. "Is he dumb?"

"Winston, move to the rope beside me slowly."

They stood by the winch and grabbed hold of the line, pretending to pull. Then Martin grabbed onto his end and did the same. The German looked at them and then at the water that was nearly at their feet. Suddenly, he understood. He nodded and put his gun down. Then he joined Martin and reached for the line.

Together, they raised the boat over the railing and the hoists slid the craft out over the water. Then they lowered it until it touched the sea. Quickly, Martin released the ropes and the boat fell free.

Before the German could do anything more, Winston picked up the man's gun and aimed it at him. There was absolutely no reason he could think of to allow a member of the infamous SS to live a second longer than was necessary. His finger closed around the trigger. The German soldier stared at him with frozen eyes. But Winston couldn't do it. He couldn't kill in cold blood the man who had just helped them.

"Get aboard," Winston shouted at him," gesturing with the rifle.

The German and then Kesi clambered into the craft while Martin held onto it, one hand on the boat, the other on the railing. Fortunately, the wind appeared to have decreased substantially. The worst of the storm seemed to be skirting them.

Then they heard shouts and a moment later Sterne and three men appeared on the aft deck. Two of the soldiers began to fire at once. Martin let go of the lifeboat, which immediately started to float away from the freighter. He picked up his rifle and made two quick shots, killing two of the Germans. The remaining soldier and Sterne ducked for cover.

"I'll keep them from firing," Martin cried to Winston. "You're going to have to swim for the boat."

Winston nodded. "One thing I do well is float. Don't wait around too long, Martin." Then he made an awkward leap into the water, disappeared, bobbed back up like a life buoy and began to dogpaddle to the boat where, somewhat to his chagrin, he was helped aboard by the German soldier.

Martin looked back at the remaining two men. He could see part of the soldier's head. Taking careful aim, he shot the man dead.

Water now flowed around his waist in great swirling whirlpools, licking quickly up toward Sterne, who suddenly seemed to realize his own predicament. Martin launched himself into the sea and swam hard for the lifeboat even as the water rose over the aft deck. He caught up to it some thirty feet from the ship and was helped aboard.

Kesi and the German had installed the oars and they pulled the craft farther away from the sinking ship.

They could see Sterne, standing alone now, staring at the water as it rushed toward him. He looked as if he still didn't want to leave his gold behind. He'd been seeking it for more than forty years and now it was sinking right beneath his feet.

At the last possible moment, he made his choice. Casting his gun away, he leaped into the water and began to swim toward the boat.

"Uh-oh," Martin said. He took Winston's rifle and sat back in the bow of the lifeboat. He nodded to the German soldier, who'd been watching what was happening even as he operated the oars. Now he put the oars down and moved to the rear of the craft. In a moment, he fished Lord Sterne out of the water, dripping like a wet rat.

"Kesi, tell them to sit together in the back and not move."

She managed to make the German soldier understand. Sterne sat beside him, showing no more fight. Winston crawled forward to where Martin sat and took the gun from him. Then Martin moved to the center of the boat and joined Kesi at the oars.

Despite the relative warmth of the ocean, they were all shivering, as much from exhaustion as from the temperature. Kesi and Martin rowed them a safe distance away from the ship, then they stopped and watched as the aging *Coast Princess,* with her priceless, blood-drenched cargo, sank beneath the waves.

Sterne let out a low moan and stared blankly at the ocean's surface. His eyes finally rose and came to rest on Winston. But there was no longer any hatred in them, only defeat and despair.

"Sterne, you filthy bugger," Winston said with a mischievous grin. "Say hello to my daughter. She's the one responsible for bringing you to bay. A slip of a girl, but she was more than enough for the likes of you."

43.

LORD STERNE SAT MANACLED to his chair in Captain Nevins's conference room aboard H.M.S. *Blackmore*. He'd showered and been given a change of clothes and a few hours of rest, as had all the occupants of the lifeboat. Also present were Martin, Kesi and Winston. The sole surviving German soldier was conspicuously absent.

Like Winston, Sterne was still feeling the effects of the extraordinary events of the past hours and days. Both men were too advanced in age for the sort of extreme workout they'd been put through. But both also had strong constitutions. Sterne had already regained some of his characteristic bravado, despite the loss of what he'd come to think of as *his* treasure.

"You realize," he said, "that you're responsible for the loss of one of the world's great historical treasures. So much for the idea of the British empire as bastion of civilization, holding back the barbarian German horde."

The charge was so ridiculous that no one in the room bothered to answer it.

"I demand that my comrade and I be treated according to the Geneva Convention," Sterne went on.

"Well now, *that's* an interesting point," said Winston. "The Geneva Convention applies to enemy combatants. Last time I checked, you were an English citizen, Sterne. Your complicity in working with the Nazis—out of uniform, I might add—makes you nothing more than a spy. We shoot spies."

Sterne looked ill. "I'll take my chances in an English court."

"It'll be a military tribunal if anything, but the captain and I have been discussing a slightly different disposition of your case."

"What the hell are you talking about?" Sterne said, looking from the Captain to Winston.

"We interviewed your *comrade*, as you call him, at some length. He now appears to be of the opinion that you sabotaged your mission by blowing up the cave and trapping Major Rathke and his men below, where they were undoubtedly dispatched most unpleasantly by the guardians of Mapungubwe Hill."

"That's a bloody lie!" Sterne shouted. "You can't prove a word of it." He turned and stared at the Captain. "I don't know what lies Winston and his black bitch of a daughter have invented, but . . ."

Winston stepped forward suddenly and struck Sterne a blow that rocked the man back in his chair. He raised his hand a second time but Kesi interfered.

"He's not worth it," she said, softly.

"Truer words never spoken," said Winston. He sat down heavily, but continued to hold Kesi's hand.

The intercom squealed. Captain Nevins leaned over and pushed a button.

"Captain," said a voice, "You wanted to be informed. We've made contact with a German submarine and our interpreter has explained the situation to them. They're agreeable to your proposal."

"Good. Arrange a rendezvous and prepare a copy of the transcript of our interrogation of the German soldier." Nevins turned the intercom off.

Sterne stared from Winston to the Captain. "What's going on?" he said. "What German submarine?"

Winston said, "You explain it to him, will you Martin?"

"It will be a pleasure. You and your *comrade* are being turned over to the Germans. We believe Herr Hitler will take an interest in the report from one of his revered SS soldiers regarding your failure to return with the gold. Specifically, with your attempt to sabotage the mission and keep the gold for yourself."

Sterne stared at him, his eyes growing wider at every word. "You can't send me back to Hitler! I'm a God damned British citizen, a member of the royal family. I demand to talk to the King."

"The King?" Winston exploded. "Your employer is Adolf Hitler. You'll report directly to him. Though I understand he's not treating even those he trusts very kindly these days. I almost wish I could come along to witness your explanation . . . assuming you get a chance to offer one, that is."

"You son of a bitch, Winston! You can't do this. The royal family will hear about it. I'll have you run out of office."

Captain Nevins nodded to the two sailors guarding Sterne, and they pushed him out of the room, still yelling. They could hear him all the way down the corridor.

"What an evil man," Kesi said.

"Born and bred, my dear," said Winston. "Born and bred. Doesn't say too much for that portion of the royal bloodline, I'm afraid." He looked at his daughter and son-in-law and sighed heavily. "I suppose you two will want to live in Africa once this bloody war is over."

Kesi started to say something, but Winston patted her arm.

"No. It's what I expected. The Dark Continent needs people like you two if it's going to find its way into the modern world. But you must come and meet Clemmie at least, and the rest of the family, before you return. I do believe, as Prime Minister I have the power to insist on that much."

Kesi looked uncomfortable. "You're my father and the Prime Minister. I'm doubly blessed. I would obey you in all things. But I don't believe it would be wise for this meeting to take place now."

Winston started to protest.

"No, please. Let me finish. The war will be over soon. How much longer can it go on with Hitler mad and everything collapsing around him?"

"Wars have a timetable all their own," said Winston. "They last as long as they last, and no one can say how long that will be."

"Nonetheless, my relationship to your family will be big news. A scandal. It could weaken you precisely when you can't afford to be weakened. What harm can there be in waiting until the war's over? Then, let them spew their venom. It won't matter."

He stared at her, a profound sadness in his eyes. "You are wise beyond your years, my dear. You're right, of course, though I'll find it very hard indeed to wait. I've already told Clemmie about you, you know. She's anxious to meet you. It will make me want to end this war all the faster."

She kissed him. "You see, I've given you additional incentive. The Fuhrer's days are numbered."

44.

Cape Town,
South Africa

May 1946

MARTIN FINISHED pounding a loose fence post into the ground and paused to take a drink of water. He stared out across the green fields of his in-laws' farm in the hills north of Cape Town. It was rare indeed for a black family in South Africa to own such a place. It would become rarer still in two years when the apartheid laws would be established. But Zeila's long association with Botha had left her in the strange position of being the equivalent of senior stateswoman. Many white politicians consulted her still concerning foreign affairs.

It was rare, too, for Martin to have time for a vacation like this. Since the end of the war he'd been appointed director of the new Center for the Advancement of the African People. Most of his time was now spent shuttling between the various capitals, coaxing and cajoling the strange mixture of kings, dictators and ministers into working together. It was a time-consuming, often exasperating and thoroughly fulfilling pastime.

This week had been a long time coming. After Kesi's stepfather died a year ago, Kesi had wanted to return to live on the farm with her mother and her siblings' families. It had been a wonderful home-coming that would today reach its climax with a visit from Winston and Clementine Churchill.

He looked at his watch. It was late afternoon, time to return to the house. The rambling, plantation-style home looked out toward the ocean, across fields teeming with animals, both wild and domestic. He found Kesi, Zeila and the other members of the family in full domestic froth, a state that had been on-going for several weeks since word had come that Winston and Clemmie would visit.

"Oh, Martin!" Kesi said. "He's here! They called from the station and are being driven up. Apparently there was some flap—the Mayor of Cape Town insisted on his photo opportunity with Winston and then there was a band and speeches. I guess by the time they got out of town, father was weighted down with so many medals and honors he could hardly walk."

He laughed. "I warned you. Just because he's no longer Prime Minister doesn't mean the world thinks a jot less of him. But it'll be good for him and Clementine to get away."

"I'm so nervous, Martin. What if Clemmie doesn't like me, or little Winnie?"

Martin leaned down and picked up his two-and-a-half-year-old son. He swung him high in the air to squeals of glee. The boy had fair hair that almost disappeared against his pale skin. He looked like a miniature Churchill, something that parents all over the world now frequently said of their newborns.

"Not like little Winnie? How could such a thing be possible? Why, young Winston Rand is the last magic act of Mapungubwe Hill."

Their new son had been born nine months to the day after they'd made such sweet love in the shelter of the stones of Mapungubwe Hill, in what they had fully expected to be the last time before the Nazis killed them. Instead, Mapungubwe had bestowed upon them the greatest gift of all.

Zeila appeared in the doorway. She was seventy-four now, two years older than Winston. Her hair was salt-and-pepper gray and her face lined from the African sun, but she was still a tall, striking figure. "Here they come," she said a bit nervously.

Kesi's two brothers and sister and their families all came out onto the broad veranda to greet the most famous man on the planet and one who, incredibly, was related to all of them. The excitement they felt could have been cut with a knife.

The large town car pulled slowly up the long drive and stopped in front of the porch. Kesi ran forward and opened the door. Clementine was the first to emerge. She was dressed simply in a light cotton dress in deference to the warm climate. She stood and stared at Kesi, taking her hands and squeezing them tightly.

"I've never quite forgiven Winston for agreeing to your proscription against acknowledging you, my dear, until the war was over. It's been one of the hardest, longest waits of my life." Her smile wandered across the assembled family members and rested upon the small figure of Kesi's son. "Winston!" She cried. "Get out of this car at once and come see your grandson."

A rumpled, dark figure from inside the car mumbled, "Well, I would if you would just get out of the way, old girl."

And then Winston was there with them, his presence affecting them as though a powerful floodlight had suddenly been turned on. He hugged Kesi tightly, saying over and over, "It took too long, too long, too long for the war to end, and then all the loose ends to tie up. Sometimes I think being leader of the opposition is more work than being Prime Minister. But we're here at last!"

He shook hands with Martin, clapped him on the shoulder and went down the line being introduced to everyone. He picked little Winnie up and jiggled the boy under the chin.

"They really do all look like you, Winston. Newborn babies, I mean," said Martin.

"I rather hope *I* still look like *them*," said Winston. "Hope for it more every year, my boy." He kissed Winnie on the cheek and then looked up to see Zeila standing in front of him. Without moving his eyes from her face, he handed the boy to Kesi.

"It's *good* to see you, Winston," Zeila said.

"Oh my," said Winston. "You've hardly changed . . . and look what's happened to me after all these years."

She smiled, pleased. "You forget. I've seen your picture in the paper almost every day for the last forty years. You look just as I knew you would." She turned at once to Clementine. "But it's your wife I've wanted to meet, Winston, even more than I've wanted to see you again." She took Clementine by the shoulders and hugged her. "You are the most amazing woman," she said. "Not just for your warm heart in welcoming us into your family under such extraordinary circumstances, but because you've actually had to *live* with Winston all these years."

Clementine laughed aloud. "And it hasn't been easy, my dear! We must spend lots of time discussing big Winnie . . . and little Winnie both."

Winston looked at Martin and rolled his eyes. "I think I could use a cigar," he said wistfully.

"Oh, you must be tired," said Zeila. "Let me show you to your room."

"Nonsense, my dear," said Clementine. "We haven't come all this way to lie down. Show us your lovely home. It's every bit as beautiful here as I had imagined."

After a tour of the house, they settled on comfortable chairs on the veranda. Winston had his cigar at last and alternated looking out at the magnificent view with watching his new grandson play on the floor. Clemmie, Zeila, Kesi and Martin shared the porch. The rest of the family had melted away to various chores. They would have time with Winston and Clementine during the coming week, but this, they all recognized, was a time for their sister to be with her father.

"There's so much to tell you," Kesi said. "I hardly know where to begin."

"Begin at the beginning," said Winston, one of the literary giants of his age.

"Well . . . it seems as though everything we've been through has to do with Mapungubwe Hill," she said. "That incredible place is the beginning of so much . . . including me. Did you know that one of the things Martin has worked on in his new job has been organizing the excavation of Mapungubwe?"

Winston looked surprised. "I didn't know that," he said.

"We've appointed a group of experts," Martin said. "The long-term goal is to set the area aside as a people's cultural park. It will belong to all the nations of the continent. We hope it serves as a catalyst for tourism while simultaneously educating Africans about their rich history."

"And what of the Sacred Warriors?" said Winston. "I find it hard to believe The Clan of the Bow has warmed to the idea of gift shops and guided tours."

"The clan has been dissolved. My friend Kwesi had a role in that. But in fact, the presence of hundreds of workers, archaeologists, tourists and soldiers at the site gave the members of the cult no alternative but to abandon the place. Indeed, their reason for being, to protect the site, no longer exists, now that it is under government supervision. Kwesi arranged the peaceful transfer of power, if you will. In a sense, you know, the warriors served their purpose. They prevented Mapungubwe from being looted, with the exception of what Lord Sterne took out, until Africa was ready to accept her cultural inheritance."

Winston nodded. He was down on the floor now, feet splayed wide apart, rolling a ball back and forth with little Winnie. He looked like a very large Winnie the Pooh, Kesi thought, as she watched her two Winnies happily.

"We've only just begun," Martin continued. "But already there's been the most amazing discovery."

Winston looked up. "And that is?"

"You remember the royal figures we found sitting surrounded by their incredible trove of Roman and African treasure?"

"Of course."

"Well, the mummified male figure was bound in dark linens. But when the boar's mask was removed from his head and the linens stripped away to study him, he was discovered to be a white man."

"Good Lord!" said Winston. "A white man?"

"Yes. You can imagine how the archaeologists have been going crazy trying to explain that. But it all fits in a strange sort of way. The female figure is clearly African, a Nubian queen. Already our experts are digging into the historical records and they've uncovered enough to suggest something quite extraordinary."

Kesi couldn't constrain herself any longer. She wasn't going to let Martin tell the entire story himself. "We believe there was an arranged marriage between a Roman leader and the Nubian queen. A way of cementing the bonds between those two ancient civilizations. It would explain the mixture of Roman and Nubian architecture, works of art, coins and treasures. There must have been a great cultural and trade exchange between them. A connection the world has somehow overlooked until now."

"If it holds up," said Martin, "It opens a whole new chapter in African and Roman history and makes Mapungubwe one of the preeminent ancient sites in the world."

"Quite incredible . . . and wonderful," said Winston.

"Oh, and another thing," said Martin. "We've begun to recover the gold lost when the *Coast Princess* sunk. It turns out she's in shallow waters and the work is going very smoothly indeed."

"I can almost hear Lord Sterne turning over in his grave," said Winston. "To think that *his* treasure might finally cause someone some good."

Martin looked at him thoughtfully. "Have you any information at all about Sterne? Any idea what happened to him?"

Winston shrugged. "None at all. There's been no information, and not for lack of my inquiries. He simply disappeared. A fitting end to the man, if you ask me. Like Hitler himself, no body found, no memorials. They both earned their rightful place, likely burned in a pit somewhere."

"Oh, Winnie, must we have more talk about people burning in pits?" said Clementine. "Hasn't there been enough of that?"

"It must never be forgotten!" he said forcefully, "what the Hun did to the Jews and so many others. But," he said as he struggled to his feet, "I suppose this is hardly the time. I want my daughter and Zeila . . . and little Winnie here . . . to show me around their wonderful African farm."

45.

Kent, England

May 1947

WINSTON WAS BUNDLED up against an unusually brisk spring breeze as he sat outside his home at Chartwell. His painting easel had been set up in a corner of the gardens where he could look past the grave of Rufus, his recently deceased pet dog, and out over the gently rolling Weald of Kent.

Just twenty-five miles from Westminster, Chartwell had been purchased by Churchill in 1922 at a cost of five thousand pounds. He and Clementine proceeded to put another thirty thousand pounds into repairs and alterations over the next fifteen years. Then the home was mothballed for the duration of the war, during which No. 10 Downing Street and the official country residence of the Prime Minister, Chequers, became their homes. After the war, Chartwell was purchased for the National Trust by a group of Churchill's admirers, providing he agreed to make it his home for the rest of his life.

He was attempting to craft a landscape of the gardens filled with asters, sweet peas, larkspurs, Spanish iris, gladioli, Canterbury bells and sweet Williams. The flowers surrounded *Mary Cot,* the charming brick playhouse he'd built for his daughter Mary. He was looking forward to showing young Winnie the playhouse when he and Kesi came to visit next month.

He loved his gardens. The eccentric mix of formal terraces, lawns, brickwork, rockeries, earth and waterworks, trees and pasture set off the huge Victorian house in precisely the right manner. This was the place where he felt most at peace in the world. Here he could paint, write, build brick walls, smoke cigars and drink port to his heart's content. The House of Commons seemed far away.

He paused, brush poised, frustrated over a bit of hedge that wouldn't come to heel to his artistic vision. At the sound of footsteps, he looked up to see an unwelcome figure striding toward him down the rows of delphiniums.

Sir David Petrie had left his position as head of MI5 the year before. Winston hadn't seen him since and couldn't imagine why the militarily erect, rather stern-looking former intelligence chief was here.

Petrie stopped to one side of Churchill and gazed over the former Prime Minister's shoulder. "Something not quite right about that hedge," he said.

Winston sighed. Most of the officials he'd once elevated to high office now felt free to take liberties in their comments about his painting and writing, even his brickwork. It was one of the hazards of being out of power.

"It's called modern art, Petrie! It's not supposed to look exactly like what you see. It's the latest thing," he said petulantly.

"Of course, sir. I wonder if I might share a few words with you."

Winston looked at him with exasperation. "The war's over. You're out of office, I'm no longer Prime Minister, and no one gives a damn what we think." He threw his brush down. "Oh all right, pull that lawn chair over and sit down. I can't stare up at you. It hurts my neck."

Sir David did as he was bade and leaned forward slightly, his elbows resting on his knees as he spoke.

"It's true I'm no longer at MI5, but I still have sources inside that consult me occasionally for advice and keep me informed in return."

"More than my mine do," Winston grumbled.

"There was a rather disturbing communiqué intercepted by intelligence the other day. One of my former aides knew that it would be of interest to you and felt you should know about it. He told me and . . . here I am."

"Well, what is it?"

Sir David sat back in his chair and smoothed the flawless crease in his pants. "This is rather awkward, sir. The communiqué in question was directed to King George. It was signed by Lord Sterne."

Winston felt as though a hand had him by the throat. He couldn't breathe. His eyes locked on Sir David, and it took several long moments before he was able to speak.

"Lord . . . Sterne . . . is alive?"

"So it would appear."

"He's written to the King?"

"Indeed."

"Where did the message originate?"

"From Berlin, the Russian sector."

Winston was silent. He stared across his lawns and wondered if there might not be something immortal about his old enemy. "What did the message say?"

"In its entirety, it said: 'With your support, am returning to England. Will reside on my family estates and maintain low profile. Appreciate your intervention on my behalf.'"

Winston looked stunned. Sir David gazed off at the gardens for a few moments. Then he said, "We in intelligence sometimes intercept things we'd rather not, sir. In fact, as you know, MI5 is proscribed from pursuing matters that relate to the royal family. Nothing further will result from this, and all records of our interception have already been destroyed."

Winston nodded. The enormity of what he'd just heard made his heart beat faster. It was long a truism that royalty stuck together through thick and thin. But this was too much . . . if true. He could hardly believe it of King George, whom he admired greatly.

"I appreciate the risk you've taken in telling me this, Petrie. It must not have been an easy decision for you."

"I confess the affair has made me reconsider how much I want to continue to be in the loop, as it were. I've found that the cloak-and-dagger stuff appears much more . . . ephemeral . . . once one is on the outside of government looking in. We had to do many unpleasant things during the war. It was necessary. But now . . . I don't know."

Winston stared at him. "By God, Petrie, there may be hope for you yet," he said.

Sir David stood up and nodded. Without another word, he turned and walked slowly down the rows of flowers. He paused briefly to look out across the Weald. He had more time for such things now.

As soon as he was gone, Winston turned his head toward the main house and yelled at the top of his voice, "Clemmie!"

46.

Buckingham Palace

May 1947

"AH, WINSTON," said King George. "It's good to see you." He shook Churchill's hand warmly. "Come sit over here. I tell you it's not the same without you as Prime Minister. I haven't the foggiest notion how the British people could have done that to you."

Winston sat heavily. "The people will have their say. It's what the whole bloody war was all about, I suppose. But I can't pretend it didn't hurt to be thrown out like that."

King George reached over and patted his knee. "Believe me, they know what you've meant to this country . . . every single citizen, the royal family perhaps more than any. Who can understand the vagaries of politics? But your name is writ large in the history of mankind, Winston."

"Thank you, sir." He shifted uncomfortably in his chair, a frown coming over his face.

King George leaned back and ran a hand through his thinning hair, one of many nervous mannerisms his subjects had come to recognize. "I know why you're here, Winston," he said.

Churchill looked up, his eyes questioning.

"Yes. When Intelligence uncovers something regarding the royal family, it's proscribed from doing any further investigation, but it sends us a report on the matter. I suspected someone would leak the information to you."

"I find myself in an awkward situation, sir. It's not my place to question your actions. But in this one matter, I have the strongest possible feelings. Lord Sterne is a traitor to his country. He tried to kill the Prime Minister . . . me . . . and my daughter as well. Yet, two days ago I learned that Sterne has been allowed to return to England to live . . . and that he did so with your help."

The King stood and paced across the room to the huge floor-to-ceiling windows that looked down across the gardens of St. James Park.

"The man did thirty years in a South African prison. You can hardly say he has gone unpunished."

"By every right," Winston replied forcefully, "He ought to be tried at Nuremberg and hanged. That is how serious his crimes were. If he had succeeded in bringing vast wealth to Hitler, it could well have affected the outcome of the war. At a minimum, it would have cost many more lives . . . American lives as well as British."

"The gold never reached Hitler, Winston. Sterne claims it was never his intention to deliver it to him. He was rescuing it to bring it back for the British people . . . to help in the war effort if it was needed, otherwise to go to the British Museum. In fact, he says, by recruiting a substantial force of SS soldiers to pursue his goal, he took those men out of the war effort, while at the same time distracting Hitler with dreams of a fantastical treasure he would never see."

Winston stared at him with incredulous eyes. "You can't seriously believe that."

"I do not. I believe what you have told me about the matter, Winston. I've known you a long time, and I've known few men more honorable or truthful."

"Then arrest the bugger!" Winston pounded his fist on the arm of his chair.

"I wish it were that easy. The fact is, after you sent him back to Germany to face Hitler, the Fuhrer put him in prison instead of having him killed. Who knows why? But Sterne remained there until the end of the war. For God's sake, Winston, the man was liberated by Russian forces marching into Berlin." King George crossed the room and sat down in his chair. "So what do we have? A member of the royal family who says he was really working to bring the gold to England in support of the war effort. The Nazis capture and imprison him as though he's an enemy combatant, perhaps even a spy. One could almost say that you provided Sterne with the perfect alibi by sending him back to Germany."

Winston stared at the King with a look of unabashed horror.

"Suppose . . . just for the sake of argument, that I refuse him permission to return to England. Suppose further that he then implicates the royal family in some fashion. It wouldn't be hard. Imagine a member of the royal family declaring that he was work-ing under the auspices of the King to try to steal the treasure of a sovereign African nation. Suppose . . . he was to suggest that the King even came to an agreement with Hitler to share that wealth. I've known Sterne at least as long as you have, Winston. He's calculating and devious enough to do any of these things. Such a scenario could bring down the monarchy."

Winston stared glumly at the white knuckles of his hands where they gripped the arms of his chair. Would this nightmare never come to an end?

"So what you are telling me . . . is that Sterne will simply live out his life as some sort of revered former POW? A war hero? An elder member of the royal family . . . riding for the hunt and attending the Queen's tea at Ascot?"

The King sighed. "He'll receive no special invitations from the House of Windsor, Winston. But as a member of the royal family, he can't be kept from certain functions such as you mention."

Winston slumped in his chair. He felt as though everything he'd been through for the past six years had somehow been turned upside down. It was as if he'd fallen through the looking glass. How could he tell Kesi and Martin . . . and Zeila . . . such ghastly news?

He felt old beyond his years. He looked up at King George, who was watching him with a sympathetic frown. He realized the King looked much older than he remembered as well.

"It was a tiring drive coming in, Sir," Winston said, rising slowly. "I'll say goodbye."

47.

NEWS ITEM, page twelve, the *London Times*, October 16, 1947—

Major Martin Rand, a leading figure in the African resistance movement against the Nazis, was welcomed today by King George at Buckingham Palace. Major Rand was knighted by the King for his service during the recent war and for his continuing work as Director of the Center for the Advancement of the African People. In attendance at the presentation were Major Rand's wife, his father-in-law, former Prime Minister Winston Churchill and half a dozen members of the Nubian tribe in full, traditional native dress. Following the ceremony, at a news conference, Mr. Rand outlined some of the work he continued to do and stated he would conclude his visit to England with some personal business before he returned home.

48.

ORD STERNE guided his horse expertly across the meadow. The grass was still damp from an early-morning dew and the footing was tricky, but the big chestnut was surefooted as usual. He was a magnificent animal and Sterne took great pride in controlling him. Control was everything, he thought, in both man and beast. The Nazis had that much right, at least. He lined up the approach to the final jump over a five-foot hedge, brokered it perfectly and then eased back, slowing to a trot.

Laura Wilms brought her own horse alongside. "That was perfect," she said, admiringly. "I wish I could control them the way you do."

He nodded slightly, accepting the compliment as his due. "They sense who is master," he said. He looked at her with open anticipation in his eyes. She was the spoiled, fortyish wife of one Harry Wilms, a down-on-his-luck barrister who was just beginning to realize that he wasn't making enough money to afford such a luscious creature. Sterne had taken in the entire situation of this poor couple almost the moment he'd met them. It had taken little effort for someone of his talents to dangle the suggestion that he might send considerable legal business to Mr. Wilms. The man had positively fawned over him ever since, even insisting that his wife go riding with Sterne since the barrister didn't like horses. After all, Sterne was a bona fide war hero, a dashing figure that the papers had led the public to believe had figured in some mysterious way in the successful outcome of the war. Harry Wilms could hardly believe his luck in coming across the distinguished-looking, silver-haired gentleman.

Bedding Laura Wilms would be little enough in the way of challenge, but the firm thigh Sterne had rested his right hand upon while helping her up onto her horse this afternoon suggested the effort would be well worth it.

All in all, life had not been unkind to him, he mused, as they rode back toward the main house. Though he'd lost the fortune that had consumed him for so many years, his personal estates had survived the war in surprisingly good shape. They now produced an income that allowed him to live as a gentleman should, though not, alas, in the style he'd once envisioned.

At seventy-seven years of age, he was still in excellent health. With a bit of luck, he might enjoy another decade of dalliances with the likes of Laura Wilms. He doubted his old nemesis, Churchill, still had that kind of spirit in him.

"Perhaps you'd like to share dinner with me this evening," Sterne said. "Seems a shame to make that long drive back to London on an empty stomach. My chef is really quite good."

Laura beamed at the invitation. Dinner with a Lord! And a war hero to boot. What harm could there be in it? Hadn't her husband told her to butter the man up, after all?

It took another thirty minutes to reach the main house, a large, Tudor-style mansion that had been in Sterne's family for centuries. He was the last of his line. His two sisters had been barren, and children had never interested Sterne in the slightest. His own interests, comfort and satisfaction had ruled his long life.

It was already twilight when they handed their reins to the stable boy and went inside. Sterne ordered their meal set out on the glass-enclosed patio. Laura went to clean up while Sterne spent a few minutes in his study looking at papers before showering and changing into a comfortable smoking jacket. He poured himself a glass of claret, admiring its fine quality and aroma.

Fine things. All his life he'd enjoyed them. Now, after all the hardships, the years as a prisoner of the Boers and then the Nazis, they were his once again. He intended to suck the marrow out of whatever years were left to him. Who deserved it more?

He opened the glass doors that led to the terrace and strolled down onto the lawn. It was a warm fall evening. He listened to the crickets and peepers as he wandered about his home. The house was constructed of the finest limestone and had always given him a sense of permanence and power. He rounded the corner of one wing and paused outside the glassed-in patio. Laura was already inside, seated at the table. She looked radiant, her golden hair flowing around her shoulders. She wore a light silk blouse that emphasized her full figure. He would have her this night.

He felt completely content here beside his magnificent home on this splendid, warm night, staring at the beautiful woman waiting for him inside. Perhaps he'd take her for a stroll before dinner and make love to her on the grass. Just like he was a boy again!

He tossed the last bit of claret onto the lawn, turned toward the terrace and suddenly felt strong hands grab him. In the dark, he could see nothing. A hand that smelled very unpleasant clamped over his mouth and then he was being carried away . . . away from his home, from his dinner and from the woman waiting so expectantly inside.

He seemed to float above the ground, carried aloft by many hands, the blackness all around broken only by the stars that twinkled on and off as they were blotted out by tree branches. They moved quickly down the sloping lawns, through his rock garden and past the pool with its fountains tinkling. He couldn't imagine what was happening to him, but then, as they left the house behind, the men carrying him began to chant. Softly at first, then growing in strength until, suddenly, Sterne knew who they were. A ribbon of fear gripped his insides and he wanted to retch.

Away from the main house, the darkness was even more total on this moonless, starry night. Where were they going?

He could hear the soft padding of bare feet. The chanting was now loud as the men stopped finally beside a large boulder. Sterne's shirt was torn from his body and he felt himself being lowered onto the cold, damp rock, felt the pull of the rope binding his wrists and ankles, heard the pounding of stakes into the soft green lawn. *His* lawn!

Then, suddenly, flames flickered and he turned his head to see a fire the men had lit nearby. It must have been prepared that very afternoon. He might have seen it if his ride had only come this way. By the firelight, he watched as huge black Nubian warriors, faces and chests painted with white slash marks, a strange set of tattoos lining their shoulders, added wood to the growing pyre and then laid an iron grate over the flames. He looked at it in puzzlement. They were going to cook something?

Finally, one of the warriors, a fierce, greasy-looking fellow, appeared, hovering over his head. The man held a shining blade up in front of Sterne's face so he could see it clearly, then lowered it slowly until it rested lightly upon the English Lord's throat.

The last thing Lord Sterne saw before his head was nearly severed from its body was the golden knife blade flickering in the twilight.

He wondered if the gold was real.